Praise for the DragonCrown War Cycle

Fortress Draconis

"What a splendid story; it grabbed me and wrenched me full force into a gripping adventure. And the wonderful thing is, there are two more books to come." —Dennis L. McKiernan, author of *Once Upon a Winter's Night*

"I think that Michael A. Stackpole is incapable of writing a book that isn't imaginative, intelligent, and sympathetic. On top of that, FORTRESS DRACONIS is ambitious, even for him. It can hardly help being exciting and satisfying. When future readers name the writers who followed the Asimov-Clarke generation, and the Zelazny-Silverberg generation, they'll have to mention Michael A. Stackpole." —*Stephen R. Donaldson*

"A compelling and engaging escape." —*Publishers Weekly*

"With a deliciously evil antagonist and some truly remarkable supporting characters, this is a terrific read." —*Booklist*

"A powerful epic fantasy that is wholly grounded in the gritty realism of battlefields and sacrifices." —*Romantic Times*

When Dragons Rage

"Intriguing [and] complex . . . worth the wait." —*Publishers Weekly*

"Addicts will devour [*When Dragons Rage*] swiftly and demand more."
—*Kirkus*

"Enough sex, love, bloody battles, and high adventure to keep reading lamps lit well into the wee hours." —*Booklist*

The Grand Crusade

"This is fantasy on the most epic of scales, with plenty of bloody conflict and treacherous double-dealing." —*Publishers Weekly*

BOOKS BY MICHAEL A. STACKPOLE

THE WARRIOR TRILOGY
Warrior: En Garde
Warrior: Riposte
Warrior: Coupé

THE BLOOD OF KERENSKY TRILOGY
Lethal Heritage
Blood Legacy
Lost Destiny

Natural Selection
Assumption of Risk
Bred for War
Malicious Intent
Grave Covenant
Prince of Havoc
Ghost War

THE FIDDLEBACK TRILOGY
A Gathering Evil
Evil Ascendant
Evil Triumphant

Eyes of Silver*
Dementia
Wolf and Raven
Once a Hero*
Talion: Revenant*

STAR WARS® X-WING SERIES
Rogue Squadron*
Wedge's Gamble*
The Krytos Trap*
The Bacta War*
Isard's Revenge*

Star Wars®: I, Jedi*
Star Wars®: Dark Tide
Star Wars®: Onslaught
Star Wars®: Ruin

THE DRAGONCROWN WAR CYCLE
The Dark Glory War*
Fortress Draconis*
When Dragons Rage*
The Grand Crusade*

*published by Bantam Books

BOOK ONE OF TH

BANTAM BOOKS

A Secret Atlas

AGE OF DISCOVERY

Michael A. Stackpole

A SECRET ATLAS
A Bantam Spectra Book / March 2005

Published by
Bantam Dell
a division of
Random House, Inc.
New York, New York

This is a work of fiction. Names, characters, places, and incidents either are the product of the author's imagination or are used fictitiously. Any resemblance to actual persons, living or dead, events, or locales is entirely coincidental.

Cover design by Jamie Warren Youll
Map by Michael Gellatly

Book design by Glen Edelstein

Library of Congress Cataloging-in-Publication Data
Stackpole, Michael A., 1957-
A secret atlas / Michael A. Stackpole.
p. cm. — (The age of discovery ; bk. 1)
ISBN 0-553-38237-3
I. Title.

PS3569. T137S73 2005
813'.54—dc22 2004046388

Printed in the United States of America
Published simultaneously in Canada

10 9 8 7 6 5 4 3 2 1
BVG

To Senator John McCain
For his courage, good sense, and willingness to do
the right thing, not the expedient one.

Acknowledgments

Books like this have one name on the cover, but are a team effort. The author would like to express his thanks to Anne Groell for her editing expertise and hard work; and Howard Morhaim and Danny Baror, agents extraordinaire, who made writing this book possible.

Two books in particular were helpful. *The Island of Lost Maps* by Miles Harvey sparked part of this novel as I mulled over a passing comment or two in that book. *1421: The Year the Chinese Discovered America* by Gavin Menzies came along later and let me fill in some gaps in my knowledge before I wrote the book. His staff at *www.1421.tv* were gracious enough to find a quote for me that allowed me to estimate the size of a ship like the *Stormwolf,* and for that I am very grateful.

Turasyndi
OPASLYNOT
Ixyll
Solaeth
Dolosan
TELARUNDE
SYLUMAK
Dreonath
EOLOTH
Irusviruk
Dark Se
Iireath
Lurenyon
Tejanmorek
Ceriskoron
Ummummorar
(Five Princes)
Gloysan

Wastes
Deseirion
FELARATI
Tirat
MELESWIN
Black River
(Helosunde)
DEJAROTH
RUI
FECISTOR
GRIA
URISOTI
MORIANDE
ASATH
Gold River
Nalenyr
GLOYSAN
Erumvirine
Moryth
Green River
KELUWAN
Hyreoth
Eastern Sea
Miromil
1" = 150 miles

A Secret Atlas

Chapter One

32nd day, Month of the Bat, Year of the Dog
9th Year of Imperial Prince Cyron's Court
162nd Year of the Komyr Dynasty
736th year since the Cataclysm
Imperial Road South
Nalenyr

Moraven Tolo reached the crest of the hill a few steps before his traveling companions. The half-blind old man who wheezed up behind him gasped involuntarily. He looked back as his grandson and great-grandson joined him, then gestured at the city in the distance. "There it is, Moriande, the grandest city in the world."

The swordsman nodded slowly in agreement. The road ran down the forested hillside and glimpses of it could be seen twisting through the Gold River valley to the city. It had been years since he'd seen Nalenyr's capital, and it had grown, but was still easily recognizable. Wentokikun, the tallest of the city's nine towers, dominated its eastern quarter, and using that as a landmark made fixing the other places easier.

The old man, his wispy beard and hair dancing in the light breeze, nodded toward Moriande. "The biggest tower, there to the east, is the Imperial Palace. I may not see well now, but I see it clear. It makes me remember when I last saw it."

Moraven remained silent, though the sight of the capital filled him with much the same awe as it did the rest of the pilgrims. Moriande's growth reflected the change in the world. As wild magic decreased in civilized lands, and trade brought prosperity, Moriande became a symbol of hope. While people always feared a return of the Time of Black Ice and the magic that had spawned it, they dared believe it could be held at bay. Moriande had grown not because of magic and superstition, but because of a victory over it.

The pace of that growth had surprised Moraven, and it clearly had accelerated in recent decades beneath the Komyr Dynasty. Many times over the last week Moraven had heard about how the old man had come to Moriande eighty-one years earlier, for the first grand Festival celebrating the Komyr Dynasty. It had survived nine cycles of nine years then, and twice that now. With this being the ninth year of the current Prince's Court, people knew that the Festival was a double blessing. The old man's hope to capitalize on that blessing was the reason for leading his scions on the long journey north.

The city was so huge that it seemed far closer than a two-day walk from where they stood. The Gold River split the white sprawl down the middle, with a broad oxbow curving to the north. Six of the city's nine towers stood in the northern half, and the other three—including the Prince's Dragon Tower, Wentokikun—lay on the southern side. Equally magnificent, though harder to see at that distance, were the nine soaring bridges arching over the sparkling river. Their height allowed even the grandest ship to pass beneath them with ease, and their width made the Imperial Road look like a game path.

Matut, the old man, tousled his great-grandson's hair with an arthritically twisted hand. "I was ten when I came to the Festival. You are but nine, as old as the court and a tenth my age. I'm sure the gods will make something of that. Your little problem will be dealt with easily, Dunos."

The little boy nodded solemnly. His right hand rubbed at his withered left arm as he looked over at Moraven. "It will be as my grandfather says, won't it, swordsman?"

Moraven crouched and gave the brown-haired boy a nod. "He is correct, but as my Master's Master told him, 'The gods grant the tools and talent, yet yours is the effort.' The gods will heal you, I have no doubt, but you will have to work."

"I'll work. Then I can be a swordsman, too."

"We might need more than a swordsman in the mill, son." The

boy's father smiled and tapped a belt pouch that rang with the muffled sound of coins. "We will do this right, make our offerings to the gods, then enjoy the Festival."

"Of course, Alait, of course." The old man chuckled himself into a wheeze. "There will be pleasures a young man like yourself and our friend here can enjoy. I was too young last time, and am too old this time."

Rising, Moraven smiled and smoothed his long black hair at the back of his neck. "You are of a blessed age, grandfather. There will be many who will seek your touch for fortune's sake."

"May they all be as comely and soft as the Lady of Jet and Jade." The old man looked at him with rheumy brown eyes and flexed a stiff hand. "It might be I don't see so well anymore, but I *can* feel."

Alait laughed and Moraven joined him. Dunos looked puzzled, and a richly robed merchantman's wife sniffed. She had often done so when conversations had revolved around Matut's stories of the Festival and all the carnal pleasures he'd seen there. She, they had been informed, was going to the capital at the invitation of "people" who, they were also told, would get her husband an imperial appointment—though she had always remained vague on what it was and why he wasn't with her.

The rest of the traveling company was a fair mix of people from within and without Nalenyr. Four were entertainers coming up from Erumvirine, while the rest were from Nalenyr itself. They'd all agreed that traveling in a company of eighteen was a very good omen, and numerous offerings had been made in the shrines scattered along the roadway to ensure the favor of the gods. Each made offerings according to his means, with the peasants clad in brown or grey homespun being a bit more quiet and circumspect in their devotions than the more extravagantly dressed. And many made extra offerings for Dunos in payment for little chores he performed on the road.

The merchantman's wife had neither made offerings for Dunos nor employed him, running him off with waves and snorts. In his grandfather's words, she had been "Loud in prayer, but in offerings spare."

Moraven Tolo fell into the middle of the two groups, being neither rich nor poor. Black woolen trousers were tucked into leather boots and his shirt had been made of undyed linen. Only his quilted sleeveless overshirt of white silk, with the wide starched shoulders and the black tigers embroidered breast and back, hinted at any prosperity. It wrapped closed and was belted with a black sash.

He'd slipped his sword into the sash, only just having reclaimed it from the boy. Dunos had proudly carried it for him, and Moraven had made offerings to the gods in recompense. He alone in the company bore a sword, though he was not the only one armed. Two of the farmers had flails, which they carried over their shoulders.

Matut's eyes half lidded and the old man shook. "It was here it happened on that first trip. I remember it now."

Dunos clutched at his grandfather's left hand. "The bandits?"

The merchantman's wife hissed. "Be quiet, child. Don't give the gods ideas."

Moraven glanced further down the road as three figures—two male, one female—slipped from the woods to the center of the road. "The mind of gods was not the womb of this idea."

The female bandit, wearing black beneath an overshirt of scarlet and gold, drew her sword and led her two companions lazily toward the pilgrims. To her left the smaller one, wearing a motley collection of greens and browns, fitted an arrow to his recurve bow. He hung back slightly and positioned himself for a clear shot.

The third figure wore a ragged brown robe that might have come to midshin on most men, but barely covered the tops of his thighs. A long tangle of unkempt hair matched the giant's scraggly beard. Dirt caked every inch of his exposed flesh and drew black lines beneath his fingernails. As imposing as he was, however, the long-hafted mallet he carried made more of an impression. With a head as big around as a melon and an irregular darkness staining the face, it was clearly intended for crushing skulls.

The bandit woman tried to smile, but a scar on her left cheek curdled the expression. "We welcome you to the Imperial Road. We are your servants, who keep it open and free of banditry. Surely you will want to show your appreciation."

Conoursai, the merchantman's wife, waved them aside with a courtly gesture full of arrogance. "This is the Prince's highway. His troops keep it clear."

The highwaywoman shook her head. "Clearly, then, they are

negligent in their duty, *grandmother*." She offered the honorific to shock Conoursai, and was rewarded with an offended hiss. "But, as we are not the Prince's troops, we must be highwaymen. Will you pay tribute and be honored or suffer as victims?"

Matut moaned. "This is how it began last time."

Moraven patted him on the shoulder. "This has long been known as a place where people stop in awe to look at the city. Bandits sneak up unawares."

The little boy stooped and picked up a rock. "I'll fight them."

"No need, brave one." Moraven Tolo moved again to the fore, slipping effortlessly past Conoursai. He motioned to the two farmers to stay back. Taking a position in the center of the road, he bowed toward the bandits.

"I am *xidantzu*. I wish harm to come to none. These people are under *my* protection. It will cost you nothing to walk away."

"Xidantzu." The woman spat contemptuously and plucked at her overshirt. "The last wandering meddler coming through here gave me this and those he protected gave us their gold."

Moraven's eyes sharpened. The scarlet overshirt had bats on the wing woven into it. He knew the man to whom it belonged. "Did you steal it, or was Jayt Macyl slain?"

She gestured with her sword to the west, then swung the blade in a short arc. "There are pieces of him all along here. He was Sixth Rank only. I am Pavynti Syolsar, and I am ranked Superior."

He considered for a moment. Jayt Macyl had indeed been a swordsman of the Sixth Rank. Her defeating him might well make her Seventh Rank, or just someone who had gotten lucky. He was tempted, given her relative youth, to believe it was the latter, but he also knew appearances could be deceiving.

"I am Moraven Tolo of the School of Jatan."

The bandit woman snorted. "Macyl was of *Serrian* Jatan. This holds no fear for me."

Moraven shook his head. "Macyl studied under Eron Jatan. My Master was his grandfather."

Her face slackened slightly. "Phoyn Jatan?"

"Yes. I am somewhat older than I appear." Moraven did his best to ignore the murmurs coming from his traveling companions. "If you still wish to fight, name your terms."

"I am not afraid of you." Pavynti's brown eyes narrowed. "To the death, of course."

He nodded. "Draw the circle."

That stopped her for a moment. It also brought gasps from his traveling companions and a joyous shout from Dunos. His father cut that short by clapping a hand over the boy's mouth as he dragged his son back. Most of the company likewise retreated, putting the crest of the hill between themselves and the combatants. Those who did not drew little circles around themselves or dug out previously hidden talismans against magic, and one farmer slid off a horsehair bracelet, which he held up to one eye so he would be safe as he watched the fight.

"The c-circle?" Pavynti's expression tightened.

"You heard me correctly." Moraven slid his sword, still in its wooden scabbard, from his belt. "It would be best."

Shaken, she began to toe a line in the roadway's dirt. Her companions, understanding the import of his request, acted. The archer loosed an arrow and the giant bellowed and began to charge. By the time the giant had passed Pavynti, the archer's second and third missiles were also in the air.

Moraven Tolo twisted his right shoulder back, letting the first shaft pass harmlessly wide. The second tugged at his overshirt's sleeve, passing through it, but missing flesh. He slid forward a half step, letting the third arrow pass behind him, then ran at the giant, clutching his sword midscabbard in his left hand.

The giant's mallet rose above his head and his mouth gaped in a horrid display of misaligned, yellowed teeth. Black eyes shrank. Veins throbbed in his forehead and neck. His incoherent war cry took on the bass tones of a water buffalo's challenge. The mallet, its haft bending beneath the incredible power of the stroke, arced up and smashed down at Moraven.

Ducking low, Moraven moved inside the mallet's arc. He plunged the hilt of his sword into the giant's middle. Planting his right hand on the lower part of the scabbard, he pivoted the sheathed blade into the man's groin. As the bellow rose into a squeak, Moraven lifted and twisted, flipping the giant over his shoulder. The man smashed down on his back and bounced once. Another spin let Moraven crack the giant in the head with his scabbard as a fourth arrow flew past.

Completing the spin, Moraven let the sword shoot forward until the hilt filled his right hand. He tightened his grip, deliberately letting momentum bare the blade. The heavy wooden scabbard flew off in a flat arc and cracked the archer's left hand. As the swordsman intended, it crushed fingers against the bow and knocked the fifth arrow flying. The archer screamed, dropping his weapon, and turned away with his broken hand nestled beneath his right armpit.

Moraven Tolo's sword came up, the silver blade pointing straight at Pavynti's throat. "Have you finished that circle yet?"

She threw her sword aside and dropped to her knees, then fell to her belly with her face in the dirt. "*Jaecaiserr,* forgive this wretched one for her arrogance."

"Which arrogance was that, Pavynti? Claiming ranks you do not have? Believing those who travel to the capital are your prey?" Moraven let his voice get cold and deeper. "Or the dishonorable arrogance of letting your friends attack me before we could engage in our duel?"

"All of them, Master."

"Up. Remove that overshirt. Take up your sword."

Disbelief widening her eyes, the woman rose, dusted the overshirt off, then removed it. Hesitantly she leaned over to pick up her sword, and a little circular silver talisman fell forward, dangling on a rawhide thong. She slowly straightened. "Do I continue drawing the circle?"

He shook his head. "Scorpion form, the first."

Pavynti blinked, then moved into that stance. He nodded then called another form, and another. She flowed through them quickly enough, doing best with Crane and Eagle, least well with Wolf and Dog. He kept her at it for a full nine minutes, which was all the time it took for his traveling companions to crest the hill again. The two farmers positioned themselves to thump the giant soundly if he regained consciousness.

When she was dripping with sweat, he called a halt, and she dropped to one knee. He could tell she was tempted to stab her sword into the ground and hang on to the hilt, but she knew better than to show that level of disrespect to her weapon. Breathing heavily, she glanced up. "What else would you have of me, Master?"

"The answer to a question."

"Yes?"

"You have Jayt's overshirt, but not his sword. What became of it?"

The flesh around her eyes tightened. "I am a bandit, Master, but not a barbarian. The blade was sent on to his family, for their shrine."

Moraven said nothing, but crossed to where the archer cowered and kicked the bow into a tangle of thornbushes. Resheathing his sword, he slid it back into his overshirt's sash and waved the archer further from his weapon. By the time he turned around again, Conoursai had advanced and raised her quirt to lash the bandit.

"Don't do that."

The merchantman's wife sputtered indignantly. "She was going to kill us all. She should be punished. You should kill her."

Moraven slowly shook his head. "A life broken can be mended. A life taken cannot."

"Then break her." The woman gestured imperiously, though not quite as confidently as before. "Have the farmers thrash the giant and the archer."

"They struck at me, not you. Their fate is in my hands."

"By what authority?"

Moraven frowned, then looked past her to where Dunos had collected Macyl's overshirt and neatly folded it. "Why can you not be like the child? As it is said, 'One action accomplishes more than ten thousand words.' "

"Her action was to slay us."

"No, her action was to show respect to a fallen foe. Her words, as yours, are nothing. Now, be silent, lest I be forced to act." He turned from her scowl and eyed the archer. "How much have you stolen from the Festival pilgrims?"

"Not a prince's ransom. Not even his petty spending."

"It is still too much. You and your giant will take all you have stolen and go to the Festival. You will give alms to the beggars until you have nothing, then you will leave for the west."

"But there are Viruk and Soth there, and wildmen. The chances of our survival . . ."

". . . Are better there than here." Moraven smiled. "Chances are excellent I shall never see you again if you go west."

The archer thought for a moment. "It *is* very crowded here. West, then."

Conoursai snorted with outrage, but said nothing. Moraven continued to ignore her and turned to Pavynti. "And now your fate must be decided."

"My lord's will be done."

"You will go to the town of Derros, south, on the Virine coast. You will present yourself at the School of Istor. You will tell the Grandmaster I have sent you to join his school. He will see to your training. When he releases you, you will be *xidantzu* for nine years. You will wander and entertain bandits as you have been entertained."

"Yes, Master." Again she put her belly to the dirt in a deep bow.

"Care for your companions tonight, then go tomorrow. This is my will."

The farmers, between the two of them, lifted the mallet and broke the haft. The others in the group started forward again, following the farmers and allowing Conoursai to join them. All of them gave Moraven wide berth. Moraven moved past the bandits, but did so slowly, waiting for the old man and his kin, who were bringing up the rear.

Moraven smiled at the boy. "When you get to Moriande, you will deliver that overshirt to Macyl's family. They will honor you for it. Ward it well."

"I will." Dunos nodded, then narrowed his eyes. "Are you really a Mystic?"

"Dunos, hush." Alait settled his hand on the back of the boy's neck. "Don't be offended, Master. He is just a boy."

"I'm not." Moraven crouched again, looking the boy eye to eye. "I have studied many years and am blessed with skill. I am *jaecaiserr,* but you cannot believe all the stories." He reached out and caressed the boy's lifeless left arm. "If I could use my magic to heal you with a touch, I would have done so on the eve we met. My magic is not for healing, to my regret. Others have that skill, and you will find them in Moriande."

The boy nodded solemnly. "Thank you, Master." He looked up at his father, and the two of them moved on.

Matut reached out a hand and rested it on Moraven's shoulder as he rose. "A moment more of your time, Master."

The swordsman nodded and let the two younger men get further down the road. "What is it, grandfather?"

The old man kept his voice low. "In this place, when the bandits stopped us nines of nine years ago, a young man of our company challenged them. He told them to draw a circle, and they did."

"And what happened?"

"He slew them all. An autumn breeze works harder stirring leaves than he did slaughtering them. He did not wear your name, but he did bear the crest of the black tiger hunting."

"That would be something hard to forget."

"I never have." The old man sighed. "If my eyes were good, I could see that you are the same man, untouched by the years. Why didn't you kill them this time?"

"As you agreed, grandfather, that was something hard to forget." Moraven's blue eyes gazed again toward Moriande. "I haven't forgotten, and I *have* learned."

Chapter Two

36th day, Month of the Bat, Year of the Dog
9th Year of Imperial Prince Cyron's Court
162nd Year of the Komyr Dynasty
736th year since the Cataclysm
Anturasikun, Moriande
Nalenyr

Keles Anturasi leaned against the marble balustrade in the elevated garden at Anturasikun. The stone felt cool beneath his hands and he knew, almost by touch, where it had been quarried and how long it had taken to reach the capital. *Solaeth, shipped over the Dark Sea, then down the Gold River.* He smiled to himself, his hazel eyes bright in a handsome face with sharply sculpted cheekbones and a nose that had been broken once when he was a child. He'd known many a happy day in the garden, and knew today would be happier still.

He looked over the city, casting his gaze to the southeast and toward the Imperial Palace. Through his mind flashed half a dozen routes for getting from the Anturasi stronghold to the Prince's demesne. He could travel through the wide streets that now thronged with Festival visitors, or wend his way through warrens, alleys, and places where, were he wearing his own Festival finery, he would have been prey. He had traveled them all since he was a child, learning the city fearlessly—or at least fearing it less than incurring his grandfather's wrath if he did not.

That was an Anturasi's lot in life. His family had shown a talent for cartography, which was all but useless in the Time of Black Ice. It didn't matter that you knew how to get from one valley to another when you had no idea what sort of horror you might find there. As the world emerged from the years of ice, snow, and wild magic, the Anturasi gift took on greater significance. Until the time of his grandfather, however, Nalenyr had neither the leadership nor the resources to exploit it.

Fifty-six years ago—when his grandfather was only his age and the world was smaller—a tiger-sized wolf was ravaging herds in the northern mountains. The then–Naleni Prince—Prince Cyron's father—was set to go hunting and had a dream that he would slay the beast. Try as he might, year after year, the Prince failed to fulfill his dream until Qiro Anturasi performed a minor miracle. Qiro had undertaken a survey of the area and presented the Prince with a map that took the Prince directly to his prey. The Prince slew the wolf and granted Qiro a private audience as a reward.

The story had become part of family legend, along with other tales of Qiro's subsequent travels west to reclaim the Spice Road. Though he failed in that latter mission, the Prince still showed great favor to the family. Qiro moved to its head, eclipsing his own father. He browbeat his brother, Ulan, into absolute obedience. Qiro's iron-willed control of the family soon extended to all Ulan's progeny and his own grandchildren. Keles and his siblings knew very well what Qiro expected of them and complied at one level or another.

At my level, compliance; at Jorim's, none. Nirati cannot, though she does what she can. Keles shivered. His sister did not have to worry about Qiro's ire, and both the older siblings did what they could to shield Jorim. Without their efforts, Qiro would have broken him, chaining him to a drafting table beside his cousins, shutting away someone who lived to explore the world.

Keles knew, someday, there would be no protecting Jorim and that even he would fall under his grandfather's suspicions. Qiro had usurped his own father's place. Ryn Anturasi, Keles' father, had fought horribly with Qiro until his death. The old man clearly expected that Keles or Jorim would try to replace him and, if the family's fortunes were to be maintained, one day one of them would.

Not something to think about. Not today. Not before the Festival. Not before she gets here.

Keles cleared his mind of dire musings and studied the city again. Bright pennants and brighter coats of paint made the city new again. It had been a good year, with a number of sailing vessels returning to the capital, their holds bulging. They carried exotic items from places as far as Tas al Aud and Aefret, including dyes for clothes, spices, artworks, and strange animals for the Prince's preserve. Envoys from distant nations likewise took passage on the Prince's Wolves, sailing to Moriande to celebrate the dynasty's anniversary.

The Imperial duties levied on those cargoes would easily pay for the Festival. More importantly for the Anturasi, since those ships used charts created by Qiro, a percentage of their profits came to him. While any one merchant might profit when a ship returned, Qiro profited when *any* ship returned. This fact was not lost on anyone, least of all the Prince.

The crunch of footsteps on the gravel at the garden's edge brought Keles around. A shaven-headed servant in brown bowed. "Pardon, Master Keles, but Lady Majiata Phoesel has come."

"Please, bring her here." The invitation was but a formality, for he could see Majiata waiting in the shadows of the tower's entrance. Formalities had to be observed, however, as she was nobility. Despite their being betrothed and of intimate acquaintance, familiarity would not do. He bowed low in her direction and waited until the hem of her blue gown came into view before he straightened, fighting to hide a smile.

Taking tiny steps, she entered the garden, bypassing stone planters brimming with the finest examples of *bhotri* in the capital—outside the Imperial Palace, of course. Several of the plants had been grown by *jaecaibhot,* whose skill reached magical proportions. The miniature pine tree at her right elbow perched on a rock and trembled with a breeze that went unfelt. Other dwarf trees would produce bountiful harvests of pea-sized fruit as succulent as their normal-sized cousins regardless of the seasons, so skilled was the Mystic arborist in the Anturasi employ.

Majiata, as always, surrendered little in comparison to the brilliant blooms in the garden. Gold silk trousers and sash complemented the deep blue of her robe. A sapphire set in gold rested at the hollow of her throat, and smaller examples of the same stone in gold settings shone from her earlobes. Her dark hair had been gathered and swept up, restrained by a gold chain around her brow, with a sapphire dangling at her forehead. While her features were not as delicate as those of most hereditary nobility, she had an undeniable beauty. Heavy eyelashes and lids blackened with kohl accentuated her cerulean eyes, and reminded him of how she looked in the dimness of the midnight hours.

"Welcome, my lady Majiata."

She inclined her head only slightly in his direction, giving him the first inkling of trouble. "You are kind in your greeting, Keles."

"Mai, what is wrong?"

He took a step forward, raising his hands toward hers, but she did not return the gesture. For a moment he thought it might be that she objected to his attire, for his bright yellow shirt did not match the gold of her robes, and his trousers and overshirt of green were far less rich in hue than her gown. He let his hands drift back to his sides and lifted his head, straightening his spine.

No anger flashed in her eyes, but he fully expected it. Her reply came softly, but even whispered it was less a question than a statement. "You have not told him yet."

"No, darling, but don't be angry." Keles smiled broadly. "It is not easy to tell my grandfather anything. You know this."

"But you have not even tried." Her left hand emerged from the opposite sleeve, letting the diamond ring he'd given her glint in the sunlight. "If you truly loved me, you would have told him what I asked you."

"Mai, you know I love you." He clapped his hands together and wanted to leap with the joy in his heart. "I've thought of something much better, my dearest. It's perfect."

"Perfect, my darling, is for us to be together, not separated as you go off on the *Stormwolf*. I know that your grandfather has reserved a great honor for you by sending you to sail around the Eastern Sea. I know there is much to see and explore. I know you dearly want to do that, but you will be gone for a year, two, *five*! What of us all that time?"

"I know, I know, but that is what is perfect about my plan, Majiata." He looked at her with hazel eyes full of enthusiasm. "You took my ring knowing what I would be doing, what my life would be like. And I want to be with you, so I have found the perfect solution. I've made the arrangements. You can come *with* me in the fleet, on the *Stormwolf*."

Her gaze flicked up as she whispered breathlessly and a tremor ran through her. "Come *with* you?"

"Yes, darling, yes, it will be perfect." He took her hands in his, squeezing them. "Istor Araset is the *bhotcai* who will be with us, and you can learn much from him. Think of the new plants you will see, the new places! We will walk where men have not been before. We will taste exotic fruits. We will see animals and vistas no man has ever laid eyes on. You *will* be a great help for me and to me. We will even have a cabin to ourselves. I won't command the ship; Anaeda Gryst will do that, but she is a brilliant captain who has sailed to Aefret and back again faster than anyone else. She's willing to take you with us . . . What's wrong?"

His voice petered out as she withdrew her hands from his.

"*With* you?" She looked at him with shock and pain in her eyes. "Do you love me so little as to even suggest that?"

Keles blinked in amazement. "W-what do you mean? I love you so much I want you with me."

"But you don't think of me at all, do you? You think only of yourself." She opened her arms wide. "You would take me from family and friends?"

"I will be your family."

"And if you die on the trip?" She turned away from him. "You describe all the wonders, but you forget the horrors. The diseases. The lack of water. Stale food. Storms. Storms sufficient to snap a ship in half. You'll sail south, maybe to find these fabled Mountains of Ice, but what if you do? You'll spend months with your teeth chattering, losing fingers and toes to frostbite. Do you want me to lose fingers and toes, Keles?"

"No, you don't understand . . ."

"And freezing is the least of our worries. Don't you see that? Don't you know why I want you here, in Moriande, learning from your grandfather?" Her voice became glacial. "Have you forgotten what happened to your father? What Qiro did to your father?"

"M-Majiata, you know better than to believe old wives' tales."

"And you denigrate the truth by labeling it fable." Her eyes slitted. "You were all of seven when it happened and I was barely beyond suckling at my nurse's breast. Your grandfather sent your father off on such a journey. Qiro was jealous of him and your father defiant, so your grandfather had him killed. Your father, the *Wavewolf,* everyone on it, *dead*!"

"No, that is not true. Not true at all." Keles scrubbed a hand over his face, then looked imploringly at her. "Don't you see, Majiata? I have to go on the *Stormwolf*. It is my duty to my family, to ensure the future. *Our* future. Can't you understand that?"

"I understand completely, Keles. I understand how selfish your love is—that you put the Anturasi before your love of me. I want you here not only so he cannot kill you, but so I can help you."

She clasped her hands together, looked down, and spoke calmly in a small voice, a helpless voice. "You know that growing flowers is not my true talent. That lies at court, using my influence with my family to help shape the court's thinking. I can do that for you. I want to be a help to you, but if you are going to abandon me, I am powerless to promote you. And perhaps you think ill of me, but I do think of the Anturasi fortunes. There are ships that go out without Anturasi charts. But with my help, laws can be passed so that will never happen again. Don't you want that?"

"Of course I do, Mai."

"But I think you want adventure more. You want to be sent away from here. Away from me. Why is it you want to be sent away from me, Keles?"

The sob that choked her last word raised a lump in his throat that prevented him from speaking. He lifted his hands and settled them on her shoulders, but she shrugged her way free, dipping her head as she began to weep. Keles froze, uncertain what to do. His guts knotted and his empty hands flexed.

With all the time in the world I could not think of the right thing to say.

"The answer to your question, Mai Phoesel, should be obvious."

Keles turned as his twin sister entered the garden. As tall as he was, with lighter brown hair and green eyes, she had sharp features that had earned her the nickname of Fox when they were children. Though she had since grown into a beauty, that vulpine nature still lingered, though more in the tightness of her eyes and the quickness of her mind than in anything else. Lest anyone forget it, however, her black robe did have running embroidery of foxes gamboling.

Mai turned and snorted. "Spying again, Nirati?"

"Hardly necessary, since you always read from the same script. I have said nothing to my brother before. I speak now because what you ask affects my whole family. It is not that I love you any less than the family, dear brother, but her meddling has gone too far."

Keles frowned. "Really, Nirati, I don't think . . ."

"You *do* think, brother, when given the chance, but you don't see when you are being used." His sister pointed at Mai, who seemed to have shrunk a little. "She wants to help you, of course. She mentions ships that sail without Anturasi charts. Well, her family's trading company has long done without them. Her father came to our grandfather after you were betrothed and demanded access to charts since we were 'practically family.' Grandfather told him to come back when she was actually wedded to you and her belly swollen with a child we could prove was yours."

Mai gasped in horror and Keles moved to comfort her.

"Don't bother, brother, she's not worth it. Her only failing in this matter has been because of her vanity." Nirati's eyes sharpened. "She was supposed to have conceived your child by now, but she failed. Was it that you dreaded morning sickness, Majiata, or feared becoming bloated and ugly—as ugly as you are inside?"

"Neither." Mai stroked a hand over her belly. "You're a fool, Nirati. Two nights ago your brother and I lay together. Even now his child is growing in my belly."

"No, little Mai." Nirati shook her head, her brown locks a shimmering curtain spilling over the shoulders of her gown. "For one who prides herself in a paltry talent at *bhotri,* you have long since neglected your studies. You must have noticed the tinge of bitterness in your night's-cup of wine before you slept. It was tincture of clawfoot."

"You *poisoned* me!" Mai's mouth gaped in horror, then looked at Keles. "Your sister tried to kill me."

Keles looked at his sister and the fury on her face burned through the outrage Mai's plea had spawned in him. "You are exaggerating, Mai. She would have done you no harm."

"I did her no harm." Nirati shrugged nonchalantly. "Technically it was a servant of yours, bought and paid for with Anturasi gold, who administered the drug, but it was prepared with consummate skill—skill far greater than you possess."

"At least I have a talent, Nirati," Majiata snarled.

Keles stepped between them, turning to face Majiata. "Stop. Go no further."

"Again you deny the truth, Keles. Everyone knows your sister is to be pitied. She's talentless. No skill at mapmaking, no skill with plants and herbs. Others who have known such shame have had the good grace to destroy themselves."

Keles' hands knotted. His words came precise and clipped. "I told you to go no further. There is more than one type of shame, Majiata. Remember, Empress Cyrsa was late come to her talent."

"Your sister is no Cyrsa."

"But she is my sister and I love her." He lifted his chin. "If you love me, you will stop. Now."

Majiata hesitated, her blue eyes flicking as she measured her responses. Keles wanted her anger to break, for her to ask his forgiveness. With every heartbeat that she did not, he realized his desire was in vain, as his earlier happiness rotted within him.

"Is that it, then? You choose your sister over me?"

"I make no such choice. I love you, I love her, I love you both. I do not choose." He frowned and his voice slackened. "And you should not make me choose."

"Oh, no, Keles, I could never make you choose. But clearly I never had a chance here at all, did I?" Majiata's eyes welled with tears. "I offered you everything. I offered you a future of your own, Keles, and you will not permit yourself to grasp it."

Nirati came up on his side. "No, Majiata, you offered him an illusion. *His* future was to be *your* future, for the benefit of *your* family. To you he was no more than a stud who could draw maps."

Mai slapped Nirati, snapping her head around. She raised her hand again, but Keles caught her by the wrist. "Don't."

Mai screeched in fury, wrenched her hand free, and clawed at his face. Keles fended her off and she retreated. Her fingers hooked spastically and anger knotted her face into ugliness. "I won't have you, Keles Anturasi. You and your family will always be prisoners here. I will have no part of it. Our engagement is *ended*!"

She stormed back toward the tower, but Nirati darted after her and caught her by her robe's sash. "The ring."

"What?"

"The ring. You broke the engagement, Majiata. The ring remains here."

Mai turned and looked at Keles, tears painting her cheeks with black. "Will you grant me nothing for my love?"

Keles looked down, his guts twisting slowly around an icy core.

Nirati laughed harshly. "You deserve nothing, Mai."

"Fine." She tugged the ring free and hurled it against his chest. It bounced off. "I want nothing of the Anturasi. You are dead to me."

Mai waited for a moment to hear any reply he might have, but Keles remained silent. She shook her head, then stalked off in a rustle of silk and a flash of blue that seemed to take the rest of the color from the garden with it.

Nirati bent to retrieve the ring. She stood slowly and held it out to her twin. "She was not worthy of you."

Keles started to speak, but his dry throat closed. He swallowed hard, then frowned at his sister. "What you did was cruel."

"To her? It was better than she deserved. For months she has bragged that she had you right where she wanted. She said you would be trapped here in our home, while she was free to enjoy the court and life in the capital. She would bear you children, but her family would help raise them, and she knew you would grant her that freedom. She had it all planned out."

He resisted the urge to cover his ears with his hands. "Couldn't you have just told me?"

"Could we?" Nirati laid a hand on his upper arm. "You saw in her the sort of woman she *could* have become, were she not grasping, greedy, and venial. You would not have listened. You did not. Mother cautioned you against sleeping with her, but you went ahead and did so anyway."

He slowly nodded. "I know it was foolish." He sighed heavily. "It's a good thing, I guess, that Mother prepared the tincture of clawfoot and bribed a servant to give it to Majiata."

Nirati laughed. "We didn't bribe any servant and we certainly didn't poison her. What I said was a trick. I told her a servant in the Phoesel household was giving her clawfoot. You know she will not rest until she determines who it was. And that will prove an impossible task."

"But . . ." He pointed off across the river toward the Phoesel compound. "Majiata and I *have* been sleeping together. If she wasn't . . . if you weren't . . . then she *could* be pregnant."

"Keles, my dear brother, we did not dose Majiata." Nirati caressed his cheek. "Mother is very good. You never recognized the taste of snipeweed in your night's-cup, did you?"

"I just thought the wine was a bit off. This time of year, before the new vintages are out . . ." He stared down at his empty hands. "I've been a fool, haven't I? I had convinced myself she would come with me, that she loved me."

"Maybe part of her did, Keles." Nirati rubbed his arm. "Mother and I didn't want to hurt you, but we knew she would hurt you more. She would hurt all of us. And it was better our acting than Grandfather. He never would have let her sail with you. You *do* know that."

"Well, I was thinking I might not actually tell him."

Nirati lifted his chin and looked him in the eyes. "Keles, you will be communicating with him, mind to mind, during your journey. I know I don't have that talent—though we did work hard, didn't we, to try and see if I did? What I know of it, though, is that while you don't actually converse, Grandfather can rummage around in your mind. Do you think you could have hidden her presence from him?"

Keles winced. "Once at sea he wouldn't have recalled us."

"In one of his rages? You really think he wouldn't have?"

"No, you're right, he would have. Or ordered her put ashore." He exhaled slowly. "It wasn't my best plan."

"Keles, you're smart and disciplined and methodical, which is why someday you will replace Grandfather." Nirati held up the ring and let sunlight flash in rainbow glints from it. "Majiata didn't let you think. When you have time, you will see things the way the rest of us did."

"You're right, I'm sure." Keles swallowed hard, then sighed. "I just hope she will be well."

"Majiata?" Nirati shook her head. "No, I won't say it. It's good that you are still concerned, though you should not be. I think, brother dear, she will recover."

The look on his sister's face told him what she refused to. *She thinks Majiata will have a new suitor by the end of the Festival. Perhaps sooner.*

"I'll have to tell Captain Gryst that Majiata won't be coming on the trip."

Nirati raised an eyebrow. "Did she actually say she'd let Majiata on her ship?"

"She said she'd find a way to get her on board."

"In a crate, no doubt. From what I hear of Captain Gryst, she would not have put up with her nonsense for long." His sister smiled. "Of course, load some ballast in the crate and dump it over the side . . ."

"Nirati!"

"I'm sorry, Keles." She gave him a warm smile. "I just didn't like her and I am glad this is over—though, with her, I know there will be repercussions. Nothing we can't live with, though."

"Repercussions." Keles shivered. "What can I expect from Grandfather and Jorim?"

"Nothing from Grandfather. He was insulated in the matter, save from the demands of her father. But it is not like he hasn't dealt with angry merchants before." Nirati shifted her shoulders. "Jorim didn't approve of her, but said nothing. The last fight he was in, however, was with her cousin."

Keles winced. "Does Grandfather know about the fight?"

"Not yet, but he will."

"Can't we . . ." Keles read her expression. "What is it?"

"The Prince is coming here, tonight, to speak with Grandfather. You and Jorim are to be there as well. There will be no disguising that Jorim has been in another fight."

Keles shook his head. "It's Festival. Things should be going well, not poorly."

"Cheer up, brother. Not everything is bad."

"No?"

"No, indeed." Nirati gave him a broad smile. "Just think, your night's-cup will now be sweet again. Perhaps it's not much, but . . ."

"I know, Nirati." He kissed her on the forehead. "There are times when that will have to do."

Chapter Three

36th day, Month of the Bat, Year of the Dog
9th Year of Imperial Prince Cyron's Court
162nd Year of the Komyr Dynasty
736th year since the Cataclysm
Inn of the Three Cranes, Moriande
Nalenyr

As the low tapping came at the door, Moraven Tolo felt his heart beating faster than it ever did in combat. "You are welcome."

The latch rose and the door swung open silently on freshly greased hinges. A young man with black hair and bright blue eyes stood on the threshold, snapping off a deep bow. Moraven bent to match it—not to honor the boy, but the man who shuffled into the doorway in his wake.

Phoyn Jatan had never been a tall man, and age had stooped him so that he barely topped five feet. His hair, thinned to wisps, no longer benefited from being dyed. The grey threads did little to hide the liver-spotted scalp, nor did the grey robe hide how skeletally thin he had become. His shuffled step and the way he leaned heavily on a gnarled walking stick mocked the lithe and fluid warrior he had once been.

Moraven sank to a knee. "Your visit honors me, Master, more than words can express."

Jatan's voice suffered little from age. "That you would journey here at my request honors me, *jaecaiserr*."

Moraven straightened up, but remained half-kneeling and

gestured to the room's low cot. It had been pushed against the wall and he'd demanded every pillow in the inn in preparation for the visit. "Had I expected to receive you in my chambers, Master, I would have chosen a place more suitable."

The old man waved away his apology as he shuffled to the bed and seated himself. The young man closed the door, then took the walking stick and knelt at Jatan's right hand. "I asked you to come to me during the Festival. It begins tomorrow, but I desired to see you sooner. Thank you for indulging me."

Moraven read the man's grin and the playful light in his eyes. "How did you know I was here?"

Jatan settled back against the mountain of pillows. "Must you ask, Moraven? I like that name, by the way. Very strong. It suits you better than the others."

"Thank you, Master." He brought his other knee down and settled back on his ankles. "But that does not answer the question."

Jatan turned to the youth. "Study him, Geias, for this is the mien and focus of a Mystic. He is a better example than I."

Moraven looked at the boy. "But my Master is a better example of how to evade. If he has a scar for each prince beneath which he has lived, it would only be because he has carelessly let a cat scratch him in the last week."

The old man laughed. "I have missed you, Moraven. As *my* Master often said, 'Better the sharp swordsman than the sharp blade.' "

"Then, lest I become sharper, your answer to my question?"

Jatan nodded slowly. "I would tell you that I felt you, four days ago, as you dealt with the bandits on the road, but you would tell me I was remembering a time before."

Moraven remained silent, but raised an eyebrow.

"No, I know that you, of all my students, would not believe it, even if it were true." The old man coughed dryly. "A boy with a withered arm came to the *serrian* two days ago, bearing Macyl's overshirt. He'd brought it to the family, and they wished us to have it. The boy and his family thanked me profusely for my student—one whose name I did not know—and how he saved them."

"It was a simple matter, Master, but one that will grow in the telling, I fear."

"It already has, but not badly. They reported evidence of *jaedun* in how you disarmed the archer." The old man smiled. "I am not certain they were wrong, though I discount reports of lightning flashing and thunder clapping. You have not become *that* powerful, have you?"

"If lightning and thunder were possible, you would have long since displayed it, though perhaps not to as unworthy a student as myself."

"You were never unworthy, Moraven." Jatan coughed again. "You were always clever."

"Not always, Master. Were that true, I would not have come to you as I did." Moraven shifted on his knees and reached for his leather traveling bag. "I did manage to find some *wyrlu* in the west. It is of Virine manufacture, if you wish, Master."

"Geias, there is no reason you will mention this to your mother."

The youth nodded.

The old man smiled and rubbed his hands together as Moraven produced a bottle, uncorked it, and poured an amber liquid into two small cups. "Eron's wife takes good care of him and the other students, but she *fusses* over me."

"I seem to recall other Mistresses of House Jatan who fussed similarly." Moraven handed him one of the cups. "I have no complaint, for without being fussed over, I would not have recovered."

Jatan sniffed at the liquor, then tossed it off in one gulp. His eyes screwed shut for a moment, then he swallowed hard. He coughed again, but only lightly, then spoke in a harsh whisper. "You underestimate your vitality."

"No, Master, I am aware of my mortality."

Moraven Tolo had first met Phoyn Jatan in Moriande, awakening on a sleeping mat in the Soshir Estate. He'd been lying there facedown, his chest swathed in bandages. He had no recollection of who he was or whence he had come. Things around him felt strangely familiar, but also quite alien, as if a hundred rice-paper paintings had been chopped into pieces and fitted together with no particular scheme.

The only thing he knew about himself was that he had been horribly wounded with a sword. The slash had taken him on the left side, stopping a handwidth shy of his spine. An inch or two of the scar remained visible on his chest and a finger of it along the flank. The blow should have killed him; but he was left alive to wonder if he had been struck in the back because he was a coward running from battle, or if enemies he now could not recall had genuinely intended to kill him.

Phoyn Jatan and his wife of the time, Chyrynal, had nursed him to health. Jatan built the sword school around him in his old Master's estate—which Moriande's growth had since overtaken. It became apparent that whoever he had been, he had been a swordsman of no mean skill. This spoke against the idea of cowardice, but Moraven worked hard to ensure this charge would never be leveled against him again. It was the reason the bandits had been slain on the road to Moriande eighty-one years previously, and countless others had died beneath his blade before then.

"Mortality, Moraven, is a concern for all of us." Jatan held the cup out for a refill. "Once I knew a man claiming to be a student of mine was here, I sent students out to seek a swordsman of skill. Do you know of a young man who calls himself Desheil Tolo, and claims to be your cousin? He wears the leopard hunting as a crest and speaks the southern dialect."

"No, but there was the business down in Erumvirine that might have caused him to choose that name." Moraven poured more of the grain alcohol for his Master. "Did he take it in my honor, or shall I be required to strip him of it?"

"Eron is making inquiries." Jatan sipped at the liquor this time. "The boy you sent, tell me his story."

"I did not send him."

"Moraven, please." The old man shook his head. "My Master told the tale of flying a hawk against forest doves. His hawk stooped and knocked one from the sky, which fell and hit a peasant's cook pot, spilling thin broth on a fire. The peasant demanded payment for his supper, since it was Master Virisken's hawk that began the loss. Your sending the boy to Macyl's family began this chain."

Moraven frowned, then drank and let the liquid burn its way down his throat. "As I recall, Master, *your* Master paid the peasant, then demanded the money back from him in payment for the dove, which the peasant's family were then roasting. When the peasant said the dove was from the gods and refused to pay, Master Virisken slew him for blasphemy."

"True, true, but the Empire had not been divided into the Nine at that time, so things were different. And your attempt to evade *my* question was bold but in vain."

"There is not much to tell. They come from the south, a day's walk from Erumvirine, and are millers. The boy had ventured up the millstream and found a place where the bank had been eroded. It opened into a little hole and he crawled in. Something was shining there, glowing with a blue light. The boy reached for it with his left hand." Moraven shrugged. "He remembers nothing else. His father found him floating down the stream and thought he was dead, but only his arm was withered."

The old man's brows furrowed. "Do they suspect how it changed him?"

"I think they saw nothing beyond the withered arm. They say they tried to find the place where he was hurt, but there were rains, the stream flooded, and all signs were gone. Still, the site was a mile upstream and they credit the gods with the miracle that he did not drown. They really did not want to speak of any of it, and only told me what had happened after they learned what I am."

"They alone would associate with you once your status was revealed?"

Moraven nodded. "Hardly a surprise."

"No, memories of the Time of Black Ice remain sharp, even in the minds of those who did not live through them." Jatan beckoned for more *wyrlu* and his hand quaked as Moraven refilled his cup. "In some ways, I bear my Master anger. He rode with his best warriors to join Empress Cyrsa in the Turasynd Campaign. It was even his idea to take the Imperial treasury in the wagons and travel northwest, along the Spice Route, to draw the barbarians away from civilized lands. He and the others went off to die, but me he left behind to protect Nalenyr. I do not think he knew what they would unleash."

Moraven nodded slowly. The Empire's best warriors had traveled with the Empress to prevent the barbarians of the Turca Wastes from destroying the Empire. Warriors of sufficient skill—such as he, Master Jatan, and Virisken Soshir—could reach the state of *jaedunto*.

Their skill connected them with *jaedun*—the magic that flowed like a river through everything. When they fought, especially against other *jaecai,* excess magic leaked out. Many were the circles outside villages where duels were fought to contain the magic, and odd were the effects therein. Snow might never melt despite the hottest summer, or rain might always fall there without a cloud in the sky. Men bred horses and dogs in those circles, hoping the wild magic would create a superior beast; but they always did it in the dead of the night, lest their neighbors learned they were playing with magic.

The Turasynd, living in the northern desert, cared little about the consequences of magic. It could do little harm to their barren homeland, and great good if it made their herds fertile or crops bountiful. When their population grew too big, a shaman bound the tribes together and invaded the Empire. The Empress lured them north and west, away from the centers of civilization, then engaged them in a grand battle the likes of which had never been seen before or since.

Jatan's eyes focused distantly. "The wild magic came in towering clouds that cloaked the sky and hid the sun. Snows came—foul black snow carried on savage winds that could peel the flesh from man and beast. Better that death, though, than what would happen if the magic in those storms touched you. The boy traded a withered arm perhaps for the ability to breathe water, or to need no breath at all, but that's because the magic is weak now."

He glanced at Geias. "Back then, villages vanished in blizzards and glaciers scraped the earth down to bedrock. There are yet places in the mountains where you can see a village made of ice—houses, people, wagons, animals, all there, frozen in place as they were when a storm caught them."

Moraven nodded. "I've seen it, Master, though much is melted now. The wild magic does gather and play sometimes, but seldom in the Nine. It's just in the Wastes now—Dolosan and Ixyll, or so I am told."

"But fear of it remains—and that, Geias, is why you study hard." Jatan coughed once more, but did not drink. "Back in the days of Empire, men grew careless. We studied swordsmanship to reach *jaedunto,* but others wanted the magic faster. Prince Nelesquin and his *vanyesh* studied *xingna* to master it, to master *jaedun*. Once they had the magic, they found ways to use it to enhance their skills. They sought the simple way, and it was their folly that caused the Cataclysm."

Moraven nodded, more out of respect for his Master than belief. Master Jatan had been one of the few *jaecai* left in the Nine—the Nine Principalities the Empress had divided the Empire into for safekeeping. He had been instrumental in convincing the Naleni Prince that the *vanyesh* had to be destroyed. Moreover, the study of magic had to be eliminated. In his view, the Imperial warriors could have contained their magic and prevented the Cataclysm, but the undisciplined *vanyesh* could not.

But this is because Prince Nelesquin and your Master hated each other. You are my Master, but I see how their hatred has tainted you.

In the wake of the Cataclysm, with magic storms raging, years of no summer and countless people dying of starvation or worse, the system of schools for teaching various skills was reinforced. The common folk distrusted magic, but were assured that anyone who had learned enough to access it could be trusted. And it was true that few achieved such mastery. Even now, with the population approaching pre-Cataclysm levels, this remained constant. Still, the fear had power, and were it not for Dunos and his family, Moraven would have traveled the last two days to Moriande alone.

The school system—at least the martial schools—had also begun the *xidantzu* tradition. The best warriors were to travel the Nine and even beyond, fighting injustice and cruelty, without regard to nationality or politics. No lord could command them and, while many good students ended up in garrisons and militias, the very best relished their freedom. The creation of the *xidantzu* meant no lord could gather an army akin to that of the Empress, so the chances of a pitched battle triggering another Cataclysm became miniscule.

"It is folly, Moraven, that caused me to ask for this audience."

"Yes, Master?"

"What happened to the boy could happen to the Nine." Jatan sat forward and a pillow slipped down to prop him up. "As you have said, the wild magic has retreated. And, for some, so has the fear of what caused it. There are those who go into the Wastes. They seek weapons of antiquity, looting graves new and old, searching for those things that will build them an army."

Moraven frowned. Weapons and relics of those who had skill would not confer that skill on others—though they might be steeped in the magic of the one who had used them. They would, however, allow one to be more easily trained. He had asked after Macyl's sword because the blade itself had been in that family for generations and was very powerful. Macyl had worked hard to attain his skill and had not allowed the blade to bring him along faster than he could have gone otherwise, but he was rare.

"Master, have you seen evidence of these relics in Moriande?"

"A few, sold as curiosities and antiques, but they were very fine specimens. One or two bore signs of having been on the Turasynd Campaign." His eyes sharpened. "It is supposed that somewhere, out in Ixyll, there is the battlefield where so many died. The weapons there would be full of magic and might make someone think he could be Emperor again."

Moraven arched an eyebrow. "Not Prince Cyron. His older brother might have striven for such, but the gods had other plans for him. Prince Pyrust?"

"Pyrust, of course. Deseirion wishes to consolidate the conquest of Helosunde, then take Nalenyr. There are others, though, who might wish a new dynasty in Moriande." Jatan shrugged. "I wish only that the graves of my comrades and Master lie undisturbed, but I am too old to venture into the Wastes to ensure this. So I wish you to do it in my stead."

"Go to Ixyll?" Dread poured through Moraven. Ixyll had ever been a distant land warped by the wild magic. He believed nothing he heard of it, but also endeavored to hear little. If he ever thought of it unbidden, he exiled his thoughts to far Ixyll itself and felt well rid of them.

"Will you do this for me, Moraven Tolo?"

"Master, I would lay siege to the Nine Hells for you. I shall leave immediately."

Jatan raised an empty hand, then extended his cup once more. "If you leave now, you will not see me during the Festival. Nor will we finish your fine *wyrlu*. This duty I charge you with *is* grave, but even the men involved in it will celebrate the Festival. So shall you."

"My Master is most kind."

"No, Moraven, far from it." He raised the cup, then sipped. "I am sending you to save the world. Enjoy the Festival and remember the world at its best. It will not make you work harder, but it may bring you comfort when the task becomes impossible."

Chapter Four

36th day, Month of the Bat, Year of the Dog
9th Year of Imperial Prince Cyron's Court
162nd Year of the Komyr Dynasty
736th year since the Cataclysm
Anturasikun, Moriande
Nalenyr

His Imperial Highness Prince Cyron patiently awaited Qiro Anturasi's pleasure. The Prince had arrived at the cartographer's tower with only a small retinue of his Keru bodyguard. They, in accord with a decree handed down by his father, waited inside the base of the tower but outside the gates that led to the core. Anturasikun was a labyrinth of public and private spaces, but few were allowed into the private chambers and workshop. Though the Keru had sworn their lives in Cyron's service, even they would not be allowed past the golden gates.

It did not matter that the tower had been fashioned by the nation's greatest builders and decorated by the most celebrated artists, or that the halls housed wonders from around the world. It was a prison. Cyron's father had explained to him, twenty years earlier, why Qiro Anturasi could not be allowed out of the tower. His skill at mapmaking and his knowledge of the world made him more valuable to Nalenyr than all the Nine Principalities' known treasures. Locked in Qiro's head were the worldly details that allowed Nalenyr to prosper, so he, himself, had to be shut away.

To lose him would be to lose everything. When the Empress had divided the Empire into the Nine Principalities, she installed the late Emperor's wives and their families to rule each one. She made ambition counteract ambition and brought the most ambitious of the Princes with her on the Turasynd Campaign. While Nalenyr had not begun as the most powerful or prosperous of the Nine, the reopening of trade with the world filled its coffers. With that gold Cyron could buy troops to hold the lords of Deseirion at bay.

Qiro has given us everything, and yet we take from him freedom. It had seemed then to the Prince as if this were the ultimate cruelty, but he soon grew to understand its necessity. Qiro Anturasi's genius lay at the heart of his personality, and with it came an inability to tolerate stupidity or insubordination. This made Qiro abrupt, abrasive, and unpredictable. *It even makes him think he can keep a prince waiting.*

Cyron laughed, because he knew he would wait. And wait.

Waiting was part of life and Cyron cultivated patience, for it was unlikely to get one killed. His brother, Crown Prince Araylis, had been impatient to see the Desei forced back out of Helosunde and had paid for his impatience with his life. Reports had come back that Prince Pyrust—the man who led the Desei and who had even come south to celebrate the Festival in Moriande—had been the one who killed his brother. Though that act had won Cyron the throne, he felt disinclined to thank Pyrust, since Pyrust himself would be more than happy to kill all the Komyr and take the throne of Nalenyr for himself.

And then Qiro would find himself well matched in temperament and obstinacy.

Qiro had sent a request to the court to be allowed to leave the tower during the anniversary Festival and his own birthday celebration. The request seemed reasonable and Cyron would have been happy to grant it, save for the influx of people from the world over who had come, ostensibly, to rejoice in the dynasty's longevity. His Master of Shadows had complained of the influx of spies during Festival, and Cyron could not chance exposing Qiro to kidnappers or assassins.

Cyron found it highly unlikely that the Desei had traveled south with any intent to kill Qiro—or anyone else for that matter—but he would not have put it past Pyrust to make use of an opportunity. *He could have dreamed up any number of plots that he seeks to put in play.* To limit their ability to cause trouble, he'd made room for Pyrust's entourage in Shirikun, at the city's northern edge.

Likewise the people from Erumvirine to the south had been housed in Quunkun, and the envoys from the Five Princes nations had taken up residence in the towers corresponding to their patron deity. Kojaikun—the tower of the Dog—served as no one's official residence since Helosunde was still subject to Deseirion conquest and Helosunde's Council of Ministers had yet to select a prince. Cyron still allowed his Keru warriors to station an honor guard there. It made the Keru happy and would discomfit Prince Pyrust.

Most of the preparations had been carried out by protocol ministers and their attendants, with the Prince only nominally overseeing things. The honor guard had been posted by direct order, since the bureaucrats and astrologers had deemed it improper. They explained to him about occlusions in the heavens and Kojai's power waning, but he had little tolerance for their explanations and overruled them.

The bureaucrats sought to placate heaven, hell, and earth, while the Prince focused far more on earth. The conflict between Deseirion and Helosunde had less to do with constellations and gods than Helosunde's first prince having been born of a woman from Deseirion. She had urged her son to take her home province as the first step to becoming the new Emperor, and war had simmered on that border long before Pyrust and his father had successfully invaded. But for Naleni support of the Helosundian mercenaries, the Desei consolidation of their conquest would have been completed long since.

Politically it made good sense to placate the Helosundians, since their province served as a buffer between Deseirion and Nalenyr. But Cyron also just liked annoying Pyrust. He hoped his northern neighbor's discomfort would manifest in more of the prophetic dreams the Desei prince believed in, distracting him from any true deviltry.

A protocol minister could have delivered a refusal of Qiro's request, but the Prince overruled that as well. First, Cyron was aware that the minister likely would never make it to Qiro's presence, and certainly would wilt beneath the heat of the cartographer's reaction. More importantly, however, the Prince felt that, as Qiro's jailer, it was up to him to deliver the rejection personally.

The doors in the small rotunda where the Prince waited cracked open, and a small, bent man shuffled through them. His face lit up with a smile, and he raised his head as much as his twisted back would allow. "Highness, nine thousand pardons for keeping you waiting."

The Prince bowed deeply and respectfully. "You honor me, Ulan, by fetching me yourself. Your work is far too important for you to be dispatched on such a trivial task." Cyron purposely refrained from using the imperial "we," though his rank all but demanded it. As it was, Ulan would natter on about how familiar the Prince was with him, and Qiro would see the deference as befitting his status.

Ulan blew a long wisp of white hair from his face. "The pleasure is mine, Highness. My brother said whichever of us produced the cleanest chart of Tirat would have this honor, and I was not outdone."

"You could only have been outdone, Ulan, had your brother set pen to paper, and he still would have been hard-pressed to win."

"You mustn't say that, Highness." The old man shook his head. "But here I am telling you what you can and cannot do."

"In the House of the Anturasi, many take orders."

"They do, they do."

The old man turned and waved the Prince through the doors, then closed them and shuffled along the corridor, which led around and up to the fifth-floor workshop. The Prince walked ahead of Ulan, letting his right hand trail along a wrought-iron railing as he mounted the ramp and moved into the workshop's light. Though he had visited the Anturasi workshop many times, the sight never failed to impress him.

The ramp emerged in the center of a circular room a hundred feet in diameter. Aside from a curtained wedge chopped out of the northern point, copy desks and drafting tables, cabinets with large flat drawers and shelves packed with scrolled charts dominated the room. Pillars supported the vaulted ceiling and, around the walls, high windows allowed illumination. For fear of fire, the Principality provided magical lighting for evening work, and ghostly blue light had often been seen glowing from the tower after sunset.

Dozens of Anturasi worked at the desks. The youngest—grandchildren and great-grandchildren, all of them sprung from

Ulan's loins—fetched paper and refilled inkwells, sharpened nibs and carefully powdered finished maps. Those a bit older copied city maps or diagrams of fortifications—anything that would help them develop the skills they needed to draft the truly important work. The adults, led by Ulan, worked at the largest tables, making nautical charts of incredible accuracy. As travelers returned from voyages and provided details, maps were revised so the next purchaser would have the most up-to-date information possible.

This controlled chaos was filled with the scrape of pen on paper, the click of knife on quill, the occasional crash of an inkwell smashing, and the even less frequent oath. The Anturasi worked quickly, precisely, and as quietly as possible—as all three traits were the only way to insulate themselves from Qiro's wrath.

Qiro's domain, in contrast to the rest of the workshop, lay out of sight beyond the blue curtains hung from ceiling to floor. Prince Cyron made for the opening and, slipping through, smiled. A second curtain—white—ten feet distant, guaranteed that the secrets within would not be seen by accident. He made certain the curtains behind him were drawn tightly shut before he opened the others.

He could not suppress a gasp. A segment of the curved wall had been whitewashed and on it a map of the known world had been drawn twenty feet high and forty wide. The Nine Principalities lay at the heart of the thing, as befitting their place in the world. The Turca Wastes capped them to the north, and the vast Eastern Sea formed the eastern boundary. The provinces and wastelands were drawn in to the west, with the eastern coast of far Aefret forming the western boundary. Above it, sketched in with the faintest of detail, lay the mythical lands of Etrusia.

Before the Time of Black Ice, the Empire had traded with the peoples of Etrusia via a land route, but the Cataclysm that had broken the world had closed that path. Qiro's expedition fifty years earlier had gotten further than any other, but still showed the way was closed. Cyron and he had discussed the possibility of trying the land route again, but the successes at ocean exploration had made doing so a low priority.

So much of the ocean remained unknown, for most of the ships had gone south and then west, along well-known routes. Cyron felt certain that great discoveries would be found to the east, and toward that end the greatest ship of his fleet, the *Stormwolf,* had been created and was preparing to sail.

The Prince found the map at once remarkable and tragic. All of the details of the world that had been confirmed by the Anturasi had been painted in strongly. They had filled in much, but still more lay blank. Even areas within the Dark Sea went uncharted, and it was from there the pirates that preyed upon provincial shipping sailed. Qiro's ages-old desire to fill in these blank areas had caused him to send his son Ryn on an ill-fated voyage. But even the pain of his son's death had not blunted his hunger to explore, and just five years previously Cyron had been forced to refuse another of Qiro's requests to undertake a grand survey himself.

The Prince tore his gaze from the map and received a surprise. Qiro's grandsons, Keles and Jorim, stood with their grandfather, but a fourth man had joined them. The Prince found this remarkable because not only had he never seen anyone outside the Anturasi clan—save himself or his kin—in the workshop; Naleni decree had made it a capital crime to enter the workshop without express state permission. That the man was present bespoke his great importance, and the fact that he was wearing a blindfold indicated Qiro had not wholly lost his mind.

Qiro smiled and crossed quickly to the Prince. Tall and lean, he possessed a full shock of white hair, moustache, and goatee. His pale eyes seemed almost devoid of color, save for the pupil, giving him an inhuman look. Though he was celebrating his eighty-first birthday within the week, he moved with the strength of a man half his age. The rich timbre of his voice, however, clearly had benefited from his longevity.

"Highness, you honor the House of Anturasi with your presence. You have met my grandsons, Keles and Jorim?"

The Prince shook and released Qiro's hand, then greeted the brothers. "I do know them, and treasure them as much as I treasure you, *dicaikyr* Anturasi. Jorim, I think you would like to know that the pair of spotted cats you brought back from Ummummorar last year have mated and produced nine kittens. They are the pride of my sanctuary."

Jorim smiled. Shorter than his brother and stockier, he wore his side locks in braids and had grown a full beard after the fashion of the Ummummori. Though he wore fine and proper clothing, his hair and beard did give him a barbaric air that had caused a bit of a stir amid the Naleni nobility. A blacked eye, split lip, and abrasions on his knuckles indicated he had not abandoned the combative skills that kept him alive in the wilds.

Before Jorim could say anything, the blindfolded man laughed. "Oh, yes, very good. Cats, the *pride* of your sanctuary. Splendid joke, Highness; marvelous. Many shall enjoy it during this Festival."

Cyron frowned. "Who is this, and why is he here?"

Qiro smiled in a manner that would have taken seventy years off his age, were it not for the feral light playing through his eyes. "This is Jesbor Gryst, and he has with him something quite remarkable. I have already purchased it, and with it our domination of the world will go unchallenged."

Cyron's frown deepened as Qiro retreated to a side table and pointed to a mahogany box. The lid had been lifted, and as the Prince approached he saw that two panes of glass separated by a piece of wood had been placed over the box's lower portion. Each pane revealed the face of a clock, and each clock was set to the proper time.

"This will allow us to dominate the world?" Cyron folded his arms over his chest. "I do not think a pair of clocks will daunt Prince Pyrust's legions, and I already know very well how fast they are capable of moving."

"You don't understand, Highness." Qiro whirled away from him and approached the wall map. "Our ships, Highness, have sailed far from here. We have outlined the continent from here to Aefret and we do our best to draw accurate maps. Were we to compare this map with those from a hundred years ago, you would see quite a difference."

He pointed toward the top of the map and drew his hand down. "Our charts are devastatingly accurate in the dimensions of north and south. Why is this? Latitude is simple to calculate, Highness. Measure a shadow at noon and anyone with rudimentary geometry skills can determine how far north or south of the equator they are. It is a simple matter to determine your location.

"East and west, however, are more difficult. North and south have an agreed-upon and fixed point of reference: the equator.

We have a pole star to the north to guide us as well, and I am certain we shall locate such in the south, possibly above the Mountains of Ice, if they exist. The point from which east and west are measured, however, is arbitrary."

Cyron shook his head. "All maps have Moriande as that point. Wentokikun, to be exact."

"*Our* maps, yes, but Deseirion uses Felarati for their charts, and Erumvirine uses Keluwan as their demarcator. But which point is used is unimportant, because the problem is determining the distance between a point and another."

The Prince looked from Qiro back to his grandsons, then the blindfolded man. "But you have made surveys. You have had people pace the distance."

Qiro spun, the sleeves and tails of his gold overshirt flaring. "Exactly, Highness, but we have no one who can walk on water to pace it. Our ships, while they can mark their speed, have trouble marking the speed and direction of currents. All maps, mine included, contain a paradox, for if we take the time it takes to get to Aefret from here, we have one distance. If we mark the time it takes for the return, we have another. We have, in the past, played with the differences and estimated the speed of currents, but even so, that is inexact. A single storm can render any speed-and-direction data useless."

The Prince nodded slowly. "I believe I understand the problem. How is this the solution?"

Qiro clapped his hands. "Jesbor Gryst, please explain this device."

"Well, Highness, first I must say it is not mine. I did not invent it; my son did. You see, I repair things, and my son, Borosan, always studied what I did, but he took it further. He became interested in the new art of *gyanri,* though there is no school for it here."

Cyron nodded, then appended, "Of course," since the man could not see. *Gyanri* was the art of new magic—calculated, mechanical magic. The tradition of training to reach *jaedunto* was revered throughout the Nine, but Nalenyr and Erumvirine had the best schools and so benefited the most from it. Other nations had begun to embrace *gyanri,* in which mechanical devices used magical energy—mostly residue of the Cataclysm—to power them. A sword imbued with magical energy would allow an untrained warrior to fight skillfully, at least until that energy wore out. A hundred enchanted swords were cheaper to produce than a single *jaecaiserr*. While none of the warriors using those swords would be particularly good, few were the swordsmen who became Mystics. In a war of attrition, *gyanri* might well overwhelm masters of the old art.

"Well, Highness, Borosan had an idea for a device that would allow one to communicate via writing over a long distance. He went off with it, and told me to look for a message every noon, which I did, but no message came. My son was frustrated, for the device seemed to work from one side of a room to the other, but not when he took it far away."

"Fascinating, Master Gryst. This, on the table, is the device?"

"No, Highness; dear me, no." The man smiled, clasping his hands together tightly at his belt. "You see, my son realized that I would be looking for his message at noon in the capital, but he was sending at noon from wherever he was. If he was north or south of the capital, it would work. So, what he did was invent this clock. It is a work of *gyanri*. It uses *thaumston* to power it. He made two clocks in case one were damaged or needed more *thaumston,* and set both to the capital time. You see, when he went away, he would send the message according to the time in the capital."

The Prince's mouth hung open for a moment. Qiro had made his passion for the dual clocks apparent, but whatever it would allow him to do was nothing compared to this other device described. If the Prince could instantaneously converse with others far away, such as military commanders in the field, he would be able to coordinate defenses and stop an invasion quickly.

"Does this device work?"

"The clocks work perfectly, Highness."

"No, no, the communication device. Does it work?"

Jesbor shook his head. "My son has not perfected it. He is, even now, traveling and working on it. I think he understood some of the message I tried to send him, for his last wished your Highness the joy of the Festival."

"That's very nice of him, but if he is out somewhere, what is his dual clock doing here?"

The tinker smiled. "Oh, well, Highness, Borosan tired of hauling that big chest around, so he just made a smaller one, more accurate. Fits in a pouch. He's clever, my son."

Too clever to be out wherever he is. The Prince looked at Qiro. "The dual clock helps you how?" Cyron held a hand up and forced himself to think. "Wait, wait. If you are away from the capital, and you look at these clocks at noon where you are, you see the difference in time. That difference in time you translate into miles."

Qiro clapped his hands delightedly, but the tightness around his eyes suggested a bit of displeasure. "Yes, Highness, you have it perfectly. With this device we can accurately chart the oceans. We can venture into places where no one has gone before."

He turned back to the map and laid his hand against the blank expanse of ocean. "Untold treasures lie here, I am certain, and they will be ours. I need your permission, Highness, to outfit the *Stormwolf* with this dual clock and launch it as soon as possible. With the data we recover, our ships will be able to go everywhere. We can colonize new lands, discover new plants, animals, and treasures. Our nation will become even greater than it already is, and you, Highness, will have the means to reunite the Principalities into the Empire and rightfully sit on the Throne of Heaven."

Chapter Five

36th day, Month of the Bat, Year of the Dog
9th Year of Imperial Prince Cyron's Court
162nd Year of the Komyr Dynasty
736th year since the Cataclysm
Anturasikun, Moriande
Nalenyr

Keles fought to keep the surprise from his face and watched as his brother failed to do the same. Keles had long understood the problem with determining longitude. While a variety of clocks, from sundials and marked candles to water clocks and spring-wound clocks, did allow timekeeping, none was precise enough to allow for the measurements a grand survey required. Qiro had experimented for years with a variety of clocks, and though Keles and Jorim had carried and religiously tended to them, upon their return to the capital the time differential had been deemed unacceptable.

What surprised Keles was his grandfather embracing a device created by a *gyanridin*. *Gyanri* was so recent a development, and one best understood outside Nalenyr, that local prejudice had dismissed it. Moreover, Qiro had pointed out that while *gyanri* might create devices that gave skills to the unskilled, it would only work with crude, unintellectual tasks. In keeping with the common wisdom, he had declared it the height of laziness to rely on devices for what training would provide. He had repeatedly sent away people who came to him with devices that would copy maps automatically, or could take readings of the sun and stars.

Yet now he champions this device. The dual clock did seem the answer to countless prayers, but his grandfather's shift in opinion was so abrupt that it almost seemed the man had lost his mind. In anyone else, Keles might have thought he had simply had a revelation and relented in his previous opinion, but his grandfather was too complex for that answer to satisfy him.

The Prince smiled. "I applaud your vision, *dicaikyr* Anturasi. The existence of this device, of course, must be kept secret. I can count on your complicity in this, Master Gryst?"

The blindfolded man nodded. "Oh yes, Highness. And my son, too. I'm sure he's quite forgotten about it, now that he has his new pouch-clock. That's what he calls it, a pouch-clock."

"Splendid." Prince Cyron slipped his hands into the opposite sleeves of his overshirt. "And where is your son now? I should like to speak with him."

"And I know he would like to speak with you, Highness. It would be an honor. I know it."

"Good, have him report to me as soon as he can. After the Festival will be fine, but during would be better."

"Oh, Highness, I wish I could comply, but he's probably in Solaeth now, or perhaps even in Dolosan."

The Prince's eyebrow rose. "He's in the wastelands?"

"On his way. That's where one gets *thaumston,* Highness."

"Yes, very true." The Prince looked back at Qiro. "Perhaps you could have Master Gryst escorted down to the gate? I will see him home after we converse for a moment."

"Of course, Highness. Jorim, please do as the Prince asks."

"Yes, Grandfather." Jorim crossed and took Gryst by the elbow, guiding him from the curtained area.

"Your pleasure, my Prince?" Qiro pointed to a side table with glasses and a pitcher. "Keles, pour us some wine."

"No, thank you, *dicaikyr*."

Keles looked at his grandfather. "Will you drink?"

"No." Qiro lifted his chin and clasped his hands at the small of his back. "What is it, Highness?"

"First, congratulations on finding the dual clock and recognizing its potential. You realize, of course, that the device Borosan Gryst is testing is . . . equally valuable. Its applications, especially as concerns our ability to defend ourselves against the Desei, cannot be overvalued."

Qiro nodded solemnly. "I have seen the value in it, too, for *my* applications, my Prince. Keles and Jorim have the talent that allows them to send me images and information, mind to mind. While this might not be as accurate as I would desire, the time saved is invaluable. Such a device would let me field more survey teams and would provide a check on the accuracy of the dual clock."

"Good. Then we are of a mind."

"That being, Highness?"

"That having Borosan Gryst in the Wastes is too dangerous. I will need you to prepare charts that will allow a group to be dispatched to find him and return him to the capital."

"An expedition to the Wastes, Highness?"

"Yes, Master Anturasi. The one we have long talked about will now be mounted. It will require your charts, of course, else any chance of success is negligible."

"My charts of that area are the best in the world, but they are still not very good." Qiro rubbed a hand over his forehead. "When the Cataclysm released the wild magic, it wrought changes in what had been there before. While the centuries have brought a retreat of the magic, it is not complete. The storms cycle strong and weak, and could still be creating changes. I will make the charts—all based on *my* travels of course—but I cannot swear by their accuracy."

The Prince nodded. "That will have to do, though we will have to remedy that situation as well. If *gyanri* can create things as powerful as what we are talking about, and the Wastes are the source of the *thaumston* that powers them, we will need to find deposits and possess them, or destroy them. That is a matter of national importance."

Qiro's icy eyes glittered. "A matter of *Imperial* importance, even."

"Yes, indeed." Cyron nodded, but refused to let himself be distracted by Imperial daydreams. "I will need those charts by the end of the Festival."

"Consider it done, Highness." Qiro smiled. "I am given leave to place the dual clock on the *Stormwolf*?"

"Yes, of course. The sooner the better. The *Stormwolf* cannot leave until after the Festival. Its premature departure would attract attention."

"As you desire, Highness."

A chill ran down Keles' spine. He dared not move, lest the two of them be reminded he was there, and motioned to his returning brother to likewise be quiet. His grandfather and the Prince were making decisions that would shape the future. The blanks on the wall map would be filled in, and the vast resources of Nalenyr would grow even larger—perhaps large enough to force the other Principalities to join it or be driven to economic ruin.

Prince Cyron nodded. "Good, very good. I had come here to convey bad news, but you have made it a joyous day."

Qiro's head canted. "Bad news, Highness?"

"Yes. Your request to leave Anturasikun is denied. I will, of course, come here to attend your birthday celebration."

The old man's pale eyes flashed for a moment, then he waved a hand through the air. "Consider the request withdrawn, Highness. I have so much to do, I may even cancel the party."

The Prince shook his head. "To do that would attract attention, and we don't want that. No, things will go as planned. You and I will host the Virine and Desei. We will show them how generous we can be. In the future they will hunger for our generosity again."

Qiro smiled his predatory smile—sharp and with a flash of teeth. "As you, in your wisdom, Highness, command."

"Good." The Prince bowed, then made to withdraw through the curtains, which Jorim held open for him. "Your health, and that of the Principality."

Keles did not like the expression on his brother's face. Jorim waited for the white curtain to sag heavily shut, then pointed at Qiro. "You ancient hypocrite!"

Their grandfather's eyes sharpened. "Be very careful, Jorim. I am in a good mood. Do not spoil it."

"I don't care what sort of mood you're in!" Jorim's nostrils flared. "I told you about Borosan Gryst's device *months* ago, when I returned from Ummummorar. You dismissed it. You berated me for being stupid and lazy. You told me that I couldn't keep the clocks wound, so I could never care for such a device. And *now* I discover you have sought out the device? You bastard!"

Qiro kept his voice even, but it came with an edge. "I reconsidered."

"Reconsidered the device, yes, but not how you treated me. What is it about me?" Jorim opened his hands and flung his arms wide. "Do you think me stupid? Do you think me . . . I don't know what. Why couldn't you tell me I was right?"

"Because, Jorim, your being correct this *once* hardly excuses all the times you have been lazy and sloppy in your duty to me and this family."

"Oh, we've trod this path before!" Jorim smashed a fist into an open palm, tearing a scab from a knuckle. "You shame me and I am to be contrite. It doesn't matter that you never were going to admit your error!"

"It was not an error, Jorim. Do you want to know what I thought when you came to me? Do you?" Qiro raised an eyebrow. "Consider carefully before you answer."

Jorim sucked on the bleeding knuckle for a moment, then nodded. "Yes, I want to know."

"I thought, 'It is another of his lazy schemes, to get out of work and excuse his inattention.' Your survey of Ummummorar was adequate, but only barely so. You went, you explored, you discovered things, but your work was hasty. You allowed yourself to be distracted. I saw your face, just now, when the Prince thanked you for the specimens you provided to his sanctuary. That's good for you, but not for *us*."

Jorim licked at his split lip. "You mean *you*."

"I mean *us*. How does your brother benefit? Your sister? Your uncle and cousins? How do they benefit?"

"I do what I do for the *world*."

"You little fool, I *am* the world!" Qiro spun and Keles flinched as the old man's gaze met his in passing. "The world does not exist, *does not exist* until I place it on the map. You bring animals and plants back from places that are nothing and nowhere until *I* show their proper location. The Cataclysm left us buried in black ice. When the dark blizzards came, people died. The world became naught but snow-choked valleys. Small communities huddled within ruins of once vast Imperial cities. Our world shrank until I began to grow it again."

Qiro thrust a trembling finger at Jorim, but his gaze included

Keles. "You are my eyes and ears and feet and hands. You exist to serve *me,* give *me* information, not to indulge your whims picking flowers and trapping animals! And, worse, disgracing us here in Moriande by engaging in common street brawling. You stand there with bloody evidence on hand and face of all I have said."

Jorim's hands knotted into fists and his face flushed scarlet. As veins began to rise in his neck, Keles stepped between the two of them. He pressed his right hand flat against Jorim's breast and felt the rage trembling through his brother.

"Stop it, both of you."

"Don't try to protect your brother, Keles. He has gone too far." Qiro snorted. "I shall see to it that this is a problem no longer. From now on, he shall go nowhere."

Keles held his left hand palm up toward his grandfather. "Stop it. You don't mean that. You're not that stupid."

"What?"

"Don't pretend you didn't hear what I said." *You never heard it from me before, but perhaps it is time you did.* Keles looked at Jorim. "Back away. Calm down."

"This is not your fight, Keles. It's been coming for a long time."

"I think you've done enough fighting for now, Jorim."

A jolt ran through his younger brother. Tears began welling in his eyes as betrayal weighted his words. "You, too, Keles? Nothing I do is good enough. I am lazy. I don't do my work. I am distracted. I have no discipline. I'm not like you."

"Jorim."

The younger man hesitated, his mouth opening and closing a couple of times before the rage drained from him. "I didn't mean that last."

"You should have, Jorim. You should be more like your brother."

Keles felt anger beginning to burn hotly in his chest. He turned to his grandfather. "No, he shouldn't be. I should be more like him."

Qiro straightened up. His voice became a rime-edged whisper. "And exactly *how* do you mean that, *lyrkyrdin* Keles?"

A fluttering started in his belly. *Was it in a cold rage like this that you sent our father off on his last journey?* The use of his formal title emphasized how much he had yet to learn, and reinforced just how angry his grandfather was.

"Despite only being ranked Superior, I have gone everywhere you have sent me. I have learned everything you deigned to teach me. I have been good and dutiful. My reward for all this was to be posted to the *Stormwolf,* and yet you never chose to tell me of the dual clocks? Had you decided I would go before you knew of them, thereby exposing me to the risk of being lost or of bringing back inaccurate data, or was I just not important enough to be told of this discovery? I should have been doing the geometry and preparing to use the device."

"So you believe I think you are untrustworthy."

"Is there another conclusion I should draw from this?" Keles took a deep breath. "I don't think you trust any of us."

"Meaning?"

Jorim answered. "Meaning that you are eighty-one years old. Meaning that Ulan is not, by disposition and training, capable of taking over for you. Neither are his sons or grandsons. Meaning that our father, who could have taken over for you, is long gone. Meaning that Keles, who is best suited to taking over for you, is being sent away and not trained to be able to do what you do. You complain that what I do is not good for *us,* but you do the same thing."

"Keles is not ready to take my place. *You* are even further from it."

"Oh, you may chain me to a desk here, but I never imagined you would train me."

"Ah, so you *do* have some inkling of your limitations. Good." Qiro's eyes narrowed. "You may think it is time for a younger generation to supplant me, but I have forgotten more than you will ever know."

"But what if you forget everything without our ever learning it?"

"Stop, again, both of you." Keles looked at his brother. "I'll speak for myself, thank you."

"Then speak." Qiro and Jorim both looked up as their words echoed each other.

"I will." Keles straightened. "It's a simple fact, grandfather, that Jorim is better suited to the *Stormwolf* expedition than I am. True, I have spent more time at sea than he has, but only a little. You are sending the *Stormwolf* into the unknown, where new plants and animals and people will be discovered. I don't care that you don't care about those things; the Prince does, the nation does, and Jorim is better prepared to bring that information back than I am. I can do the surveys and the math, but he can *discover* things. You are not so foolish as to let your anger with him jeopardize what will be the most important voyage of a lifetime by letting it go without him, are you? Your anger comes from the fact that the two of you are so alike, it's disgusting and obvious to anyone but you."

"Is that so? Then what would you do?" Qiro half turned and gestured at the map. "Would you take over for me? Would you do my work, wipe my mouth, wipe my ass, usher me into my dotage?"

"No, *dicaikyr,* I would learn from you. I would do whatever you asked to guarantee that your work lives forever."

"Oh, of course, Keles, why did I think differently?" Qiro's voice rose dramatically. "You'd learn from me until that merchant-whelp coaxed you to give her family our secrets. You cannot fool me."

Keles' cheeks burned hotly. "Majiata is no longer an issue. She has been sent away, *for the good of the family*."

"Really?"

"Really." Keles found his hands had knotted and forced them open. "I have no desire to supplant you. I know I could *not* supplant you. I merely wish to become capable of keeping your work alive."

The old man nodded slowly. "We shall see, we shall see."

Jorim was about to make a comment, but Keles grabbed the breast of his overshirt and jerked him toward the curtains. Bowing low, pulling Jorim down with him, Keles spoke softly.

"Your wisdom is unquestioned, Grandfather. We serve at your whim and will."

They straightened up and Qiro inclined his head a little toward them. "Words in which you will find fulfillment or damnation, Keles. I pray you have the wisdom to know which is which."

Chapter Six

1st day, Harvest Festival, Year of the Dog
9th Year of Imperial Prince Cyron's Court
162nd Year of the Komyr Dynasty
736th year since the Cataclysm
Moriande, Nalenyr

Moraven Tolo drifted through the throngs of revelers with the ease of smoke wending through the leaves of a tree. Where others might have seen people in a riot of finery, wearing masks to disguise themselves, donning gaudy feathers to brighten their costumes and layering on cosmetics, he saw flows of energy. The crowd moved slowly at times, and in strong surges at others. By shifting his shoulders or twisting his hips, he passed through the masses with barely a notice.

He worked his way past the crowds and deeper into the city not because he felt no kinship with those celebrating. He *did* enjoy the Festival and had enjoyed it in Moriande many times before. Even if Master Jatan had not sent word to him, Moraven would have made the trek in this very special year. A sense of urgency, which fascinated him since he had long since thought he'd conquered that sort of thing, had been growing in him.

He smiled to himself. He enjoyed the spectacle and had a taste for grand things. On the road, wandering from spot to spot, he seldom had a chance to indulge it—which, he admitted, was good for the development of his soul and his art. Even so, he envied the celebrants and wondered how it had been, centuries before, back when the Empire still existed. He knew without a doubt that the Festivals had been even more ostentatious and delightful then, and if instead of traveling through Moriande's streets he could have traveled back in time to those ancient days, he would have gladly embraced the opportunity.

The Harvest Festival—save in years of famine—was always a phenomenon of excess. The hard work of the spring and summer gave way to bellies filled with freshly harvested produce and coffers brimming with money earned from selling surplus. Wines that had been laid down years before were bottled; the finest brewers vied to produce the best beers; and luxuries brought to the capital on trading ships added an element of the novel which delighted everyone. Add to all of that the influx of exotic visitors, entertainers, and merchants, and the eye could not rest for such chaos and commotion.

The crowd parted as one man juggled and another blew long tongues of flame high into the sky. Children shrieked in delight and one small dog barked from beneath the legs of its master. The scent of sizzling, well-spiced meat easily overrode the bitter stink of stale beer, and laughter accompanied it all. Here and there a steely gaze might flash in his direction, but he acknowledged none of them. While any of them might be the man who had wounded him so long ago, the Festival was not a time to battle over ancient incidents.

Moraven weaved his way along the crowded street and found the alley he had been seeking. At the mouth, high up on the wall he discerned a symbol—to almost anyone else it would have appeared to be a triangular crack in the plaster—which told him where he could find Phoyn Jatan. Moraven was uncertain why he had been summoned so soon, but he chose not to question his Master's judgment in the matter.

While some celebrants were making their way up the alley toward the street, Moraven made it through without incident. The alley opened onto a small courtyard, and another alley to the east led to a smaller street with only a few Festival-goers. The swordsman made his way along it, then entered the gate in a tall wooden palisade.

The wooden walls surrounded a small, two-story inn with a sizable courtyard in front. The sign in front had a juggling dog depicted on it and Moraven smiled. Jatan's Master had referred to Prince

Nelesquin as a juggling dog. Moraven doubted the inn's owner knew the significance of the name, and appreciated his Master's sense of humor.

A dozen young men and women clad in the black trousers and shirts of student swordsmen lounged around the courtyard. Geias waited among them, but gave no sign that he recognized Moraven beyond the most cursory of nods. The rest affected to pay him no mind, but he caught their wary glances and heard the hissed beginnings of whispers as he mounted the trio of steps to a short porch. He sat on the bench beside the door, drew off his boots, and took a pair of slippers from a servant. He surrendered his sword to another servant, then ducked his head through the low doorway and passed beneath the stairs to the second floor.

He straightened up again in the common room, and was not so tall that he bumped his head on the low rafters. Directly across from him stood the door into the back and the sleeping rooms. To the left of it sat the bar; the tavern keeper was drawing a draft of rice beer into a small bottle. He placed two cups on a serving tray and a young girl bore it to the table in the other corner.

The two people there watched Moraven carefully. The larger of them could have been a twin to the giant on the roadway save that he wore a patch over his left eye. The other—a whipcord-lean woman with long black hair braided with a red ribbon into a long queue—looked him up and down, then gave him a quick nod. He bowed in their direction briefly—in the manner of *xidantzu* acknowledging fellow wanderers—then smiled as he turned to the man seated at a table at the base of the stairs.

"Bless the Nine Gods, Eron, you look well." Moraven bowed to him and held it as the man rose and returned it. "Those must be yours down there."

"The finest *serrian* Jatan has to offer."

"Then I have passed through the midst of the finest swordsmen in the world, not the least being your son."

Eron, whose white forelock gave him the look of someone perhaps five years further into middle age than Moraven, smiled. "They were only the finest for the moment you were at their heart."

"You are too hard on your students."

"And you always depreciate your own skill."

"*That* I have to take with good grace from your grandfather, but not you." Moraven closed the distance between them and shook Eron's hand. "Have we time to get caught up, or is the Master waiting?"

Eron glanced up the stairs. "Both. My grandfather awaits, and I will join you. Step lively; it is about time for you to see this."

His curiosity piqued, Moraven mounted the stairs quickly. He took one step away from the top to allow Eron to come up, then snapped a bow at Phoyn Jatan. The swordmaster was seated at a table next to the window overlooking the courtyard. Moraven made the bow deep and held it long, only coming up when the old man wheezed out a cough.

Moraven smiled and drew from a sleeve another small bottle of *wyrlu*. "It is an honor to be in your presence again, *jaecaiserr* Phoyn Jatan."

Phoyn shifted in the large chair, resettling cushions. "I see you have not idled away the day, Moraven. More from Erumvirine?"

"I was told this was from Ceriskoron, though the bottle has the markings of a potter in Gria." Moraven looked at the table where three empty cups stood. "I see you anticipated me."

The old man smiled weakly. " 'It is the wise student who addresses the needs of the Master.' "

Eron seated himself across from Jatan. "He slept very well last night and told my wife of a magic tonic he had from a *bhotcai*. Were it not the Festival, she would not have chosen to believe him."

Moraven took the seat facing the courtyard and poured out three equal measures. "The joy of the Festival to you both."

"And you."

All three men drank, then Moraven refilled the cups, but they remained on the table. "I had not expected you to summon me now."

Jatan nodded slowly. "I had anticipated calling for you after the fourth day, but this morning something happened at the *serrian*. I may have to lay another burden upon you, Moraven."

The swordsman laid his hand on the older man's sleeve and was surprised to feel how slender and light the man's arm seemed. "As your Master told you, 'It is a burden if not viewed as a challenge. Only a fool accepts burdens.' "

Phoyn glanced at Eron. "You see, he remembers even the old lessons."

"He was your best pupil, Grandfather . . ."

Moraven frowned. "Now who is discounting his own skill, Eron? I hardly think . . ."

The old man's hand rose to silence Moraven. "It is good the old lessons are remembered, for I teach no more. Eron is the *dicaiserr* of *serrian* Jatan. Geias will continue our school. They teach well, and will be blessed if they find another student like you."

Moraven would have protested, but the look Phoyn gave him silenced the words. The old man had been a master swordsman for longer than Nalenyr had existed as a nation. True blood ran in his veins, conferring on him the same longevity as it did with Moraven and Eron, but it was his mastery of the magic of swordsmanship that had preserved him. While anyone looking at Phoyn and Eron might guess that Eron was his grandson or even great-grandson, if there were fewer than nine generations between them Moraven would have been greatly surprised.

Before Phoyn could continue, a young man in a pristine pair of white silk trousers, shirt, and overshirt trimmed in red entered the courtyard. A red sash closed the overshirt and supported a sword in a scarlet scabbard. His boots were mostly white leather, but had red and yellow scraps sewn on them in a flame motif. Red embroidery at the sleeves and along the breasts of his clothes continued that pattern. Clean-limbed, with an aristocratic cast to his features, the young man paused just inside the gateway and planted his fists on his hips.

He looked around as Eron's students hastily assembled. Into their belts were thrust wooden practice swords. The young man nodded, then looked up toward the window. His eyes tightened, and disdain stained his words.

"Again I am shown students when I have come for a master." His nostrils flared for a moment, then he let his arms slacken and he bowed precisely, though neither too long nor too deep. "I am Ciras Dejote. I come from Tirat, from *serrian* Foachin. I have been taught all they have to teach and I have been sent to Moriande to train with a master."

Moraven frowned. "Released to wander and find another master?"

Jatan shrugged. "They may just be backward on Tirat; I do not know."

Eron stood, inclining his head toward those in the courtyard. "You dishonored my students this morning. You did not deign to fight them."

"You set children before me."

"Not these." Eron clapped his hands. "Dobyl, commence."

One of the smallest of the students left the line, drawing his wooden sword fluidly and moving into the first Cobra form. His sword came up and around at a feint toward the eyes, then abruptly down in a blow angled to break Ciras' left shoulder.

Ciras twisted his shoulder from beneath the blow, then sidestepped toward Eron's student. The interloper's left elbow came up with blinding speed, catching Dobyl across the bridge of the nose. Blood gushed, staining the shirtsleeve, and the audible crack made Eron wince. Dobyl staggered for a heartbeat, then went down with both hands covering his face.

Ciras appropriated his wooden sword and moved to the attack. He beat aside one thrust, then struck that student in the face with the hilt of his practice blade. Spinning, he leaped above a low cut, then effortlessly clipped his foe in the head. A girl came next, shifting from Tiger to Dragon, but Ciras' Scorpion attack came up and smashed into her elbow. She yelped as her sword dropped from numbed fingers.

The next student in line sprang from behind her and lunged low. The wooden blade caught Ciras on the left hip, but he pivoted quickly on his right foot, moving inside the lunge before the student could recover. Had the blades been steel, the wound he took would have slowed him down, but would still have allowed him to lay his blade against his foe's neck. Since the swords were wooden, Ciras earned a bruise, his foe kept his head, and the Tirati was free to face Geias.

Eron's son took a step back and dropped into the Scorpion stance. Ciras countered with Tiger, so Geias shifted to Mantis. Ciras stamped his right foot impatiently, inviting an attack, and Geias gathered himself to answer the challenge.

Moraven rose to his feet and grabbed Eron's arm. "Your son knows better than to attack."

Eron raised a hand. "My son knows his duty. Watch."

Geias leaped a pace left, then slashed his way forward with cuts from high left to low right, then across and down again. He repeated the pattern three times and Moraven readied himself to watch Geias dropped as easily as the others. Though he was better, his repetition meant Ciras now had his measure. *Tiger flows into Scorpion and he'll catch Geias right across the ribs.*

As if Ciras had plucked the strategy from Moraven's mind, he moved left and began the transition in forms. By the time Geias had completed his diagonal slash, Ciras was in position to strike. As Geias' sword moved across in a cut, Ciras' blade would just follow right along and exploit the opening the young Jatan had given him.

Geias, however, had Ciras' measure as well. Instead of the cross-cut, he shifted the wooden sword from his right to his left hand and pivoted on his right foot. The wooden sword came up and back around in a low thrust meant to gut Ciras. As the interloper had already begun his own thrust, nothing shy of a miracle would allow him to parry what would be a killing blow.

Ciras wrenched his body around, kicking up high with his right heel. His body straightened and twisted, his belly slipped beneath Geias' thrust. Snapping his wrist at the same time, Ciras batted away his foe's blade, then landed hard on his back. Before Geias could even begin to recover from his lunge, Ciras cracked the wooden sword hard against Geias' ankles, spilling him to the ground. As if drawn by his blade, Ciras flowed to his feet again and arrogantly kicked Geias' sword away.

Eron looked at Moraven. "You saw?"

As Moraven nodded slowly, Phoyn chuckled dryly. "He *felt*."

"Yes, I felt." Moraven sat. It had been when Ciras had kicked his right heel back and twisted. A flash, a tingle. It dazzled his skin and sank into his flesh with the pins-and-needles pain of a sleeping limb slowly awakening. He had felt it, and felt it strongly.

Jaedun had come off Ciras in a powerful wave.

Moraven frowned. "What rank does he claim?"

"*Lirserrdin.* His Master judged him Superior." Phoyn exhaled slowly and seemed to deflate a bit. "I do not think his Master knew how advanced his student was, just that he was something more than most. Had he any inkling, he would not have sent him away. Having someone so skilled would have brought great honor on the school."

"He will then bring great honor on *serrian* Jatan."

Eron shook his head. "I am a swordmaster, Moraven, but not a Mystic. I cannot teach him."

Moraven turned and looked at the old man. "You can't think of having me train him! I am not a teacher. I do not have a school."

"A school is not what he needs." The old man's brow wrinkled. "You came to me already trained and I guided you on the correct path. 'The journey is of the chosen forks, not the untraveled roads.' "

And there are roads he should not travel. Reaching the state of *jaedunto* did have its benefits, both in how the magic manifested and the longevity it supplied. It could, however, exact a fearful price because it tended to distill the *jaecai*'s personality. If one were kind, considerate, and peaceful, this would be accentuated. *If, on the other hand, he is arrogant and desirous of fame, it will fill him with bitterness.*

Ciras tossed the wooden sword on the porch with a clatter. "I require a master, Eron of *serrian* Jatan. I have beaten your best. Will you have me?"

Moraven looked at Phoyn. "You would have me do this in addition to the charge you have already given me?"

The old man shrugged. "Having a companion can hardly make the first task more difficult or more dangerous."

"You don't expect me to find that prospect comforting, do you?"

"No, I hope you take no comfort in it at all." The old man raised his cup of *wyrlu*. "The discomfort you feel now will be what we all feel if you fail at either task. Peace of the Festival to you, Moraven Tolo, and may the gods be merciful in shaping your future."

Chapter Seven

2nd day, Harvest Festival, Year of the Dog
9th Year of Imperial Prince Cyron's Court
162nd Year of the Komyr Dynasty
736th year since the Cataclysm
Anturasikun, Moriande
Nalenyr

Keles ignored the growled "Go away," and entered his brother's chamber. Jorim shot him an angry glare but, reflected in the mirror, it lost some of its power. The younger Anturasi struggled with tying the gold silk tie, but it was more than that which fed his foul mood. Keles knew that, but also knew he had to settle some issues with his brother or the party that evening would be even more of a disaster than it already promised to be.

"Let me help you with that."

"I can do it myself."

"Yes, but not before snow flies, which means you'll be late for the party."

Jorim snarled. "I don't want to go anyway."

Keles rested his hands on his brother's shoulders and slowly turned him around. "If you don't go, you will disappoint Nirati and our mother. Both have worked hard to fashion the compromise that has let you keep your beard and your braids. I know you don't mind upsetting our grandfather, but their feelings must be respected."

"Certainly. Respect their feelings, but not mine." Jorim let his hands fall from the golden length of cloth, but they slowly balled into fists. "Why is it always everyone else's feelings that matter and not mine?"

Keles took the tie in hand and snapped it against the high, starched collar of his brother's shirt. "By that you mean to ask why I don't respect your feelings. I'm sorry you felt betrayed."

"No, you're not. You knew it would hurt."

"Fair enough, but I also knew I had to sting you to make you stop. I betrayed you, yes, but I stopped you from betraying yourself."

Jorim frowned. "Read that from my mind, did you?"

"Don't joke. I can only touch your mind when we are both concentrating, reaching out, and you know that. And, unlike Grandfather, I don't have the will to work past what you want to share. Nor do I have the desire. I do respect your feelings that much, and respect *you* that much."

"You respect me, do you?"

Keles sighed slowly. Once they had left their grandfather, Jorim had broken away from him. "I know I betrayed you, but this runs deeper than that. What is going on?"

Jorim's hands came up, batting his brother's hands away, then he half turned toward the mirror. "You *mocked* me in front of the old man."

"I did no such thing."

"No, of course not, from your point of view." Jorim crossed the small chamber and flopped down in a chair that almost tipped over backward. "Keles the wise and thoughtful. Grandfather will give *me* the *Stormwolf* because *you* suggested it, not because I earned it—even though I did."

"So? You're getting what you want."

"You don't understand." Jorim pounded a fist against the chair's arm. "Why don't you listen to me? Do I know I would be better on the *Stormwolf*? Of course I would. I speak twice the languages you do, and I pick them up very easily. I have a catalog of animals I've seen, and I'm very good at drawing them in case we can't bring back specimens. I know your *bhotcai* and I've worked with some of the crew before. I'm perfect for that trip and I *should* have it, but I wanted Grandfather to give it to me because *I* made a case for it, not you."

Keles pressed fingertips to his temples. "That makes no sense, Jorim. You'll get it. What matter if I ask?"

"Haven't you listened?"

"Yes. Have you?" Keles nodded emphatically, then brought his hands down and open. "There is something else going on here. Are you afraid that Grandfather will keep you here and break you the way he has Uncle Ulan? Is that it?"

Jorim shifted his shoulders uneasily. "No, I hadn't thought of that. Thanks for sharing."

"Jorim, you know he couldn't do that. You're too strong for him to break."

"You think so? Really?"

Keles nodded. "Really. He'd try, but you would defy him. It would be all Nine Hells rolled into one for the both of you."

"Heh." Jorim's expression brightened for a moment, then soured again.

"Then if that's not it, Jorim, what are you afraid of?"

Jorim scowled, then hunched forward with his elbows on his knees. The silk of his overshirt and trousers rustled as he moved. "I'm afraid that if Qiro sends you, you'll be lost like our father."

"What?"

Jorim looked up, his face tightening as his eyes grew wet. "I was trying to save your life by taking that trip for myself."

Keles shook his head. "You can't believe our grandfather would send me off to die. You can't believe he did that to our father."

"I can and do, Keles."

"You weren't old enough to remember . . ."

"Neither were you. I was two years old; you were five. I don't remember our father. You and Nirati do, and she says you're his spitting image. Others have told me that you're very like him except in one way. All right, maybe two ways. First, you don't fight with the old man, at least you didn't used to."

Keles sighed. "I've stood up to him before."

"Sure you have. You've told him a map you'd drawn wasn't good enough."

"It wasn't."

"Telling him you were wrong before he tells you isn't standing up to him, Keles." Jorim shook his head. "You're more talented than our father was. Ryn *thought* he was Qiro's equal, and maybe he was. But you're better. You can surpass Qiro. And Grandfather can't have that, so he's going to try to kill you."

"That makes no sense." Keles raked fingers back through his dark hair. He wanted to deny that his grandfather could be that cold-blooded, but the way he treated Ulan showed how hard-hearted the old man could be. *Did he kill our father? Will it be "like father, like son"?*

"It makes sense, Keles. You're the best able to replace him and keep the family business going. If you surpass him, he could be forgotten."

"That's not possible."

"No? Prince Araylis should have been our leader, but now his younger brother occupies the throne. How many people remember him, or their father, Prince Jogisko? In nine years of prosperity, Cyron has begun to eclipse them. It will happen to Qiro, and he fears it."

"You're forgetting one thing, Jorim." Keles lowered his voice. "What if Qiro reaches the state of *jaedunto*?"

"Not possible."

"But might he not be there already? Look at him. Ulan is younger than he is and looks twice as old. Yes, we are all True Bloods, so we live longer than other Men, but we do age. He hasn't."

Jorim shook his head adamantly. "*Jaedunto* is possible in many things, but cartography? It is a thing of the physical skills, not scribbling on paper. Qiro is just well preserved. Uncle Ulan looks as he does because he's served under Grandfather. No, the old man will not know magic immortality. He'll live for a while longer because they want him in neither the Heavens nor the Hells, but he will die and you will be greater than he."

"That is clearly not what he assumes, on either count. He certainly *thinks* he is that good at what he does."

"It's another of his delusions."

Jorim ignored the comment. "I think he assumes he has another eighty-one years in him, perhaps longer."

"Let him assume what he wants. He's still going to die. It's not as if he's a Viruk."

Jorim snorted. "By disposition he is."

Even Keles had to laugh at that. "I'll not argue. But, that aside, somewhere deep down he knows he's mortal. If you or I can be as good as he is, our ability to work expands all he can do, and he has to see that. If Nirati had talent, then . . ."

"If Nirati had talent, he'd destroy her."

Keles blinked. "How can you say that? She is his favorite. You or I would have to argue to get you on the *Stormwolf*. If she suggested it in a whisper, you'd be on board so fast you'd not be able to catch your breath."

Jorim slowly stood. "I can say it, brother, because she does not threaten him. She has no talent for surveys and mapmaking, so he forgives and indulges her. Thank the stars that she has our mother's sense, else she'd be spoiled and worthless. Rather like Majiata."

"Don't try to deflect me." Keles approached his brother and took the tie in hand again. "Tonight Grandfather will announce our missions."

"To his glorification . . . Hey, not so tight."

"Sorry." Keles eased the knot ever so slightly. "He will announce that you are going off on the *Stormwolf* . . ."

"You *know* this, or you're speculating?" Jorim half closed his eyes. "You had Nirati talk to him, didn't you?"

Keles smiled. "She thought she owed you a favor. She'd done me one in driving Majiata off."

"What did she say he would have you doing?"

"Nothing." Keles shook his head, finished the knot and patted his brother on the chest. "When she asked for a hint, he became coy and refused to tell her."

"He'll probably keep you here and find ways to make you miserable."

"Please tell me you have not been reading his mind."

"As you said, that requires cooperation, and he and I are definitely not cooperating." Jorim turned and faced the mirror. He made a couple of minor adjustments to his brother's handiwork, then smiled. "Thank you. I couldn't have done it without you."

"Yes, but you know that's not true about the *Stormwolf*."

Jorim frowned. "How do you plot that course?"

"It's simple. The work is important, and the dual clock is a key component. I would be a bit more diligent in taking measurements and doing the calculations than you, but you have one very special qualification that I do not. What would you do if the clocks stopped working?"

The younger man closed his eyes for a moment, then nodded. "Well, I had assumed that I'd run a water clock occasionally just to see if the clocks were keeping good time. I'd maintain speed and direction logs and have the ship backtrack so I'd have data in both directions to account for current, then I'd look for any *gyanridin* who could help me fix them."

Keles smiled. "You see, you've already thought about what you would do. I wouldn't have the first clue. My skills run to calculations and making maps. I'm not as flexible as you. And I'll tell you one other thing. I know why you and Grandfather so often butt heads like those spiral-horn sheep you saw in Tejanmorek."

"Oh yes? Why?"

"You suggested that Grandfather fears me because I remind him of our father."

"I'm not the only one who has said that."

Keles took his brother by the shoulders and turned him around again. "You and he fight so much because you remind him of himself."

"What? You're insane."

"No, I'm not. You know the stories of him at your age. He traveled, he did surveys, and he brought things back to the Prince's father much as you do." Keles smiled slowly. "He just never went as far, saw as much, or brought back anywhere near what you have. In fact, he only made one long journey off to the northwest and it was a failure. Then his father died and Grandfather was brought into this gilded cage. The freedom he'd known was gone."

Jorim took a half step back. "And you're looking at a life of being trapped here, too, aren't you? The *Stormwolf* would have been your greatest adventure, your great escape."

"Perhaps. It could have been my greatest disaster, too. In some ways that would have been better." Keles shook his head. "After a nightmare expedition, Anturasikun would look very inviting."

"But don't you hate the idea of having to live the rest of your life here, trapped? Won't that kill you?"

Keles shook his head. "It won't kill me, Jorim." *But it* would *kill you, little brother.*

Jorim frowned heavily. "You'll be as good as dead. You'll be the person who creates the maps that allow others to go further than anyone before, and yet you will be limited to this little scrap of Moriande."

Keles felt a hand squeeze his heart. Being trapped in the family tower did frighten him. Certainly it brought with it security, but security without freedom was useless. *To never again look upon a sunset in the mountains, or see gaily plumed birds winging through rain forests . . .*

"I guess you'll just have to bring the world to me, Jorim. It is what I will be called upon to do. If we are lucky, you and I, we will become *jaecaikyr* and live a good long time. Perhaps the Prince will let us take turns here, being each other's eyes and ears elsewhere, bringing back the world. If that is not the case, then I will have to depend upon you, your children, my children, and perhaps Nirati's children, to do that for me. It is an eventuality I am willing to accept, for the good of our family and our nation."

"Protecting me again, brother?" Jorim smiled, then waved a hand toward the door of his chamber. "I know that's what you were doing in the map room. That's what you've always done. Nirati distracts Grandfather, and you appeal to reason. It drives me utterly mad, but I know I benefit from it."

Keles reached out and tugged on a braid. "You benefit from it, and you make us work very hard, you know that?"

"That's what little brothers are for. It says so in all the stories."

"And here I thought you preferred being unique." Keles preceded him from the room. "One thing, tonight. Please, no fighting. There's still blood in your eye, and that bruise is not quite in keeping with the color scheme."

"Yeah, the purple isn't quite Imperial, and the yellow edges are just not the right shade of gold." Jorim's hand landed heavily on his brother's shoulder and squeezed. "Fear not, brother, I will be on my best behavior. If what you have told me is true, I don't wish to give Grandfather any cause to change his mind."

"Good." Keles let himself exhale loudly. "This is his night. We let him have his way, and things will be perfect."

Chapter Eight

2nd day, Harvest Festival, Year of the Dog
9th Year of Imperial Prince Cyron's Court
162nd Year of the Komyr Dynasty
736th year since the Cataclysm
Anturasikun, Moriande
Nalenyr

Nirati found she was having difficulty breathing, and it was not just because of the corset into which she had been laced. She was a slender woman already, and the corset had been used to shrink her waist to an impossibly tiny circumference. Her handmaiden had pulled it tight, admonishing, "Lass like you, Mistress, don't need to be breathing, since all the men will think you're breathless because of them." Nirati had laughed at that, and the servant used the exhalation to tighten it just a bit more.

Nirati looked out through the tower's Grand Ballroom, which was only half-full, and felt a bit dazzled. The evening's colors were purple and gold—purple for the Prince and gold for the Anturasi family. She, her brothers, cousins, mother, and grandfather all wore predominantly golden robes, overshirts, and trousers, with purple ribbons as decoration. The Prince and his household would reverse that, and everyone in between would wear whatever struck their fancy, with gold and purple accents as befitted their ties to the family or Crown.

Or depending on what sort of impression they wished to make.

The Prince, though not yet in attendance, had already made

a strong impression. He had allowed some of his Keru bodyguards to be stationed at the gate, front door, and the ballroom entrance. Drawn entirely from the women of the exile population of Helosundians, the Keru pledged themselves to the Naleni royal house, eschewing marriage and children, leading an ascetic life filled with training and guard duties. *And odd rituals, if the whispered tales are true.*

Without exception, the women wore their golden hair braided with a white ribbon, in mourning for their lost homeland. Though quite handsome, few among them would have been described as beautiful because their features were as strong as their bodies, and their hard-eyed stares lacked warmth. Each wore a sword and carried a spear, but was polite and respectful—although Nirati wondered if they would retain that demeanor when the Prince of Deseirion appeared.

The rectangular ballroom had a row of tall windows along the western wall that allowed a wonderful view of the night sky. Opposite them, to the left as one entered, tables had been set up and laden with all manner of viands. Merchants and traders who wished to curry favor with the Anturasi had gifted much in the way of wine, cheese, and other exotic foods. Her grandfather's taste for heavily spiced food had also been represented at the centermost table, with cooks preparing and bringing out dishes that filled the air with delightful scents in much the way the musicians in the room's southwest corner filled the air with sweet sounds.

As she surveyed the chamber, her eyes were naturally drawn to the catwalk running around the entire room a good fifteen feet above the floor. Six feet wide, save at the southeast corner where it became a triangular platform, its golden bars formed a lattice that separated anyone up there from those below. In the southeast corner stood a chair and small table, along with two Keru guards. The door in the east wall would be the one through which her grandfather entered and from which he would eventually announce the *Stormwolf* expedition.

She smiled slightly because she knew the posting would please Jorim beyond measure. Her only worry was that her grandfather, through preoccupation or deliberate action, might make the pronouncement in a way that would set Jorim off. While she loved her little brother dearly, he did have a temper, and her grandfather's celebration was not the place to let it flare.

She shivered because a display of temper could do more than ruin the party. She could not remember her grandfather's sixty-third birthday feast, but Qiro and Ryn Anturasi had gotten into a shouting match. From all she'd heard, Ryn had only been defending himself. The fact that he'd left on the *Wavewolf* the next day without ever exchanging a civil word with his father—and had then disappeared—kept rumors alive that Qiro had had him murdered.

Nirati looked over at her mother and smiled. Siatsi Anturasi wore a robe of gold, with broad white bands trimming it at the hem, sleeves, and edges, and a purple sash holding it closed. Taller than Nirati, though not as tall as any of the Keru, her mother had gone from being a slender girl to mature woman without any diminution of beauty. She wore her black hair up and secured with golden sticks. She'd powdered her face white, and used gold to add a sparkle of freckles over her cheeks and nose. Gold paint also emphasized her eyelids and lips, giving her the look of an alabaster statue come to life.

Her mother was an interesting woman, for she had managed to prosper within the framework of two families dominated by strong patriarchs. Her own family, the Isturkens, had been prosperous merchants who had married her off to Ryn Anturasi hoping to gain some sort of benefit from Qiro. They had continued to prosper until her father died and her elder brother, Eoarch, had taken over the business. His gambling habits extended beyond the gaming tables, and lost cargoes and ships drove the family to the brink of ruin.

When Ryn died it had been expected that Siatsi would function as Qiro's hostess, but she declined and instead returned to her family and took over for Eoarch in all ways save for the trading company's public face. She bargained with Qiro for maps in return for allowing his grandchildren to visit and be trained. Nirati had even heard it said that her mother had become one of Prince Araylis' mistresses in return for favorable customs duties on certain shipments, but she had never asked after the veracity of those remarks.

She and her mother had worked hard preparing the celebration and smoothing things over between Qiro and Jorim. They'd both agreed to act on Jorim's behalf without consulting him. Jorim sometimes did not know what was good for him, and would eventually come around to their point of view.

Several gasps from near the entrance caused Nirati to turn. She did so slowly, not because her robe restricted her movement—there would be dancing later, after all—but because calm patience in the face of any emergency was the hallmark of a successful hostess. She braced herself for anything from a splash of spilled wine to Jorim's entering awash in blood. Despite her preparation, her breath did catch in her throat.

The Keru at the door had stepped aside to admit the Viruk ambassador and her consort. Ierariach of Clan Nessagia likely would not have elicited the gasps herself. Her ebon eyes always attracted comment, as did the thick flow of her jet-black hair, which she wore unrestrained. Her pale green flesh, on the other hand, did make her inhuman nature apparent. Of average height, she had chosen to wear a gown of sea green that complemented her complexion. Her concession to the evening's color scheme came in the form of a large amethyst set in gold that she wore as a spider-shaped pendant above her ample bosom.

But her consort *was* enough to take the breath away, and guarantee nightmares. Had he stood up straight, he would have topped eight feet easily, and Nirati suspected that his outstretched hand could touch the bottom of the catwalk. He wore only trousers and a sleeveless overshirt that let everyone see the bony plates on his long, slender arms. The hue of his flesh matched hers on throat, chest, belly, and the insides of his arms, though it deepened to a pine green over the rest of him, including his face. His black hair was as long as Jorim's and could have benefited from similar braiding, though that would have entailed plaiting it down the length of his spine. His fingers and toes ended in sharp claws. The hooks on his elbows and the thorns on his head appeared not quite as sharp as the claws, but when he smiled, an ivory row of needle-sharp teeth reinforced the idea that while he carried no weapons, he was far from defenseless.

Nirati strode forward at a pace that would allow her to reach the Viruk at the same time as her mother. Siatsi stopped ten feet from them and bowed. Nirati matched her in depth and duration—which were both considerable given the Viruk relationship to Men. They straightened in unison and smiled.

"*Dicairoun* Nessagia, you honor us with your attendance."

The ambassador smiled, but not without a little effort. "We were most pleased to receive the invitation to celebrate the life of the man who has recovered much of the world that was lost."

Nirati kept her smile in place. Most of the people hearing those words would think the ambassador referred to the Cataclysm and the resulting loss of contact with the rest of the world, but Qiro's granddaughter knew better. The Viruk had, millennia before, ruled over an empire that encompassed all Nine Principalities, their provinces and more. The men who lived there had been enslaved, along with other races, to serve the Viruk.

The Viruk capital, Virukadeen, had been located in what was now the heart of the Dark Sea, but had been destroyed in a cataclysm of Viruk manufacture. The Viruk who lived away from the capital, administering the provinces, suddenly no longer had the legions of Viruk warriors to secure their positions. Revolts followed, and Viruk rule was overthrown in places. Human freedom did not always last, but just over two thousand years ago, the True Bloods had come in a vast armada, invaded the Viruk Empire, and driven them out of what became the Principalities. Within the provinces, pockets of Viruk population still existed, though scattered and isolated. Far Irusviruk—the Viruk nation from which the ambassador had come—neither invited nor tolerated human interlopers. Peace between the races, for the most part, reigned—though did so uneasily the further one got from the Principalities.

Siatsi clearly had not missed the implications of the ambassador's greeting. "The world is a vast place. Not all that was lost can be discovered, and some things discovered may never have been lost—such as the pleasure your presence brings to me. May your visit be blessed, and the peace of the Festival yours to enjoy."

The consort bobbed his head and again flashed teeth. Nirati felt he was no more used to smiling than Ierariach was, but just enjoyed watching the human reaction to his grin. A shiver descended her spine as a thin ribbon of spittle began to roll down over his jaw. Fortunately, his thick black tongue licked it back before it could reach the floor.

The ambassador nodded. "We will enjoy your hospitality. Thank you."

As they moved away, Siatsi took her daughter by the elbow. "Watch your brother when he gets here and keep him away from the Viruk. The story that Jorim slew two warriors while in Ummummorar is not unknown. I doubt anything will lead to violence this evening, but Jorim would offer a duel if challenged."

"But the ambassador wouldn't . . ."

Her mother shook her head. "The Viruk have a very strong caste system. Her consort, Rekarafi, is a warrior. And they will do anything to uphold the honor of the Viruk."

"Why did Grandfather invite them?"

"Having the ancient ones here to venerate the anniversary of his birth feeds his ego."

"But putting Jorim at risk . . ."

Siatsi raised a sculpted eyebrow. "It may not. It could be that Rekarafi would view the slain Viruk as provincial barbarians, much as we see the wildmen in the Wastes. If we are lucky, those slain were his enemies—but I do not wish to chance it. Remember, our Viruk guests are not only old enough to remember the coming of the True Bloods, they likely remember the fall of Virukadeen. Such long lives make them view us much as we would sand midges—something we could swat without a second thought. And I don't want Jorim swatted."

"Had you swatted him when he was a babe, he'd be less likely to cause trouble now."

"And had I swatted you as a child, perhaps your tongue would not be so sharp."

Nirati laughed. "I merely take after my mother."

"And she will take after you if you do not perform this duty." Siatsi sighed. "And be watchful for other deviltry. Your grandfather has been in a foul mood, and I would not put anything past him. Avert disaster where you see it."

"Yes, Mother." Nirati nodded toward the wine table. "Speaking of which, perhaps you wish to see to Uncle Eoarch. That's his third cup of wine in an hour. If he's heard the Viruk rumors, he's likely to set up a duel just so he can wager on it."

"Thank you." Her mother kissed her softly on the cheek, then headed off to intercept her brother.

Nirati watched her go, then turned to study the next guests arriving. A young woman accompanied a man roughly twice her age and it took Nirati a moment to recognize her. She would have done it faster, but the woman's handsome escort distracted her. When she saw who it was, she wished for a dozen more Viruk. *Oh, Grandfather, you have been causing trouble.*

Nirati moved to cut them off as they entered. She let her voice drop to a frosty tone. "I had not thought to see you here, Majiata. I would have thought you had *some* self-respect."

Majiata began to answer, but her escort stopped her. "You will forgive me, please, for the fault is mine. I am newly come here. The invitation from your grandfather was unexpected, and it was suggested Lady Majiata might be free to attend."

He spoke very precisely, and with a Desei accent. His purple silk overshirt had been trimmed in gold, though his shirt and trousers were midnight blue. The white sash belting his waist suggested mourning, but knotted the way it was it signaled his status as an exile. *Which would make him . . .*

Nirati bowed appropriately for one of his status, but held it longer than required out of deference. "Forgive me, Count Aerynnor, for being so rude. You are a most welcome guest. My grandfather will, no doubt, be pleased you took his suggestion to heart."

The man returned the bow and tugged Majiata down with him. As he straightened up he smiled slowly, white teeth splitting his black beard and moustache. Light blue eyes sparkled in a handsome face. The short scar over his right cheekbone only accentuated his good looks. That he had paled at her reaction to Majiata endeared him to Nirati, and she'd always found the Desei accent intriguing.

"Please, you will be calling me Junel. My title hardly pertains, as my family's lands have been seized by the Crown."

"I had heard stories to that effect, Junel." Nirati smiled, liking how his name felt in her mouth. Majiata's discomfort only helped accentuate Nirati's satisfaction. "Are you aware Prince Pyrust has said he will attend?"

Junel frowned for a moment, then gave her a quick nod. "I had assumed so, since he is here in Moriande. Until you mentioned it, though, I had not considered how I felt. I will not cause you any difficulty in this matter. I thank you for the warning. It was most kind of you. If there is a service I can render you, you have but to ask."

"Two services. Simple, both, but I ask you to indulge me."

"As you are my hostess, I would offer you two services, even if both were complex."

"Thank you." Nirati smiled. "The first is that you keep Majiata away from my brothers, either or both of them."

Junel looked at Majiata. She blushed, and he nodded. "And the second?"

Nirati looked straight into Majiata's eyes. "Save the last dance of the evening for me, Junel."

Chapter Nine

2nd day, Harvest Festival, Year of the Dog
9th Year of Imperial Prince Cyron's Court
162nd Year of the Komyr Dynasty
736th year since the Cataclysm
Anturasikun, Moriande
Nalenyr

The first two things that happened as he entered the Grand Ballroom did not surprise Keles Anturasi at all. The Keru guards had let him and his brother pass without notice, which made him share a secret smile with Jorim. The Keru, being tall, strong, and alluring, had long been the fantasy fodder for many a Naleni youth. While all of them knew the Keru did not engage in carnal adventuring, stories of illicit affairs abounded—always having happened to the friend of a friend, thus escaping verification because of the remove—so the adolescent dreams never died.

Once inside, his brother immediately slipped away, which Keles had anticipated. Jorim started off on an arc through the crowd defined by the prettiest women present. He angled his way around toward the dance floor near the musicians, for Jorim's reputation as a dancer had many anticipating his invitation.

The second thing was his sister approaching him, filling the vacuum Jorim had left. The visible concern on her face braced him for some sort of trouble. "Good evening, Nirati. Joy of the Festival to you."

"And you, brother." She linked her arm in his and drew him toward the room's northwest corner, where the crowd thinned. "Mother has asked me to keep an eye on Jorim. The Viruk ambassador brought her consort, and he is a Viruk warrior. Mother is afraid that he may have heard tales of Jorim having slain Viruk on his travels. If he were to challenge Jorim . . ."

"Jorim would accept. And either way it turned out, there would be trouble. Do you wish help on that assignment?"

"No, but it will keep me occupied the whole of the evening, I fear. I do need to warn you of something else, though."

"What?"

"Majiata is here. She arrived with a Desei noble exile of the Aerynnor family. Grandfather sent him an invitation and suggested he bring Majiata. He seems rather gracious, whereas she is . . . herself."

Keles felt a barbed serpent begin to coil in his guts. "Do you want me to stay away from her? I really don't care that she is here." He put emphasis on his latter statement, hoping both of them could be convinced it was true.

"I trust you to use your judgment and all will be well." Nirati kissed him on the cheek. "Actually, I want you to have fun. I'll keep Jorim out of trouble for tonight, at least. After that, he's *your* responsibility for the rest of the Festival."

"Great." Keles sighed, but smiled. "You have as much fun as you can as well. I'll be careful and keep my eyes open."

"Good. I love you, Keles."

"And I you, Nirati. Go."

His sister departed in a flash of gold silk, but Keles remained in the corner for a bit. The knowledge that Majiata had chosen to attend his grandfather's birthday celebration surprised him. In the short time since she had been forced to return his ring, he'd let himself think back over their courtship. While they had been affianced for two years, during a considerable amount of that time he'd been traveling in the west, completing a survey of the navigable stretches of the Gold River. Back in the days of the Empire one could sail from the Dark Sea all the way to the coast, but the glaciers that had come in the Cataclysm's wake had deposited much debris in the river. The

Prince wanted to know what work would have to be done to make the river suitable for trade again, and Qiro had entrusted that job to Keles.

When he was in Moriande and not working, he had attended social gatherings. On the latter occasions Majiata had been with him and had been a perfect companion. She was polite and witty, rescuing him when he would let his enthusiasm carry him into detailed explanations of things that bored others to tears. When they were alone—and there had been precious little privacy outside of bed—Majiata had surrendered the maturity she had shown in public and become demanding, requesting gifts and throwing childish tantrums. He'd felt guilty for having spent so much time apart from her, so he weathered her moods, thinking that it would all be better once they were married and living together.

But recently he had begun to see what Nirati had likely seen from the beginning: these things would never get better. While some people are capable of change, most are not. Majiata had no motive to change because Keles acceded to her every demand. And her family was certainly telling her that what she was doing was right.

Keles shivered. In many ways it would have been easier had humans been as the Soth were rumored to be. The Soth went through each life stage with a period of hibernation in between. Like caterpillars that emerge as butterflies—though the Soth changes were not nearly as pretty—they reached points in their lives where radical changes were necessary. As legend had it, they found a place to hibernate, took months or years to reorder their thinking, then molded their shapes to suit and emerged new creatures, facing the world more wisely.

And the Soth Gloon are even supposed to be able to see the future—though to be seen by one brings dire consequences. He smiled. *One must have seen me when I was first introduced to Majiata.*

He wished he could just put Majiata out of his mind, but it wasn't that easy. He could remember her smiles, her coos. While she'd not been very attentive to his needs, he still craved human contact. He wanted someone to look at him with eyes full of desire in the middle of the night, and the feeling he'd not know that again sent a trickle of fear through his bowels.

He shook his head, watching his brother move from knot to

knot of giggling women. Jorim was all but a *jaecai* in the art of flirtation. He had an exotic air about him because of his hair, the bruise on his eye, and the stories he engendered. He was wild and unsafe, and the civilized women of the capital craved that.

Whereas I'm just safe.

Keles sighed. Women had never flocked to him as they did his brother—which was part of the reason he'd fallen so hard for Majiata. She had played him well, making him feel desired. And while he did want someone to share his life with, part of him wondered how he would ever know if he was being played, or if the interest was genuine.

The sharp crack of Keru spear butts on the floor announced the arrival of someone important. Keles glanced at the doorway, half-expecting to see Prince Cyron and his attendants, but instead he saw a single, tall man clad entirely in midnight blue, save for a gold ribbon swirling down his left arm. Prince Pyrust of Deseirion waited for the Keru to bring their spears back upright so he would not have to bow his head to get past their spearpoints. He waited, but they did as well, relenting only after the time one would have held a bow of respect for one of Imperial rank.

The man moved into the ballroom entrance then paused, giving the Keru the chance to watch his unprotected back. He reached up with his left hand to stroke his goatee. Though it and his light brown hair were shot with white, he did not look terribly old. Even at a distance, Keles saw that the Prince had lost the last two fingers on his left hand. A large ring of state rode on what would have been the middle finger.

Even Keles knew the story of that ring. While the conquest of Helosunde had taken place well before Pyrust ever took the Desei throne, the royal line of Helosunde had not been eliminated. After Pyrust became prince, they led a strong incursion into Helosunde and Pyrust himself had headed the army that opposed them. In his travels he was ambushed and wounded, losing both the fingers and the Desei ring of state. He survived, however, and in the subsequent battle shattered the Helosundian force, killing the Crown Prince. The new ring of state that he fashioned for himself came from the coronet he'd pulled from the Helosundian Prince's head.

Keles started to move toward the Prince to greet him, and the

Prince, seeing him, strode in Keles' direction. He even held up a hand to stop Keles from leaving the corner. At ten feet the Prince stopped, allowing Keles to bow, and the bow was returned respectfully.

Pyrust looked him up and down. "You clearly are an Anturasi. Keles, I assume?"

"I am honored, Highness."

"The honor is mine. I dreamed of meeting you."

"A pleasant dream, I hope."

"Quite." The Prince approached and smiled carefully. "Anturasikun is lovely. I dreamed I was walking through it with my brother, Theyral. He would have been much taken with this place."

"I did not know you had a brother, Highness. Did he not come with you?"

"No, he is dead." Pyrust raised his half hand. "I'll thank you for your as-yet-unexpressed sympathy. I feel his loss sometimes. And do not regret your not knowing him, for my family is obscure. Your family, of course, is well-known outside Nalenyr, and your work is the envy of cartographers everywhere. I see well why Prince Cyron guards you so jealously."

"The Prince's concern for our welfare is much appreciated." Keles felt a bit uncomfortable. "Would you like some wine, Highness? I would be honored to fetch some for you."

"In a moment perhaps." Pyrust stepped closer, his voice dropping, his hand resting on Keles' forearm. "I have heard of the work you did in your study of the Gold River. You know the Black River runs through the heart of my nation?"

"Yes, my lord." Keles agreed even though the Black River had long formed the boundary between Deseirion and Helosunde. "It is one of the three great rivers."

"You needn't be polite, Keles Anturasi, for I can see your unease."

"Forgive me, sire."

"Perhaps I will have cause to at some point, but your unease is good. It is a measure of your loyalty." Pyrust's hand came up, fingering one of the purple ribbons hanging from Keles' shoulder. "I have need of a survey of the Black River."

"I am afraid, Highness, that I would be unable to undertake such a venture."

"Oh, yes, of course. I'd not ask that of you. I was hoping, by reputation, that you knew of any cartographers, here or in my realm, whom you would trust with such a task." Pyrust gave the purple thread a tug, then let it go. "Of course, if ever you found Nalenyr a place where you no longer felt you could live, accommodations could be made in my realm."

"Your Highness is very kind. I understand Deseirion is a beautiful nation."

"It has its charms, though you know well that the glaciers that clogged the Gold River scraped portions of my realm down to bedrock. This is why the Desei are so tough—we work very hard to grind out an existence. As such, we are most eager to improve our situation. As I said, your help in the matter of the Black River would be greatly appreciated. If you *were* to undertake the expedition, I'm certain your family's knowledge of my realm would be increased. Perhaps you will discuss this with your grandfather?"

"As my lord wishes."

"Very good, thank you. Now, I will take some of that wine, if you do not mind."

Keles nodded and guided the Prince toward the wine tables. He steered him away from his uncle Eoarch, to where the best wine waited. Keles himself took a cup filled with a Desei vintage, though he often found them too dry and bitter. Pyrust chose one of the sweet wines from Erumvirine, and they toasted each other's health.

Several Naleni nobles approached and introduced themselves, freeing Keles from his duties as host. He didn't drift very far away, in case he was needed, but Majiata and her escort stood just to his left. They conversed with another couple who looked vaguely familiar, but Keles could not remember their names. Next to Majiata stood the Viruk ambassador, her consort hulking beside her menacingly. His attention seemed drawn to the dance floor, and Keles knew without looking—primarily because of the song being played—that his brother was already entertaining some young woman.

Things happened very quickly from there, and while Keles had flashes of memories, it was not until later conversations with his family that he was able to fully reconstruct the events. Thinking back, he had tried to find any sense of foreboding. There was nothing—no unease, no warning from the gods, nothing—so events unfolded without warning. And very painfully.

Up above, in the room's southeast corner, the Keru guards hammered the butts of their spears against the floor. This heralded the arrival of his grandfather. Qiro would make his appearance, be applauded and lauded. After that Prince Cyron would arrive, speeches would be made, and the celebration would continue in earnest.

At the sound Majiata had turned and stepped back, looking up as she did so. She bumped into the Viruk ambassador who, at that moment, had just raised her wine cup to her lips. The collision poured the cup's contents down over the Viruk's bosom and robe, staining it as if with blood. Ierariach hissed a curse in her native tongue which needed no translation.

Majiata's own arm had been jostled with the impact, sloshing wine from her cup over her own sleeve and gown. Outrage purpling her face, she heard the oath and turned. In a quick explosion of anger and utterly without thought, she slapped the Viruk for her insolence. Fury narrowed her eyes and she even began to demand an apology from the ambassador.

But before a single word had left her mouth, the Viruk warrior pulled the ambassador back behind him with one hand and raised the other. His claws hooked and the hand quivered, high in the air. Keles remembered that clearly: the talons silhouetted against the ceiling. Then the hand came down and around in a sweeping slash that was intended to rake Majiata's entrails from her body. So large was he in comparison to Majiata, the blow might even have cut her cleanly in half.

The Desei count grabbed Majiata and spun her about. Wine sprayed like blood. He tried to impose himself between her and the claws, but even his most valiant effort could not succeed. Majiata, locked in her rage, resisted him, dooming herself.

Keles, seeing it all unfold as if he were a Soth Gloon and reading the future, reacted in an instant. He dove and hit the Viruk in the flank with both hands. The impact shocked him, snapping his wrists back. He'd have had an easier time toppling a stone obelisk, but his effort was not wholly in vain. He did manage to knock the Viruk off-balance enough that the swipe would have missed Majiata cleanly.

Unfortunately, his dive carried him within the circle of the Viruk's blow. The heel of the Viruk's hand caught Keles square over the left shoulder blade, bowing his back. The cartographer left his feet and flew into the crowd, scattering people before slamming down hard. He landed on his chest and bounced once, then flipped over and skidded. He felt the cold stone against his back, which meant the claws had ripped through overshirt, shirt, and flesh. He looked back along his trail and saw blood smeared on the floor.

Oh, this is not good. He tried to catch his breath but couldn't. He attempted to sit up, but couldn't do that, either. Mercifully, before panic completely possessed him, he blacked out as the first silver agonies began to gnaw into his back.

Chapter Ten

2nd day, Harvest Festival, Year of the Dog
9th Year of Imperial Prince Cyron's Court
162nd Year of the Komyr Dynasty
736th year since the Cataclysm
Anturasikun, Moriande
Nalenyr

Prince Cyron had been waiting with his entourage just outside the Grand Ballroom. He would have been content to have gone in immediately, but his Minister of Protocol had been very precise in explaining he should enter after Qiro Anturasi had been welcomed. In that way, Qiro would be seen as being more important than Prince Pyrust, would be acknowledged as host, and yet be seen as subordinate to the Crown.

While much of that struck Cyron as silliness, he abided by it. His father had seen his impatience with such shows of manners, but pointed out that it was such manners that were the ligaments and tendons of society. *If I ignore them, others will do so as well, and so the whole of society will collapse.* He was not certain he entirely believed his father's words, but during the high Festivals, observing convention did provide a certain amount of ceremonial excitement.

Screams from within the ballroom suggested another kind of excitement. The two Keru guards at the door bolted into the room and the Prince's head came around fast enough that he saw a limp body in gold on the downward part of an arc. The guards, snapping orders and brandishing their spears, cleared a path to the origin point of that arc. Cyron cut around to where the man had landed. The violence had stunned many of the crowd to immobility, so the Prince's path was not obstructed, and he reached the bleeding man's side quickly.

Keles Anturasi? The Prince couldn't have imagined what Keles could have done to have been subjected to such an attack. *Jorim, certainly, but Keles?*

He dropped to his knees on the man's left side, while a young woman knelt at Keles' right. The Prince recognized her as Nirati and saw her gown had already grown red at the knees. She was desperately trying to roll her brother over, and the Prince helped her accomplish that task.

Four ragged slashes had been torn in Keles' overshirt low on the left side of his back. They ended before his spine and welled with blood. No blood spurted, which the Prince knew was good. No artery had been severed, but the amount of blood soaking his clothes and smeared along the floor left no doubt the wounds were deep.

Cyron pulled his own overshirt over his head, tugging it free of the sash, and laid it over Keles' back. He pressed his hands to the wounds and Nirati did likewise, despite the paleness of her face and the quiver in her lower lip. Her mother slid through the crowd and knelt at the Prince's side.

"Thank you, Highness, but I will . . ."

"No, Mistress Anturasi, no." Cyron lifted his head. "Where is my physician? *Geselkir!* Get over here, or you and your entire school will forever be barred from Crown service."

A portly man wearing formal robes of purple that featured a lengthy train and impossibly long sleeves appeared at the head of the blood trail. "Highness?"

"You have work to do, *now*."

The man lifted his hands; the overlong sleeves hung limply to his knees. "But my robe!"

"It will be your shroud if Keles Anturasi dies."

One of the Keru poked the physician in the backside with the butt of a spear. The man waddled forward, his gown's train sopping up a good deal of the blood. He struggled down to his knees and took over from the Prince, then began issuing orders, commandeering various guests into service.

The Prince got up and followed the Keru to where two others stood beside the Viruk ambassador and her consort. The Keru whispered to him the story of what had happened as they approached the Viruk. The warrior had his hands lifted, and blood stained the claws on his left hand. The Prince also noticed the clear print of a hand on the ambassador's face and the wash of wine over the front of her gown. To their right he also saw a young woman hiding her face against the breast of a tall man wearing the colors of a Desei exile.

The ambassador bowed deeply and the warrior hung his head. "Prince Cyron, I profoundly regret the difficulty my consort has caused. How is the young Anturasi?"

"Bleeding." Cyron turned from her and looked at the Desei noble. "What is your woman's problem?"

"She was almost as the Anturasi is now."

"Turn, girl. Look at me."

The woman turned, never leaving the safety of the man's arms, then bowed very low. "Forgive me, Highness."

"Forgive you what, child?"

"Someone jostled my arm, Highness, and wine spilled on my gown. It is ruined. I reacted."

The girl started to straighten up again, but the Prince growled. "Keep your head low. This is a celebration where you are a guest, not a hostess. You are far too young to be a doyenne of etiquette, and certainly not sufficiently schooled in it to be disciplining those who might have done something accidentally. You turned and you struck someone much your superior. Do you understand?"

"Yes, Highness."

He glanced at the ambassador again. "It falls to me to set a punishment that will be meted out in the morning. I will accept your comments on it, Ierariach. I would sentence her to five lashes with a whip for her slap and the offense it did you."

The Viruk thought for a moment, and a moment longer when a whimper from the girl stole the first opportunity to speak. "I would not have her back scarred when what she did to me shall not leave scars."

"You are most gracious, Ierariach. Your compassion does you credit." Cyron looked at the girl again. "Stand tall, girl."

She came up from her bow, her face a ruin of eroded cosmetics. "Thank you, my lady."

The Prince untied the loose sash around his waist and kicked it away. "She may be gracious, but I am not so inclined. Your slap will not leave scars, but Keles Anturasi will have four, *if* he lives. So, you will have four lashes in the morning, then four for every year of his life if he dies."

The girl moaned and collapsed to her knees. "But that would be a hundred. I could die."

The Prince squatted and took her chin in his left hand, raising her face. He lowered his voice to a whisper. "No, child, I will see to it that you do *not* die. You will live a cripple, your back a mass of worm-track scars. Do not doubt for an instant that I will order it done. I will retain the greatest *jaecaitsae* to lash you, and if you live to be eighty-one, you will relive your punishment every moment of every day."

He wiped melted cosmetics off on her robe, then stood and looked at her escort. "You will see her home now. Tell her parents that all entreaties for mercy have fallen on deaf ears. Any more that I hear will be an irritant."

"As your Highness wishes." The man scooped the girl in his arms. He carried her well past the Viruk warrior's reach and out of the ballroom.

The Viruk ambassador raised a hand. "I, too, shall retire, as my attire is no longer suitable for a celebration. I would, however, demand of the Prince his accounting to my consort for the hurt done Keles Anturasi. Rekarafi will be punished."

Cyron looked up into the warrior's dark eyes. "You struck to protect the ambassador, did you not?"

The warrior nodded.

"Had you followed through with the blow, clawing your fingers forward, you would have torn his back open and severed his spine, wouldn't you?"

Again the warrior nodded, his eyes narrowing a bit.

"You blunted what could have been a killing blow."

The ambassador answered before the warrior could nod. "His actions still were negligent, Highness. Punishment should be exacted."

"I say this to you, Ambassador." Cyron let his light eyes half close. "I will punish the girl who offended you. To you shall fall the task of the appropriate punishment for Rekarafi."

Ierariach bowed graciously. "Your Highness is as wise as he is equitable. If I may be of any aid to the Anturasi, ask and anything within my power is yours."

"Noted. Thank you." The Prince returned the bow. "It saddens me you will not be staying longer."

"Yes, Highness, me as well." Ierariach came up from her bow, then looked into the room's upper corner. "And to you, Qiro Anturasi, joy of the Festival, health, longer life, and more prosperity. Forgive us this incident."

The Viruk's address first drew Cyron's attention to Qiro Anturasi's presence, though he should have sensed it just from the heat of the man's anger. Qiro had chosen robes of the finest gold silk and had them embroidered with purple stars. On his breastbone he wore a solar medallion, and gold specks sparked in his hair and on his forehead and cheekbones. There, in the east, Qiro shone like the sun, his pale eyes ablaze.

Cyron bowed low in his direction, then straightened. "When this dynasty was but your age, Qiro Anturasi, it was a provincial domain with no true understanding of its own geography. Now, at twice your age, Nalenyr again ventures to realms that never existed before you placed them on maps. You are our most important citizen, and with you and your future goes our prosperity and happiness. We celebrate your birthday with all due respect and adoration."

The anger in Qiro's eyes abated slightly, but Cyron knew something was still wrong. He had no idea what it could be, but the feeling of difficulty only increased as Qiro began to speak. His voice remained even, though slightly tight, and filled the large room with ease.

"Prince Cyron, you are far too kind to suggest I might have had so strong and pivotal a role in Naleni history, for I am a simple scribbler on parchment. It is my family—my brother, nephews, grandnephews, and even great-grandnephews—who bring the charts to life. Some might see me as a gold mine, but they are the miners, and what would one be without the other?

"But I have not forgotten my own grandchildren. Nirati is my joy. She brings light into my life with songs and riddles and gentle admonishments when, as set in my ways as I am, I can be harsh."

Qiro began to pace, and Cyron instantly recognized the strong stride and quick turns as those of a caged predator growing slowly more agitated. "At my age, it is customary to cede the family business to the next generation. My son is long gone, so it would fall to his sons to inherit the mantle I wear. Either of them is worthy, for while my brother and his progeny are the miners of gold, my grandsons are the prospectors that find new veins to be mined. Without them, the mine would soon be exhausted."

He gestured casually toward the dance floor. "Jorim is more than a cartographer. He is an explorer and adventurer. He brings back more than maps. He brings animals and flowers, fruits, medicines, spices, and anything else he can stuff into a holdall. He also brings back foreign customs, which then become the fashion or serve to outrage the fashionable. I gather, for him, either outcome is acceptable."

Mild laughter greeted that comment, which Qiro acknowledged with a nod. "I would have preferred to have Jorim here with me, training to replace me, but a grand expedition must be undertaken. Prince Cyron has graciously built and outfitted the *Stormwolf* for a long voyage of discovery. There is no one better suited to serve on that ship. To Jorim I grant passage. Not only will this ship return to Moriande with untold riches of cargo and tales, but the knowledge of the world it provides will solve many mysteries."

Cyron lifted his head and straightened his back, hearing his vertebrae pop into place. His sense of unease began to spike. The first part of the speech had been delivered as if scripted, but Qiro had deviated quickly from it. The prince suspected that Qiro meant to reduce Jorim to servitude and captivity within Anturasikun, punishing him for the gods alone knew what offense. *And if Jorim had not been intended to get the* Stormwolf *in the first place, it would have gone to Keles.*

Qiro smiled slowly as he stopped his pacing. "I had thought Keles would perhaps enjoy remaining in Moriande to help me with my work, but now I see he is a young man, full of fancies and a sense of romance that leads to adventure. There is another trek I have long contemplated. I wished myself to go again, but was never granted permission to do so. Highness, you and I have discussed it many times, but had decided it was an expedition that could never take place."

The old man clasped his hands at the small of his back and began lecturing the guests as he had often lectured Cyron. "As we all know, before the Cataclysm, the Empire traded with nations far to the west along the Spice Route. This route wended its way from the Empire through the provinces of Solaeth and Dolosan, through Ixyll and beyond. It was into Ixyll that Empress Cyrsa—for whom our own prince is named—led the Turasyndi hordes and destroyed them, unleashing the Cataclysm. This, common wisdom held, closed the Spice Route forever. But over the centuries the chaos of excess magics has receded. It is all but unknown in Solaeth and rare in Dolosan.

"Keles, my strong, brave grandson, will recover from his wounds. Of this I am certain. He is too strong-willed for mere scratches to do him in." Qiro nodded confidently as people applauded—politely and sparingly—and the Prince could not determine if they applauded the journey, the idea of Keles' survival, or for fear Qiro would see they were not applauding.

"Once Keles is well, he will survey the Spice Route with the same skill he surveyed the western reaches of the Gold River. He will go into what, for over seven hundred and twenty-nine years, has been a realm of the unknown. He will conquer it, or be consumed by it, and I have no doubt which it shall be."

The old man clapped his hands, then took a cup of wine from the arm of his chair. Raising it, he took a moment to let his gaze sweep over the crowd. "Knowledge is our victory over the world, and is worth any price we could possibly pay."

The Prince had no cup, and was glad for it. He locked eyes with Qiro and knew instantly that the old man intended that Keles should die. Cyron hoped it was reasons and conflicts that had long lain hidden within the Anturasi clan that bred such hatred, for the alternative betokened a madness in the old man that Cyron did not know how to battle.

If you are killing Keles because his wounding upstaged your entrance . . .

The Prince shook his head. *It couldn't be that. Not even the gods could be that capricious.*

Qiro inclined his head toward the Prince, then drank.

No, no god could be that capricious. But a man who thinks he is a god could be so with ease.

Chapter Eleven

3rd day, Harvest Festival, Year of the Dog
9th Year of Imperial Prince Cyron's Court
162nd Year of the Komyr Dynasty
736th year since the Cataclysm
Moriande, Nalenyr

Moraven Tolo made his way through the graveyard in the shadow of Grijakun. The area had been sculpted with small hills and hollows, and had copses of trees and hedges that screened many a mausoleum from another. He passed the resting places of poets and priests, merchants, nobles, and warriors. Each had offerings placed in front of them: some had food, many had candles, and others had piles of *faetsun*—the fanciful paper money that the priests would later gather and burn. As smoke it would rise to the Heavens, and as ash sink to the Hells, so their recipients would have it to spend in the afterlife.

He carried with him a small jug that had been swaddled in cloth to keep its contents warm. While summer had not yet passed into autumn, the night had been cool. As he expected, he found Ciras Dejote sitting cross-legged in front of the tomb where he'd left him, his sword still sheathed across his thighs. The younger man made to rise when Moraven deliberately trod upon and snapped a stick, but the *serrcai* motioned for him to remain seated.

"It has been a long, cold night." Moraven squatted and placed the jug before Ciras. He pulled the lid off and the steamy scent of spicy chicken broth filled the air. "Would you share my breakfast?"

The younger man shook his head, though his stomach's growling told the truth. "Please, Master, eat. If there is anything left over, then I shall partake."

"Very well." Moraven sat and replaced the lid on the jug. "Do you have questions for me?"

"No, Master."

"No? Your mouth lies better than your belly. We met on the first night of Festival. I agreed to take you on as a student. You were most eager, yet you have no questions?"

"No, Master."

"Again, no? You came all the way from Tirat to find a swordmaster. You were given to my care when it was the *serrian* Jatan you wished to enter. No questions?"

"No, Master."

Moraven let any pleasure drain from his face and voice. "If you have no questions, I can teach you nothing. You might as well return to Tirat. Do you not wonder why you were given to me?"

The younger man hesitated, then nodded. "I do wonder."

"And?"

"And I assumed Grandmaster Jatan sought the best for me, so put me in your charge."

"Very good." Moraven lounged back against the corner of the tomb of a poet. "Have you come to question that assumption?"

"No. Yes." The man's shoulders shifted uneasily. "I am certain you know what you are doing."

"No, you are not, but that's good. Neither am I."

Ciras blinked away shock, then looked down to hide his reaction. Moraven gave him a moment to compose himself. When the man's head slowly came back up, the swordmaster continued, letting the hint of a smirk tug at the corners of his mouth. "If you have questioned *dicaiserr* Jatan's decision, then you have questioned other things, too. What have you questioned?"

Ciras opened his mouth, then snapped it shut. The drowsiness that had marked him before evaporated. "Master, I mean no disrespect."

"But?"

Ciras opened his hands to take in the whole of the cemetery. "Why am I here?"

"Why do you think you are here?"

"I don't know. You told me to wait here. I have waited. I have not stirred an inch. I have been vigilant. I have looked for ghosts and thieves and those who would steal relics, and I have seen nothing."

"Nothing?"

"Of course I have seen some things." Ciras set his sword aside and stood. He wavered for a moment, resting his hand on the tomb, then shook his legs and took a few halting steps. "I saw kin and admirers bring offerings to those whose monuments are here. Most were quiet; some laughed."

Moraven let his smile broaden. "Laughed, did they? Why would they do that?"

The younger man's eyes widened. "Do you not know where you put me?"

"Tell me."

Ciras prodded the tomb with a toe. "This is the monument to the poet and playwright, Jaor Dirxi. Do you know who that is?"

Moraven shrugged. "I might remember a poem or two."

"He is famous for his satires about warriors. His poems ridicule what we are and do. His plays make us into buffoons. Some think them funny. They turn the natural order on its head. They exalt farmers over swordsmen; they equate fighting off locusts with defending the Empire from barbarian hordes. Save that a Naleni princess was his lover, he would not be here and his work would be forgotten."

"And you didn't like them laughing at you, a warrior, standing vigil at his tomb?"

"No, I did not." Ciras stopped his pacing and stared down at Moraven. "But I preferred that to the humiliation I received last evening when you bid me stand vigil in the courtyard of the Three Pearls."

"You didn't like that duty?" Moraven raised an eyebrow, then pulled the lid from the jug again. "I spent last evening there myself and quite enjoyed it."

"How could you? The Three Pearls is one of the most notorious houses of prostitution in Moriande—nay, even the whole of Nalenyr."

"More like all nine of the Principalities."

"Even worse, then," Ciras snarled. "Not even a house of entertainment, just a house of whores, coming in from trolling the streets, finding men and women of dubious character, questionable sobriety, and soon to be diminished wealth. They saw me there, teased me, touched me, and whispered all manner of lewd and lascivious suggestions. One even served her customer right there in front of me, moaning, groaning, and making other noises ill suited to the human throat."

Moraven sipped some of the soup and let its warmth spread through him. "I know she did that. I paid her to do so."

"You *paid* for my humiliation?" Ciras' eyes narrowed and anger crept into his voice. "Was that your aim, then, to humiliate me? Or did you have me stand guard there so the brothel's owner would reward you for my service?"

"And, if that were true?"

"That would be reprehensible."

"Would it? Why?" Moraven sprang to his feet and rested a hand on the hilt of his sword. "If I am your Master and hire you out, am I not entitled to your wages?"

Ciras hesitated. "Yes, but—"

"But what? Is it wrong that I collect your wages in congress with gutter whores if I so choose? You would let me take food from a farmer for your service. Why not what others have to offer?"

"But, Master, you are *serrcai*!"

"Meaning?"

"You are better than that! You are better than that just as I am better than sitting vigil in a graveyard while the whole of the city is celebrating the Harvest Festival. My family is Tirati nobility. We have money. On the second night of Festival we throw a huge ball for the richest and wisest and most celebrated. Had you come to Tirat, you would have been honored at that ball, Master. You would have been given anything you desired. You would not have had to settle for gutter whores. We would have bought you the finest courtesan on the island. We would have brought one from the mainland for you. My family would have done that. They would have."

Moraven again arched an eyebrow. "But not now?"

"After how I have been treated in your service? Why would they? You have disgraced them, me, and yourself. I had never imagined I could be so poorly used. I trusted Master Jatan and he turns me over to you, a jokester who consorts with poxed gutter whores while paying them to tempt me with their foul bodies. You are worthy of respect, or should be, but I can find nothing but contempt for you."

Moraven drank again, then set the jar down. "You may stop now."

"Stop? Why would I? You asked if I had questions, so I have them." Color flooded Ciras' face. "Why did you have me guarding a whorehouse? Of what possible use was that? And why have me here standing vigil over the grave of a poet who hated what I am?"

"Stop. Now." Moraven held his right hand out, palm up. "Sit."

The edge in his voice drove Ciras to his knees. He bowed his head and laid his hands on his thighs. "As you wish, Master."

Moraven dropped to his knees as well and kept his voice low. "The use of what I have required from you, and what I *will* require from you, is that these things allow me to learn about you. The more I know about you, the better I will be able to correct your errors and make you into the *serrdin* you should be."

He moved the jug of broth closer to Ciras. "Drink. You are hungry and thirsty. But slowly. It is hot."

"Yes, Master."

"Let me tell you what I have learned so far, Ciras." Moraven let the man drink and lick away the droplet of broth hanging from his lower lip before continuing. "You have a romantic view of being a swordsman. I have little doubt you have killed—probably bandits and thieves who were besetting good folk. They probably even deserved to be dead. You see yourself as part of a grand heroic tradition of the sort exalted in songs, poems, and stories, rendered in statuary and in paintings. You know the works of classical Imperial authors, like Jontze and Viron Dunnol—more the latter since he was himself *serrcai*. You cling to the Nine Virtues, eschew the Nine Vices, and intend to pass the Eighty-One Tests of an Imperial *serrcai*. How many have you already passed?"

Ciras barely looked up, but pride infused his words. "Thirty-one, Master."

"More than one a year." Moraven smiled. "And more than I have."

"What?" Ciras all but dropped the jug of soup. "Master!"

Moraven's eyes narrowed. "Still your tongue, for when it is working your ears are not."

He waited for the man to fall silent again, then continued. "You wonder at the postings I gave you. They were exercises in becoming a swordsman. They encompassed rules—those you imagined, and those that exist without your comprehension. And they had grander lessons attached to them. You failed the lessons and followed only the rules you acknowledged. Let me explain.

"The rules you acknowledged were those you have accepted from your reading and previous training. You accept that, as your Master, I can give you an order and you feel honor-bound to abide by it without question. I told you, last night, that I wished you to 'stand watch here.' You took the words to mean you were to be rooted to this very spot—one that was cold, subjected you to ridicule, and left you hungry."

Ciras frowned, but did not voice a question.

Moraven smiled. "Very good. You were hungry, yet you sat here in a place where people bring food to the dead. You are in a place of plenty, yet you were wanting."

"But, Master, the food is an offering to the dead, and to the gods. To take it would be—"

"Would be what? Didn't you see vermin come and nibble at sweetcakes and fruit?"

"Yes, of course."

"Did the gods smite them? Did revenants rise to protect those offerings?" Moraven lowered his voice. "The priests of Grija are seldom skeletal, though they serve the god of Death. Do you think all that food is burned as sacrifice?"

"No, but . . . It is *wrong*."

"Very good, Ciras. This speaks well of your character that you are willing to endure discomfort when something runs against your moral code." Moraven nodded encouragingly and bade him drink more soup. "You must remember, however, there are times when circumstances require you to deal with things in ways different from those you might have intended. Rare is the transgression that cannot be repaired afterward. In fact, all but one can be fixed."

"And that one?" Ciras closed his eyes and crimson burned his cheeks. "Forgive me, Master. Here I sit at the focus of the answer."

"Yes. Why did I have you sit here last night, in a graveyard, when all about you could hear the sounds and see the lights of Festival? Because those who are here once enjoyed Festival. What you and I do can take that away from them."

"If you will forgive me, Master, that makes sense. Why, then, the House of Three Pearls?"

"I would have hoped that would have been obvious, too." Moraven sighed. "There you saw the ardor that burns at the core of all people. Each of the Nine Virtues denies a drive that the Nine Vices embody. Lust is one—which in a house of entertainment is renamed desire and therefore acceptable. The point is that people have drives—urges that they may or may not be able to control. If they can control them, it may only be for a little while. You controlled yours that night, but you were under no directive to do so. I told you 'stay here,' nothing more. Had you asked for a bed, they would have put you in the same small room I slept in last night."

The swordmaster raised a finger. "At the Three Pearls you saw the strength of lust. Here I hoped you might truly reflect on the truth beneath Jaor Dirxi's poetry. He *did* ridicule warriors, but did so because of his terror of them. He and many others were terrified in that day and age that warriors would dominate the world, and that Cataclysm after Cataclysm would be unleashed. Many a warlord and bandit prince had second thoughts about actions they intended, for fear Jaor's sharp wit would lampoon them.

"So, these two nights were for you to learn that people will do much to defend or to obtain the objects of their desire, and that their fear of death will prompt them to many things, including acts of courage. All to avoid death. Without understanding those lessons, you will not understand people. Without understanding people, you will never be able to separate those you must kill from those you need not."

Ciras' expression softened, then he nodded.

"One more thing, Ciras."

"Yes, Master?"

"You mentioned your family."

"Yes."

"Are they here?"

Ciras shook his head. "In Moriande? No, Master."

"Do they know you are here?"

"No."

"Do they have influence here?"

"Not really."

Moraven flowed to his feet, drew his sword, and let the quivering blade slap the underside of Ciras' chin. "Could they prevent me from killing you this instant?"

The young man swallowed hard. "No, Master."

"Very good." Moraven resheathed his sword. "All you are, Ciras, is *what* you are: what you can do, how you can make the world better. Money, rank, family—even your past—are immaterial. We are each of us utterly alone in the world. If we cannot find within ourselves the strength to deal with the challenges the world presents us, all the strength from outside will not save us."

Ciras nodded and appeared on the brink of asking another question when two guards in the Prince's livery approached, leading an elderly man wearing the formal robes and wispy beard of protocol functionary. Moraven stood as the old man mounted the little hill.

The functionary bowed. "Have I the honor of addressing Moraven Tolo?"

"I am he." Moraven returned the bow, making it of a depth and duration suitable for the Prince himself.

The old man drew an ivory paper scroll from his sleeve and handed it to the swordmaster. He held out a small bronze stamp so Moraven could check its design against the red wax seal, then he broke it and read.

"Minister, there must be some mistake."

The old man shook his head. "No, *serrcai,* there is no mistake. You will report to Wentokikun on the sixth night of Festival. There you will display your skills in a duel."

"But I made no offer to do anything of the sort."

"It does not matter. The display of your skills was offered to the Prince as a gift to honor the dynasty's anniversary."

Moraven smiled. "A gift? Who offered my services so?"

The old man's head tilted to the side. "The Lady of Jet and Jade."

"Ah, of course." Moraven smiled warmly. "Her request is my command."

Chapter Twelve

3rd day, Harvest Festival, Year of the Dog
9th Year of Imperial Prince Cyron's Court
162nd Year of the Komyr Dynasty
736th year since the Cataclysm
Wentokikun, Moriande
Nalenyr

The confining weight of the layered robes of state struck Prince Cyron as heavier than the lamellar armor he donned for battle. He would have gladly traded the purple robes—embroidered as they were with a menagerie of the gods' earthly avatars, dragons ascendant—for his armor. Having the dragon mask shielding his face would have been a grand bonus, for a single slip of expression could be his undoing. *Much better the cut of a sword than so simple a mistake.*

The doors to the long reception chamber opened slowly. Eight pillars, each depicting one of the gods of the Zodiac, neatly divided the room into three equal parts. The Dragon Throne on which he sat represented Wentiko—the ninth star sign—and clearly subordinated all the other gods. A wide red carpet trimmed in purple ran from the edge of the throne dais to the door. Only those of royal blood were permitted to walk the wide carpet between the pillars. For a commoner to set foot on it would be an offense before Heaven and against the Prince, resulting in dire catastrophes that his astrologers and ministers could catalog with precision. The trespasser would have to be killed to prevent them—and in any number of horrible ways which his ministers could also enumerate.

The ministers would be witness to all, but from their positions on the reed mats in the outer thirds of the room. His own functionaries would take up positions at the right side of the room, and his visitors would be opposite them, also at their Master's right hand. They would be matched in number, ordered equally by age, so everything remained in harmony and balance.

Aside from the fact that I hate their Master and he hates me.

Cyron kept his face utterly impassive as Prince Pyrust of Deseirion centered himself in the doorway. He was likewise hampered by ceremonial robes, with dark blue predominating. His had been embroidered with a far simpler motif that involved Hawks and only two other of the gods. Dogs, which were the symbol of Helosunde, rimmed the hem of his garment so that with each shuffled step, he crushed one beneath his feet. On his robe's skirts, breasts, and, no doubt, back, a gigantic hawk bore a clawed worm in its talons, asserting the supremacy of Deseirion over Nalenyr.

Cyron found the display as ill-mannered as he did bold—but at least he had refrained from giving the worm a red mane matching Cyron's dead brother's hair. Another might have taken Pyrust as crude or stupid for wearing such a garment during this particular Festival, but to do that would be to underestimate Pyrust. Regardless of Naleni money and weapons being placed in the hands of Helosundian rebels, the Desei maintained their grip on the conquered Principality. Cyron doubted, despite the peerlessness of his Keru guards, that Helosunde would ever again be free, which meant Pyrust would be coming for Nalenyr sooner rather than later.

But while Pyrust was a formidable opponent, he did have flaws. The greatest among them was his belief in prophetic dreams. Cyron had long since gotten past such superstitious nonsense, but he still listened to court astrologers and soothsayers. It appeased the ministers and that made his life easier. *Now, if Pyrust would just do the same, all could be well.*

As Pyrust stepped onto the carpet, his ministers filed into the room and took their places. Cyron's followed suit, as if each side were a well-practiced dance troupe. The Prince knew each of them was watching the others, evaluating, guessing, and cataloging nuances that would later be turned to advantage during negotiations. Had they put a fraction of this energy into actually making the vast bureaucracy function, all the Principalities would be years ahead of where they currently were.

When Pyrust reached the halfway point of the carpet, Cyron stood and laid the horsehair-tipped wand of state on the arm of his throne. A minister twitched when he did that, disappointing Cyron. He'd half hoped the man's heart would seize and he could put someone in that position who had not been old when his grandfather ruled.

While Pyrust's face had remained a stone mask, his step faltered for a heartbeat when Cyron put his wand down. One of the Desei ministers saw that and stiffened, evening the score in the protocol duel. Pyrust came on, lengthening his stride ever so slightly, kicking Helosundian dogs as he came, then stopped at the last pair of pillars and bowed.

"On this occasion of your dynasty's anniversary, Prince Cyron, I and the Desei wish you all prosperity, longevity, and joy."

Pyrust held the bow deeply and long enough to impress Cyron. *I could almost believe he is sincere.*

He waited for his northern counterpart to straighten up, then he bowed—not nearly so deeply. To do so would have been unseemly given the location and circumstance of their meeting. He did hold the bow as long as Pyrust's, however, and the eldest Naleni minister did begin to grey about the face.

"You are most welcome, Prince Pyrust." Cyron looked at his ministers. "I would have a chair brought for the Prince."

The oldest minister grimaced, and a hand stole to his chest. The two most subordinate ministers did stand and shuffle to the door to take a small seat from a Keru guard. They conveyed it to the front of the hall and set it up at the line of pillars at the right. Bowing deeply to both Princes, they retreated with tiny steps, but managed to move quickly regardless.

Pyrust turned his back to his own ministers and hazarded a smile. "A campaign chair. How thoughtful."

"Your Highness is known for being comfortable in one." Cyron nodded slightly. "I would have made it a saddle but bringing a horse in here would have had its difficulties."

Pyrust did sit, though stiffly. "So I understand."

Cyron sat and arranged his robe around his legs so the flat central panel was in clear display. It showed a hawk being savaged by a dog. It continued the insult his remark about the horse had started, since legend had it that Pyrust's grandfather, when he took the Helosundian capital, had ridden into the palace's reception hall and smashed his face against a rafter, spilling him from the saddle. Much was made of that as an ill omen for the Helosundian occupation.

"I was pleased you accepted my invitation to visit during the Festival this year. I hope you will find it a pleasing experience."

"Far more so than some, but I am glad you find amusement at your own Festival."

The Naleni prince frowned, which deepened the slight groan from his ministers. "I am not sure I understand."

Pyrust smiled wolfishly. "You clearly enjoyed terrifying that girl last evening. You had her whipped this morning as well."

"I did enjoy the former, but not the latter." Cyron's eyes tightened. "You have seen her type before—born into privilege, but with no sense of the responsibility that comes with it. How would you have handled things?"

"You know the answer to that. I would have had her whipped right then and there. No chance for appeal. I would let everyone understand the severity of her offense and the justice of her punishment. Punishment delayed serves little purpose."

"Perhaps, but that was not my thinking."

"What *were* you thinking?"

The younger man smiled. "I was thinking to give her a chance to learn from her experience. I gave her eight hours to think about the lash tasting her flesh. Had she become contrite, had she apologized—had she come to accept her punishment this morning and admitted the justice of it—I might well have forgiven it in the spirit of the Festival." He shrugged. "She was not contrite. Her kin came and demanded I forgive her in the name of the Festival. I offered them the chance to take her place, but none wished to do so."

The Desei prince frowned. "We may think you Naleni are degenerate, but I would not have imagined that your sense of morality had decayed such that even her father would not take her place."

"No, but I did mention that my *jaecaitsae* would add a lash for every year she had lived, and that made the total unacceptable. Her escort, however, did make the offer. He was one of yours, so perhaps you are right about us, or you are just morally superior."

Pyrust snorted. "You say that only because he has been exiled, so is no longer one of mine. Had he truly been, you would have said it was a sign of intellectual morbidity."

"Or true love."

"Often the same thing."

"Alas." Cyron did allow himself a smile. "She was led to a public square, stripped to the waist—which I think bothered her more than the threat of a lashing—then whipped. The *jaecaitsae,* on my instruction, did inflict enough pain with the first lash that she passed out. The other three were lighter, and only one left a small mark, tracing the line of a shoulder blade. She will never see it, but her handmaidens will."

"You think that is justice?"

"It is enough justice for me. There was nothing that could change her into a productive citizen, so she serves as an example. I could have hoped for more, but I will settle for that." Cyron nodded once. "I know you would have been more ruthless, but I did what I thought was best. Our opinions clearly differ on that. And they will into the future, I am quite certain."

"You speak frankly."

"In my court, that is welcome."

Prince Pyrust nodded, then slapped his hands on the arms of the campaign chair. "As you have made me feel comfortable and permit me some familiarity, my brother, I would suggest we drop all pretense. You know I had no choice but to come to celebrate your dynasty, for your father came to Felarati to celebrate a similar anniversary twenty years ago."

"My brother came with him."

"I recall having met him." Pyrust's eyes tightened slightly. "A brave man, your brother."

But not your superior. You measure me by him, and find me lacking. It is dangerous to disabuse you of that notion, but far more so to let you maintain it.

Cyron smiled. "Let us cast aside pretense. I want you to know I do not see your attendance here as any acknowledgment of my nation's superiority, even though my dynasty is nearly twice the age of yours. I also thank you for the gift of the fine woods and carvings that you had sent to us."

The northern Prince stiffened. "I would hope you do not read the wrong thing into the simplicity of our gift."

"I do not." The Desei had sent fine hardwoods, well seasoned, that the Prince's artisans drooled over, and the finished goods that arrived had won admiration from all who saw them. Cyron had even kept a small traveling chess set for himself before distributing the rest of the works among his ministers and friends. The only difficulty with the Desei gift was its overall size, for they should have offered much more than they did.

Cyron leaned forward. "You are aware that Erumvirine sent a million *quor* of rice to us as a gift?"

Pyrust's eyes hardened. "News of their largesse runs rampant throughout Moriande. Even the deaf and the dead know of it."

"And news of your lean harvest is likewise known." Cyron deliberately chose the word "lean" because the truth was so harsh it could have whipped flesh from the bone. It had been a dry year, and the Black River had not flooded, so the rice crop all but failed in Deseirion. With a *quor* being enough rice to feed a man for a year, the Desei harvest had left them with barely half a *quor* per person.

"It is my intent, Prince Pyrust, to honor the Erumvirine gift by distributing their black rice among my people."

"Your people, then, will be fat and happy."

"Happy, indeed, for that is what I wish for them." Cyron pressed his hands together, palm to palm, and rested his chin on his fingertips. "I intend to take a million *quor* of our gold rice and send it north, to Deseirion."

Pyrust covered his surprise well, but only with suspicion. "Why would you do this?"

"I would have thought my motives transparent." Cyron exhaled, straightening up. "Your people will suffer this winter and some will die. If your harvest next year is as bad—which my astrologers suggest is quite possible—you will have one choice. That will be to move south with troops and take what you want and need from my nation. The thing of it is that after a year of famine, your army will be weaker, so you will have to move now, this year, and within the next month, or the disaster cannot be averted. A fool would wait until next year, and you are not a fool."

"You say I am not a fool, but you seek to bribe me with food."

"I don't think a wolf is a fool, but if food cast out to it will keep it from entering my home, I will feed it."

Pyrust's face closed for a moment, then he nodded. "You put me in a difficult position. Food is what my nation needs immediately, and you offer it. Not freely; I expect a price of some sort. Since you are also not a fool, I know that price will be dear. But you also know the inequality of food is not the overwhelming disparity between our nations. I have dreamed of what is. As you explore and trade with the rest of the world, you grow more wealthy. If I let you bribe me with food and gold, I will grow dependent on you; and then when you cut me off, my nation collapses."

"I will not dispute your reading of the future, Prince Pyrust, but I will maintain it is but one future of many."

"Ha! You wish to reunite the Principalities into an empire just as much as any other prince. Only you would buy us instead of take us."

Cyron raised an eyebrow. "Peaceful consolidation of an empire is a vice?"

The northern ruler hesitated. "It's not the way of things. Your brother knew that. Your action reduces the rest of us to slaves. It destroys our spirits."

"And being conquered doesn't?"

"Those who survive a war of conquest are cowards. Those with spirit will have died in the defense of their nation."

The Prince of the Naleni nodded. "Let me explain things to you carefully, then. I will ship grain north, but only at intervals. If your army invades, the warehouses and way stations will be burned. I will draw you south with my army while my fleet burns Felarati. The Helosundians have far more people under arms than you imagine, and as you move south, they will move in behind you, cutting off your supplies. Your army will starve. Once I have crushed your army, I will move north with food and win over your people, establish a Helosundian regent for Deseirion, and unite all three realms under my banner."

"It sounds good when you say it, my brother-prince, but crushing my army will take more than a long march and rebels running through mountains." Pyrust held his hands up. "But the future you outline *is* possible. It will profit neither of us. This leaves me asking what you will demand for the rice?"

"My ministers will meet with yours, but what I want is a cessation of the Helosundian campaign. I want you to withdraw your troops from the field."

The Desei leader thought for a moment, then nodded. "You could have gotten more from me. A pact of nonaggression for five years."

Cyron shook his head. "You would not honor it, nor would I have trusted you to."

Both leaders fell silent, but the echoes of gasps from ministers filled the air. The two men did smile at that.

Pyrust frowned. "Your defense of your realm would work whether or not you were willing to give me food. Why, then, do you not let me starve?"

"Because *you* will not starve, my brother." Cyron shook his head ever so lightly. *Why don't you understand?* "Your people will starve. My desire is to save them from pain and death."

"But they mean nothing to you."

"But they should, shouldn't they?"

"There are some who would argue in favor of that point, yes." Pyrust stood slowly. "I am not one of them. The power we have is power to exercise for the glory of our dynasties. It is not enough to survive. We must prosper, and others must be made to bow and acknowledge our superiority."

Those could have been my brother's dying words. Cyron rose as well. "This could be true, Prince Pyrust; but if it is, it won't be happening this year."

Pyrust smiled. "No, but there are many years to come."

Chapter Thirteen

3rd day, Harvest Festival, Year of the Dog
9th Year of Imperial Prince Cyron's Court
162nd Year of the Komyr Dynasty
736th year since the Cataclysm
Anturasikun, Moriande
Nalenyr

Keles Anturasi became aware of the buzz of murmured voices as he woke, almost because of their abrupt silence as he stirred. The stinging scent of smelling salts still filled his head and he sneezed, once—violently—reigniting the ripping pains in his back. He felt tightness, where his flesh had been stitched closed, but it felt as if red-hot wire had been used for the sutures, and ground glass had been bound into his wounds.

He gasped and wanted to cry out, but his dry throat and thick tongue prevented it. He lay on his stomach and tried to lift his head, but even that simple movement sent a pulse of pain through him. He bit at the pillow and managed a growl as a fat man's pale hand brought smelling salts near him again.

The man's voice came distant and disdainful. "He must lie still or he will reopen the wounds. He has slept long enough for the poultices to draw most of the poison, and for the lacerations to begin to heal, but things are still delicate."

Keles couldn't place that voice, but his mother's followed. "You are certain he will be well?"

"My lady, I *am* the Prince's own physician."

"I know this very well, Geselkir, but the question is how hard do you wish me to use my influence with the royal house on your behalf?"

"Well, really!"

Keles smiled, despite feeling as if his insides were drifting within a shell of pain. His mother did not often reveal her steely nature. On those few times she did she invariably got her way.

"You are still of the opinion that he cannot be taken to attend the healing tomorrow evening?"

"Under no circumstances. I was adamant at the start about that, and have not changed my mind." Disgust infused the physician's words. "The healing is superstitious nonsense, and dangerous as well. The Prince's pet may be docile, but he was not always so. He could revert at any time. To allow one of the *vanyesh* to live is unthinkable."

"It is not the *vanyesh*'s life which concerns me, Geselkir."

"Keles should remain quiet for several days. I will return to remove the stitching. Keep the wounds clean, change the poultices often, and he will do very well. If there is redness, especially if it spreads, you will tell me."

"You will see it yourself when you visit him."

"My lady, if you think . . . yes, of course, as you desire."

Drawing in as deep a breath as he could muster, Keles studied the pain in his back. He discovered a dull ache in his ribs lurking beneath the fiery lines in his flesh. The sharper pain in his back throbbed—four distinct lines of it, each in its own time as if a fiddle string was being plucked at random. He let his breath out slowly, hoping some of the pain might fade, but instead it just thrummed in a new, jagged melody.

He opened his eyes and caught a glimpse of a rotund man still wearing a Festival robe. The brownish stains at the knee and on the sleeves were obviously blood, and undoubtedly his. Keles dimly recalled some sort of commotion, but his throbbing skull prevented him from being able to remember anything clearly.

Keles tucked his chin toward his chest and looked at his mother. She, too, wore the gown from the previous night. He knew she hadn't slept, but she looked as beautiful as ever. Beyond her stood his sister, likewise pretty, but wearing everyday clothing. She had not slept much either, but Keles was certain their mother had sent her off to bed at some point.

Keles tried a grin and it worked. His voice did, too, in a croak. "How long have I been sleeping?"

From near his head Geselkir offered, "Not long enough."

Siatsi smiled at her son. "You will sleep more, but it was important we wake you now. Thank you, *dicaifixtsi,* you are excused."

"If you think for one moment I approve of what you are going to do, you are sorely mistaken, Mistress Anturasi."

"Your concern is noted."

"I don't think you understand. You have made him my responsibility. The Prince has made Keles my responsibility. What you are about to do—"

"—is necessary." His mother's voice remained even, but her expression was unrelenting. "You give me no choice. You've said he cannot go to the healing, so I must bring it to him."

"It is dangerous nonsense, worse than subjecting him to the *vanyesh*. You risk your son's life."

"Have you changed your mind about the healing?"

"No, and I resent your questioning my judgment in this matter."

"Do you?" Siatsi's chin came up. "Exactly how many claw wounds from a Viruk warrior have you treated?"

"Well . . ."

"Would that be *none*?"

"I have seen them." His voice grew small. "After death."

"Wait outside."

"Gladly. I shall not be a party to this."

Keles waited for the doctor to leave, then looked at his sister. "Water."

His mother held her back. "Not yet."

"But I need water." Keles fought to speak clearly, but his throat closed.

Siatsi squatted down to bring her face on a level with his. "You need something else first. Nirati, please bring our guest."

His sister departed without a word and quickly returned leading the Viruk ambassador. At the sight of her, a flutter began in Keles' belly. She came close enough for him to catch a hint of her scent, and perspiration immediately blossomed on his brow and upper lip. His breathing came harder and his lower lip trembled. His stomach clenched and he almost lost control of his bowels.

Ierariach stood back away from him. "The *nesginesfal* is in him. I can prevent it doing any lasting damage, if you please."

His mother nodded. "Please."

"Stand away from him." The Viruk came no closer, but as his mother moved behind her, she pressed her hands together, palm to palm, with fingers pointing toward him. She crossed her thumbs—he wasn't sure why he noticed that, but he did. Then her hands shot away from each other like stags leaping away from dogs.

The air between her hands shimmered, much as it did above a sun-baked rock. Her form rippled and shifted, then a blast of heat slammed into Keles. It poured into him along the stripes on his back, liquefying the ground glass and searing his flesh. Hot bile from his stomach burned up into his throat and how he refrained from vomiting he did not know. The pain, which had been sharp, melted into soft flows, but that only lasted for a heartbeat or two. The heat spiked, hurting him enough that he cried out, then went limp. Strength drained from him as a chill seeped through damp sheets and into his skin.

Keles labored to breathe. He shivered a bit and wanted to roll onto his side so he could draw his knees up, but he could not. Each breath felt as if he were lifting the whole of his family's tower, and each exhalation sounded as if it might be his last.

He would have been worried that it would be, save for his mother's whispered question. "What do we do now?"

The ambassador spoke plainly, but also in subdued tones. "The poultices will not hurt. Keeping the wounds clean will be good as well. He should remain in bed for several days—I know his grandfather will not wish this, but I have an ancient chart that might buy your son the time he needs. Mild meals, and no meat to anger the blood."

His mother nodded. "Your magic has cured him?"

"Some." The ambassador nodded toward him. "The venom may yet have some residual effects."

"What do you mean?"

"I will show you." From the sleeve of her robe she drew a handkerchief and used it to mop the perspiration from her brow. She stepped toward him, then brought the kerchief to his nose. "Can you smell my scent, Keles?"

He breathed in, though not deeply, for fear of starting the fire in his back again. At the first hint of her scent, however, his gorge rose and he could not restrain it. He vomited over the cloth and her hand. Worse, his bowels let loose and his bladder as well. His body convulsed. He threw up again, then aspirated a bit of vomit, which started him coughing.

The ambassador whipped away the pillow and held his head as he vomited one more time. He coughed again, hard, and the pain exploded in his back. He choked, coughed, and couldn't breathe. He fought for air, unsuccessfully, and with agony wracking him once more, the world narrowed and became black.

Chapter Fourteen

4th day, Harvest Festival, Year of the Dog
9th Year of Imperial Prince Cyron's Court
162nd Year of the Komyr Dynasty
736th year since the Cataclysm
Ministry of Harmony, Liankun
Moriande, Nalenyr

Pelut Vniel looked up from the small table at which he knelt. A long rectangle of rice paper lay on it. The black pinecone he'd quickly brushed there glistened wetly. He set the brush down and smiled as Kan Hisatal bowed.

"Thank you for coming so quickly, Minister Hisatal."

"It is my pleasure to answer your summons with alacrity, Minister." The heavyset man held his bow for a second more than required by protocol, then took one step forward and sank to his knees at the edge of the floor. "How may this one be of service?"

Pelut did not answer as his clerk, Iesol Pelmir, knelt and cleared the low table. The clerk—a slight and bald man—meekly and precisely set the table aside without disturbing the painting, then shuffled over to Hisatal and gave him a pillow on which to kneel. The clerk withdrew to his corner, where he knelt on the bare wooden floor, and Hisatal's hesitation betrayed surprise that the clerk remained.

This pleased Pelut. Hisatal had come expecting a private conversation, as many of their conversations prior to his departure on the *Stormwolf* had been. Neither of them wanted a witness to what was said. Iesol's presence suggested that either the minor clerk was soon to be elevated, or that what was to be said would be safe for wide currency. *Neither is true, but if he assumes it is, he will be looking for hidden meanings. He will be off-balance, and I want that.*

Pelut looked up. "We have several things to discuss, you and I, concerning the future. *Your* future, and how it shapes the nation's future."

"May it be of benefit to both of us."

And you think I do not know all the nuances of your statement. Pelut resisted the urge to smile and instead slipped his hands into the sleeves of his robe, thereby emphasizing his superior stature. As with any member of the bureaucracy, he wore a blue robe with a gold sash. While the two others wore cotton, Pelut wore silk, and his cuffs and hem were decorated with wide gold cloth bands. All three had the Naleni dragon embroidered in purple on the ends of the sash, but Pelut also had it on the gold bands at his sleeves. He was in a position of power both of them hungered for, and Hisatal especially needed to be reminded of that fact.

"The most important first, then . . ."

Hisatal nodded, betraying himself. "I do not think Keles Anturasi's being shifted from the *Stormwolf* should affect the expedition in any way. Its outcome will be the same."

For you, yes. Pelut cocked his head to the right. "No, Minister, the *most* important first."

The heavyset man's mouth snapped shut and his jowls jiggled. He glanced down quickly and color rose to his cheeks. "Forgive me, Minister."

"Your error is understandable, Minister." Pelut straightened his head but did not smile. "The most important item is the Prince's notion of sending grain to the Desei. He has done this despite our best attempts to dissuade him. Grand Minister Lynesorat was less than forceful in making our case to the Prince. This leaves us in quite a muddle."

Hisatal nodded gravely. "The Helosundians have initiated protests over many ministerial contacts. They have spoken to me even though they know I am leaving. They see this as Prince Cyron's subsidization of the enemy and are not pleased."

"I have heard, but that is a problem of their own making. They maintain their Council of Ministers beyond any practical purpose."

Hisatal frowned. "But without leadership, Helosunde would collapse into disorder. It is our purpose to maintain order."

"But we must do this within the shell of the state, Hisatal. Leaders, princes, make *decisions*—but we provide them the choices from among which they select. Leaders come and go, but the bureaucracy is eternal. To those outside we are the instrument of state, carrying out the dictates of the leaders. To the leaders we are eyes and ears, hands and feet, making it possible for them to administer their nations. Before the time of Emperor Taichun, the Empire was in chaos, with warlords fighting warlords and the Emperor's dominance measured by how widely his army ranged."

Pelut's blue eyes narrowed. "The Helosundian Council governs in its own name, allowing resentment to be directed at the ministers. Neither Prince Cyron nor Pyrust need heed them since they cannot speak to them as peers. If the ministers feared poor leadership, their retaining power could be understood, but they fear losing it and the riches it brings them."

He let a bit of an edge enter his voice and Hisatal found within himself a shred of dignity that prompted a blush. It had not been difficult for Pelut's agents to learn that Hisatal had entered into a series of agreements with shipping houses and cartographers to give them information about what the *Stormwolf* discovered. It would make him and his family very wealthy, and that wealth could be used to guarantee patronage that would vault him into the Ministry's upper echelons.

"You are correct that we must maintain order, but *how* we do that is just as important. You cannot divorce the two things." Pelut slipped his hands from his sleeves and held them out, palms up. "The people cherish stability and cling to hope. They hope things will get better. They believe that if they work hard and are diligent, they may someday be blessed with *jaedunto*. With that comes fame, fortune, and many other benefits."

"More realistically, we know that *jaedunto* is a mere fantasy for most. As good as we can be, as hard as we study and work, such a thing is not possible for us. There are rumors, yes, and Taichun's

Grand Minister Urmyr might have achieved it. But he was a celebrated warrior before becoming a minister, and his life has largely been mythologized. He existed, and his precepts are still followed."

Pelut looked over at Iesol. "Which of his sayings would apply here?"

The young man bowed his head. "Book Seven, Chapter Four, Verse Twenty-seven. 'And holding up a nut, the Master said, "We take nourishment from the kernel, discarding the shell." ' "

Disdain flashed over Hisatal's face. "Yes, looking at the truth of a thing is important, but you are saying we hide the truth of things from the leader and the led respectively."

"Because Urmyr's words were for *us,* not them." Pelut let a smile tug at the left corner of his mouth. "The rice is a problem because of Helosundian protests, as well as protests from the inland lords who will still have to send rice to Moriande. It is a problem because Pyrust's army will not starve. We will need to initiate an effort to divert eight percent of the grain into stores from which we can disburse them as needed."

Hisatal nodded. "A wise precaution, Minister."

"And a bold undertaking. I will be making the delivery of the rice *your* problem, Minister."

The man's head came up, shock widening his eyes. "But, Master, I am prepared for the journey. Things have been made ready. My things are already aboard the *Stormwolf.*"

Pelut shook his head. "By the time you return to your home you will find they have been restored to you."

"You cannot—"

"I can and I have. I have because you violated Urmyr's saying." Pelut allowed disgust to fill his words. "Iesol, the quote about the perils of greed. The bathing one."

" 'And the Master said, "The just sip from the river of Reward, the greedy drown in it." ' "

"But, Master—"

"You are a fool, Hisatal, and had I known you were such a fool, I would not have appointed you to the *Stormwolf* in the first place. Were you expected to find a way to enrich yourself? Of course. I fully expect that you will divert one percent of the rice into your own treasury, and do I dispute that? No. I know you will do it, I know you will share your largesse with me and the others who are appropriate. That *is* the way of things. We reward those who help us.

"But in doing what you did with the *Stormwolf* you became enamored of the shell and neglected the kernel. I placed you on the *Stormwolf* so you could befriend Keles Anturasi. You were to win his trust and be his helper. This was not so you could steal his secrets, but so you could influence him in the future. His grandfather will not live forever and Keles will replace him. What matter gold in your pocket today, when the world could be yours tomorrow?"

"I did not think, Master."

"Wrong. You thought, but you did so without discipline. If there is no discipline, there is no order. If there is no order, there is only chaos. Chaos destroyed the world and only we, the bureaucracy, have been able to remake it by establishing order."

Hisatal bowed deeply, pressing his forehead to the floor.

Pelut allowed him to remain down until sweat began to drip on the floor. "Enough."

"Thank you, Master."

Pelut shook his head. "You are Fifth Rank, Hisatal, and you have forgotten all you learned when you were but Third as is our friend here. 'The house stands, but dry rot invites the disaster of a breeze's caress.' Do you know that?"

"Yes, Master."

"Have you not listened, or have you become truly stupid? Iesol, the citation."

"Book Three, Chapter Eight, Verse Four in *Meditations on collapse*."

"I knew that, Minister. It is that I am distracted."

Pelut half closed his eyes. "Undistract yourself, Minister, or I shall find the means to provide you focus. I would assign you to join Keles Anturasi in Ixyll, but you are as unsuited to that expedition as he is. He is being sent off to die. Though you have displeased me, I see no reason to have you die quite so soon."

"Thank you, Master." Hisatal's mouth hung open for a moment more, and Pelut knew he was searching his memory for a suitable Urmyrian quote.

Pelut declined to restrain himself. " 'The wise man is content to be thought a fool, rather than to speak and have the opinion confirmed.' "

Hisatal just nodded, once, curtly, and said nothing.

"We have an immediate problem, Hisatal, which is this: we need someone on the *Stormwolf*. As Jorim will never head House Anturasi, it need not be someone important. Indeed, the most competent and wily must be retained, as the next two years will prove most tricky. Have you a candidate who might suffice? Someone loyal to you, perhaps?"

Hisatal sat back, but before he could say anything, Iesol cleared his throat.

Pelut glanced at him from the corner of his eye. "You have something to offer?"

" 'And the Master said, "Though the neighbor's fruit looks more plump, the wise man harvests his own crop." ' "

A smile slowly grew on the elder minister's face. "By this you mean?"

"Master, Minister Hisatal will require his retainers to deal with the gift of rice. You have in your household one who could be your agent on the *Stormwolf*."

"Whom did you have in mind?"

"I would advance myself, Master." The man bowed low and stayed down.

Pelut played a hand along his jaw. Iesol was useful and even competent at a variety of tedious tasks, which few mastered and fewer cared to remember once they had. He could have gone far save that he lacked any dynamism. He could neither command nor inspire and until offering his services now had never exhibited anything beyond the most mundane of ambitions.

"You have concluded no arrangements to profit from the expedition?"

"No, Master."

"You are fleeing no entanglements or feuds?"

"No, Master."

"Raise yourself, Iesol. Look at me." Pelut shifted around to face the functionary. "Why do you wish to go?"

"I have seen the ship, Master. I know the glory it will bring

Nalenyr. In my soul I know I could perform no greater service to our nation than to contribute to the expedition's success."

"You think you can make a contribution?"

" 'Without kindling there is no fire.' "

Iesol's use of Urmyr's words stung Pelut, and he should have broken him for being so bold. He did not because he knew the man was not being bold, merely earnest; and rewarding him with a position Hisatal wanted would reinforce the need for Hisatal to adhere to the codes promulgated by Urmyr. *Besides, I can rid myself of him later.*

"Do you imagine, Iesol, that your action will cause this Ministry to recognize you upon your return?"

"My place is to serve, Master, not to dream."

"Reward shall be considered, *if* I am pleased with your work." Pelut put emphasis into his words, so Hisatal would know they were for him, too. "Serve me well, the both of you. The future is known only to the gods. If I am blessed, so shall you be. Through me you serve the nation. Do not be a disappointment."

Chapter Fifteen

5th day, Harvest Festival, Year of the Dog
9th Year of Imperial Prince Cyron's Court
162nd Year of the Komyr Dynasty
736th year since the Cataclysm
Xingnakun, Moriande
Nalenyr

Nirati shivered as she strode toward the hulking dome of Xingnakun. The structure, built on the city's northwestern quarter, had once been an outdoor amphitheater. Construction had long since enclosed it with a mushroom cap, and eight buttresses sent arched arms to cross over the center. A tall spike rose from the intersection and there, at the top, a blue *gyanri* light burned. Barely visible in the day, at night it rivaled the lights high on the nine bridges—though most people fingered their talismans when they caught sight of it, even accidentally.

Her shiver had nothing to do with the day, for it had dawned bright and warm. It came from her experience that morning, setting out from Anturasikun and walking through the streets. While they were crowded for the Festival, people moved out of her way as she went. Some dug for talismans, others toed small circles in the dirt, while the few who knew her looked past her as if she did not exist.

Another time she would have been offended, but circles could hurt her, even social circles, so having friends turn away was more of a blessing than a curse. *Besides, I could not abide the pity in their eyes.*

It was not hard to tell that she and others were bound for the

Tower of Magic and the healing. Because circles could be proof against magic, their robes had been specially woven of coarse cloth, with snags and dropped threads. No sash closed them; instead, square buttons or short ties were used, with hard knots and no loops. Sleeves were slashed from shoulder to wrist and none of those wandering northwest wore jewelry. Rings, bracelets, and necklaces had circles and had to be eschewed.

More noticeable than the robes, however, had been the effort to disguise the circles in their faces. Black crosses slashed diagonally over both her eyes, and another in red decorated her mouth. Some people clipped their nostrils closed and stuffed cloth in their ears, but Nirati thought that an unnecessary precaution.

Drawing closer to the dome, she entered a bizarre realm where merchants had set up small booths or sold things from the backs of wagons. Circles abounded, large and small, from the tiny talismans many wore daily to hoops large enough to circle the waist. One man offered crystal disks through which things could be watched safely, while others touted potions and unguents that would ward folks from magic, or do for them immediately what the magic might do later. One man offered to store money for those who had come with purses laden with circular coins. She doubted he or his wagon would be there after the ceremony, but she admired his boldness.

He lost most of his business to another man who, with hammer and anvil, just squared coins up for a sliver from each one.

In a few places knots of hale and hearty individuals pointed and laughed at the sick and injured shambling forward. "Good luck, old One-leg," or "Not enough magic in the world to heal you," they'd call, then dissolve into laughter. One stepped along with a lame man leaning on a crutch, mocking his limp. Nirati hoped the man would be healed, then come back and beat his tormentor silly.

If any of them recognized her, they probably wondered what she needed healed. It wasn't obvious, but she needed the greatest healing of all. Nirati had no talent and while everyone told her she just had yet to discover it, she had long since lost the ability to believe them. Even Majiata had a talent, and her squandering it angered Nirati. Even as poor with plants as Majiata was, she could have been more help with Keles' care than Nirati.

Nirati snarled and refused to let herself sink into self-pity. She had done what she could. She'd sat with Keles while he slept, softly reading to him from the tales of Amenis Dukao. He'd always enjoyed the stories when he was a child—all three of them had—and he'd slept easier as she read. Her attending him let her mother get sleep, and that, too, was a blessing. But Nirati would have given an arm to be able to do more.

A blush rose to her face as she came into the area around Xingnakun and saw a young boy with a withered left arm. *At least I have an arm to give.*

Someone she took as his father crouched beside him at the edge of the first stone circle surrounding the dome. The man tousled the boy's hair. "Dunos, you know I can't go in with you, but you'll find me waiting here for you. Don't be afraid."

"I'm not really, Father." The tremble in the boy's voice undercut his reply.

Nirati walked toward them and bowed. "Peace of the Festival to you both. Might I ask a favor?"

The man rose, then bowed, and his son joined him. "Peace with you as well, my lady. What would you have of us?"

She smiled at the father, then pointed at the vast and empty courtyard around the dome. "It is distant yet to Xingnakun, and I worry about being able to make it without an escort. Might I be so bold as to ask your son to accompany me?"

The man nodded, then wiped a smudge of black on his son's cheek, keeping an eye line crisp. "Dunos would be pleased to accompany you."

The boy nodded and Nirati took his hand in hers. "Thank you. I shall have him lead me back here. I am Nirati."

"This is Dunos and I am Alait. I will find you here. Thank you."

"Bye, Father."

Nirati and the boy crossed the courtyard. A granite circle broke the line of the cobbles every hundred yards. Black at the outside, then grey and white, the circles warned people to stay away. Whereas the other streets and courts in the capital teemed with people, Xingnakun's courtyard remained empty save for the broken wandering toward it. In the midst of a Festival full of joy and hope, the hopeless and desperate trickled in slowly.

Dunos looked up at her. "Why are you going to be healed, my lady? You look okay."

"Not all of us have visible injuries."

"Are you talking woman stuff? That's what my mother calls it before she tells me to go help my father."

Nirati smiled. "Perhaps. I just hope I bear my trouble as well as you do."

Dunos nodded, then let his withered arm swing forward. "Once I get this healed up, I'm going to be a swordsman."

"That's a fine ambition."

A little tremor ran through his hand. "Have you seen Kaerinus before?"

She shook her head. "You can only do this once, Dunos." She'd heard from many that the omen of the years combined with a spike in the cyclical magic activity promised much from this ritual. It was thought that if a dead body could walk into Xingnakun this year, Kaerinus might even cure it.

"Why do you ask, Dunos?"

The boy shrugged. "Well, it's not that I'm afraid, you know, but I have heard stories. He was with Prince Nelesquin in Ixyll. He's the last of the *vanyesh*. He lived through the Cataclysm. He's really old and he's a monster."

"I've heard all those things, too." She gently pulled him in front of her as they started up one of the narrow ramps leading to an entryway. The entrances were all circles, unbroken, with a low lip so one had to step over them. Though she had never seen it herself, she had heard stories of magical energy guttering out of these holes during the ceremony.

He stepped in first, then held her hand as she crossed. "I think, Dunos, that he might be a monster, but if he is willing to heal people, he is not entirely bad."

The boy nodded, then looked back again. "For the healing, you're not going to have to get naked or nothing, are you?"

She smiled. "No."

"Okay. I'll have to take my robe off, so he can see my arm."

"Okay."

They strode through the tunnel and paused at the top of the

steep stairs. Back in Imperial times the area closer to the earthen circle would have been reserved for the nobility. Dunos tugged her toward the left, preparatory to climbing up to the higher reaches where the poorer people gravitated, but she shook her head.

"We'll go down and get closer."

"But my father said—"

"You're my escort, remember?" She winked at him. "We'll get closer so we get a good healing."

Nirati started down, intent on taking a place right at the circle's edge, but she stiffened. Majiata had preceded her and stood there, head high, black hair shining. Her robe, while poorly woven and cut, had still been made of silk. Not wishing to speak with her, but interested in watching her, Nirati chose a place several rows back and directly behind.

More people filed in and Dunos looked around, his eyes wide. He freed his hand from hers and waved to a man. Nirati turned and looked at him, wondering why he had come since he looked no more injured than she was. He moved easily down and toward them from the row in front.

Dunos smiled hugely. "Why are you here, Master?"

"We all bear our wounds, Dunos."

The boy nodded. "This is Nirati. She's here for woman stuff."

The man smiled. "I am Moraven. Peace of the Festival to you."

"And you." Nirati smiled, but kept her voice low. At the mention of her name Majiata's head had half turned. *Just ignore me, Majiata, or I'll go down there and give you some bruises that will really need healing.*

From somewhere deep in the building's bowels, drums began to pound. Nirati actually felt the vibration before she heard it, but as the crowd quieted, the echoes filled the dome. As each sound rippled through the throng, waves of fear rose in its wake. In a few places, people started to run toward the exits. Their fear became contagious and still others fled.

Nirati expected Majiata to run, but she didn't. She did glance back again and Nirati realized her game. *As long as I am here, she won't run.* That reason alone would not have stopped Nirati, but if she'd left, the boy would have gone, too. *And he needs this more than I.*

Yet her resolve to remain faced stiff opposition, for remaining there—inviting the attention of a magician—had, since the Cataclysm and even before, been considered foolhardy. Kaerinus was the last of the *vanyesh* and, having existed for so long, clearly had reached a mastery of magic that allowed him to work miracles. It was said the gods remained in the Heavens for fear he would find them and send them back.

The sort of power he could wield had destroyed the world. It had triggered the Time of Black Ice, killing millions—flattening mountains, erasing cities and towns, and threatening humanity with extinction. Stories of wandering *xingnaridin* frightened children into good behavior, and rumors of them banded men into mobs. The dome had been created to contain Kaerinus' power against the fear that he could initiate another Cataclysm.

A light grey mist began to pour from a circular entrance across the arena. Little tendrils of intense blue color played through it—part flame, part lightning—that cracked when they winked out. Nirati's flesh tingled. The fog deepened, filling the opening, then a blue light built inside it. Fire flickered faster, and little spiderwebs of lightning flashed.

All around her people exposed their injuries. Dunos clumsily tore at the buttons on his robe. She bent to help him slip it off and noticed the blue lightning playing up and down beneath his flesh, outlining veins and arteries. In front of them, Moraven took off his robe, revealing a hideous scar on the left side of his chest. Nirati and Dunos both stared at it for a moment and she wondered how someone strong enough to survive that could ever imagine himself needing healing.

Beyond him, Majiata let her robe slip down to beneath her shoulder blades. She clutched it modestly closed at her breasts and Nirati shook her head. *That makes a circle, silly girl.* Had it been anyone else, Nirati would have said something, but looking at the red worm of a scar on Majiata's shoulder blade disgusted Nirati. Majiata's stupidity had earned her that scar, and her stupidity would see to it that it remained.

A gasp rose as Kaerinus emerged from the tunnel. He wore a purple cloak with a high collar that hid the lower half of his head. A hood covered it and shadowed his face, but could not hide the blue fire burning in his eyes. No decoration adorned his cloak, though azure lightning cascaded down from his shoulders.

Two things became immediately apparent to Nirati and knotted her stomach. The first was that Kaerinus' head had not been bowed when he left the tunnel, nor had his shoulders been stooped, but now he stood at least ten feet tall. His shoulders, she felt certain, would have brushed either edge of the tunnel. Even as she made that judgment about his size, he grew larger—until he could have dwarfed a Viruk warrior with ease.

The second thing she found even more frightening. He moved forward at something slower than a gentle walking pace, but gave no sign of moving. She could not see foot or knee press against the cloak. Instead, he drifted forward on the grey fog. He could have been the figurehead on a ship sailing serenely down the Gold River.

Then, suddenly, in the center of the earthen circle, he stopped. The cloud around him did not continue to roll forward; it stopped, too. He remained unmoving for a heartbeat, then slowly spun. Some people shrank from his gaze—a few broke, others fainted. Dunos slipped his hand into hers and squeezed and even Moraven shifted his shoulders uneasily. As her gaze met the mage's, she felt a hint of recognition, but only a cursory one. *As if he is a trader inspecting livestock, nothing more.*

The drums faded and the lightning no longer pulsed through the fog or his cloak. The light in his eyes shifted from blue to purple. The fiery tongues twisting through the fog likewise changed, matching his eyes. From somewhere within his hood—or in *him*—words rose. Nirati didn't think she was even hearing him speak, and the idea of words seemed wrong as well.

Is this what my brothers share with our grandfather?

Images boiled through her mind quickly. She caught sight of a boy's hand reaching for a glowing crystal. She felt the weight of a lash against her back. The searing-hot pain of a sword slicing flesh drew a line over her ribs. Those things she guessed came from Dunos, Majiata, and Moraven; so she assumed the other things came from the rest of the crowd. Beneath them all, however, came a chorus of screams—Men, animals—all in pain, horrible pain.

Nirati found herself screaming as well. Everyone did, filling the dome with a horrible sound that doubled back on itself, increasing and pulsing, drilling through her more powerfully than the drums.

They had shaken her physically, but this reached inside and touched her pain, her fear. Before, she had been unlike anyone, for she had no talent, but here she now was like everyone—she was broken and was afraid she could not be fixed.

The fog around Kaerinus thickened into tentacles that lashed out full of sizzling electricity. One thick rope hit a crippled crone, lifting her off her feet. Purple lightning wreathed her limbs, shocking them straight. Her head flew back, her dowager's hump vanished as her spine untwisted. She shrieked and the fog left her a crumpled heap, vapor rising.

Again and again the tentacles flicked out, swirling to the left. A lower disk of fog spread out to fill the arena. Kaerinus rose with it and the tentacles spun faster, stirring the fog so it would slop over the arena's edges. One wave crashed into Majiata and her scar burned so intensely Nirati could not look at it. Majiata screamed and dropped her robe, her back bowing, then her whole torso snapped forward. For a moment it looked as if she would pitch headlong into the opaque vapor roiling below, but she clutched at the edge and sagged down, half-naked. Purple fire filled vacant eyes as she sprawled sloppily—looking as if she were drunk and had been ravished by a Turasynd horde.

Nirati had but a heartbeat to relish Majiata's dishevelment before a larger wave surged up and engulfed her. In an instant it felt as if she were naked in a stinging steel rain. She looked down, expecting to see her flesh freckled with blood, but her eyes no longer registered reality. She saw herself as a child again, viewing herself from both a distance and within her skin. She was walking hand in hand with her grandfather through the gardens of Anturasikun. The sun shone on them both, and the sting melted into warmth.

She half remembered the incident, but it crawled from her memory with the reluctance of a Soth ripping free of its cocoon. Qiro let her hand drop and turned to face Ulan. Only her uncle was much younger than now; her grandfather was still his powerful, white-maned self. Ulan unscrolled a chart for Qiro to inspect. Before she had enough time to even begin to recognize shapes, Qiro savagely berated Ulan.

Nirati did not hear the words, but rather saw them as arrows flying straight into her uncle. They ripped into his chest and blood gushed. One transfixed his skull and another sank in through his left eye. A small bolt pinned his tongue to his lower jaw, and yet another emasculated him. Ulan crumpled the same way the chart crumpled in Qiro's hands.

She looked up at her grandfather, tears forming in her eyes. She bent to pick up the map and smooth it, but Qiro took it from her hands and threw it away. He smiled at her, turning her from Ulan, and led her deeper into the gardens. Flowers poured from his mouth, though they were ghosts of those blooming around her.

And around her heart slid an armored sleeve. She did not say it then—she had not known the words to say it then—but now she knew. *I determined then I would never let him hurt me as he did Uncle Ulan. I am not without talent. I hid from my talent.*

That knowledge exploded in her. Everything she had tried to do had been a failure. She had worked diligently at it, but never had connected with anything. *I'd not let myself connect. I did not want a talent. I did not want to be judged, to be skewered and crumpled. Perhaps I never needed healing.*

Her vision returned to her and there, in a grey sea, she saw the purple light burning in the arena's heart. Kaerinus had risen high enough that the fog could fill the dome and touch everyone. *Is that it? Did I never need the healing, or was this the healing I needed?*

She felt his awareness sweep past her, but she got no reply. Instead, she felt herself beginning to drift upward. She glanced down and saw her body. Around her, as if phantoms, she saw Dunos and Moraven, even Majiata. Of others she became only dimly aware. When she looked up again, Kaerinus had become a black pearl with purple fire swirling around its middle. It rotated down as if an eye, with a fiery purple pupil mirroring what had become the corona. It saw her. It saw her and she saw herself reflected and distorted in the orb's dark surface.

She reached a hand out and traced a finger over the sphere. She felt something ancient in there, and knew she should fear it, but she did not. She caressed it again, and the illusion of a smooth surface vanished. Tiny glass teeth tore at her flesh. Violet lightning lashed her. She yanked her hand away, screaming as she severed contact.

Her eyes snapped open as Moraven and Dunos both crouched

beside her. She started trembling, then bit her lower lip. "W-what happened?"

Moraven smiled uneasily. "I suspect it was different for each of us. One moment we were locked in the magic. In the next, it and Kaerinus were gone."

Nirati let them help her into a sitting position. She looked toward where Majiata had fallen. "What of that woman?"

"She wandered out, dazed."

Dunos nodded and lifted her robe in his right hand. "She forgot this."

Nirati half smiled, but stopped quickly. Dunos' arm remained withered. She glanced at Moraven and saw the end of his scar. "I'm sorry."

"For what, Mistress?"

"You still have your scar, and Dunos . . ."

The boy frowned and tears glistened in his eyes, but none rolled down his cheeks. "It's okay."

Moraven leaned across Nirati and caressed Dunos' left arm. "Have you forgotten what I said on the road, Dunos?"

"You said I would be healed." His lower lip trembled. "You can't always be right, Master."

"I was not wrong, Dunos." The man's voice, though soft, carried confidence. "The magic promised only to heal us, not give us what we want. It gave us what we need."

"But I wanted to be a swordsman."

"And you may yet be." Moraven smiled, then tapped the boy on the head. "First, though, you have to find out what was healed. That will tell you your true destiny."

"Yes, Master. Thank you."

Nirati looked at Moraven. "Have you been given what you need?"

He shrugged. "Perhaps."

"That doesn't sound very definite."

Moraven smiled, stood, and helped her to her feet. "Healing is always a process, magical or not. It will take time for me to figure out what has changed. The same for Dunos. Do you know, Mistress, or will you need time as well?"

"I think I *will* need time." Nirati paused for a moment, then nodded. "Time to heal, then time to discover what it is my healing will allow me to do."

"Best fortune in your search." The swordsman shrugged his robe back on. "You're embarked on a journey most never realize they need to take. If that realization were the only thing you got today, you would have been the most fortunate of us all."

Chapter Sixteen

6th day, Harvest Festival, Year of the Dog
9th Year of Imperial Prince Cyron's Court
162nd Year of the Komyr Dynasty
736th year since the Cataclysm
Anturasikun, Moriande
Nalenyr

When Keles awoke again he found himself in a larger bed within a dim room. The sheets were fresh—likewise the straw in the mattress. He could smell the poultice and other herbs. Their scents did not make him want to gag. He felt stronger somehow, and though he noticed the pain in his back, the tightness of the flesh across the wounds superseded it.

He turned his head and found his mother sitting in a chair beside the bed, concentrating on embroidering an emblem on cloth. She looked up as the rustle of bedclothes betrayed his movement. "How do you feel?"

"Thirsty."

She poured him a small cup of water, then held his head, raising the cup to his lips and only allowing him tiny sips. He wanted to suck it down greedily, but knew it would come right back up, so he settled for allowing a cool trickle down his throat. He drank as much as he could, then nodded, and she withdrew the nearly empty cup.

"How long have I slept?"

"A long time, which is good. It's the Festival's sixth day."

Keles concentrated. "The Prince's ball is tonight."

Siatsi laughed lightly and brushed hair back from his forehead. "Your brother and sister will represent us well."

"You should have gone, Mother."

She shook her head. "And have every crone in the nation asking me how you were, what I thought of what happened? No, that would not do. You *are* the talk of Festival, Keles, but I need not be the one doing that talking."

Keles nodded, or thought he had. He did hear the rustle of pillowcase against his cheek. "I remember the ambassador. What happened?"

Siatsi sighed. "I'm certain your brother has told you of frogs and toads in Ummummorar that exude a poison. Wildmen use it to hunt with, but it protects the creatures from predators."

Keles nodded.

"The Viruk apparently have a similar thing. Just as our sweat becomes acrid when we are nervous, so their personal humors change. When the warrior cut you, his claws poisoned you. Mildly, of course, but you were poisoned nonetheless. The ambassador's magic was able to deal with the more virulent aspects of the venom, but some things will take time to work out. It could be a year or more. Until then even the scent of a Viruk could make you sick."

"Luckily there will be no Viruk on the *Stormwolf*."

"Lucky for some, Keles, but not for you." In quiet tones Siatsi told him what had happened that night and of his grandfather's pronouncement. Keles' skin puckered as she spoke. He did not so much fear the trip as he did his grandfather's wrath. The *Stormwolf*'s voyage *might* have been meant to kill him, but a trip into the depths of Ixyll surely would.

Even in the dim light he could see how his mother had paled, and her fingers quivered as she stroked his hair. "I have spoken with Qiro, but he is adamant. I cannot shift him, no matter how I try."

"Give it time, Mother."

"Dear boy, there is not that much time in the world." She frowned. "I could tell you all the ways in which he felt compelled to act, but the simple fact was that he made that pronouncement at his birthday celebration. Princes heard him. For him to relent now would be a dishonor. It would suggest one or both of you are weak, and he will tolerate neither."

"Do you think he wants me dead?"

"He is capable of it."

"Did he want my father dead?"

Siatsi frowned for a moment, then sighed. "The years and rumors have made it easy to accept the simple answer, but Qiro and Ryn were more complex. Your father pushed his father hard. Your father had a gift, one greater than Qiro's, if you can believe it, and Qiro realized that Ryn would be able to cement the Anturasi place in history if he would focus that gift. But your father was not patient. Like your brother, he had other interests. Qiro tried to focus your father on cartography. That led to the last voyage.

"Part of him probably *did* want your father dead, for they fought furiously. And part of him mourned piteously when your father died. He grieves still."

"Does he want me dead?"

"No. He wants you to return after doing your work." She smiled. "Your grandfather is not entirely heartless."

Keles frowned. "He has condemned me to a journey of over two thousand miles as the hawks fly. I will be traveling through lands where wild magic has held sway and heroes refuse to go. The only people who venture into the realm of Ixyll are the insane, or the *gyanridin,* who *act* insane. I will have to cross the Dark Sea, risking storms and pirates, and I'll be passing close enough to Irusviruk to see many more warriors. Some will be kin to those Jorim killed, and all of them will make me ill. Grandfather may not be coldhearted, as you say, but he is showing me little of his warmth."

She laughed.

"I did not think I was being funny."

"No, Keles, I know that."

"Well?"

Siatsi smiled. "Rumor had it that Majiata had described your journey similarly, but without regret."

"She did?" His heart ached slightly. "You didn't tell me if the Prince had her lashed."

"He did. She fainted and bears naught but a tiny scar on her back. Your sister saw it when she went to the healing ceremony."

Keles blinked. "Nirati went? You let her go?"

"It was important to her to go." His mother sighed. "Nirati's been here by your side a lot, Keles. She does all she can to help, and she has been a great help, but she feels her lack of talent. She watches me mix herbs and roots for your poultices and would give anything to be able to do that. She went hoping she would find her talent."

"I keep telling her she's like Empress Cyrsa. She *will* find her talent."

"I know, Keles. I agree, but Cyrsa's story is one that salves the wound for children."

"How did it turn out for her?"

His mother shrugged. "She said it was good, but talked more about a little boy from the south. You talk to her, see what you can learn."

"I will. So there was no change?"

"There might have been, but she said it might take time. You know your sister. She's no more patient than your brother in most things." Siatsi smiled. "In fact, she is impatient in everything save dealing with your grandfather."

"That's true, but I would rather she followed your footsteps than his."

"So would I, but she would gladly be a cartographer. You'll have to be kind to her. I think had she found a talent for mapmaking, she would have offered to go in your place."

"If anyone is less suited to go than I am, it would be Nirati."

His mother smiled. "I agree, but your brother didn't."

"No?"

"He said you were equally ill suited to it. He said if it didn't kill you or maim you, the journey would drive you insane. Then he said he would give anything to be going in your place."

Keles managed a chuckle. "He would, wouldn't he?"

"Yes, but he knew you'd not let him—though he did advance a plan where you could trade identities."

"Wouldn't work. As I send information to Grandfather he would know of the deception."

"Jorim agreed that was true, but thought if the deception were maintained, only the family need know."

"No. Too many others would know, from the crew of the *Stormwolf* to whoever accompanies me." Keles sighed. "Unless Qiro changes his mind, or the Prince issues orders to the contrary, I shall be bound for Ixyll."

His mother nodded solemnly. "Jorim said you would feel honor-bound to go."

"He knows me well." *But does he know me well enough? He doesn't think I can even* survive. *Is he right?*

Keles had made journeys for years, and had conducted surveys, but always close to or within Nalenyr. It had not been because anyone thought he could not have gone further, but because things like the survey of the upper reaches of the Gold River were vital, and Keles remained focused on the task at hand. Being able to focus like that had made him successful, but he had to wonder how useful that skill would be on a trip into places where magic could and often *did* warp the landscape.

He laughed. Even wondering about *that* showed his focus—and the problem with it. The wild magic out there warped *everything*—plants, animals, relics—and yet he was concerned about the geography. It was not going to be a mountain becoming a plain that would kill him, but the weirder, less predictable curiosities in that land.

He smiled at his mother. "Jorim will take a trip that will test his skills to the utmost, for he will have to do what I do well and what he does well, both at the same time. On the other hand, I will have to learn to survive the way he does and how to change quickly and adapt, as fast or faster than the realm into which I wander. Not an easy job for either of us."

"Indeed not." Siatsi smiled, then kissed Keles' brow. "Sleep. Heal. That is what you must do now, if you are to stand any chance at success later."

"Do you think I will succeed, mother?"

She nodded. "Beyond the ability of any of us to dream."

Chapter Seventeen

6th day, Harvest Festival, Year of the Dog
9th Year of Imperial Prince Cyron's Court
162nd Year of the Komyr Dynasty
736th year since the Cataclysm
Kojaikun, Moriande
Nalenyr

"Sister, you worry too much." Jorim Anturasi slowly shook his head as they passed through a gantlet of Keru guardswomen to reach the large reception hall in Kojaikun. "The least the healing could have done was cure you of that."

Nirati quickly stuck her tongue out at him.

The sixth day of Festival was always given over to the honoring of heroes. To make a point and annoy Prince Pyrust, Prince Cyron had chosen to hold it in the tower most associated with Helosunde. Prince Pyrust had sent his regrets and the Helosundians viewed that as a victory of sorts.

Nirati, wearing a green silk gown with yellow, red, and blue birds embroidered on it, gave her younger brother a hard stare. "There is not a night of heroes I can recall when you did not end up in some sort of fight."

"Youthful indiscretions."

"Would that a healing could cure you of those." Her expression softened ever so slightly. "Mother has entrusted us with the family honor, so please be careful."

"Yes, Nirati, I will." Jorim paused with her at the doorway to the long, rectangular hall. It had been finished entirely in blond wood, with lighting coming through panels papered over with ivory rice paper. The color of the wood reminded everyone of the Keru and their dedication to the Prince's service.

He surveyed the room and the gaily robed guests, then gave his sister a smile. "I see no Viruk, so I doubt there will be trouble."

Nirati's green eyes became slits. "You remember what you were instructed to say about that?"

Jorim sighed. "Keles is resting comfortably, full recovery expected, in no danger, won't even see the scars, looking forward to his journey—which he doesn't even know about unless he's come awake in the last hour."

"Jorim!"

"I *know,* Nirati. I will not say what I should not."

"And you won't get into trouble."

He gave her a hard stare, but she had learned well from their mother. *And I have always been her younger brother, which gives her an advantage I cannot undo.* While she might be hard on him, she was also protective, and that was something he was reluctant to surrender no matter the cause.

"I won't get into trouble."

"Thank you." She leaned in and kissed him on the cheek. "Now, go have fun."

"As if that's possible. I'm going, I'm going." He smiled into her reproving glare, then moved into the hall and let himself drift. Not for the first time he studied the gathering the way he viewed savage peoples. He didn't do it with a sense of superiority, only curiosity.

I bet even they don't know what they reveal about themselves, they are so busy playing their games. To Jorim, a great deal was obvious just from a casual glance. The most important people had taken up positions around the room where they could be seen easily, but not cut off. Rarely was anyone with true power in a corner, though several people who wished to be perceived as having power had taken up positions there.

Lesser personages usually had someone with them—someone of a higher social station—to lend them some sort of legitimacy. Had Jorim chosen to extend an invitation to various women of his acquaintance, he, too, could have had someone on his arm. Women would have fought for the honor—not to be seen with him per se, but to be seen by older men who might take them as mistresses, or dowagers who were looking for someone to bear grandchildren for them. As he watched, that very scenario played itself out a dozen times or more.

Politics and politicians ran a circuit through the room. Likewise the social pressures caused currents, and gossip of both varieties raced. Courtiers and sycophants jockeyed for position awaiting the arrival of the Prince, in hopes they would be able to get a word with him, or at least be noticed.

While friends did meet friends at the gathering, the greetings were brief and fulfilled the minimum demands of social intercourse. There would be time for true friends later in Festival, after the day of Mourning and before the glory of the Prince would be celebrated. On the night of heroes, all those gathered wished to be seen as heroes, so acted in a way they thought full of mythic import.

Jorim didn't see himself as a hero, though he hoped some people did—and he acknowledged that as a paradox springing from self-deception the moment it occurred to him. He had gone places, seen and done things that few in the room could match. While many of them would thrill to his exploits and claim that someday they would like to do the same thing, they preferred the safety of their homes and stable lives. He couldn't blame them for that, and he didn't despise them for it.

He just knew it wasn't for him.

There were those who would claim that it was hatred or fear of his grandfather that prompted him to go so far away, but they were wrong. First off, they didn't understand that his journeys required him to be very close to his grandfather. The skill for cartography ran strong in the Anturasi bloodline, and with that came the ability—through training and study—for both Jorim and Keles to enter a sort of mental communion with their grandfather. By concentrating very hard and holding information in their minds for a time, they could share basic data with him. He would immediately add it to his maps of the world. Sketching in vast vistas had to wait for their return; but distances traveled, the height of mountains, and other such information could be transmitted over the miles.

Keles was much better at it than Jorim, primarily because he had worked so hard to train his twin. In Nirati's case the training had been for nothing, since she did not possess that skill. That was not all bad. It meant Qiro did not see her as a threat and, therefore, saw no reason to put her in danger. Jorim, while being able to send information to his grandfather, was not as precise as Keles, and whenever he returned to Moriande, he braced himself for discipline.

No, Jorim went out into the world not to escape his grandfather, but because he loved experiencing the variety of things out there. He allowed his curiosity to govern him, and trusted in his luck to keep him safe. No matter how close he had come to death, his desire to see more and do more had not been squelched.

And now I get the Stormwolf. The ship's keel had been laid before he went on his last expedition. Jorim had fully expected that Keles would be given the honor of that trip, and that had made him jealous. That was why he'd mentioned the Gryst device to Qiro, in the slender hope it might win him a berth on the ship, too.

Jorim was at once elated and apprehensive about the trip. It would allow him to sate his curiosity. They would be going into a part of the world no one knew existed outside fable and legend, from the Mountains of Ice to whatever lay beyond the Eastern Sea. He would be able to discover things, bring back samples, and add to the world—shaping and defining it with every mile traveled. What was rumor would become fact, what was legend would be proved true or false, and whatever was unknown would become known. He would be there to make all that happen, to the greater glory of his nation and his family.

At the same time Jorim had hoped Qiro would keep Keles close and train him to take over. He'd looked forward to actually communicating data to his brother instead of his grandfather, for he was certain the bond would be tighter and allow for a faster exchange of more information. And speed in the race to discover the world could not be underestimated.

Keles' journey into the wastelands scared Jorim, for he'd gotten far enough into the wilds to see places where the Cataclysm had changed things, albeit centuries ago. The wild magic unleashed when the Empress's troops had met the Turasynd hordes had exploded out of Ixyll and washed over half the known world. Skies had darkened, and black snows had fallen early and deep. The histories told of years without summer, which is when the die-off of peoples began. Before the Cataclysm, the Empire had boasted tens of millions of people. Within a decade, the Principalities had been reduced to maybe hundreds of thousands. Most of them clustered in the central river valleys of the three largest Principalities, while others clung to existence however they were able.

Unpredictable weather, coming from the northwest where titanic magical storms raged, had battered the Principalities for another century, with the nine days of the Harvest Festival being the closest approximation to summer. Imperial civilization all but collapsed, and chaos would have reigned had the bureaucrats not maintained order. While the histories of those hard times praised the ministers and functionaries, Jorim realized they must have been much like their modern counterparts. While annoying, they had served a purpose, and that purpose kept people alive long enough to begin a slow recovery.

Jorim knew his dismissal of their efforts was overly harsh, and based on discussions he'd had with Keles when they were younger. Keles had said that just maintaining order and organizing shipments of food was a heroic effort. Jorim had replied that the ministers had been too complacent, seeking order above all else, thereby smothering the sort of ambition that might have allowed the Principalities to recover faster. Each brother had to allow that the other might be right; but with no way to prove their arguments, it became a difference of opinion they both acknowledged and somehow found comforting.

Jorim got himself a small cup of wine and sipped it as he moved through the crowd. He looked for others who, like him, remained detached. A few, by their dress, were foreigners who knew no one. Others were famous or infamous, depending upon how one chose to view them. He found the Lady of Jet and Jade along a narrow wall, protected by several of her protégés.

He hid a smile behind his cup. She was still gorgeous despite her years. He'd heard stories suggesting she had been the concubine to princes even before the Komyr dynasty was founded. He wondered if that were true, or if the woman presiding over the House of Jade Pleasure inherited the title and assumed a role as part of a legend. He was not certain why she would be considered a hero, but many were the heroes who visited her house of entertainment.

I wonder if the Prince will send me to her when the Stormwolf *comes back*? He considered approaching her and introducing himself, but her aides seemed very selective. So he kept his distance and saved himself the humiliation of being turned away.

Wandering further, he noticed two men in the crowd, the younger one holding a cup of wine but not drinking, the older one watching with restless eyes. The younger one's belt had been knotted with a swordsman's knot, but neither of them wore swords. No one would be allowed to do so in the Prince's presence, so this came as no surprise, but the younger man looked uneasy. Even with that discomfort, however, he did seem more accustomed to such grand surroundings than his companion.

Jorim looked through the crowd again and discovered a couple more individuals who looked equally like swordsmen, but they stood with their employers. None was as watchful as the older man, but he put that down to a familiarity with such gatherings and their confidence that nothing untoward would unfold. Anyone mad enough to start trouble there would find it ended by the Keru.

No one in this city is that insane, save perhaps Kaerinus. Jorim, as with every child in Nalenyr, had grown up fearing the last of the *vanyesh*. He'd once asked Keles why the sorcerer had been allowed to live, if everyone feared him so, and his brother just gave him a hard stare. Then he lowered his voice, and said, "If they *could* kill him, don't you think they would have? He can't die."

This had made him more terrifying, and Nirati's description of him hadn't eased Jorim's mind at all. The official story, which people told but did not believe, was that he had returned from the west with his mind shattered, reduced to that of a child. While incredibly powerful, he wished only to heal and do good things. *If that were true, however, why would the Naleni princes keep him captive in Xingnakun?*

Not for the first time, the parallel between Kaerinus' fate and that of his grandfather struck Jorim. The sorcerer had been imprisoned because of the harm he might do, and Qiro's freedom might be similarly harmful. Were his charts to fall into the hands of the Virine or the Desei, they could compete with Nalenyr. The Naleni economy would collapse, but before that, Prince Cyron would have to go to war to destroy his enemies.

Jorim took a big swallow of his wine. Perhaps Keles had not been so wrong. While it might take a great deal of effort for Jorim to hack his way through a swamp, capture some lizard, and bring it back to the Prince, the more heroic effort might be required to make sure there was a Nalenyr for him to return to. *When I come back on the* Stormwolf *how much of Moriande, how many of these people, will still be here?*

He looked around, uncertain how to answer that. He pushed the dark thought away. He could think on that tomorrow, on the day of Mourning. Tonight was a time to celebrate and enjoy. *As this might be the last night of heroes any of us ever sees, I shall make the most of it.*

Chapter Eighteen

6th day, Harvest Festival, Year of the Dog
9th Year of Imperial Prince Cyron's Court
162nd Year of the Komyr Dynasty
736th year since the Cataclysm
Kojaikun, Moriande
Nalenyr

Nirati let her brother go reluctantly. She felt confident he would not seek trouble, but also she knew there were times when it sought him. Still, at this gathering, he was more likely to be lionized as a hero and questioned about his exploits than to be challenged by someone in his cups. She wished him a night of peace because the coming voyage would likely afford him few.

She moved into the room and around to the left, taking a course that would not bring her around to Jorim until the far side. The robe she had chosen had all the artistry of the one she'd worn at her grandfather's party, but not the formal cut. The silken trousers beneath allowed her freedom of movement that would make dancing a pleasure instead of a battle against gravity and the entanglements of a longer robe. She'd even done some of the embroidery herself and took pride in it.

She took a good look at the embroidery and tried to evaluate how good she was at it. Since the healing, she'd been reexamining her life, looking at the world with new eyes. *My talent is there, I'm sure. Now I just have to find it. But where?*

She caught sight of the Lady of Jet and Jade and wondered at her skills. So many possibilities opened up. Nirati might be able to do *anything. Could I be a concubine?* She wondered what it would be like to be one of the Lady of Jet and Jade's students. Would it be possible to be so learned in the art of love that it would become a magical experience? For Nirati, whose carnal experience was limited to the inept fumblings of servants and drunken noblemen, that idea seemed as wondrous as it was distant.

She knew the stories about those who were *jaecai*—the legendary masters of any discipline. It was said their lives were extended and their vitality increased as they perfected their skills. Looking at the Lady's flawless beauty, the delicate serenity with which she stood against a wall sipping wine, Nirati wondered how old she truly was. Had she really been the concubine of the prince whose dynasty fell to the Komyr cohort? The woman barely looked older than she—save for her silvery eyes, which had an ancient, alluring quality.

"I would guess eleven enneads, would you not?"

Nirati's head came around, a rebuke on her lips that remained unspoken as she recognized the voice. "Count Aerynnor, would you think me so common as to be speculating about a woman's age?"

"I beg your pardon, my lady Anturasi." The black-haired Desei bowed his head. "I betray my rustic nature with such thoughts, and my lack of manners by attributing the same to you."

"If offering me one of those cups of wine would be an apology, sir, I should be happy to forgive you." Nirati smiled and accepted the cup he passed to her. "Have you come alone? Is poor, dear, frail Majiata up from her sickbed yet?"

The man smiled easily. "Shall we drink to her health?"

"The Lady of Jet and Jade? Please."

Junel Aerynnor's smile broadened. "I can see that keeping up with you will not be a simple matter."

"Oh, you meant Majiata?" Nirati raised the cup. "May she soon be feeling herself again."

"Indeed." He drank. "She was supposed to accompany me tonight, but she heard a rumor that the *jaecaitsae* who disciplined her would be here, demonstrating his skill. She thought that would be too much for her."

Nirati smiled. "I doubt he would be asking for volunteers. Did you see her punishment?"

The Desei noble's face closed. "I did; I felt it was my duty. Your brother took the stripes that should have been mine. I confess to quailing as the Viruk moved. So quick, so large."

"You may have quailed, my lord, but I was there. I saw you act, and saw no hesitation. You spun Majiata around and shielded her with your body. Had my brother not acted, his stripes would indeed have been yours."

"I shall be certain to thank him. He is recovering, I hear?"

"Yes, he is, thank you. He would enjoy it if you came to visit. I sit with him often to let my mother rest."

"I shall pay my respects then." Junel sipped at his wine. "The Prince would not allow another to accept Majiata's punishment, but the *jaecaitsae* cut her only once, and her family has sought every manner of salve to see that it will not scar. She even went to be healed by the *vanyesh*."

"It didn't work?"

"I have not looked that closely, but I have seen no disfigurement. But Majiata and her family see through the lens of disgrace." Junel grimaced. "I took no pleasure in watching her punishment, but there is yet a part of me which believes she had long been due such treatment."

Nirati smiled. "Are you abnormally perceptive, or is this a trait shared by your countrymen?"

"I simply learn, my lady." He smiled uneasily. "I would have been hard-pressed not to hear the tales told of Majiata since the party. What the rumors suggest, I have seen. On my last visit, she asked only if her scar had made her hideous. When I mentioned that I had heard your brother fared well, but would bear four scars, she said she was glad of it."

"She wanted my brother in order to advance her family. It took him a long time to see it. You are lucky to have discovered it so quickly."

"Her family has graciously provided me lodging, so I would have to be blind not to have discovered it." Junel glanced around the room. "I am seeing many things that are new. Coming from Deseirion, there are things here I have not seen before—and am not certain I understand."

"Such as?"

He inclined his head toward the Lady of Jet and Jade. "While we have such individuals in Deseirion, I do not think one would be welcomed at such a celebration. Not that she isn't beautiful—and not that many present would not visit her domain and avail themselves of her skills—but they would not want it known."

Nirati sipped her wine, savoring the sweet bite. "In Nalenyr we have a bit more freedom. It fuels us."

The count frowned. "That could be taken many ways. Please, explain."

"Carnal desire, my lord, can be approached in two ways. One is to deny its existence, to claim that fidelity is the highest standard possible and turn a blind eye to the covert assignations many enjoy. By making it forbidden, one increases its allure, and that is what makes it such a destabilizing influence. Most would not care if one enjoyed liaisons outside of marriage provided that the marriage was not put in jeopardy by it."

"Since so many marriages are really dynastic alliances, they have little to do with those who are involved in them. This is certainly the attitude and reality in my nation."

"Here it is viewed for what it is: a sensual experience. We all acknowledge that variety is to be desired. If one only eats one food, or drinks one wine, hears only one song, or smells only one flower, those things quickly become lifeless. No one limits themselves in that manner for anything save physical attraction and desire, clearly running counter to how we function as people. By having the Lady of Jet and Jade as an outlet for such desires, with all parties knowing what is expected, boredom is avoided, as is destabilizing influence."

Nirati looked at him past the rim of her cup. "If you forge an alliance with Majiata's family, I'm sure you'll need the release."

Junel raised an eyebrow. "You are even more perceptive than I thought, Mistress Anturasi. But, tell me, you are not suggesting that there is never a marriage destroyed because a client and a courtesan fall in love?"

"No, but that shift in affections could occur no matter who is involved, for whatever affection was present in the marriage would have long since died, else the desire and need for emotional fulfillment would not have been present."

"I am very impressed with your argument." He nodded respectfully. "You think deeply and express yourself very well."

"It's years of having debates with my brothers. We have discussed every issue from as many points of view as possible. It is great fun." Nirati swirled the wine in her cup and looked down. "You've not been here long, but you already know of the Lady of Jet and Jade. Have you considered engaging her services?"

"I? Well, no, but . . ."

Nirati covered a smile as she saw the man blushing. "What is it?"

He snapped his mouth shut, then looked down. "I would lie if I did not say that I have not entertained the idea. You will think me provincial, I suspect, but it goes back to where our conversation started. I would be uneasy being with someone who could have known my great-grandfather."

She hesitated for a moment, then nodded. "I understand that, though some maintain the best wines are those that have aged to perfection."

"Very true, but there are also those who enjoy younger vintages."

Nirati sipped again and felt herself relaxing in the Desei count's presence. He knew few people and seemed content to talk to her, yet his presence kept others away, and that was good, too. She didn't mind that the people who saw them together would probably accuse her of stealing Majiata's suitor. Half of them would think it served Majiata right, and the other half would speculate as to what this would mean concerning the Anturasi maps, the Desei, and the fortunes of House Phoesel.

But she found the count easy company. She slowly guided him around the room, filling him in on who was whom. She refrained from outright gossip, but indicated which people were feuding with others. The only time she relayed salacious information was when his eyes grew distant and she imagined all the facts becoming a jumble in his head.

Before she saw her brother again, a gong sounded and the room fell to silence. A half dozen Keru guards with long spears bearing purple dragon pennants cut a path through the crowd. Prince Cyron walked in their midst and mounted a small dais at the far end of the room. The guards took up positions around it and the Prince bowed to those assembled.

The bow was returned by all present. Nirati held the bow for the polite count of fifteen, extended to twenty since this was the dynasty's anniversary, and was willing go to thirty because of the Prince's punishment of Majiata. But when she reached twenty-five, one of the Prince's cousins rose and, with audible relief, the others in the room followed.

The Prince opened his hands in greeting. "Welcome to you all. This is the night of heroes, which is especially hallowed in a nation of heroes. All of you present are worthy of that title, or will earn your place in their ranks. Our nation and our course is one that will both demand and reward heroes. I know none of you will shrink from that calling."

Two protocol functionaries produced a chair for the Prince and set it up in the center of the dais. A minister of protocol—a senior underminister by the cut of his robe—came forward and addressed the crowd. "Entertainments have been provided for this evening, spectacular entertainments."

As he spoke, he moved into the crowd and shifted his ceremonial staff from vertical to horizontal. The crowd withdrew slowly as he grasped the staff in his right hand and began to turn, describing a circle. "If you please, respect the circle drawn, and you will see things of which most only dream."

The count, through stern glances and an open-faced refusal to understand those with a Naleni accent, did not withdraw as others pulled back. Instead, he placed his hands on Nirati's shoulders and brought her in front of him, placing her at the front rank of observers. She smiled, realized that the last time she'd had so clear a view was with her father's hands on her shoulders.

The entertainments were more than fantastic. They started with four Keru who performed a ritual dance with spears. Pennants snapped, the spear butts cracked crisply on the stone, and the shafts whistled as they were spun about. The women moved so precisely, with strength and fluidity, they seemed more animal than human. When confederates lofted apples and other fruits into the air, the spear blades skewered or split them, filling the air with sweet fragrance.

Jugglers followed, then acrobats whose ability to pile themselves higher seemed limited only by the ceiling. Contortionists twisted their limbs into patterns that it seemed would never come undone, and dancers flowed into and through music until their bodies were little more than vibrant blurs.

Each entertainment surpassed the one that preceded it—as impossible as that seemed. The minister pointed out whoever had brought the entertainers, and applause rewarded them for their efforts. But the minister cut them off if they offered anything more than a few words of praise for the Prince, then announced the next act.

He kept his voice even as the last troupe of dancers melted away. "As our final entertainment, we present something as special as it is appropriate for the night of heroes. We have with us two *dicaiserr*. They will present for you a display of swords skill as has never been seen before. The Prince welcomes Moraven Tolo and the Turasynd, Chyrut Scok."

Nirati smiled. From their encounter at the healing, she knew Moraven was a swordsman. She'd taken Dunos' praise of him as childish hyperbole, but clearly the youth had been right. *To be selected to entertain here means he is very good. Perhaps he's even* jaecaiserr.

A jolt ran through Junel's hands. Nirati turned enough to look up into his face. "What is it?"

"Moraven Tolo I have never heard of, but the Turasynd I have. They may think he is here to demonstrate his skill, and he is—but not in the way one would expect."

"What do you mean?"

He nodded as a tall, gaunt, dark-haired man moved into the circle. "When he removes his shirt, you'll see the mark of the black eagle on him. He belongs to a barbarian cult. No matter what he is told, when he draws his blade, the fight is to the death."

Chapter Nineteen

6th day, Harvest Festival, Year of the Dog
9th Year of Imperial Prince Cyron's Court
162nd Year of the Komyr Dynasty
736th year since the Cataclysm
Kojaikun, Moriande
Nalenyr

Prince Cyron sat forward in his chair as the two fighters came through the crowd. The Turasynd was easy to spot, for he stood head and shoulders above the others. His clothing bespoke origins in the Turca Wastes, though Chyrut himself had been born in Solaeth. Clean-limbed and very lean, he wore a half-sleeved leather shirt that showed off arms scarred from fighting. The white scars stood out starkly on his red skin. A strip of leather circled his brows, and his long, black hair had been braided with the ends of it.

The guests began buzzing when the Turasynd moved into the circle. For most of them, he was the embodiment of terror. His people had caused the Cataclysm, and many of those assembled had been raised with threats of Turasynd raiders coming to steal them away. Even the Prince had heard tales of Turasynd infamy that had him mindful of their threat—despite the fact that Deseirion and Helosunde insulated Nalenyr.

While Chyrut looked to be no more than fifty years old, which was young even for a Turasynd, the Prince wondered at his true age. That he was a master of the sword was well documented, and some reports even hinted that he might be *jaecaiserr*. If so, he could be considerably older than he appeared. The Prince doubted he could have been one of the barbarian survivors of the Cataclysm—rumors of them did exist, but it was said they had all returned horribly warped. He could, however, have been old enough to learn his art from such survivors.

A smaller percentage of the crowd hissed because they knew the Turasynd worked for Black Myrian, one of the shadowy figures who profited from criminal enterprises in Nalenyr. The underworld lord had occasionally done a favor for the Crown—like exposing or destroying Desei spies—so the Prince saw no value in eliminating him. In return, Black Myrian kept his activities largely benign—at least when it came to enforcement.

These are odd times when one must conspire with criminals to preserve society. There really was no other way, however, and Cyron had long since resigned himself to that. There would always be those who existed outside the law, and if one of their own could maintain order, they had a use. Myrian stabilized what could have otherwise been a very chaotic situation, and the Prince's ministers valued stability above all.

The man who entered the circle to oppose the Turasynd moved with a fluid economy that seemed humble—especially on a night meant to honor heroes. He wore an overshirt of white trimmed in green, with green trousers over black boots. A black shirt and sash completed his outfit, and his black hair, which was not as long as the barbarian's, hung loose. He bowed easily to his foe, then turned and bowed deeply to the Prince.

The Prince's eyes narrowed, for the smaller man seemed overmatched, which meant he wasn't at all. The black and green marked him as the entertainment provided by the Lady of Jet and Jade, which further indicated he was present for more than just his skill. His overshirt bore no sign of national allegiance, which impressed the Prince—for in Moriande during the Festival, one was either of Nalenyr or proudly displayed signs of one's homeland. Tigers had been embroidered on the overshirt as a personal crest and Cyron recognized the crest—though the man's name had meant nothing to him.

This is *the* xidantzu *I remember.* The Prince smiled as he bowed his head to the swordsman. The Free Company had no leadership nor allegiance. Its members might act as mercenaries or bounty hunters, and in any conflict one or more could be found on either side. More than heroes for hire, they traveled as they wished and, as long as they broke no laws, they did as they wished, too. *And occasionally will serve the Crown, as long as it suits their purposes.*

Cyron wondered why Moraven Tolo traveled under a new name and had been presented as a gift from the Lady of Jet and Jade. Had the Prince known of his presence in Moriande he would have long since summoned him, but one could never be certain a *xidantzu* would obey. He glanced at the Lady of Jet and Jade, wondering if Moraven's presence was her gift to him, with the coming display of skill an added benefit.

I will find him useful, if *he survives this fight.*

The Turasynd pulled his leather jerkin off, and even the Prince gasped. It appeared as if a black eagle had been tattooed on the man's chest, shoulders, and back. The shape was correct, but light shimmered from the design. No ink in the world—even that applied by a Mystic tattooist—could have reflected that way.

A chill ran through Cyron's guts as he realized the truth. The design had not been inked, it had been *fletched.* Feathers, hundreds of them, had been plucked from black eagles. Their tips had been sharpened, then plunged into Chyrut's flesh. It had been part of some Turasynd ritual, and had been performed in a circle where—for days—Chyrut had dueled with other warriors. Their fights had released magical energy the ritual had trapped and channeled into a force that fused the feathers with his flesh.

Cyron had heard of such things, and had dismissed them as wild tales from the Wastes. But for someone to subject himself to such magic willingly . . . The Prince shook his head. He'd even found the risk of the healing ceremony unacceptable, but that tradition predated his dynasty and doubtless would continue well after it.

Two Keru moved to the edge of the circle. Each bore a sword and handed it to the closest combatant. The Turasynd used a slightly curved Turasyndi saber. It came to a sharp point that could be used for lunging, but had been primarily made for sweeping and crushing strokes best delivered from horseback. A pair of green cords ending in satin tassels dangled from the hilt, but the worn scabbard suggested the blade was old and had seen much use.

Moraven Tolo accepted his sword, which surrendered length and breadth to his opponent's weapon. He slid the slender scabbard into his sash, so the hilt rose at his left hip. Nothing decorated its pommel. Just the way he put the blade away without looking marked how well he had grown accustomed to its presence.

Both fighters bowed to the Prince, then to each other. As they straightened, Chyrut bared his blade and tossed the scabbard aside. He roared and slashed the air. People at the edge of the circle withdrew, and one man fainted. Hatred twisted the Turasynd's face, and even the Prince's breath caught in his throat for a moment.

Moraven Tolo did nothing. He did not draw his sword. He did not smile. But the Prince could see this was not the same as ignoring his foe. While he did not move, his blue eyes studied the barbarian—measuring him, judging him.

The Turasynd sailed in, aiming a slashing blow at the smaller man's head. Had it landed, it would have trimmed Moraven's skull at the level of his ears, but it never came close. The smaller man ducked his head and drove forward, passing beneath the cut. Had he drawn his sword and pivoted on his right foot, he would have been able to slash through the barbarian's middle, from back to front.

Chyrut flipped his right wrist and pivoted on his right foot. Feathers lifted on his right shoulder, aiding him in the turn. He brought the blade around in a backhanded cut that should have split Tolo's spine. But Moraven had, by that point, drawn his sword and thrust it down behind himself, blocking the slash. The swords clanged and the smaller man flew forward, tucking into a roll and coming up at the edge of the circle furthest from where he had started. He turned quickly, his blade coming up in a guard that covered him from navel to crown.

Again the barbarian roared and charged, but Moraven did not wait for him. They met in the center of the circle, not standing to exchange blows, but flowing through an intricate series of exchanges. The Prince's scalp tingled and the hair stood on his arms as the two combatants lunged, cut, blocked, parried, spun, and leaped. The fighters' forms blurred and their blades became silver-grey phantoms, appearing and disappearing almost faster than the eye could follow.

The Prince had, as was to be expected, studied the way of the sword. And while never as good as his brother, he knew enough to be able to unravel some of what he was witnessing. The two of them *were* master swordsmen—and perhaps even more. Their actions required more skill than he had ever seen. They seemed to anticipate each other, with Moraven Tolo again and again turning a blade or sidestepping a cut a heartbeat before it would have opened him.

As Cyron watched, he became aware of one other factor in the battle that made it all the more spectacular. The Turasynd, mindful of the fact that this was just a demonstration of skill, fought without fear that his enemy might actually hurt him. Both of them had such control that the only way blood would be drawn would be by accident, and Chyrut left himself open over and over again to speed cuts at Moraven. The smaller man parried, blocked, and evaded, but never riposted no matter how vulnerable Chyrut left himself.

Frustration boiled in the Turasynd. He snarled and redoubled his efforts. His blade screamed through the air, and metal rang with a peal that would have drowned out a signal gong. Sparks flew as he attempted to batter his way through Moraven's guard. His size, the weight of his blade, and the pure fury of his attacks threatened to overwhelm his foe.

Moraven gave ground, but this only seemed to further antagonize the Turasynd. His slashes became more wild and determined, and came close to wounding a few spectators who had crowded back close to the circle. The blades twisted through the air, seeming to have lost all rigidity.

The barbarian cried out in triumph as he whipped his blade through a diagonal slash. A triangular tidbit of cloth hung in the air for a second, then fluttered to the floor. It had come from Moraven's right sleeve, and the Turasynd roared as if it had been the *xidantzu*'s heart that had been pricked.

No one moved. All eyes studied the ragged piece of cloth. It lay there, slightly rumpled, dark against the light wood. For everyone in the room, save the Turasynd, it seemed a dire prediction of a return of the hordes, and the destruction of life as they knew it.

Then the tip of a single feather floated down to land on the cloth.

The Prince rapped his knuckles on the arm of his chair. His protocol minister looked at him, caught his nod, then clapped his hands. "The entertainment is ended."

If the Turasynd had been able to hear him above the din of applause, he did not heed the command. Moraven Tolo leaped above a low slash that shaved curls from the floor, then blocked the return cut. He fell back, slowly arcing around the edge of the circle. The Turasynd followed, then slowed beside the protocol minister.

The minister again announced that the entertainment had ended.

Chyrut's left hand came around in a backhanded slap that spun the minister full circle before dropping him. As his body hit, the Turasynd drove at Moraven Tolo again. His saber came up in a two-handed strike designed to cut the man in half, yet left his belly open.

The Prince squinted, not really wishing to see the aftermath of Moraven's obvious avenue of attack. While he didn't object to the Turasynd's death, having him kneeling there keening as he tried to stuff entrails back into his stomach really would put a damper on any festivities. Still, Moraven Tolo really had no choice. *It is just a matter of how he chooses to do it.*

The Turasynd's sword began to fall. Moraven Tolo reversed his grip on his sword, letting the blade rest along his forearm and extend past his elbow. He danced forward, inside the arc of Chyrut's blow. Another step in and a sidestep to the left would let him slash right across the barbarian's stomach. Tolo's body would even shield much of the audience from the spectacle. *Had I his skill, that's how I would do it.*

Even the loud thud of Chyrut's sword chopping into the wooden floor could not completely disguise the sharp crack of Moraven's pommel smashing into the barbarian's jaw. The larger man's head snapped back, then his knees buckled. Moraven Tolo spun outside the circle of his foe's arms and brought his blade up high at his left shoulder. The Turasynd wavered for a moment, almost holding himself up on his hands, and with the flick of an arm Moraven could have taken his head off easily.

Chyrut tried to say something, but his misshapen jaw did not function well. He pitched forward onto his face, the feathers on his back rippling briefly. The Turasynd's breathing was labored, but the smaller man seemed barely winded.

A young man came from outside the circle and lifted the barbarian's blade from the floor. Moraven frowned for a moment, then dropped to a knee and laid his sword on the ground before the Prince's dais.

"The entertainment is ended, Highness."

Cyron stood and nodded down at the man. "Was he a worthy foe?"

"One of the best I have ever been given the opportunity to fight."

"Were you ever really in danger?"

The swordsman canted his head slightly. "In the circle, one is always in danger. Your foe can only hurt you as much as you allow him to. And any mistake can be your last."

The Prince smiled. "Thank you, *dicaiserr* Moraven Tolo. Before you leave Moriande, I would appreciate your calling on me at Wentokikun."

"You honor me." Moraven Tolo turned and glanced at the younger man who was fiddling with Chyrut's sword. "If my aide learns manners by then, might I present him to you, Highness?"

"Indeed, yes."

Moraven's words brought his aide's head up. The man quickly knelt and laid the sword on the ground. He bowed, but did not raise himself until Moraven lifted his heel as a signal. The younger man then straightened, but did not leave his knees.

The Prince opened his arms. "I thank you all for being so attentive during our entertainments. I would have you continue to enjoy the bounty this harvest has brought our nation. You have seen heroes here tonight, and from them we can all learn. First, we know that our best effort can only be produced through dedication and practice. Second, that to fail to do our best means we have been defeated before we begin to act."

Chapter Twenty

6th day, Harvest Festival, Year of the Dog
9th Year of Imperial Prince Cyron's Court
162nd Year of the Komyr Dynasty
736th year since the Cataclysm
Kojaikun, Moriande
Nalenyr

At the Prince's word, the musicians struck up a tune, and the circle that had contained the night's entertainment slowly filled with people dancing. Keru came and took both swords and the Turasynd swordsman away. Moraven Tolo allowed himself to smile at the congratulations offered, then melted into the crowd with Ciras in his wake.

When Moraven stopped, Ciras moved around in front of him, bowing deeply. "I beg your pardon, Master. I did not mean to be an embarrassment."

"This I understand. You may be able to redeem yourself." Moraven kept his voice low, then pointed toward an unoccupied corner. Without a word, Ciras preceded him there. When the youth positioned himself to watch the room, Moraven took him by the shoulders and turned the younger man to face him, reversing their positions.

"Forgive me, *Serrcai* Moraven Tolo."

"Perhaps. Tell me what you are to be forgiven for and why you did it."

The younger man's brows tightened. "I was presumptuous enough to assume you would present me to the Prince."

"Why?"

"I am of the nobility of Tirat. I assumed you would present me, as I would be presented to nobility." Ciras' head came up. "And this is a contravention of the lesson you taught me in the graveyard. Here I am nothing."

Moraven smiled. "That is all well and good, from your point of view, but you must see it from mine. Do you think me so poorly mannered that I would not have presented you to the Prince?"

"No, Master, but—"

An upheld hand cut off Ciras' reply. "Then what reason would I have for not presenting you?"

The young man's brow furrowed with concentration. "I am at a loss, Master."

"I do not think you are." Moraven allowed himself to lean back against the wall. "You saw everything you needed to, and you know all you need to puzzle this out. Concentrate. What did you see?"

"You defeated the Turasynd monster, but that was not a question even from the beginning."

"Why not?"

Ciras' eyes widened. "How could you have had a moment's doubt? The man was strong and fast and big, but he had no *classical* training. He showed no recognized forms, he did not flow from attack and defense. He just attacked relentlessly. As you said, he knew you would defend yourself and not kill him, so he did not have to worry."

"But was he trying to kill me?"

"No. Wait . . . was he?"

Moraven nodded slowly. "That was his intent. The Black Eagles and *xidantzu* have little love for each other."

Ciras smiled. "That's a known fact even in Tirat."

"Usually their conflicts occur in the provinces. I've not fought them, but I've talked to those who have. You might think him an undisciplined fighter"—Moraven held his right hand out to display where his sleeve had been trimmed—"but he was good. Better than most."

"If you say so, Master."

"You don't believe me?"

"It is not that. He was good, but not good enough to have done as well as he did."

"That is also true. What does this tell you?"

Ciras wrapped his left hand around his right fist and pressed both hands against his mouth as he thought. Moraven watched his eyes narrow and widen again as he reviewed the fight in his head. A realization began to dawn on Ciras' face, then several more things fell into place.

"Oh, Master, I am truly sorry."

"Tell me."

"The sword. It must be one of those which has been enhanced by a *gyanridin*. I touched it, you feared it might affect me, so you had me put it down and used my breach of etiquette to draw attention away from the weapon." He rubbed his hands against his robe as if to rid them of the weapon's taint. "Is that not it, Master?"

"Very close, Ciras, very close indeed." Moraven pressed his hands together, fingertip to fingertip. "Many fine warriors followed the Empress into the Wastes to destroy the Turasynd. Their skill led to the Cataclysm. They were all slain."

"You do not believe that the Empress and her surviving guards will return when we need them?"

"Perhaps, but if they have not returned in seven centuries, why would they return now?" Moraven did not allow his apprentice to answer. "While a weapon does not improve when wielded by the best swordsman, one that has been used by a superior swordsman can make it easier for another to attain higher levels of skill. It is an aid to the obtaining of *jaedunto*."

"I know, Master. I used such a blade for some of my training."

"Excellent. Then you will understand the importance of what we saw here. There has been a rumor, which Master Jatan shared with me, that, in the Wastes, certain caches of such weapons have been found. I saw enough of the Turasynd's weapon to know it dates from before the Cataclysm. Someone has been seeking these weapons out."

"The Desei?"

"Perhaps, or others. But what of that I have just told you does not make sense?"

Ciras thought for a moment. "There should be no vast caches of such weapons. They would have been entombed with their owners or sent back to their families. They would not just have been piled up."

"And this means?"

"Any number of things." Ciras frowned. "At the very least, someone is out there digging up graves. And that means—"

"Go ahead."

Ciras shook his head. "It is foul beyond imagining."

Vrilxingna, the darkest of arts, and most dangerous. While it was common knowledge that even the most skilled magician could not raise the dead, it did not mean the dead were wholly useless. *Vrilxingnaridin* made a practice of locating and despoiling the graves of those known for great virtue or skill. They would take a corpse, grind it down into a powder, and sell that powder to be inhaled. It was believed that the corpse powder would grant one the skills of the deceased. Other *vrilxingna* practices were still more unspeakable, but the idea that the corpses of the world's greatest heroes could be made into a powder that could be given to an army was enough to strike terror into the hearts of any who heard it.

"The Deathbreathers are foul, but think on what you have seen here. A lord of the underworld has announced to all present that the means to manufacture heroes are available. Helosundians would desire such wares to help reconquer their nation. Inland Naleni nobles could see this as a way to raise an army that could overthrow their prince."

"It is a good thing the Desei prince was not here."

Another voice, light, replied to Ciras' comment. "Do you not think, *Lirserrdin* Dejote, that Prince Pyrust has been given his own showing of what is for sale?"

Moraven turned to his right and bowed in her direction. "You honor us, my lady."

The Lady of Jet and Jade smiled easily, yet not without restraint. "You are the one who has honored me by acting as my gift. I trust you did not find my offer presumptuous?"

"It was yet another honor."

She held her left hand out to him, and he took it in his right. "Let us walk. You will be entertained, *Lirserrdin*." At her word two of her aides each took Ciras by an arm and steered him toward the dancers, while others created a circle around Moraven and their Mistress.

"Should I be angered that you have not come to see me, or shall I assume that you thought, with your new name, I would not recognize you?" Her words came sweetly and softly, wrapping in jest the hurt they conveyed. "I have often wondered if you have stayed away from Moriande because of me."

Moraven slid her hand to the crook of his elbow and led her through a set of double doors to the small courtyard garden. Strains of music followed them. The garden, dark and empty, carried the scent of night-blooming flowers. Their perfume complemented the scent she had chosen to wear.

"Not because of you, but because of the tragedy of my last visit. Whenever I thought I would return, an omen reminded me of it." He smiled at her. "I have thought the gods strove to keep us apart."

"And so fearing the gods is why you have spent nights at the House of Three Pearls after you did arrive?"

"Do not affect that hurt tone with me, my lady."

"So formal and cold."

"And now you seek to deflect me." He closed his eyes. "Is there a familiar name you wish me to use?"

"For you there is always one." Her hand came up and she delicately caressed his cheek. "You are never far from my thoughts. I do like your new name. I shall use it, Moraven. It suits you much better. It bespeaks more deliberation, a passion that is subsumed but available."

"And your name, Paryssa, has always meant passion to me." Moraven looked down into her perfect face, with its pale, infinite eyes. Thousands had looked into those eyes over the years, but how many of them had seen what he had? Beguiled by her beauty, seduced by her certain movements, the skills she employed with the same facility as he did a sword.

He shivered, the memory of their first union bringing a flush to his cheeks. He had been young yet—not as young as Ciras, but young, and so was she. He had fought a duel over her honor—less because he was concerned for it than that the man he fought deserved death. It was not the first time he'd felt the magic of the sword, but it was the first time he remembered its remaining with him so long, and the first time he was certain it would not leave him.

She had reached that same place as they coupled. Together they attained a height neither had known before, and it thrilled them. And each time after, it came faster and harder, shaking them. For any two people who had stumbled upon it accidentally, the ecstasy would have been addictive. It would have consumed them utterly, but the two of them had the discipline of their art to fall back on. In the same way as it opened them to the possibilities, it dictated how they were to avoid consumption.

Her fingers lingered on his face, then she slid them down to grab hold of his robe and laid her face against his breast. "We both know why you have stayed away, and why I have not come after you. On a night like this, however, a night to reward heroes, would it not be more wrong for us to be apart than together?"

"Yes, it would, though my status as a hero may demand a few things more this evening."

"Such as?"

He lifted his hand to her chin and tilted her face up. "Jatan told me of the rumors about the Wastes. You clearly chose me to oppose Black Myrian's champion to alert me to what is going on. You and Jatan did not collaborate?"

"No, Moraven. I was led to believe that you visited him to be given your apprentice." Her grip tightened on his robe. "I did collaborate with Black Myrian. A favor was repaid, but I would have demanded more had I known his man would try to kill you."

"Black Myrian wanted to let everyone know what he could get, but did so before the Prince, and on this night, to let Cyron know he could be counted upon to forestall trouble."

"But for a price. His loyalty is for sale."

"Prince Cyron knows that."

The Lady of Jet and Jade kissed his throat. "Black Myrian has treated with many of the inland nobles. The capital merchants grow fat with profits, but the provincial lordlings see very little of that money. They were reluctant to invest in trade ventures initially, and the merchants are now loath to reward them for withholding money in the past. The lordlings want the spices and other goods that come in, but lack the gold to pay for them.

"On top of that, they feel the Prince is far too concerned with Helosunde and the Desei problem. The harvest this year was quite abundant, but the Prince did not reduce taxes. Had the lordlings kept more grain, they would have been able to trade more. Instead, the Prince takes their grain, and still demands their troops to defend against Deseirion. There are some who think a private army will keep them safe from the Desei, if they ever invade. Others believe an army will be needed to overthrow the Prince if he does not become more realistic."

Moraven nodded slowly. "I imagine, in the city, there are also merchants who have not profited as much as others and so feel a private army of their own would be useful to disrupt the business of others. The only thing that keeps the tensions from soaring out of control is the general prosperity that trade has brought?"

"Yes. The Prince is aware of the discontent, and is forcing some merchants to take on rural investors if they want to use Anturasi charts. Those who don't have had horrid luck—to the point where several houses of cartography have been ruined. All it will take, however, is a disaster with an expedition the state is mounting. The economy will crash, and the knives will come out."

"And that would be the *Stormwolf* expedition?"

She smiled up at him. "For one who has not been in Moriande for a long while, you understand the politics well."

"Moriande today, Kelewan ages ago." Moraven frowned. "The difference then was that swordsmen were being bought, so the forces gathering were easier to see. Here it would be weapons and dust, which could hide an army in a warehouse with no mouths to feed and no one the wiser."

"Do you have a means to deal with this?"

"Not as yet, no." He bowed his head and kissed her forehead. "There is much more to learn, but I have a little time. The *Stormwolf* cannot fail before it is launched."

"And you will spend some of that time with me?"

Moraven lowered his mouth to hers. "Could there be better use than spending it with you?"

Chapter Twenty-one

6th day, Harvest Festival, Year of the Dog
9th Year of Imperial Prince Cyron's Court
162nd Year of the Komyr Dynasty
736th year since the Cataclysm
Shirikun, Moriande
Nalenyr

Prince Pyrust lifted the lid of the small ebony box on the table in his suite's parlor. There, nestled in a swatch of red velvet, he found nine metal figures, gaily painted save one, with the tallest measuring two and a half inches. This one—the one painted black except for the face and the white hawk emblazoned on the breastplate of the armor—he plucked from the box and held in the light of the nearest candle. He turned it left and right, marveling more at the artistry of the sculpting than the painting, for that had clearly been done quickly.

He smiled. "They are more kind in their treatment of me this year than in the past. Is that because I am here, or is it an edict from Cyron?"

The other person in the room sat in a corner, cloaked in shadow, a hood pulled up so naught but a few wisps of long grey hair could be seen. Her voice, though quiet, crackled with age. "This we are not certain, Highness. Cyron is not as given to issuing edicts as his father was."

Pyrust set his simulacrum on the table and pulled out Cyron's piece. The robe he wore had been painted with exquisite skill and looked even better than the garment worn at their meeting. The gold of it would have been all but blinding in brighter light. The artisan had taken great care to portray the hawk beneath the dragon as being in great distress, with feathers flying.

"I find it curious to hold him in my hand so easily now, but to have difficulty controlling him in life."

His guest slowly shook her head, but no light fell across her features. "Control is an illusion. He thinks he controls you now."

"Does he?" Pyrust set him down as well, taking minor satisfaction that his figure was taller than that of the Naleni Prince. "His offer of food was not one I could refuse. Along with it came conditions of behavior. I violate them at my nation's ruination."

"Do you, my lord?"

"Is it not obvious, Delasonsa? Your agents are the ones who have brought me an accurate picture of the state of my nation. The bureaucrats hide things in statistics and the manner in which they let reports filter to court. They dole out bad news in degrees."

"It is their means of maintaining order, for bureaucracy breaks down in the face of chaos. They see themselves as the real keepers of order in the world, the heirs to the Empire the Empress abandoned so long ago. She split political power among the Nine Princes, but the mechanism for maintaining the Empire fell to the bureaucrats. Save that it would be the ultimate invocation of chaos, they would have supplanted the Princes long ago."

She gestured, the tip of her finger with its long crooked nail barely escaping a heavy sleeve. "You were not surprised Prince Cyron knew of the harvest. You supposed, not incorrectly, that Helosundian agents brought him that news. Bureaucrats confirmed it, however, as they sought to open negotiations on your behalf with his bureaucrats. Information was flowing through those channels well before the harvest failed."

With his maimed left hand Pyrust stroked his goatee. "Those same channels will convey information about any invasion I was to make. It is those channels that tell him about my attempts to hunt down the Helosundian rebels."

"In part, yes, but we have been taking care of those problems." Her hood shifted. "It is both a blessing and a curse to have the bureaucrats. Yours are greatly efficient, duplicating or triplicating every report, sending them on through different couriers, demanding dated receipts so things can be tracked. When you desire something done, it gets done."

"Yes. I use the same system in the field with troops."

"Of course you do, Highness, which is why your campaigns have been successful, and will continue to be so in the future."

"You need not flatter me, Mother of Shadows. I rely upon others for that." Pyrust turned back to the box and pulled out the figure of Qiro Anturasi. He held it up as he turned back. "Here is the key to the future."

"Would you have me slay him?"

Pyrust focused beyond the white-robed figurine to the huddle of rags in the chair. "You have oft asked me to give you leave to kill him. What is this personal animosity you bear him?"

"None, Highness." She chuckled lightly. "It is the challenge. Anturasikun is as secure a prison as Prince Cyron and his father could devise. Getting in is not simple, and getting out is less so. For me to slip in, slay him in a manner that made it appear he died naturally, and escape again is probably the hardest task imaginable."

"Save escaping from the Nine Hells."

"Or Nine Heavens. Yes, Master."

Pyrust studied her for a moment. From his earliest memory she had appeared thus: an aged crone shrunk by the weight of centuries. His father had said she had seemed the same to him, so Pyrust doubted she truly looked like that. But still, it meant that she was very likely *jaecaivril*—so masterful in the shadow arts that the merest touch could kill. She had long run the mechanism of state security in Deseirion—both the visible forces and those that dwelt exclusively in the shadows, most of whom were of her blood. Generations of them.

I do not doubt you could *kill Qiro Anturasi*. He let the figure of the man slip into his fist and tightened his grip. "I hate denying you that challenge, but as long as he has his vulnerabilities, he is more useful alive than dead. Besides, he is merely contributory to the problem we face. His entire family would have to be wiped out, and all of their charts destroyed, and even that would only slow Nalenyr, not stop it.

"Explorations bring trade to Nalenyr, and that results in gold with which the Prince can train and maintain an army of Helosundian mercenaries to harass me and defend his nation. It puts him in a position to hire an even larger army, if need be. Any assault I could begin would be bogged down in Helosunde fighting mercenaries. He brings Naleni troops up, and mine starve before we can win even a foot of Naleni soil."

"Hence your financing expeditions into the Wastes and the study of *gyan*. If you can recover enough artifacts or the machines can be perfected, you could create an army that would overwhelm his. It becomes a race. He wants more gold; you seek the means to take his gold from him."

"I do not like such impasses." He set Qiro down next to the other two figures in the set. "I like them less than Cyron's jerking a leash and my having to heel as if I were some cur."

"There *is* an advantage to that, Highness."

"Yes?"

The crone gestured vaguely in the direction of Kojaikun. "He believes himself a hero on this night of heroes, and he believes you a cur secure at the end of a leash. He has told you that if you are hostile, you will starve. Do you think he really cares if you continue your campaigns in Helosunde or not?"

Pyrust frowned. "True. His proxy war in Helosunde bleeds me but does not bleed him. It can only be to his benefit if we continue fighting."

"And if you continue fighting, he will assume you are stupid, since you risk cutting off the grain heading north. You know he will delay shipments to you, but he dare not do that to his allies. If you are successful in stealing their grain, he will divert shipments to them, but you shall be fed nonetheless."

"This gets me nothing."

"On the contrary, it gets you much."

Pyrust's head came up. "It shows him I am predictable and stupid."

"Which he will be more than willing to accept. After all, he already believes you follow dreams." She pointed to the box of figures. "Draw out the two Guards figures: the Cloud Dragon and the River Dragon."

Knowing she had a point and assuming it would be of value, he turned to the box and pulled out the two figures that represented the most elite of Naleni troops. Save for the colors and insignia painted on their armor and shields, the pieces were identical. They had been cast from the same mold and differed only in color.

"They are the same."

"Indeed, they are. There is no way to tell them apart save for their uniforms."

"Exactly, my prince. You have the Shadow Hawks and the Mountain Hawks operating in Helosunde. They cross the river and strike at various points in punitive expeditions. What if you used the same troops, but differed their uniforms? What if the bureaucrats still sent the same reports, indicating where the units were, their strength and their disposition? You would, in essence, free one unit from observation."

"And one unit consumes half the fodder of two, so I can hoard some of what we capture. This I understand. To what end, though?"

"I would have thought it would be simple, Highness." Her laughter mocked him. "The Naleni assume you will never defeat them because they can buy well-trained troops to oppose you. You, it is assumed, need *gyan*-worked swords to equal them, or relics or troops fueled with corpse dust and other unsavory things. As we have discussed in the past, such troops would be useful at the start, engaging Naleni troops, pinning them so your better-trained and disciplined troops could sweep past and seize valuable targets."

"Agreed."

The crone stood and hobbled forward, her head bent low and her dowager's hump visible above the set of her shoulders. "What if you used your troops to provide your rabble some very basic training? Enough to establish discipline? Instead of sending them into battle to die, you send them into battle with some chance of survival. You can take them and train them into an effective force. You need not worry about any becoming overly skilled, since you will be simply teaching them how to march and follow orders."

Pyrust frowned for a moment, then slowly nodded. "Those who show promise could be brought to schools and further trained. Yes, this might well work. The basic discipline could even be disguised as an effort to establish local militias to protect villages against marauders looking for food in a time of famine. Cyron would take this as a further sign of disorder and it would make him underestimate me more."

Delasonsa moved past him and tapped the Anturasi figure on the head with a finger. "While Prince Cyron believes you are turned inward to stave off disaster, we find ways to threaten his monopoly on world knowledge. Plans, as you know, are unfolding. You spoke to his grandson, Keles?"

"Yes, just a preliminary talk. I sensed no willingness to come out of his grandfather's shadow."

"No, that one is loyal. The other is wilder and can be tempted, though sending him off on the *Stormwolf* will take him outside my influence."

Pyrust smiled and set the guards on the table. "You have yet been frustrated in your attempt to infiltrate an agent onto the ship."

"It would have been a waste of time regardless. Someone of sufficient skill to duplicate the work Jorim Anturasi will be doing would have been instantly recognizable. Their ability to communicate back to us what they had learned would have been questionable, and their discovery a disaster. Instead, I think using the time the ship is gone to compromise people who will have information during its absence and upon its return will provide us a much greater reward for our efforts."

"What of our attempts to get Anturasi charts, or even the charts of other houses?"

She laughed. "Anturasi charts are better guarded than the Naleni treasury, so we have not been successful there. The other charts have come to us, but our people have seen their like before. They have noted something interesting, however."

"Oh?"

"We have our own coastal charts for much of the waters once claimed by the Empire. There have been changes down through the years, such as the shift of sandbars that create navigational hazards. What is curious is that the newest charts either do not show these or have indications of hazards where there should be clear water. The conclusion is inescapable: the Anturasi have gotten their own agents into the other houses, creating charts that bring disaster for those who use them."

The Desei prince picked Qiro's figure up again. "Craftier than I would have imagined, then."

"And, as you said, Highness, he is vulnerable." She turned and flicked a finger toward the west. "Keles Anturasi will be traveling to the Wastes. I shall have agents following him. I will seek to slip one into his company, if it is possible. I am less concerned with what he will learn than placing him in situations that keep him beholden to us. If we can earn his trust by saving his life, splendid. If we have to take him and hold him, we can do that as well. At the very least we will have him in our control, and that will give us a means to control Anturasi."

Pyrust slowly nodded. "There is, of course, one other thing we could do."

"Say the word, Highness, and it shall be done."

"Not yet." Pyrust set the Anturasi figure down, then flicked a nail against Prince Cyron, knocking the figure onto its back. "I will save killing him for a more crucial moment. It is not something considered lightly."

"Since the Empire's division, assassins have not claimed a crown."

"To the best of your knowledge, Shadowmother."

He caught the flash of teeth from within the hood. "No other has better knowledge, Highness. It has not yet been done by an assassin. I *would* know."

"So you would." Pyrust nodded easily. "It is a strategy that will only work when the time is right. At a time when many things hinge on him, when all the pressure is on, that's when I will take him. It won't matter if he is the hero of heroes or not. All that will matter is that he is dead, and in the chaos that follows, it will be the sword of a warrior, not the pen of a bureaucrat, that reclaims order."

Chapter Twenty-two

8th day, Harvest Festival, Year of the Dog
9th Year of Imperial Prince Cyron's Court
162nd Year of the Komyr Dynasty
736th year since the Cataclysm
Anturasikun, Moriande
Nalenyr

Keles Anturasi set aside the book and rose slowly from his chair as his brother entered the sunroom. The surprise on Jorim's face gratified him, and made Keles determined not to show the least twinge of discomfort. He forced a smile and straightened, despite the lingering pain in his back.

"You're up quicker than anyone expected, Keles. Are you sure that's wise?"

"Yes, I feel wonderful. Thank you for asking." Keles let his smile grow. "The Viruk ambassador's magic has had a good effect on my back. I have to be up and around because if I'm not, I'll be trapped here for Grandfather to vent his fury upon."

"Has he actually visited you?"

"No, but he has sent Ulan with more dictates than Urmyr has for bureaucrats. I'm well sick of it."

Jorim nodded and tugged at the black sash on his green robe. "I can understand that. While I feel sorry people have to work on provisioning the *Stormwolf* during the Festival, I can't wait to be heading downriver and away. The journey cannot begin too soon."

"Give me at least a couple more days, then I will be able to travel upriver and get away myself."

"Gladly." Jorim moved past and picked up the well-worn, leather-bound volume from which Keles had been reading. " 'The Memoir of Amenis Dukao'? You're not considering this research for your journey, are you?"

"No, but it does have value." Keles eased himself back down into his chair and motioned for his brother to seat himself on the footstool. "We enjoyed it as children. Nirati had been reading to me from it, and I find it comforting now. As well, there is some truth in there. Dukao did travel through the Wastes and fought alongside the Empress against the Turasynd."

"Value? May the gods be merciful." Jorim dragged another chair around, seated himself, and put his feet on the footstool. "Keles, Keles, Keles, what am I going to do with you?" He rapped a fist against the book's cover.

Keles held his hands up. "I know what you're going to tell me. The book is a compilation of earlier legends, all framed with a story about how scavengers found a handwritten memoir in the Wastes. They brought it to an author who transcribed it, then the original manuscript mysteriously vanished."

"Right. Kyda Jameet is a pseudonym of some Virine noble who'd never been further north than the mountains and no closer to the Ixyll Wastes than the shore of the Dark Sea, and he plucked Dukao's name from history because no one knows that much about who he was."

"We've argued all this before." Keles sighed. "Still, some of the observations about conditions in the Wastes are true."

Jorim sighed and his brows arrowed sharply toward his nose. "There are parts of Ummummorar and Tejanmorek that felt the fringes of the Cataclysm. Things get pretty strange there. And where you are going will be worse."

"Which is exactly what it describes here."

"But not well, dear brother. Where I have been, and have *seen* the effects, they were more than Jameet ever dreamed. I have seen a tree—one single one in the midst of a forest—that was turned to crystal. It has leaves which, when they fall, revert to normal matter.

It has fruit which, when plucked, decays immediately. The flowers smell sweet, but, when picked, die in the blink of an eye."

"But here he talks about such things."

"Yet insufficiently. I've seen a tree, he describes a grove, but you'll ride through forests of crystal—and worse." Jorim opened the book to a plate showing the hero in armor. "Amenis Dukao was lucky. He died in the grand battle. He made his way to Kianmang well before his brothers, and was there to welcome them to the Warriors' Heaven when they fell. He never saw, much less had to survive, what the Cataclysm did to Ixyll."

Keles nodded, hiding a smile at his brother's slowly smoldering anger. He knew he could play with him like that for a while longer, but he didn't want to trigger an outburst. "Your point is well-taken. Still, the stories might prepare me for what I will see."

Jorim, it appeared, was in a conciliatory mood as well. "That's true. And, truth be told, I wish you had a hero like Amenis Dukao to accompany you out there."

"I can handle myself."

Jorim set the book aside, planted his feet on the ground, and leaned forward. He rested his elbows on his knees and clasped his hands together. "Keles, two things you must know are true. The first is that I have the utmost respect for all you have done. The survey of the upper reaches of the Gold River is flawless. I envy your ability to see in such detail and to be so exact. Second, you must know that I am sure you will be just as diligent, if not more so, in this trek. The work you produce will be stunning; there is no doubt about it in my mind."

"But?"

"But I worry about you."

"Jorim, I'm the older brother, I'm supposed to worry about *you*."

The younger Anturasi smiled for a moment. "Keles, you are a cartographer. I am an adventurer. The survey you'll be making into the Wastes is one that really calls for an adventurer."

Keles pointed toward the river. "And the *Stormwolf* voyage won't?"

"Yes, it will, but not as much." Jorim stood and began to pace. "I've been in the wilds, Keles. You can take nothing for granted, nothing at all, and out in the Wastes it will be worse. You are an indifferent swordsman. You once were a passable archer, but you've let that skill atrophy. Out there you will be defenseless."

Keles sat back, bringing his hands together and pressing index fingers to his lips. His brother's genuine concern stoked the fear that had been smoldering in his belly. Aside from what was written in books like the memoir, or any of its similarly fanciful cousins, which delighted children and disgusted most adults, he knew nothing of what he would be facing. His brother's comments were accurate concerning his skill with a sword, and he made a mental note to have a bow and arrows included in the supplies he would take with him.

Though Jorim was right, Keles didn't want to deal with that point immediately, so he did the only thing he could: he deflected the argument.

"You're wrong, Jorim, when you state that my journey will take more of an adventurer than yours. At least I know what to expect. You have no clue. There could be anything out there, or nothing. You could fall off the edge of the world."

Jorim laughed. Those who were not conversant with maps and the world often subscribed to the superstitious notion that the world was flat and had edges. But they knew it was a ball and one of a finite size. Their grandfather had even calculated it and, based upon those calculations, the *Stormwolf* had been fitted out for a two-year journey.

"There could be anything out there, and probably is." Keles deliberately widened his eyes. "Cannibals. Demons. Monsters. You'd best be an even better swordsman than the stories make you out to be."

Jorim bit back a response, then nodded slowly. "I have thought of that, you know. Whatever is out there was enough to kill our father. I don't think it will get me, but I am aware of the danger. As for cannibals, monsters, and demons, I was told those lurked in Ummummorar and other places. I never found any of it to be true, so I'm not terribly worried."

"You're not?" Keles frowned. "Then why did you come here to see me?"

"I think I'm too much of an adventurer for the *Stormwolf,* Keles. I'm good at leading folks into the unknown, reading the land, hunting for animals."

"Which is exactly what you will be doing."

"But not while we're on the ocean. The ship has a captain, and she's very good, so what use will I be? You'd find a way to do something useful."

"Come here. Sit down." Keles pulled his feet from the footstool and this time his brother accepted it. "You'll do what is required of you on the journey, Jorim. Your job is to track longitude and latitude, then lead expeditions into the places you find. That's your role, and you had best be as bold and breathtaking as you can when you fulfill it. That's what they will expect. You are being sent on the greatest adventure of all time. Our father is a giant in my eyes. I loved him dearly, but even he would bow to you on this voyage."

Jorim frowned, swiped at a tear. "Allergies."

"Of course."

"Does this wisdom come with being just two years older?"

"Well, that, and having a little brother who so often needs it."

"Uh-huh. If you were *that* wise, you'd have avoided the sharp side of a Viruk's claws."

Keles laughed. "Very true indeed." He nodded toward his brother. "I have listened to what you've said. I will have a bow taken along with me, and I will practice."

Jorim's smile broadened. "I'm glad to hear that. I already took the liberty of having my second-best bow stowed with your gear. I'd have given you the best, but you won't be up to drawing it for a while. The one I'm giving you will put an arrow through armor at forty-five yards."

"You're giving me your bow so I won't get close enough to have to use a sword, right?"

Jorim leaned forward and patted his brother's knee. "Keles, let me put this to you gently. You're so bad with a blade that an apple doesn't get worried when you approach it with a paring knife."

"I am not *that* bad."

"Close. Doesn't matter, though." Jorim ducked a hand inside his right sleeve and it emerged holding a ring of jade with an inch-long flange that curved in toward the far side. "This thumbring is something I found here in Moriande. It once belonged to Panil Ishir. He's even mentioned in your memoir there—though that's probably the only fact in the book. He was one of the finest archers in the Empire.

Practice with this, and you'll be shooting better than ever in no time."

Keles took the smooth stone ring and fitted it over his thumb. The flange protected the pad, and was worn where it had been used to draw a bowstring back. The cool jade didn't tingle with magic or otherwise betray service to an ancient hero. But he had no doubt it would work as his brother suggested, helping him refine his skill, and he knew his brother must have paid dearly for it.

"This is too great a gift for me to take into the Wastes, Jorim, and you're more likely to need it where you are going."

"Nonsense." Jorim closed his brother's hand around it. "You'll need it, I'm sure of that."

Keles sighed. "I will take it, but only because I have an ulterior motive. Panil Ishir is one of those who supposedly survived the battle. He's out there with the Eternal Empress, ready to serve her on her return should ever the Nine Principalities require succor."

"Oh, really?" Jorim burst out with a laugh. "You should go back to reading the memoirs. They are much more believable than the stories of the Sleeping Empress."

Keles shifted his shoulders uneasily and felt a twinge in his back. "You're not looking at it correctly. The tales make sense."

"You're delirious, but I'd love to hear your reasoning—flawed as it is."

"It's not flawed at all. The Imperial forces must have been victorious; otherwise, the barbarians would have long since overrun the Principalities. She and the others were trapped in this new place that is changed because of the battle, with monsters and other things that are as much of a threat to her Empire as the barbarians ever were. She and the survivors stayed out there eliminating these threats, and still remain there. Had they not, the monsters would have long since overrun the Principalities. It's all very logical."

"It would be if you weren't basing things on a fallacy. You assume monsters aren't here from the Wastes because they've been killed in the Wastes. *If* monsters ever existed, and *if* they were killed in the Wastes, it does not follow that it was the Empress and her troops who did the killing. And while they were all great heroes, I doubt many of them will have survived the centuries since then—if any."

"Kaerinus did."

"He was not a hero."

"Immaterial." Keles smiled sheepishly. "If one of them did, and he is Panil, wouldn't it be great to return his property to him?"

"If he doesn't take you for a grave robber and shoot you first, yes." Jorim shook his head. "There are times, Keles, when I wonder about you. Perhaps that Viruk venom has softened your head."

"Hey, you used to believe this as fervently as I did."

"Sure. Then I grew up. One of the reasons I envy you your journey is that I know you'll see things far more fantastic than the Sleeping Empress."

"But maybe I'll see her, too."

"Maybe you will. In the wilds you hear stories. They're nine times more fanciful than the memoirs." Jorim frowned for a moment. "It is odd, though, that *something* kept the Viruk from using the Cataclysm as a means to reestablish their Empire. They take to the cold better than us, and survive magic better. They could have returned, but they didn't."

"See? It could have been her."

"Or *they* could have been killing the monsters you say she has been slaying."

"Could be. Not much of a comfort if it is." Keles' mind flicked to a greater problem that his brother's comment raised. Fear flared in his stomach. "The battle released enough magic to change this world. What if it did more?"

"Like?"

"Like open a hole into another world so that things from there came pouring through? What if the Viruk did spend the dark years fighting for their very survival against whatever came from that place?"

"Well, Keles, if *that* is what happened, I've only two things to tell you. First, learn to shoot really, really well." Jorim's eyes tightened. "Second, watch your back. You *don't* want anything following you home."

Chapter Twenty-three

9th day, Harvest Festival, Year of the Dog
9th Year of Imperial Prince Cyron's Court
162nd Year of the Komyr Dynasty
736th year since the Cataclysm
Wentokikun, Moriande
Nalenyr

Prince Cyron dismissed his attendants and the minor minister with a wave of his hand. "I shall finish dressing myself. Minister Delar, you will wait in the corridor until Master Anturasi and I are finished, then you shall conduct him back to the ball."

The minister bowed silently, waited for the dressers to exit before he did, then slid the door closed.

The Prince tugged at the shoulders of his overshirt, then glanced up at Keles Anturasi. The young man looked pale and just a little afraid, both of which were understandable. Cyron smiled, shifted his shoulders, and lowered his hands. "Does it look good?"

"Yes, Highness." Keles—wearing a simple overshirt of black, adorned with his family's crest in white, over a green tunic and green pants—cleared his throat. "Yes, Highness, it is spectacular."

"But not what you would have expected me to wear?" The Prince moved to a pair of chairs with a small round table set between them. The table had a box made of dark wood centered on its circular top. He motioned for the cartographer to take the other chair. Keles bowed abortively, then sat, uncertain of himself.

"Please, Keles, be at ease. I've not asked you here to discipline you. I consider you a friend, and I have been concerned about you. My physician has kept me informed of your progress. He does not like Viruk magic, but he has grudgingly testified to its efficacy." The Prince seated himself, going so far as to extend his legs and cross his booted ankles. "You honor me by coming here with your family tonight. I even understand that you will head up the river as your brother sails down in the *Stormwolf*."

"Yes, Highness." Keles frowned and eased himself back in the chair. "Highness, I am honored you consider me a friend, but this puzzles me. You know my brother far better, and I would have expected he would be here instead of me."

"And he has been, but not tonight. This is *your* night." Cyron opened his arms to take in his dressing room. Rich golden wood predominated, save where strips of dark wood divided the doors and walls with a geometric pattern. Mobile panels blocked off doors, screens hid corners, and well-fitted doors concealed closet space. Aside from the chairs and table, the room contained very few furnishings, and most of that practical, such as armatures for the hanging of robes and a small cabinet for storing wine and drinking vessels.

"I invited you here to know I really do appreciate the great lengths to which you have gone for Nalenyr, and to which you will go. May I speak frankly?"

Keles blinked, his light eyes wide. "You need not ask my permission for that, Highness."

"But no word of this meeting must ever pass your lips."

The cartographer clasped his hands over his heart and likely would have sunk to his knees save for the lingering effects of his wounding. "Never, Highness."

"Good." The Prince sat forward, leaning on the left arm of his chair. "I was appalled when your grandfather sent you on this mission to Ixyll. It is true that he and I had discussed the necessity for sending someone there. That used to be the area through which trade was carried on with the Far West. For us not to know the state of things would be foolish. If that way were open, the *Stormwolf* expedition—and the knowledge it recovers—could be redundant. Still, given what few reports do come from there, we were fairly certain the way would remain sealed for another ninety years or so. That would give us the time needed to profit from trade and find another way to put the Empire back together.

"His choosing you, and invoking my name in doing so, put me in a difficult position. As you know, your grandfather can be . . . *contrary* at times."

Keles laughed and his manner relaxed. "You are very diplomatic, Highness."

"I try to be, but with you I can be very open. Your grandfather defies me from time to time, with increasing frequency, and were he not so vital to Nalenyr, I'd have him publicly flogged. Now, isn't that something you'd like to see?"

"See? There are times I would like to help."

"Well, I doubt you will get the chance, but you can help in other ways." Cyron's voice dropped in volume, forcing the younger man to lean forward. "The mission you are undertaking is of vital importance, and you will hear rumors about it. Rumors I have started. The rumors will indicate that you are too valuable to be left to go out into the Wastes, and that is true. People will be led to believe that you will be secretly recalled to court."

"I'm not certain I understand, sire."

"It is for your safety. A show shall be made of your departure. I have already obtained someone to impersonate you. I have assembled an entourage to travel upriver, both to draw attention to your double, and to keep others from getting too close. The company will make slow progress and attract much attention. Our enemies will watch that group. And you, disguised and on the same boat, will pass unnoticed."

"Forgive me, Highness, but would it not be more prudent to send me out on another boat?"

"No. Our enemies will be working so hard to learn what they can from the actor, they will have little attention to spend studying much else. Moreover, their focus on your double will allow others to identify them."

"I see, Highness." Keles lowered his hands and tightened his arms around his stomach. "You think there will be danger on the trip? I mean, beyond the dangers out there?"

Cyron laughed aloud. "You are an Anturasi. You will be seen as being the key to your grandfather. You are also invaluable in and of yourself. I know Prince Pyrust spoke to you about undertaking a task for him."

"I refused, Highness, instantly and without equivocation."

"Calm yourself, Keles, I know that. I know you love your family and nation, and I know I can trust you." Cyron's voice grew softer again. "I *can* trust you, can I not?"

Keles winced, but dropped to a knee and bowed his head so low he almost hit it on the table. "In anything, Highness."

"As I expected. And thank you. I knew my trust was well placed. Now you need to understand something from me." The Prince drew back, his eyes sharpening. "I will see to your safety. You must trust me on that, regardless of what appearances seem. I will keep you safe and you will gather the information your grandfather wants. There may be another service or two I require, and if the opportunity arises, I will communicate my needs to you."

Cyron flicked his right hand up and Keles rose, seating himself on the edge of his chair. The Prince laid his hand on the wooden box on the table. "You know the legend about my great-grandfather, that because he had played war games with toy soldiers as a child, he was able to take the throne and establish this dynasty? While others drilled and learned swordplay, a sickly child marched armies through battles and learned the skills to make those swordsmen most effective in combat."

"Yes, Highness. My brother and I used to fight many battles with soldiers when we were young. My father, and sometimes our grandfather, would show us the Festival figures, though we were never allowed to play with them."

Cyron smiled. "I don't think anyone ever played with them, which is a pity." He opened the box to reveal nine figures on a bed of velvet within. "You know, then, that the Prince gives a set to each family invited to this final celebration. Aside from the sculptors, painters, and myself, you are the first to see this year's figures. We made only the number of sets required for this evening, and all that are unclaimed will be destroyed."

"They are beautiful, Highness."

"I think so, too." Cyron smiled slowly. "Each year I determine who will be cast."

"It is a great honor to receive a set, Highness." Keles slowly shook his head without taking his eyes from the figures. "To be cast as one is unimaginable."

"Allow yourself to imagine, Keles Anturasi." The Prince lifted out the figure of Qiro Anturasi. "Your grandfather, as invaluable as he is to us, was cast this year in honor of his eighty-first birthday. You and your brother will be cast upon returning from your missions. So much greater will your contribution to Nalenyr be that such an honor is easily within your grasp."

Keles' expression of awe slowly dissolved as he met the Prince's gaze. "If my grandfather were to guess that were possible, he might do the unthinkable."

"True, so we shall not let him know." Cyron replaced Qiro in the box and closed it again. "That secret shall remain as safe as these figures are. And I shall keep you equally safe."

"Yes, Highness. Thank you."

The Prince opened his hands. "You shall return to the party and enjoy yourself. Tell the assembled that I'd heard a story of a jungle cat the color of red sand with black stripes and, while you are not your brother, I dearly wished you would capture me a half dozen for my sanctuary. Something like that will suffice for most, and those it won't satisfy will be smart enough to know you could not be saying anything anyway."

"Yes, Highness." Keles rose from his chair and bowed.

Before he could straighten up, the Prince rose and clapped him on both shoulders. "That you bow despite your injury marks the depth of your soul, Keles Anturasi. Your future and that of our nation are intertwined. They will grow together into prosperity. Never forget you are loved and respected, and your return is anxiously awaited."

Keles nodded, rose, and withdrew from the room.

As the door slid shut behind him, Prince Cyron turned to a screen that had concealed one corner of the room. "We will be undisturbed now."

Moraven Tolo, dressed in black and white with black tigers embroidered on his overshirt, emerged from behind the screen. "I have listened as you bid me, Prince Cyron."

"I beg your forgiveness, *serrcai,* for making you a party to that deception, but I needed you to hear two things. First, you would agree, he really has no idea of the sort of difficulties he will face. He is naive and will need protecting."

The swordsman bowed his head. "You wish me to do that?"

"I would not presume to reduce you to the role of a mercenary, *serrcai*. I think you will find that in your mission for *dicaiserr* Jatan, having a cartographer along will be of great aid."

"The wisdom of your words cannot be denied, Highness." Moraven turned and looked back toward the door. "I will not be alone in seeing to his survival?"

"You have your apprentice."

"True, Highness, but you evade my question."

"He will not travel alone." The Prince slipped a folded paper packet sealed with red wax from the interior of his overshirt. "I will have another service I require from the both of you. You will open this only when you meet him again in Gria."

The swordsman's eyes narrowed. "I do not begrudge you a service, Highness, for we both know I owe a debt of honor to your family. You want two things from me—great, difficult things. You do presume much."

Cyron killed the smile beginning to tug at the corners of his mouth. "The other evening you did a favor for a friend in entertaining me. I ask you to pay your debt to the House of Komyr. And the House of Komyr will now be indebted to you."

Moraven bowed his head slightly, but brought it up far too quickly. "It will take more than casting me as a toy to pay this debt."

"Some debts can never be paid, Moraven Tolo, but let us worry about the service being performed first." The Prince forced his expression to soften. "In your wanderings, you are able to shield a few from disasters. On this journey, you will find the means to prevent war from destroying many. I will stand the debt, but we both know that I shall not be the only one to benefit from your actions."

"Were it for any lesser reason you asked me to do this, I would refuse you, Prince Cyron." Moraven bowed respectfully. "I hope my efforts will succeed."

"As do I." A shiver ran down Cyron's spine. "If you fail, there may be no House of Komyr left to honor its obligation."

Chapter Twenty-four

9th day, Harvest Festival, Year of the Dog
9th Year of Imperial Prince Cyron's Court
162nd Year of the Komyr Dynasty
736th year since the Cataclysm
Wentokikun, Moriande
Nalenyr

Keles was not surprised that his sister was the first person to find him after he returned to the Festival celebration. Plenty of people had seen him drawn away, doubtless wondering if he were being singled out for some honor or an upbraiding. When he returned without some visible sign of the Prince's favor, most people decided to ignore him.

"Why are you so concerned, Keles?" Nirati took his arm and rubbed a hand over his back. "You're frightened."

He glanced at her, realizing she was correct. "I thought you couldn't read my mind."

"Only your face." She smiled bravely at him. "And even if we were able to communicate that way, you know I would not be able to read your mind, just that which you wished to send me."

"I wouldn't wish to send you any of this." Keles led her over to a side table, where servants poured him a small porcelain cup of sweet wine. He drank, then purposely shrugged his shoulders and tried to let tension drain from his body. "The Prince did nothing to scare me. In fact, he did everything he could to be reassuring. I actually do take heart in what he told me, and you should, too, Nirati. Do not fear for me."

His sister's blue eyes narrowed as she accepted a cup of wine. "If I promise not to worry, will you tell me what he said?"

"I cannot. He forbade me to reveal anything he said to anyone. I'd give you the story he told me to tell others, but you'd see through it in a heartbeat."

Nirati regarded him for a moment over the curved rim of the cup. "Tell me why you are frightened, then."

"That's a little more difficult." Keles drank again, thinking that if he gulped the wine he might find some euphoria. He also realized that was actually the last thing he needed. That wouldn't make his situation any better; it would only put off what had to be faced.

"In talking to the Prince I truly came to see the enormity of the task ahead of me. Jorim pointed out the dangers accurately enough when we spoke the other day. I figured they would all be things that an arrow or two could handle."

His sister laughed. "All things considered, shooting well won't hurt."

"I agree, but the Prince made it apparent that there was more going on. My mission is not just a way for Grandfather to banish me for spoiling his birthday party. It actually has value, and could be crucial to Nalenyr. He took what I'd seen as little more than a family squabble and broadened it."

She nodded. "He raised the stakes, making the price of failure much higher."

"As if the possibility of dying was not enough. Yes."

"And you want me not to worry?"

Keles leaned in and kissed his twin on the forehead. "No, I'll do enough of that. I want to know you are back here in Moriande having fun, breaking hearts, and finding someone who will be a brilliant addition to our family."

Nirati's eyes sparkled. "I think I have the harder task, given that Mother and Grandfather will be watching over me. Still, there are possibilities."

Keles turned and followed her gaze. Just entering the hall were Majiata Phoesel and her family. Along with them came a tall man who, by his dress and demeanor, embraced his Desei heritage. The man was handsome, and certainly the type that had attracted his sister in the past. When the count had visited him, Keles found him to be intelligent as well, which was good; his sister would suffer no idiots.

"Tell me, Nir, do you want the Desei because of him, or because he is with *her*?"

He felt a shock run through Nirati. "Your lips are moving, but I hear Jorim's words."

"You're not answering the question."

"One of those reasons suffices, but the other makes it that much more fun, brother dear." Her eyes slitted as Majiata broke from her group and approached them. "I'll let you speak with her alone."

"Could be she is coming to warn you off."

"She can send me a letter—if she learns to write." Nirati kissed him on the cheek and wandered away, not even acknowledging Majiata with a nod as she passed.

Keles nodded as Majiata reached him. "Pleasure of the Festival to you."

"And you." Majiata clasped her hands at her waist. "I am pleased to see you have recovered from your injuries."

"Am recovering, but it is expected I shall heal fully."

She hesitated for a moment, clearly expecting something, then glanced down. "I am recovering from my injuries as well."

"Your injuries . . . Ah, yes, I heard you were at the healing. I was unconscious." Keles imagined a red scar on what had previously been soft ivory skin. He recalled her near panic, once, when a blemish had appeared on her chin. It struck him as curious that he didn't want to offer her succor or sympathy, but wished to see the scar so he could forever erase the vision of her beauty from his memory.

Her gaze came back up and her face became a smooth, ivory mask with a splash of color at lips, cheeks, and eyes. "In the spirit of the Festival, I wish you to know that I bear you no ill will for what happened to me. I absolve you of all guilt in the matter. It was not your fault."

"Not my fault?" Keles frowned. "I'm afraid I don't understand."

"You needn't feign ignorance, Keles. Despite your rejection of me, I know you intimately, and you me. I know what you are feeling inside."

"And what, exactly, would that be?"

"Many things. Regret and anger chief among them." Majiata kept her voice even and quiet, prompting the scandalmongers in the crowd to edge closer to hear. "You regret having sent me away and regret not having been able to keep me safe."

"I thought I *did* keep you safe." Keles held his cup out for a servant to replenish. "That, or I got these scars for nothing."

"Oh, not *that*." The dismissive tone of her voice coupled with disdain, and put a twist in her mouth that was not attractive. "That you were not able to tell the Prince you would have excused me the whipping."

"What?"

"You are not so cruel as to wish me harmed, though you are the man who broke my heart."

"I broke your heart?" Keles drank to give himself time to think, trying to pierce her logic. "You are the one who came to break things off with me, remember? You are the one who refused to accompany me on the *Stormwolf*."

"But, you see, had I agreed, I would now be bound for Ixyll."

He screwed his eyes shut for a moment, hoping her words would make sense as he reviewed them. "But, had you agreed to join me, I would not be bound for the Wastes."

"You see, so it is all your fault, Keles."

"But you said it wasn't my fault."

"No, I am *forgiving* you." Frustration had begun to rise in her voice, but she gained control of it. "I want you to know I will always love you."

He drained his drink and, in the moment of solitude afforded him by the cup eclipsing her, things made a crude sort of sense. Majiata had always been self-centered, but had never before ventured so far into fantasy. He would have put it down to her having been whipped, save for the calculation he saw in what she was saying.

Quite simply, she and her family were hedging their bets. Leaving things on good terms with him would make further relations with his grandfather possible. It might also be seen as something that would please the Prince. Moreover, when he returned—Keles refused to think of it as *if*—he might very well have found an overland route to the trade of old days. In that case still being friendly with him would directly enrich her family.

He lowered his cup again and a smiling servant refilled it. "Majiata, I have something I must say to you."

"Yes?" Her reply came in a husky hushed whisper reminiscent of words spoken postpassion, in the dark of the night. "Tell me, Keles Anturasi."

"I see many things right now. Things about you and about me. Truths that cannot be denied. You say you love me, and will always do so." He pressed his left hand to his breastbone. "I also feel something."

"Yes, Keles?" Her words came breathlessly, and her expression changed to one of expectation. "What do you feel?"

"Frankly," he began, his heart racing, "I feel sick."

"Oh, poor Keles."

"No, I think you mistake me. I feel sick that I was for so long deceived about you, your feelings, and your aims. You clearly thought, perhaps from the beginning, that you could use me as a toy. You could play with my feelings, even as you are trying to play with them now. That with a coo and a whisper and a kiss and the spreading of your thighs, you could win a prize from me. My eternal adoration? My family's wealth of geographical knowledge? The fortune that has earned us? I don't know what you thought you would get. What I was offering you *was* my heart, my devotion, my *love,* and you spurned it.

"And now you come to me and tell me that you *forgive* me and that I shouldn't feel *guilty* for your having been whipped? Right now, Majiata, right now"—his voice began to rise and he exercised no restraint—"I wish you'd gotten the full measure of the Prince's threat. I'd have been dead, but that would have been fine. Better me dead and you broken than your believing in your delusions."

All color had drained from her face. "You are not well. Clearly the Viruk venom has addled you."

She turned to leave, but he grabbed her with his left hand and spun her back. "Not so fast."

"Unhand me."

"Not yet, for, in the spirit of the Festival, I would tell you something." He held her tightly in that one hand, certain his fingers would leave bruises on her upper arm. "I *would* be inclined to forgive you for the scars on my back and the fact that I'm being sent into the Wastes, but my doing that would require a few things from you. First would be an acknowledgment that you *are* responsible for what happened to both of us. Yes, I acted to safeguard you, no denying that, but I never would have had to act were you not unthinking, petulant, and so self-absorbed that you believe the world is centered on you."

Her eyes went flat, and he knew nothing was getting through. It didn't matter, though, for he had an audience and other ears to fill. "Well, Majiata, the Anturasi know, better than anyone else in the world, that all creation is *not* centered on you. We explore the world. We broaden it. Those who are capable of seeing outside themselves understand what a wonder that is. We make the world bigger and that just makes you smaller. Of course, making you smaller than you make yourself is tough, but you know what?"

He tossed off the last of his wine with relish and deposited the cup in her hands.

"I'm going into the Wastes . . . happily . . . joyously . . . all because I'll be very far away from *you*."

Chapter Twenty-five

3rd day, Month of the Dog, Year of the Dog
9th Year of Imperial Prince Cyron's Court
162nd Year of the Komyr Dynasty
736th year since the Cataclysm
Stormwolf, Moriande
Nalenyr

Jorim Anturasi planted fists on his hips as he mounted the deck of the *Stormwolf*. The massive ship rose and fell ever so slightly under his feet. The Gold River's sluggish current did pull at the ship, but its sheer size and weight made it resistant to the river's efforts to move it. Above him, purple silk sails hung furled from crosstrees on each of nine masts. On other ships, some of the nine would be purely ornamental, but on this ship there was nothing that was not meant to be functional.

"If I could beg your pardon." A slight voice came from behind him. "You are blocking the gangway."

"So I am." Jorim stepped aside and watched a small man come aboard, bent almost double beneath an overstuffed bag. He wore a good blue robe and, despite having lost most of his hair, looked young. He certainly wasn't a sailor or soldier. *What is he doing here?*

The Anturasi grabbed the bag and lifted it from the man's back with one hand. "Have you a concubine hidden in here?"

The little man straightened, his face tight with surprise. "No, I have only necessities." His voice took on a bit of an edge. "I do not require your aid with it, either."

Jorim bit back a riposte. The blue robe had a yellow sash, which was not unusual for one who functioned as a minor clerk in a ministry, but the ends had been embroidered with a coiled dragon. That meant the man had some sort of court appointment and if someone so unsuited to the voyage were on the ship by court choice, he was not a quantity to be made sport of until his measure had been taken.

Jorim set the bag on the deck. "I beg your pardon. I am Jorim Anturasi."

"And I am . . . did you say *Anturasi*?"

"Yes."

The man snapped forward in a deep bow. "Forgive me for speaking sharply to you, Master."

Jorim took him by the shoulders and forced him to straighten up again. "No forgiveness necessary. You were telling me your name."

"He would be Iesol Pelmir." The new voice came from a tall woman with dark hair and hazel eyes. Though she was slender, neither her voice nor stance suggested weakness. Despite her relative youth, she wore a captain's robe. It and her mien underscored her strength of personality. "I would see the both of you in my cabin. *Immediately.*"

"As you will it, Captain Gryst." Iesol fell in behind her, then hesitated, torn, half-turning back for his bag.

Jorim hefted it again and swung it easily onto his own back. Iesol's look of horror was reward enough as Jorim followed the two toward the ship's stern and the cabins below the steersman's deck. He deposited the sack in the narrow passage outside the captain's cabin and followed Iesol.

He'd expected a cramped cabin, but found himself pleasantly surprised. The rear bulkhead had been made of shutters which, when open as they were now, admitted light and air while affording a wonderful view of Moriande and the river. Lamps hung on chains from rafters above the edges of an ancient desk. Off to the right lay the captain's bunk and wardrobe. The area to the left of her desk had been set with a table and chairs, clearly serving as a dining and entertaining area.

But Captain Gryst offered neither Iesol nor Jorim a seat. The little man glanced around nervously, but Jorim calmly planted his feet and clasped his hands at the small of his back. He had an idea what was coming and braced himself for it.

Anaeda Gryst positioned herself behind her desk, allowing the cityscape to silhouette her. She rested her hands on the desktop and studied papers filled with long columns of script. Her voice began low, but in it Jorim could hear the commanding tone of a leader.

"This is a talk I expected I would only have to give your brother once, Jorim. You might require it *twice,* but you'll not get it a third time. In lieu of that, I'll be leaving you on the nearest rock with fresh water. As for you, Minister Pelmir, I never expected to be giving you this talk at all. I understand that Minister Hisatal has new duties that require him to remain on dry land; hence you have been foisted on us."

"Yes, Mistress."

Her head came up quickly and the small man shook. "When I want you to speak, Minister, I will invite you to do so. I did not ask you a question, nor do I require confirmation of something I already knew. I have no idea why *you* were chosen to replace him—what evil, perceived or real, you performed to get this berth—but . . . Yes, you wish to tell me?"

"Is that a question?"

Her eyes tightened and Jorim began to find her attractive. At least ten years his senior, her flesh had been darkened by wind, sun, and sea. Her hazel eyes were of the kind considered handsome within the aristocracy, and the sense of character that shone through them was riveting. Unlike the women of his class and society, she had steel in her spine and a mind attuned not to artificial nuances, but to those things that could and did make the difference between life and death.

"Tell me, Minister."

"I-I asked to be assigned to the *Stormwolf.*"

She turned her head slightly to the left and said nothing for a moment. Then, coming upright, she regarded him openly. "Interesting. That makes you even more of a candidate for this talk, so I'll begin. This is the *Stormwolf.* I am her captain. On this ship, my word is law. If an event is entered into the ship's log, it is a fact. If it is not, it never happened. I will require meticulous care be given to the log and account books, but I will review and edit as I see fit. The Prince, in his wisdom, wishes to know all but needs not be burdened with details of no consequence."

Her gaze shifted from the clerk to Jorim, and he felt a jolt. "You are an adventurer. Your passion, your life, your vocation demand you take chances, and I will expect you to do just that. On land. You do that on my ship and I'll have you clapped in irons and stowed below with the ratters and other livestock. Is that clear?"

"Yes, Captain."

"This ship has over a thousand crew, plus a hundred and eighty concubines and ninety distinguished scholars, guests, and assorted others. To actually *sail* this ship I require four hundred and fifty. Attrition can and will occur, but it is my intention to keep it to a minimum. I want to come back with at least ninety percent of those I go out with, and if we come back with more, I will be very pleased.

"This ship is as much a village as it is a vessel. The sailors have been drawn from the best of the Naleni fleet. All have volunteered. All are hoping for riches and glory, but they know all they'll be certain of getting is food, water, and older. I don't know what your thoughts are on the chances for riches and glory. I don't care. What I care is that you're not going about spreading stories that promise much and deliver nothing."

She pointed at Jorim. "You, very specifically, are going to be a problem. You have very little to do while on board. I suggest you find something to do. Learn how to play an instrument. Visit every concubine we have. Join the scholars in intellectual discussions. Do *something,* because if I find you to be disruptive, I will find you something to do. And I can guarantee it will not be pleasant.

"As for you, Minister, I will run you ragged. If you get a chance to draw an idle breath it is because you are shirking duty. You will be available to me at all hours. You will report instantly, you will draft orders, follow orders, and report back promptly and accurately. No excuses, no tardiness, no laziness."

Iesol bobbed his head.

"Has either of you anything to say?"

Jorim nodded. "Permission to speak, Captain."

She eyed him up and down, then nodded. "Granted."

"First, I wish to apologize for not having reported before this. I know we will sail with the tide tonight. But I have spent much of the time leading up to this closeted with my grandfather and I have with me the best possible charts."

"Very good."

"Second, I fully acknowledge you as the Master of this ship, and I shall obey you in all things—save one."

Anaeda Gryst's eyes narrowed. "Did you not listen to what I said?"

"Please, Captain." Jorim held a hand up. "No disrespect intended, but I have orders from the Prince to attend to the device in my cabin without failing. If my obligation to deal with it is, in my opinion, more important than your current order, I will do my duty to the Crown."

"We will discuss that point more, Master Anturasi." She folded her arms beneath her breasts. "And you, Minister? What have you to say?"

Iesol bowed his head to her. "I understand all you have said and will obey. I am not the person who was meant to be here, but I will work very hard to prove to you that fortune has been kind in appointing me to this position. If there is any service you require of me, Captain, I shall not hesitate to acquit it."

The hint of a smile curled the corners of her mouth. "You are from which Ministry?"

"I have studied for Protocol, Etiquette, and Diplomacy, as well as Regulation, and have all the training for Accounting and Economics. I most recently served Harmony."

"You did not answer the question."

His shoulders slumped a bit. "As yet, Captain, I have not been acknowledged by a Ministry."

Jorim felt a tug at his heart for the small man. As with any trade, a person studied and worked hard to be accepted into his occupational community. Captain Gryst had proven, through her past voyages, to be worthy of the great command she had been given. Though Jorim's grandfather often was displeased with him, he, too, had been accepted as a cartographer in his own right. In both their cases, the laws of the land dictated the minimums they could be paid, the sort of treatment they would receive, their social standing, and the like.

Iesol had not yet been acknowledged. While he could and clearly did function as a clerk or employee—probably for the very Ministries that would not acknowledge him—without their sanction he had few, if any, rights. Had he a powerful patron, his position in a Ministry could have been assured, which would pave the way to a known and stable future. Without it, however, he worked at the whim of others and could be used as a pawn in any manner of political situations.

"Were you promised acknowledgment if you returned?"

"Not precisely, Captain, but the indications were strong."

She nodded. "As I said, my word here is law. Serve me well and, if the voyage is two years in duration, you will have served the Maritime Ministry for long enough that they *must* acknowledge you. They have reciprocity with the other Ministries. It seems likely the one who gave you this chance did not think you would survive the voyage. If you can, they will have been fooled."

Iesol nodded slowly, as if unable to believe what he had heard.

"That's very good of you, Captain." Jorim smiled easily and gave her a nod.

Her face closed. "Did I give you permission to comment?"

Jorim bowed. "No, Captain."

"Very good. Remember that, Master Anturasi." She turned and patted the sternpost. "The *Stormwolf* is the greatest of the Naleni Wolves. The voyage we will undertake will live forever in the annals of history. Do what I tell you to do when I tell you to do it, and we will make it back to Moriande. Disobey me and the ship *will* get back. You likely will not. Am I understood?"

"Yes, Captain."

"Good. Minister Pelmir, please collect your belongings and report below. You will be shown to your cabin—which you will share with two young apprentice sailors. I doubt either will be good for much, being yet children, but perhaps you can teach them something useful like writing and addition."

"Yes, Captain." Iesol bowed and kept bowing as he shuffled his way backward out of the cabin.

Captain Gryst came around from behind her desk, then sat back on it. "Master Anturasi, you *are* going to be trouble, aren't you?"

"I will do my best not to be, Captain."

"I hope so." She pointed a finger at the deck, and for a moment he thought she was indicating he should kneel before her, which he just wasn't going to do. "The device that was installed in your cabin, I know what it is."

"How?"

"Fear not. The state secret is safe. Borosan Gryst, its inventor, is my cousin. He told me of his desire to create such a thing. My uncle installed it here. I know what it will allow you to do, and why the Prince has given you the orders he has."

Jorim smiled. "I am glad you understand its importance."

"I do, but I have a problem." She regarded him openly. "As I said, my word is law on this ship—even overruling the Prince. I cannot and will not have you obeying him when I need you obeying me. If you fail to do that, not only could you put the ship in jeopardy, but you could find yourself in trouble. This crew contains many people who have sailed with me for years. Defy me, disobey me, and someone might take it into his head to discipline you in a manner that would show how much respect they have for me."

"I hadn't looked at it—right, you didn't ask for a comment."

"You're learning." She held up a finger. "You would disobey me to obey the Prince, I know that, so I need to deal with that problem. Therefore, I now issue you an order: without fail you are to see to all your duties concerning that device. *Without fail,* do you understand me? This standing order will supersede any other order you are issued."

The cartographer smiled slowly. "I understand you perfectly, Captain."

"Good." Her dark eyes hardened. "What I said before I meant. I will remind you once that you're not to be a disruptive influence on my crew. After that, I leave you behind. The only thing you are uniquely qualified to do here is make maps and communicate the information to your grandfather. I can make maps; I can use the device my cousin made. If the Prince has to wait to get his maps, I'm sure he won't mind as long as they arrive and are accurate."

"And if you don't get them back to him, Captain?"

She smiled easily. "It will be because the Eastern Sea has swallowed us whole, Jorim Anturasi. That's the only way we won't be returning. Obey me and you'll be with us when we get back."

Chapter Twenty-six

3rd day, Month of the Dog, Year of the Dog
9th Year of Imperial Prince Cyron's Court
162nd Year of the Komyr Dynasty
736th year since the Cataclysm
Catfish, Moriande
Nalenyr

Keles Anturasi stood by the rail on the river vessel *Catfish* as it slid past the *Stormwolf*. The tall, long ship, with its many masts and swarming crew, mocked the small, flat-bottomed boat that trios of oarsmen propelled up the river with broad sweeps of long oars. Further upriver they would pole the ship through shallows, but rowing was the only method of moving against the current when in the deep channels dredged for ships like the *Stormwolf*.

The sun had begun to set, so he knew his brother was already on board. He felt a pang of envy, and another of loss, both of which surprised him. Going on the *Stormwolf* had been something he'd been looking forward to, but he didn't live for it the way his brother did. Even when they'd said their farewells at the family tower, Jorim's anticipation kept distracting him.

Keles would have preferred to see his brother to the *Stormwolf*, or have Jorim visit the *Catfish*, but that was not permitted. Keles had been ordered by the Prince to dye his hair Helosundian blond and grow a beard. With three days' growth it was not much, but did alter his appearance somewhat. He'd also taken to dressing in robes of coarse material and had confined much of his conversation to grunts and short sentences.

True to his word, the Prince had found an actor who looked enough like Keles to make Siatsi pause. Nirati had come to the *Catfish* to see the actor off and had played her tearful part exquisitely. She'd given Keles himself barely more than a glance when he boarded.

Keles tried not to pay too much attention to those who were supposed to be accompanying him, but the deception fascinated him. He found the actor to be pompous, playing him like an effete noble. The fake Keles lectured about the river, quoting directly from the report Keles had written, but he kept putting the emphasis in the wrong places. It annoyed Keles, but he did admit that everyone was paying attention to the pretender, while he sank back into the crowd unnoticed.

Keles likewise kept his eyes open for any Desei agents who might be watching, but so far the only northerner he'd seen was Count Aerynnor, who conducted his sister back to Anturasikun. Still, just as he was trying not to look Naleni, he knew the Desei would be trying to look like anything but themselves, so his observations were bound to be fruitless.

His life, he realized as the *Catfish* wiggled its way against the current, had become very complex. Not that it hadn't been complex before, but that had been *controlled* complexity. He had been given problems, like the Gold River survey, which had very clear success and failure parameters. The problem had been manageable and he had managed it very well.

The problem he now faced was not manageable at all. He could barely even define it. He was going into the unknown, opposed by unknown forces, aided by unknown forces, with future-but-unknown work for the Prince in the offing. About the only known quantities were guesses based on rumors and legends, and those were worthless. The only thing he could be certain about was that he had enemies who would do him harm if they discovered his identity.

He glanced down at the deep green water and contemplated throwing himself in, but it was just a passing thought. *It would make things much easier, but it would also mean I lose. And I don't want to lose.*

"It is good to meet a kinsman on this boat."

Keles turned, then looked up. The woman who had spoken had

long hair that hung in blonde ringlets. Her slender, well-formed nose and high cheekbones combined with a strong jaw and pale blue eyes to make her very pretty, but the vapid expression she wore did not fit her face. The life burning in her eyes belied it, and the obvious deception put Keles on guard. In addition, though her simple, oversize robe of brown wool tried to soften her outline, there was no hiding her broad shoulders.

"Yes. A comfort."

"I am Tyressa Joden."

Keles shivered. "I am Kulshar Joden." He stiffly offered the name the Prince's ministers had supplied him, not at all liking that she had used the surname first.

"I know." She smiled slightly, then glanced out at the water. "Ah, Wentokikun. Do you suppose that man up there at the window might be the Prince himself? He would watch to see Keles Anturasi off, don't you think?"

"Perhaps." Keles' mind raced. "Or one of the Keru."

Her smile broadened a little. "Perhaps. We have the same name. I don't believe in coincidences, do you?"

"No, I do not." He looked around and saw no one nearby. "You are Keru?"

"And entrusted with your safety, yes." She kept her voice low. "You should continue your quiet ways, as your accent will never pass as Helosundian. You're berthing below with most of the other passengers while your double will get the second-best cabin aboard. You'll want to be very careful."

"Are there enemy agents on board?"

She snorted. "If there are any active ones, I will find them and deal with them. You must be wary, though, for anyone could see something odd. And if they let their puzzlement slip to someone else, that person, or someone they talk to, could be in communication with the enemy."

Before he could ask, she added, "And the enemy could be anyone."

Keles smiled ruefully. "I am glad you were able to narrow that down for me."

"I'll do my best." She pointed a finger toward the river's south shore. "How far do you think it is to the bank?"

Keles shrugged, but studied the distance for a moment, then answered. "Sixty-seven yards, give or take."

"Precisely. You've just given yourself away."

"What?"

"No one save a cartographer or surveyor would estimate the distance the way you just did. Most would say 'a middling bowshot' or 'further than I can throw a stone.' "

"But you're here to protect me."

"And how do you know that?"

Keles quickly reviewed their conversation and felt his stomach fold in on itself. He began to slide back along the railing away from her. "I guess I don't."

Tyressa grabbed him by the shoulder and he tried to bat her hand away, but he couldn't break her grip. He wanted to take that as confirmation that she *was* Keru and there to protect him, but the only thing it signified was that he was in trouble.

"Stop, Kulshar." She loosened her grip, but only a little. "I was told to tell you the sculptors won't include your beard, and the painters will work with brown."

A sign from the Prince. Another shiver rocked him and her hand fell away. He shook his head. "You are going to have to work hard with me, right?"

"I will, yes, but there are advantages. I *know* you can learn. I *think* you will take orders."

"Yes, to both of those."

"Good. You're like the Prince in the first, and I wish he were like you in the second."

Keles smiled. "Is that why you are here?"

"What do you mean?"

"I'm on this trip because I earned my grandfather's ire."

"I have no grandfather. He died in Helosunde."

"I'm sorry to hear that."

Tyressa turned and leaned on the rail. "Why is that? You didn't know him. From what my family has said, he makes your grandfather look pleasant."

"I still won't say I'm happy for you." He turned and leaned his elbows on the rail, too. "But you know what I mean and you're evading the question."

"What question was that?"

"Why are you on this trip?"

She said nothing, but nodded in the direction of Wentokikun. "I was given an order. I am here."

"That's it?"

She looked at him sidelong. "That's all you need to know."

He frowned. "Maybe I need to know more."

"That is all I want to tell you."

"But, if I'm to trust you . . ."

Tyressa shook her head. "You don't have to trust me. You just have to trust that I know what to do and how to do it, and that I will do my duty. Anything beyond that is immaterial. The Prince trusts us. Why should you be different?"

"If he asked that sort of question, would you answer him?"

"That, Kulshar, is a hypothetical question with no validity, so it gets no answer."

"I see." He fell silent, letting the scent of cook smoke supplant the river's heavy, sour miasma. "I'm sorry. I didn't mean to make you angry."

He waited for a reply and when he got none after a moment or two, he looked over and saw she'd drifted away. Keles considered going after her, but hesitated. It was probably for the best he didn't, since that could attract attention. Moreover, she could have been off to check something he didn't notice. He felt frustrated and helpless, and that sank him back to the night of the Prince's celebration.

He'd made his bold statements to Majiata and waited for her reply. He expected she'd scourge him, but it would have been worth it. In an instant, he'd seen how shabbily she'd treated him, and his resentment had been immediate and strong. He'd braced for her to strike back hard, fully shocked and petulant.

Instead, she'd just looked at him and begun to cry. Tears welled in her eyes, then gushed down her cheeks, melting cosmetics in a dark stain. He imagined, just for a moment, that this was all for effect, but then tears splashed down to soil her gown. Her lower lip trembled and her nose began to run. She looked up at him, her moist eyes summoning up a torrent of guilt.

She said nothing.

Keles had immediately been of two minds. The first was certain he was being manipulated. How could someone who had used him so ruthlessly be so vulnerable? He knew this was just another ploy, another way to get under his skin and make him hurt.

The other part of him just melted. This was the woman he had loved, and he'd been cruel to her. He'd reduced her to tears, which was bad enough, but he'd done it there, at the Prince's Festival, where everyone could see how he had shamed her.

He wanted to reach out and hug her, offer some sort of comfort, but he couldn't raise his hands. She looked so small and weak, so hurt by what he had said, that he questioned his vehemence, his certainty. *Could I have been wrong all along? Maybe she does love me.*

The two halves of his mind warred against each other, which left him standing before her frustrated and impotent. Not doing something was worse than doing the wrong thing, but how should he act? He could turn his back on her, walking away, but that would have been even more cold and callous. Yet standing there just increased the awkwardness and made it so very much worse.

Keles had instead turned toward the wine table and held his cup out to be refilled. He had intended to offer her some of the wine, but when he turned back, she had already retreated, cutting swiftly through the crowd, audible sobs accompanying her tears. People looked from her to him—a few with surprise, but more with anger on their faces. One and all they seemed to be saying, "She might have had it coming, but did it have to be *now*?"

Jorim had rescued him. His younger brother had approached, gotten a cup of wine, then pulled him aside. "Are you all right, Keles?"

Keles had drunk, then nodded. "Yes."

"What happened?"

"She came to forgive me. She told me it wasn't my fault."

Jorim laughed heartily and spoke perhaps a bit louder than he might have otherwise. "*She* forgave *you*? You, the one who prevented her from being clawed into sweetmeats? She *forgave* you?"

The effect of his brother's words had been immediate, both in Keles and the surrounding audience. Gossipmongers immediately repeated his remarks, countering what they'd said when watching the drama unfold. What had been an emotional encounter shifted into one more entertainment for the evening.

The change in Keles was one he now reexamined as he stared

down into the waters. He'd steeled himself to accept that what the people in that room felt about him didn't matter. He'd done nothing wrong. She'd chosen the confrontation and he'd just dealt with her as best he could.

Here, too, what he thought of his guardian and what she thought of him likewise didn't matter. They both had missions to fulfill, and would do so. Tyressa would keep him safe, he would complete the survey for the Prince, and that would be that.

That seemed right to him, but after a moment's reflection he located the flaw in his thinking. What Tyressa thought of him, and what she thought about how he conducted himself, were very different. There were things he could learn from her, especially about being observant. While she might be charged with his safety, he couldn't cede that responsibility to her. Not only did he owe it to himself to be observant, but he had to think ahead to a time when she might not be there to help him.

To this point in your life, Keles, you have been sheltered. Just because he'd learned to deal with his grandfather didn't mean he was prepared to deal with the world. There were going to be folks, like Majiata, who wanted certain things from him—such as his knowledge or even his death. He needed to be wary of them.

Do any less and you'll not be worth the lead it would take to cast you. He smiled. *Any less, and you'll not even be worth the dross that spills out of an overfilled mold.*

Chapter Twenty-seven

14th day, Month of the Dog, Year of the Dog
9th Year of Imperial Prince Cyron's Court
162nd Year of the Komyr Dynasty
736th year since the Cataclysm
Jandetokun Inn, Moriande
Nalenyr

Nirati slipped the hood back on her white mourning cloak as she entered the Jandetokun Inn. Those gathered in the common area on the main floor slowly quieted as they realized someone in mourning was in their midst. Since she had thrown the cloak back and wore no tear tracks drawn in black down whitened cheeks, the others became instantly aware that the person being mourned was not a family member. Their conversations began again, but at a low murmur that would remain sober until she left.

She found their deference a comfort, for she still remained in shock. The death had been so brutal—at least, this was the impression she'd had of it from gossip and whispers. Those of her cousins who talked about it didn't think it was the sort of thing a young woman should hear, so she dwelt in ignorance. This left her imagination free to conjure up all sorts of ideas. While she wanted to suppose that what she made up was worse than reality, somehow she didn't think it was.

Nirati also found herself feeling guilty. She might have, once, thought of Majiata as a friend. Majiata had been younger than she and always a bit aloof. Nirati had tried to like her when Keles began courting her, but they had never developed a deep friendship. Nirati's hopes that they could become as sisters died quickly, and that left her with a crystal-clear vision of what the woman was doing to her twin.

That Keles had remained ignorant of how horribly she was treating him came as no surprise to Nirati. Her twin had the tendency to see the best in people, acting as if they had risen to fulfill the idealized role he'd pictured for them. The reality was often quite different.

But at least he learned to deal with Majiata. Their confrontation at the Prince's celebration had pleased Nirati. It marked a shift in Keles' attitude. She hoped it would stand him in good stead in the middle of the wildlands—though she dreaded the inevitable conflict it would cause when he returned and had to deal with Qiro directly.

Try though she might, she could not project what Keles' reaction to the news of Majiata's death would be. Before he had started to grow, she would have imagined that it would have hurt him deeply. He would have felt, somehow, it was his fault, and he would try to make amends. With her death, the Phoesel family might have gotten maps and concessions that even her wedding to Keles would not have gained them.

Now, however, his reaction remained unpredictable. It was possible he could revert to his old ways and become overly kind to her family, but Nirati doubted that. Likewise she didn't think he would laugh at the news or hoist a glass in favor of her killer. She didn't think he would swear vengeance on the thing that had done this either—Jorim would have, but not Keles. But, however he chose to deal with it, she resolved to be there to help him.

She put her twin out of her mind as she mounted the steps to the rental rooms above the inn's main floor. Though she had not been there before, she knew unerringly which room she was bound for. Others might have put this down to her family 's skill with cartography, but it was less complicated. Her informant had been very specific in his instructions, as well as in relating that the resident did not want to be disturbed.

Topping the steps, she turned left and moved toward the front of the building. She knocked gently on the middle door and waited. She heard nothing, so she knocked again, more loudly. When that brought no response, she hammered her fist on the door, then spoke in a very clear voice. "It is Nirati Anturasi. I am not leaving until I speak to you, and I'll beat on this door until my fist is bloody."

That brought some noise from within. Beneath the edge of the door light flashed, indicating the heavy curtains had been drawn back. The agonized gasp that accompanied the light suggested the person within had enjoyed too much drink and too little sleep.

"The door is open."

Nirati slipped the latch, but hesitated in the doorway. While light flooded in through the window, the room still had the sour scent of nightsweats and bodies long unwashed. She would have expected things to be more disorderly, but aside from tall boots lying flopped over in the middle of the floor, gloves scattered to two corners, and an ale bucket tipped on its side near the bed, things looked relatively neat.

They contrasted sharply with Junel Aerynnor. He sat on the side of the bed, his shoulders slumped, wearing a stained linen nightshirt and two days' growth of beard. His hair needed taming and his sunken eyes were rimmed with black and tinged with red. His skin looked white enough that had he leaned over and retched into the bucket, she would not have been surprised. In fact, she almost righted it and slid it to him. She closed the door and moved to the chair by the small table beneath the window.

"I had no desire to intrude on your grief, Count Aerynnor, but you have no one else here that I know of."

He glanced at her, his lips pressed in a grim line. "The Phoesel family has no desire to see me. I was the one to bring them the bad tidings. When her father asked me to tell him what I had seen, I had no idea he wanted me to lie. In the north, perfect candor would have been expected."

Nirati seated herself without waiting for an invitation. "I heard of their reaction. The constabulary asked you to identify her instead of the family?"

He rubbed his right hand over his eyes. "It sounds so official that way. One of the constables who had attended her punishment recognized her. As he was going to her home he chanced across me. I agreed to accompany him, but now I wish I never had."

Junel's hand fell from his eyes and he stared past Nirati. "There are things men are not meant to see."

Nirati nodded as a shiver ran up her spine. "What can I do for you, my lord? If you want to tell me . . ."

He snorted. "That offer from anyone else would be an invitation to gossip. Not you, Nirati. You'd tell no one."

"So tell me."

Junel shook his head. "No, you'd have it locked inside the way I do. That's not a burden anyone should have to bear."

She slipped the clasp on her cloak and allowed it to drape back over the chair. "I think, my lord, you will find me stronger than you imagine. If it is such a burden for you now, imagine the relief at having it shared. I will bear it, and not blame you."

He half smiled. "I know you Anturasi are more hardy than the Phoesels, but even so . . ."

"I think you are feeling guilty for not having prevented this tragedy. It was not your fault."

"How can you say that?"

"I know you. You once saved her from Viruk talons. You would have done that again."

"Is that who they say did it? A Viruk. *The* Viruk?" Junel's eyes tightened. "It was enough of a mess that he could have."

Nirati nodded. The hottest gossip in Moriande suggested that the Viruk Rekarafi had slain Majiata to cleanse some blot from his honor. The authorities had asked for him to be produced for examination, but the ambassador said her consort had long since quit the city. She even submitted to a search of the embassy, but the constables could not find him.

Some wags even went so far as to suggest that after killing the girl he had set out in pursuit of Keles. Nirati shivered. She'd seen the scars on his back and had no doubt that Rekarafi would rend Keles limb from limb if he found him. *Perhaps the Prince's deception will give Keles enough time to get where the Viruk cannot find him.*

She blinked and refocused on Junel. "The Viruk is the leading candidate, but plenty of other rumors abound. One even suggests one of my brothers did it."

"Keles or Jorim?"

"Keles. They say his heading upriver was a trick, and that he could have ridden hard to join the ship after he did the deed." Nirati shook her head. "Now, tell me. What happened?"

Junel sighed and his shoulders slumped further. "It was all quite a muddle. I was living with the Phoesel family, but I knew that Majiata and I were a poor match. Her father was still upset about her having embarrassed the family and lost your brother. I was a poor second choice, and while Majiata's father was polite, he was not silent in sharing that opinion. Still, I was better than nothing.

"I had expressed my reservations about our union to Majiata and said I planned to leave her home. Three days ago, when I awoke, I found a note in her hand slipped beneath my door. She begged me to do nothing rash and to meet her in the city after dark, away from her family. She asked me to burn the note, which I did."

He frowned. "I knew I should not have agreed to meet her, but something in that note touched me. She'd always been immature and selfish, but there was something different in that missive. I resolved to meet her and left the house early so her family would suspect nothing. I went to meet her at the appointed time but got delayed. I arrived perhaps a quarter hour late, but really thought nothing of it."

Nirati snorted. "Majiata was never punctual. You should still have been early."

"That's what I thought. I waited for an hour, then just assumed she had decided to go back on whatever she had been thinking. I returned to the house and went to sleep. The next morning I got up and out early to meet the people who had delayed me the night before, and that is when I ran into the constable."

"What happened then, my lord?"

He shook his head. "You do not want to know."

Her flesh crawled at the tone in his voice. "I have to know. You're not alone in feeling guilty."

"I don't think you know what you are asking."

"But I'm still asking."

"Fine." His spine straightened, but he refused to look at her as he spoke in a flat tone. "Whatever, whoever, did this to her met her in the street. She probably knew him and went with him willingly, or he was strong enough to carry her off. He took her to a rooftop where she could easily see the southern sky and the three moons chasing each other through the constellations. It would have been beautiful. I keep reminding myself of that, hoping, somehow, that such beauty was the last thing she knew."

The strain in his voice suggested Junel knew his hope was forlorn.

"On the roof, her clothing was cut from her. She didn't fight much if at all. The constable said she would have had cuts on her forearms if she had. 'Defensive wounds,' he called them. He also said she might have scratched her attacker and they'd find skin under the fingernails. She had such long nails."

He snorted. "Of course, to do that, they'd have to find her hands."

Nirati's mouth dropped open. She'd heard no inkling that Majiata's hands had been taken. She knew of no reason anyone would do that. Her stomach began to roil.

"He cut her throat, nice and clean, almost severing her head completely. It surprised her, for she died with that shocked look on her face. Then he opened her from throat to groin and dressed her out as a hunter might a deer. He hollowed her out, and spread her organs out around her. And, as I said, he took her hands."

Nirati clapped a hand to her mouth. "No, that is too horrible."

"Horrible. Odd how a word fails, isn't it?" Junel exhaled slowly. "The constable said it would have taken an ax to take her hands off like that. Or a bite. And the cutting, that was one knife, maybe two. Or talons. Even then they were thinking Viruk, I guess.

"When I saw her, I dropped to my knees and vomited. Had I been on time, he might not have gotten her. If I had not decided that our union would be useless, she might not have felt the need to meet me away from the house. If, if, if . . ."

His lean body again bowed forward. He ground the heels of his hands against his eyes and began to sob, repeating that one word over and over.

Nirati rose and crossed to the bed, gathering him in her arms. He slumped across her thighs, his body convulsing with silent sobs. She hugged him hard, despite the stink. She stroked greasy hair and hushed him, holding on until his body slackened and his breathing came more regularly.

Then she shifted him off her and laid him back in the bed. She got up and swung his legs around. She pulled the thin blanket over him and stroked his face. In sleep he seemed a bit more peaceful and this brought the hint of a smile to her face.

Poor Junel. Compassion for him filled her, but fury at Majiata ran countercurrent to it. Majiata's death tortured Junel, and it was not right. Majiata had been unworthy of such honest feelings—and, were she alive, would have only thought of how she could profit from them. If there was something good to be taken from her death, it was that she would no longer be around to torment Keles.

I hope he does not learn of her death for a long time. I'll talk to Grandfather about that. Keles, however, is not my immediate problem.

Stooping, she scooped up the ale bucket and carried it down to the common room. The innkeeper's wife, a plump, rosy-cheeked woman, accepted it from her. "Shall I just fill it for him as before?"

"No." Nirati kept her voice firm. "You'll bring him soup when he's awake, something that isn't heavy, and watered wine. I want you to go up there and wash him, too."

The woman frowned. "He's a grown man. He can be doing for himself."

Nirati's nostrils flared. "Have you any idea who I am?"

The woman bit back a quick response. "I don't suppose it would make a difference if I did."

"It might. I am the granddaughter of Qiro Anturasi. If I let it be known that the Jandetokun Inn is favored, you will prosper. If I let it be known you have displeased us, this place will fail. If need be, I could even ask the Prince to shut you down. You understand this, I see, but you need not fear, because I am asking you for a favor, so I shall do you one in return."

"Y-yes, my lady?"

"Do as I ask with the Desei count and you will be blessed. Any bills, *reasonable* bills, for his care will be paid immediately and in gold."

"Or spices?"

"If you wish, yes, we have some influence there." Nirati kept a smile from her face, though it was clear she and the woman understood each other. "I want him sober, fed, cleaned, and groomed. I shall come back daily to see the progress and settle accounts."

The woman nodded. "I understand, my lady Anturasi. Been in this business long enough to know how to dry someone up."

"Good. One more thing."

"Yes?"

"If anyone else asks after him, you don't know where he has gone. You'll even complain about accounts left unpaid."

"Do I keep any money they give me to settle them?"

"Yes. And I will pay you to know who asks for him." Nirati nodded to the woman and accepted a bow in return. "Your cooperation will be rewarded."

"Thank you, my lady." The woman's voice dropped into a whisper. "I'll do what you ask, but why? He's just a Desei. Why help him?"

Nirati let her question rattle around inside her skull, but found no answer the woman would understand. In fact, she did not even understand her first thoughts. She just smiled and replied in another whisper, "It's an investment in the future. He owes me a dance or three, and it's not a debt I shall let go unpaid."

Chapter Twenty-eight

20th day, Month of the Dog, Year of the Dog
9th Year of Imperial Prince Cyron's Court
162nd Year of the Komyr Dynasty
736th year since the Cataclysm
Stormwolf, Nysant
Cartayne

Jorim Anturasi used the slight rise and fall of the *Stormwolf* as a means to quiet his mind. He sat on the deck in his cramped cabin, legs crossed, spine straight. His personal logbook, containing measurements and hastily sketched maps, as well as time lists, lay open before him. In the dim light of a single candle he could make out enough to let it serve as a boost to his memory. Most things he held in his mind, however, which was where they needed to be so he could send them to his grandfather.

He regulated his breathing and relaxed, which was harder than he imagined because of the impatience that kept coming from Qiro. Each day, as close to Naleni noon as possible, Jorim had composed himself to send information. The experience had never been a pleasant one, but of late it had been even less so. Qiro had changed, and not for the better.

When Jorim had first learned telepathic communication with his grandfather, things had flowed easily, much the way the massive *Stormwolf* rose and fell rhythmically at anchor. His grandfather had been welcoming and gentle, prompting recollections or details in a wordless manner. Jorim always sought to communicate as much as he could. He'd been eager to please his grandfather, and reveled in any encouragement he'd gotten.

But now Qiro regarded any lack of information as an act of conspiracy. His gentle prompts had become sharp jabs. The few times Jorim had been too exhausted to muster a defense, his grandfather had raked through his mind, leaving a blinding headache in his wake.

Even when his grandfather invaded his mind, Jorim had little worries about his secrets being betrayed. Numbers communicated very easily. Subjective concepts, such as beauty, or even a color, did not get conveyed as precisely. Even when he had worked with Keles, there had been mistakes, despite their closeness. The emotional and generational gap with his grandfather meant Qiro could get less from him, and also meant the old man cared very little for Jorim's personal adventures.

The old man just wanted more data for his maps.

With this lot, he would get quite enough. The *Stormwolf* did not travel alone. With it were a dozen other ships, which carried food and water, fodder for the cavalry horses on board, as well as other necessary supplies like lumber, cables, and sailcloth. As they approached the island of Cartayne, the fleet had been split and lesser cartographers had taken measurements as they sailed north and south. The two halves of the fleet converged at the western port of Nysant, and Jorim had worked all night combining the information into an accurate chart of the island, complete with soundings of a southern harbor and the route to it through a reef.

Reaching out with his mind, visualizing Anturasikun and his grandfather's sanctum, he reached the old man easily. Qiro began to devour his information with the fervor of a starving man falling on a haunch of venison. For a heartbeat Jorim actually saw an image of the world on the wall and watched Cartayne sharpen in definition.

He braced for a mental assault, but his grandfather broke the link with a swift finality. Jorim slumped back against the bulkhead and bumped his head—not enough to injure himself, but sufficient to shock him back to full consciousness. Sitting up, he rubbed the back of his head.

I hope everything is all right. The quick termination of their link could have meant his grandfather had collapsed. His heart might have failed, or he might have suffered a brain tremor. *He might even have been murdered.* Jorim dismissed the latter instantly, since Uncle Ulan would never have the nerve to kill him, and would permit no one else close enough to do so. The Prince's precautions would keep assassins out, so the old man was safe from anything other than natural disaster or the vengeance of the gods.

He just as easily dismissed the idea that his grandfather was ill. Jorim felt certain he would have gotten some hint of pain, shock, or panic through the link before it was broken. His grandfather's ego was such that he'd not have been able to conceal his dismay at being prey to mortal afflictions.

But it surprised Jorim that his first reaction was concern for the old man. He would have expected to feel some sort of relief, or even glee, for he had long since ceased to like his grandfather. He didn't respect him much either, save in the area of mapmaking. Outside of that, Qiro Anturasi was a creature worthy only of contempt.

A knock on the cabin door prevented him from examining his feelings further. "I'm not hurt. The thump you heard was nothing."

The door opened and Anaeda Gryst stood there. "I'm glad to hear that. We're going ashore."

"I thought . . ." Jorim scrambled to his feet and scooped his logbook up as her eyes narrowed. "As ordered, Captain Gryst. Let me lock this away first."

"Be quick about it, and bring your sword."

He opened his sea chest and deposited the log, then drew out a simple sword. Single-edged, running just shy of a yard from hilt to point, the blade resided in an unadorned wooden scabbard. The hilt was long enough to let him use the blade two-handed, but the sword was light enough that he could duel with it easily as well. Jorim had not studied swordsmanship at a *serrian,* but the Prince had seen to it that the Anturasi heirs knew enough to protect themselves. Jorim had gotten better on his own and might have been Fifth Rank if tested by a school in the capital.

"Do you expect trouble, Captain?"

"If I did, you'd see our cavalry mounted and ready to escort us."

Jorim shut the chest and locked it. "I notice you're unarmed."

She smiled slowly. "The people we'll see already know how dangerous I am. Your sword will win you a modicum of respect. That will be enough for the moment. Come, we've not a moment to lose."

He followed her from his cabin up to the main deck, and then down netting to where a small boat bobbed beside the *Stormwolf*. Five sailors—four oarsmen and a coxswain—waited for them. Captain Gryst sat in the stern, leaving Jorim the bench at the bow, which he didn't mind taking. The oarsmen pushed off the ship, then began the half mile pull in toward the shore.

Nysant had, ages before, been a Viruk outpost. Little could be seen of what once had been strong fortresses because stones had been stolen from them and mud buildings grafted to their walls like hornets' nests. The squat human buildings mocked the former grandeur. Their imprecise angles and slouching forms dragged on Viruk architecture, much as the human slaves must have dragged on the last of their Viruk masters.

When the heart of the Viruk Empire sank beneath the Dark Sea, the Cartayne colony had begun to wither. The Viruk had brought Men and Soth slaves to populate the place and work it. Gemstone mines and plantations in the interior had provided a lot of wealth for the Empire, but with no home market, the economy collapsed. The Viruk retreated, not caring what happened to their slaves.

Nysant had become, over the centuries, a center of commerce. The trade winds made it easy for ships from the east to reach the city, and the coastal currents allowed them safe passage back home. Along the way they filled their holds with a variety of things that fetched high prices in their home ports. Until Naleni fleets had begun to travel to the west themselves, Nysant had been the source of western treasures. It yet served the same role for a number of the other Principalities, and ships from the Five Princes all rode anchor in the harbor.

Jorim and Captain Gryst climbed a ladder to a wharf and headed inland. Just beyond the normal thicket of dockside warehouses, they entered a free marketplace where wares from the world over were touted by hundreds of loud voices. Textiles and spices, exotic animals and enslaved peoples all were offered for sale. Captain

Gryst stayed well away from the slave pens, where half-naked ebon-fleshed men from Aefret stood chained in a line on an auction block. The auctioneer—a mongrel of dusky skin and muddled features—solicited bids with a combination of flattery and abuse, all in the local cant. Jorim caught words here and there, and liked the lyrical flow of his voice, though the practice of trading human flesh did not appeal to him at all.

They continued on past stalls with fruits and vegetables, squawking yard fowl and collections of odd trinkets. Captain Gryst led him out through the eastern edge of the bazaar and turned north. They plunged into a dim world of twisting alleys. Despite his skill at cartography, Jorim quickly became lost, and he gained the impression that she wanted it that way.

Finally, she stopped before a small shop and entered through a doorway hung with a ragged blanket. He found himself in a small room with a carpeted floor that had been strewn with thick pillows. The carpet had come from Tas al Aud and would fetch a fortune in Moriande—likewise the beautifully embroidered pillows.

That she sat in the midst of a fortune did not seem to make any impression on the tiny, wizened woman facing them. She drew on a long pipe and exhaled sweet smoke that drifted into a low-hanging cloud. Captain Gryst bowed, then sank to her knees, drawing some of the smoke down with her. Jorim likewise bowed, instinctively holding it long enough to convey great respect, then knelt a step behind and to the right of Captain Gryst.

The old woman smiled toothlessly. "I am pleased you have returned, Anaeda. Your absence has been mourned."

"It grieved me as well, Grandmother." Anaeda bowed her head again. "I came when word reached me that you wished to see me."

"Would that you thought to come sooner, for my home is yours. But the *Stormwolf* demands more attention than I do." The old woman pointed the pipe stem at Jorim. "He is not your bodyguard. Your lover, perhaps?"

"An associate, Grandmother."

The woman snorted smoke out her nose, then clamped the pipe firmly in teeth. "You will be more forthcoming, I know." She shifted a pillow and withdrew from it a bamboo case corked at each end. She opened one end and withdrew a scroll, which she spread out on the carpet. She used her bare feet to hold two corners down, leaving it to Anaeda and Jorim to secure the corners nearest them.

Jorim fought to conceal his reaction, but Anaeda did not. She gasped, then chuckled. "This is wonderful, Grandmother." She turned to Jorim. "What do you think?"

Jorim rubbed his free hand over his chin. The rice-paper scroll measured two feet by four and clearly depicted the southern reaches of the Principalities, stretching west to Aefret. Cartayne figured prominently at the center of the map; but from their voyage so far, he knew it to be shown about three hundred miles too far west. To the south of it, however, a string of islands curved gently east to the mythical Mountains of Ice at the bottom of the world. Those islands had appeared on no chart he'd ever seen, and one of them had a city indicated. The others all had fanciful images of strange people and creatures—as did the interior of Aefret over on the left side of the map. He suspected those were more decorative than informative, but he'd seen nothing like them before, and they intrigued him.

Of course, they're likely as much fable as the Mountains of Ice.

He glanced up at the old woman. "Where was this found?"

"It was drawn from voyages."

Jorim knew better than to contradict her. "It was drawn from many voyages. Voyages that took place many years apart."

Anaeda looked at him. "How do you know?"

He traced a finger along the coast of the continent to the north. "This is a fairly recent representation of the coast. It probably came from a Desei chart because of the shape of the bay right here in southern Ummummorar. Two hundred years ago a volcano's flow extended the left edge, making the harbor larger than it once was. The coast of Aefret came from a chart their navigators use."

He tapped Cartayne. "This placement of Cartayne in the center of the map is a thing the Soth did. The island is smaller than it should be. The Soth did that to show how unimportant it was in comparison to Virukadeen. They made maps that way to flatter their Viruk masters, so this part of the chart is thousands of years old. Now, the question is, did this archipelago appear on the Soth map, or have others actually sailed south to the Mountains of Ice?"

The old woman cackled and her eyes shone. "Take him as your lover, Anaeda. Bear his children, for they shall be quick of mind."

"It is something I shall consider, Grandmother. Now, what of his question?"

The old woman pulled her feet back in and hugged her knees to her chest. The map's upper edge rolled in as she sucked on her pipe. Smoke drifted from her mouth, hiding her face for a moment, then she nodded. "I believe it was drawn from an old chart."

Jorim kept his voice low. "Do you have that map?"

The old woman canted her head and closed her eyes. The dark hollow in the bowl of her pipe brightened to a cherry red. "I believe the original could be found. What would you offer for it?"

Anaeda needn't have glanced at him, for Jorim was not going to answer even though he had a thousand thoughts of what he could give her. The captain bowed low, pressed her forehead to the map, and spoke in something barely above a whisper. "Our offering would be meager. As your chart might be of aid, so we could provide you with a similar chart. South and east there is another harbor. We have a chart of it that would let ships navigate even at night. A place where it is believed no goods could come ashore would now be open to you."

Jorim watched the old woman but caught no hint of how she took that offer. It hardly surprised him that she might have connections to smugglers, for even the composite map she had shown them would be invaluable to all sorts of people. But the offer suggested she might benefit more directly from smuggling operations.

Finally, the old woman nodded. "That will be acceptable, Anaeda."

Captain Gryst straightened up. "You are most kind, Grandmother."

"I am, child, but it pleases me to be so with you." The old woman turned to look Jorim full in the face. "You have something else you would ask of me?"

"Yes, Grandmother. Where did you find the map?"

She smiled. "There are many places on this island where the Viruk once lived. In one of them, on a wall, the world known at the time was painted. Much of the paint has been destroyed by lichen and molds, but that bit remained. I will have you taken there and you can make your own copy."

Jorim bowed low. "Your generosity leaves me in your debt."

"I accept that debt, Anturasi." The old woman laughed. "Yes, I know who you are, which is why I make that offer to you. Only an Anturasi who has slain Viruk would dare enter one of their ruins. If your heart does not fail you, that map and perhaps more will be yours."

Chapter Twenty-nine

20th day, Month of the Dog, Year of the Dog
9th Year of Imperial Prince Cyron's Court
162nd Year of the Komyr Dynasty
736th year since the Cataclysm
Asath
Nalenyr

Keles snapped out of his trance as Tyressa jerked him to his feet. She planted a kiss firmly on his lips, sending a jolt through him and leaving him disoriented and surprised. Then she pulled her mouth from his, breaking the kiss loudly, and embraced him tightly with her left arm around his shoulders.

Her voice sounded strongly above the laughter of those assembled in the inn's common room. "Enough of these river men. I am homesick. You're coming with me."

More hoots and calls accompanied them as she steered him toward the rough-hewn stairs leading up to the room they'd taken. She tightened her embrace against any attempt he might make to slip away and, reflexively, he wrapped his right arm around her waist. In an instant he knew his brother, in keeping with whatever deception Tyressa had deemed necessary, would have dropped a hand to one of her firm, round cheeks, but he could not. *I like my arm in one piece.*

He shook his head, clearing the last of the fog, and tried to imagine what had prompted her action. He'd seen nothing, but then he'd taken the opportunity to slip inside himself to send a message to his grandfather. The *Catfish* had come up the river as quickly as possible, but had been delayed by storms that washed debris into the river. When they continued, they reached Asath, which was at the lower end of a stretch of the river where glacial deposits made it impassable. Cargoes were off-loaded there and transported overland to Urisoti to continue the journey to the port of Gria.

They had arrived in midafternoon, and Keles immediately noticed that the work clearing and dredging the river was nowhere near as complete as had been reported to Moriande. He'd read the various reports and saw that the situation was little changed from when he was last there. The money set aside for the project was being squandered. Communicating the true state of affairs was vital and would only take a moment.

He'd slipped into the trance he used to reach Qiro easily and found his grandfather awake. He got a sense of things back through the link that he'd not experienced before. Impressions from his grandfather had always been strong, and while he expected ire, he got little of it. The sensations were vague and made him uneasy, but Keles could not determine why. Regardless of that, he did manage to convey the information before Tyressa had so rudely brought him back to Asath.

She said nothing even as she propelled him through the door to their room. He caught himself on the end of the bed, then cried out as his right knee slammed into the footboard. "What is the mea—"

Tyressa spun him around and clapped a hand over his mouth. Her whisper came harsh and strained. "Keep your voice down and gather your stuff. We're leaving."

He jerked his mouth from beneath her hand, but did keep his voice low. "What is it?"

"It was *you*." She released him, then gathered her baggage, which consisted of an overstuffed backpack and bedroll beneath it, a sling pouch and her sword belt. "I think your fading was taken as drifting off to sleep. Not too suspicious, though it *is* a bit early. If they didn't think you were sleeping, they might have figured out who you are."

He rubbed at his knee, then gathered up his pack, bow, and quiver then belted on his knife. "What are you talking about?"

"Four men. Two local, two from the ship. They affected not to see us. But they worked too hard at not seeing us."

Another jolt ran through Keles, one altogether different from what he felt when she kissed him. "Desei agents?"

"Perhaps. It's well-known that all river traffic stops here and goes overland to Urisoti. It would make sense to have watchers here." She crossed to the room's window and opened the shutters. "Out you go. Be careful. Drop to the street. We'll go to the livery and get horses. We'll travel tonight and steal a march on the rest of the *Catfish* company."

He frowned. "Wouldn't it be safer traveling with others?"

"Not when those others are out to get you."

"Good point." Keles limped over to the window and climbed out. He crouched without her telling him and crept along the tiled awning to the back of the building. He lowered himself, then dropped to the ground and fell back firmly on his tailbone.

Any embarrassment he might have felt at being so clumsy vanished as a four-pointed throwing star whizzed through the night and stuck, quivering, in the side of the inn. He rolled and came to his feet, then jumped away as a small man slashed at him with a dagger. Keles bumped into the post supporting the awning and tried to cut to the left, but a nail in the post caught on his pack and held him firmly.

The knife wielder's smile vanished as Tyressa leaped from above and smashed both booted feet into his face. He flew back, hitting the street hard; his knife sailed into the darkness. She landed in a crouch and came up quickly. She shifted her sword from right hand to left, then yanked Keles free of the nail.

"Run."

He took off down the alley toward the livery stable. There was no mistaking his direction; his training and blood had already let him assemble a map of Asath. Though his previous visit hadn't brought him to that part of town, his journey through it earlier had locked the details in place. Three more alleys down, then turn left and on two more blocks.

Behind him came sounds of fighting, with the occasional clash of steel on steel. He listened for the sound of Tyressa crying out, or the whirring of more throwing stars, but he heard nothing of the sort. As the din of combat grew, he was tempted to turn and string his bow, but he knew he'd be more of a hindrance than help in the dark.

He cut around the corner and the alley widened into a street. Directly ahead of him, a block and a half down, two men stood in the middle of the street. Ruffians, knives drawn or swords slipping from scabbards, bled into the street between the pair and Keles. He stopped and turned, but saw more men behind him. Tyressa had inflicted enough damage to keep those chasing her at a respectful distance, but they still came on.

She looked at him imploringly and waved him on, but then she turned the corner and realized why he'd stopped. She immediately dropped to one knee to catch her breath, then flicked her sword out to bat away a throwing star.

One of the men who had been chasing her took a step forward. "We are not required to kill you."

Tyressa stood again. "You'll get past me no other way."

The man shrugged. "Kill her. Take his legs."

The dozen ruffians began to tighten their circle. Tyressa closed with Keles. "Get ready to run again. We're going at the stables. Now! Go!"

The two of them started to sprint. Her longer legs gained her a slight lead. The brigands between them and the stable moved to oppose her. With a backhanded slash, she battered one man's sword aside and crushed his skull. She punched another man in the face, dropping him, but there was no way she could win through, especially not with the two men coming to reinforce the ones trying to stop her. The duo came with swords drawn and moved with precision their comrades lacked.

Striding forward boldly, the younger of the pair whipped his sword forward, cutting down one of the footpads. Another of them turned to oppose him, but the man struck so quickly his thrust punctured his foe's chest and withdrew even before his victim completed his turn. A parry and slash killed a third man and, suddenly, the way to the stable stood clear.

Keles darted through the opening and Tyressa joined him. The two of them turned to see the swordsmen moving to cut off pursuit. The elder swordsman turned to his companion and spoke quietly. "You did well, Ciras. Guide them to the stables."

The ruffians' leader came to the fore and spared only a brief glance for his wounded and dying confederates. "You are meddling in affairs not your own."

The swordsman smiled. "Then you know my affairs?"

"Well, no, but . . ." The head ruffian frowned. "Get out of my way or I shall be forced to kill you."

"It would seem, then, that our intentions coincide." The swordsman nodded, then slid a foot forward and set himself. "Ciras, you should be much closer to the stables than you are now."

"Yes, Master." Ciras tugged at Keles' shoulder. "My Master bid me to get you to the stables. Let us go."

"We can't just leave him alone. There are seven of them, eight." Keles shook his head. "Seven. That one went down again."

"There could be nine, or nine times nine. Come, we have to get clear."

Keles backed away along the street with Ciras, and Tyressa came as well, though as reluctantly as he did. The ruffians began to gather into a tight pack, preparing to rush the lone man opposing them. Many of them were larger than he was, and almost all were as well armed. Men wiped moist hands on their overshirts, then tightened grips on their swords' hilts. Some shifted and advanced in a formal guard, while others just hunched forward and snarled. Onward they came, inch by inch, a mob ready to destroy the man in front of them. Having drawn to within two paces, the leader screamed an inarticulate war cry, and the human storm broke on the single swordsman.

The ruffians came at their protector in a tight crescent. The two men at each end shot out and past, coming for the retreating trio. The five who remained came on as a solid wall—all muscle, steel, and snarls. Keles watched without wanting to, utterly certain that Ciras' Master would soon be dead.

The swordsman twisted to his right and moved ghostlike through the line of men opposing him. Their blades flashed in the moonlight, and in such close quarters, it seemed impossible they did not strike him. Eerily, no ringing of sword on sword sounded, and war cries swallowed the sound of footsteps in the street.

Then one of the war cries curdled into a whimper. The sound's shift mirrored the way the group's leader curled around a slit belly and fell. The swordsman emerged at the back of the crescent with the leader's sword in his other hand, then planted a foot and spun back instantly. Two quick slashes cut down the central pair of swordsmen as they turned to face him. Their blades flew as they reeled away, throat and chest opened respectively.

As their bodies thrashed on the ground, the quintet's last two fighters turned back to oppose him. The man on the right lunged, but the swordmaster slipped past the quivering blade effortlessly. A quick cut opened that man from groin to breastbone. A return slash took his head in time to silence his scream, but without erasing the expression of horror on his face.

The last man assumed a stance that betrayed some training. He stamped his forward foot and feinted a lunge. Then he pulled back, recovering from his feint, pulling his blade up to protect him from waist to crown. Sparks flew as he blocked a forehand slash. He even began to smile as the swordmaster whipped his right arm forward in a repetition of that attack. He moved to block again.

The swordmaster's second blade came around and down behind the block, severing the man's hands. Blood spurted as the sword dropped, then a third slash neatly cut the man's throat. Gurgling a sigh, the man slumped to the ground.

The last two men had slowed their charge as Tyressa and Ciras had moved to oppose them. With their comrades' deaths, their attack faltered entirely. As if sharing a mind, each chose to bolt for the safety of shadows, one going left, the other right. They ran as if the demons of the fifth Hell pursued them.

Only what pursued them was worse.

The swordsman dashed to his left and slashed, sending that man spinning to the dust with a split spine. Without pause, he whirled and threw his acquired sword. It spun in a flat arc and caught the last man in the legs. It tangled there, not cutting him, but tripping him up. He smashed face-first into a building and rebounded to flop loose-limbed in the mouth of an alley.

Without saying a word, the swordmaster drew a small knife and slit the throats of the last two men. He squatted and cleaned his blades on the tunic of the man he'd tripped, then approached them with his blades still bared. He stopped ten feet from them and bowed, both deeply and long. "You will please forgive my haste and resulting sloppiness."

Keles, utterly disbelieving what he had just seen, returned the bow. He would have matched that of the swordsman in duration, but Tyressa remained down longer, and he took his cue from her. He had the impression she would have held it for yet longer, but lingering in the corpse-littered street was not a good idea.

As they straightened up, the swordsman sheathed his weapons. "I am Moraven Tolo. This is my companion, Ciras Dejote. We do not need your names. Speaking them here would not be a good idea just now."

Keles opened his mouth, closed it, then shifted his shoulders uneasily. "How did you find us?"

"Prince Cyron arranged for us to accompany you to Ixyll. I believe, Tyressa, you have instructions from the Prince that were only to be opened in Gria?"

Tyressa nodded. "I was given such a packet."

"It contains a letter of introduction for us. We had planned to reveal ourselves to you there, but circumstances intervened."

"I understand and thank you." The Keru slid her own sword into its scabbard. "I suspected the Prince would send others."

Keles frowned. "You did? Why didn't you tell me?"

She ignored him. "Were you on the *Catfish*?"

Moraven pointed to the stables. "There will be time on the road to explain. We should hurry."

The four of them trotted to the stables. Tyressa and Keles waited while Moraven and Ciras picked out their horses. Part of the money paid to rent the horses would be returned to them in Urisoti when they left the horses with the agent there. The fees were more than the animals and tack were actually worth, so any incentive to steal them vanished.

The swordsmen had chosen well and obtained two horses for each of them. That would allow them to move fast and complete the trip in less than the five days it normally took. Keles fastened his pack to the rear of his saddle, then mounted up and joined the others.

No one said much until they were well out of Asath, which was when Tyressa repeated her question about the riverboat.

Moraven nodded. "We were."

"I didn't see you."

"You remember a young priest conducting his maiden aunt back to Gria? She had loudly exclaimed about the wonders of Festival?"

Keles blinked. He remembered the lady well, for her voice penetrated bulkheads as if they were rice paper and she repeated each story at least a dozen times. Even the actor pretending to be him grew terse with her. She had been fat and slow, complaining of gout and other maladies which, according to her, could be cured only through taking the waters in some hot mineral spring high in the mountains southeast of Gria.

"That was you?"

The swordsman smiled. "It was. Ciras was the silent, suffering priest."

Tyressa turned to look at Ciras, then back to Moraven. "If you were in disguise on the boat, why drop it in Asath?"

Ciras answered. "My Master charged me with the duty of listening to all but himself. There were two men on the *Catfish* from Asath, and they watched Keles Anturasi very closely. We were not certain why, but then when the ship docked, an official delegation met Keles and took him off to Lord-Mayor Yiritar's house to stay. We suppose that the actor did something there to let the mayor penetrate the deception."

"It wasn't what he did, but what he didn't do."

Keles hoped the darkness hid his blush. "When I was here before, I lost a bet with the Lord-Mayor. He cheated, and we both knew it, so I promised him a dozen bottles of the best brandy Moriande had to offer. I told him I would deliver it myself, and we both knew I was lying since I would never return. I'd never mentioned the incident, and had quite forgotten it. My double would not have known and likely did not respond correctly."

Tyressa shook her head. "But why send people out looking for us?"

Moraven shifted in the saddle. "The Lord-Mayor, knowing he was deceived, looked for everyone from the *Catfish*. He wanted to determine if the Prince had sent spies upriver. He may have even supposed, when he learned the actor was not you, that you were the spy."

Keles nodded. "Who better to determine that he's been taking the Prince's money and doing none of the work required? Of course, if he did, the river would be clear and his town would cease to exist."

The elder swordsman nodded. "That makes perfect sense. Thank you for solving that riddle."

"My pleasure. If you would not mind, you could solve one for me."

"Yes?"

"Can you tell me what is in the sealed orders Tyressa is carrying?"

"I do not know. I know what I believe they say, but it is speculation."

Keles smiled. "Go ahead, speculate."

Moraven shook his head slowly. "No, I think not. There may be many dangers between here and Gria. To speculate would distract us. What the Prince means us to know will be revealed when we reach Gria."

"What if we don't get that far?"

"Then whatever he would have tasked us with is immaterial, isn't it, Master Anturasi?" Moraven laughed quickly. "Let us get to Gria and prove ourselves worthy of the Prince's command."

Chapter Thirty

27th day, Month of the Dog, Year of the Dog
9th Year of Imperial Prince Cyron's Court
162nd Year of the Komyr Dynasty
736th year since the Cataclysm
Thyrenkun, Felarati
Deseirion

Prince Pyrust pulled his black cloak more tightly around himself and snarled. A glance in a looking glass reminded him that he now appeared very much like the model for the toy soldier of himself the Naleni had created. While his spymaster had told him he was not being played, and that it was good for Prince Cyron to underestimate him, being seen as a child's amusement rankled.

It was not this alone that consumed him or made his thoughts as dark as his capital city. Upon his return he had called his chief ministers to him and demanded a full and forthright accounting of the harvest. They were hesitant—so much so he had to explain that while the sons and daughters of Deseirion would continue to enter the bureaucracy, *their* sons and daughters might not be among them. He did not elaborate, letting each man's fears spur him on to action.

The full report had been even more dire than Prince Cyron had suggested. While Pyrust was forced to assume that the harvest had been underreported, even a generous estimate of supplies would have his people eating rice they needed to be sprouting and planting next spring. There was no way all of his people would survive without Naleni rice.

The ministers had even estimated a die-off of five to ten percent of the population. They did allow as how it would mostly be the old and the very young, but they cast that in the form of a tragedy. Even Cyron had seen it that way when he noted that Pyrust would not starve, but his people would.

The Desei Prince chuckled, for neither his neighbor to his south nor even the Desei bureaucrats understood the true joy of power and how it could be employed. If he deemed it necessary, he could keep the children alive, and even the ancient ones. He would simply order that food be given to them preferentially, and that if a child or elder died of malnutrition, their families would be slain, their goods divided and their ancestors' bones scattered. He need not even carry out such a threat, but just spread the story of one or two places where it happened, and gossips would carry it far and wide. Overnight the reports would universally be attributed to a village or town a valley or two away, and everyone would toe the line lest their village be hit next.

The thing of it was, however, Pyrust saw no difficulty in carrying out his order. He could simply select a perfectly innocent family or two, accuse them of having a child die of malnutrition, and destroy them. Aside from being a superior means of eliminating local political troublemakers, a single true act was better than a hundred manufactured stories.

Still, the loss of five or even ten percent of his population, provided it was from the unproductive margins of society, seemed more of a blessing than a tragedy. His people were a herd that had overgrazed their range. A die-off was inevitable, and it would be the weak who died. Those who survived would be stronger, and would not be bothered with needing to care for the weak. The whole ordeal would make his nation stronger.

While he was fully prepared to accept this purge of his people, he resisted it for one simple reason—he loathed situations that were forced upon him, by man or the gods. If he could find a way to defy either, it pleased him. Immediately upon his return to Felarati, he had put into place several plans that did begin to make a difference, both for the short term and longer.

Delasonsa's suggestion about making one military unit into two, and using the other to train villagers into militia units had begun in earnest. Pyrust had ordered villages to provide warriors for service in a local militia. He would feed those who joined, as well as provide extra *quor* of rice for the villages from whence they came. Those shipments would, of course, be delayed so the villages, which now had fewer mouths to feed, would eat off supplies that should have been made available to the Crown. The soldiers would be fed from the Naleni grain. Not only was there irony to that, but the golden rice from the south provided more nutrition than that grown locally.

He would allow the militias a month's training, then put them to work in the second part of his plan. In response to hard times and tight markets, a system of smuggling and tax avoidance always sprang up. He would move the militia into the bigger cities and use them to hunt down and destroy the criminal element. They would liberate great stores of hoarded grain, some of which they would be allowed to convey back home, giving the militias combat experience as well as the joy of entering their villages as heroes. They would be lauded as having performed a service for the Crown, which would make them see themselves as part of the state. Once they began to identify with him and the nation, they would be his to use.

Reports from the training fields suggested that perhaps as many as one in five of the recruits might be talented enough to be trained as a warrior. This hardly surprised him, both because levies were regularly called up and those who survived battle with little or no training must have had some minor talent to begin with. As well, the tools used in cutting and threshing were, in essence, swords and flails. A farmer's normal activities honed skills that were translatable into something Pyrust would find more useful. If the recruits accepted the call to further training, he paid a bonus to their families, the village and the village's headman, which helped all of them to convince young men and women to accept the honor of further training.

Most recently, his ministers reported Naleni displeasure with his troops' continuing attacks within Helosunde. The protests had come through the lowest diplomatic levels because the Mountain Hawks' attacks had all been in response to Helosundian raids. Because those raids had been easy enough to provoke, and his response to them had been fierce, neither Cyron nor his people were fooled. Still, he felt fairly certain that as much as he was being admonished to stop all operations, so were the Helosundians, and that served his purposes as well.

Pyrust closed his half hand over his goatee and tugged on it unconsciously. There had been threats that rice shipments would be delayed or stopped, as Delasonsa had predicted, but Pyrust knew he could not withdraw all pressure from Helosunde. Cyron himself had said that he would willingly toss food to a wolf to keep him away from the door. *If I do not show him fang, he will forget I am a wolf.*

The Desei Prince crossed the creaking cedar floor, slid open the door to his tower's southern balcony, and passed out into the dusk. Already, Fryl—the large, white owl-moon—had begun to rise from the sea. Its light revealed jagged silhouettes of the city's rooftops.

Fog had risen to nibble at the wharves in Swellside. A thick tentacle stole its way up the sluggish Black River, while other small feelers filled streets and alleys. Yellow lights burned in windows and atop streetlamps, but the mist soon muted them. Only the *gyanri* lights on the largest trio of bridges over the river held the fog at bay. They glowed like sapphires, and the pattern in which they had been arranged revealed to him the constellation Shiri—the hawk.

Pyrust's hands emerged from beneath his cloak as he leaned on the stone balustrade. Black stone had been used to shape the tower, for it hid the dirt and grime of the city. Likewise it contrasted sharply with the white towers of Moriande, mocking them. Felarati defied and challenged Moriande, as it had for ages, though seldom had the south felt any real threat.

Deseirion had always been a frontier province in the Empire. Its only worth, initially, had been as a place to stage troops to slow down barbarians. The early Emperors had created a string of fortresses to garrison troops, and slowly towns had grown up around them. Felarati had been the largest of these and the most vital, since supplies passed through it, up the Black River and its tributaries to the other fortresses.

A plague among the Turasynd killed enough of them to minimize their power for several centuries before the Time of Black Ice. Imperial interest in Deseirion waned as peace and prosperity waxed. Imperial support withered, but instead of retreat, the bold souls who had come to make Deseirion their home decided to stay. Prospectors found deposits of iron, copper, tin, and coal. The mineral wealth gave rise to foundries, with iron, bronze, and steel flowing south in return for gold and rice. Existence in Deseirion was not soft as it was in the south, but the Desei reveled in it.

The Emperors and other nobles also used Deseirion as a dumping place for obstreperous offspring and rebel generals. The Desei took these outcasts to their hearts, training them and molding them to survive in the unforgiving north. The people of the frontier knew they needed to be more united than the decadent provinces to the south. If they were not the strongest and purest of the Imperial people, the barbarians would come through and destroy the Empire.

When the Empress left to fight the Turasynd, leading them into Ixyll, she drew her last troops from the Desei. She gave control of the province to a small but clever man who kept Desei from Helosundian conquest by constant reports of pitched battles in which his people were the only thing that stopped hordes from pouring over the Black River. Though these battles were as mythical as the Mountains of Ice, his Helosundian counterpart—a cousin who was a grand warrior but stupid enough that he had trouble discerning day from night—prepared his nation for invasion and never furthered his ambition.

And when the Cataclysm came, it wiped out ambition along with much of the population. Since that time, Deseirion had changed dynasties every ninety to hundred and twenty years. As always, the perception in the outlying areas was that city life had softened the Prince into a southerner. Pyrust's father knew that this fate would destroy his dynasty, so he launched the attack on Helosunde. Not only did the successful invasion make pride burn hotter and deeper in the hearts of his countrymen, but being constantly caught between Turasynd and Helosundian threats meant they had little time to think about weakness in Felarati.

Pyrust chuckled and looked at his maimed hand, corpse-white against the cold, black stone. Those missing fingers had proven how hard he could be. While the hawk remained the symbol of Deseirion, his personal flags had two feathers clipped from the hawk's left wing. Four of his best units claimed to have his finger bones in their headquarters, where they were revered and worshiped much as the bones of great warriors were.

Felarati, the Dark City, spread out before him. Factories and forges belched black clouds full of red sparks into the air. Their foul stink permeated everything, muting even the finest of scents from the south. It poisoned the air, tainted the food, and soured the wine. It tainted the snow that fell, and made the Black River even darker as it entered the sea.

Pyrust saw no virtue in this state of his city, but neither did he see a way to get away from it. Out there in the factories, *gyanridin* worked on their inventions. Perhaps one of a hundred *gyanrigot* devices would actually work, and one of a hundred of those might be useful. He had reviewed plans for everything from riverboats that would row themselves to giant tripod figures that could carry troops, batter down city walls, and resist every attack. Neither of those plans had come to fruition yet, but they would.

If I can afford to continue financing them. Deseirion had spirit the way Nalenyr had gold, but it did not spend as easily or go as far. He had plenty of people traveling to the west to bring back *thaumston* to power the devices, but the west was not kind, and the supplies returning to the capital were both scant and costly.

The Prince caught the scrape of boot on stone and knew it well. He also knew he'd not have heard it, save that Delasonsa wished to announce her presence. He did not turn to face her but shifted to lean on his elbows. "What do you have for me, Mother of Shadows?"

The crone remained in her hooded cloak and back in the dim recesses of the doorway. "Many things, my Prince. Our whispering campaign among the Helosundians is working. They believe you will be forced to draw your troops back, and they are massing to punish you. They wish to celebrate the New Year's Festival in Meleswin. They will attack and slaughter anyone we leave behind, then sack the city."

"This is very good to know. This gives us two months to train more soldiers and organize its reconquest. I will lead the counterattack. I want you to determine who will be leading the Helosundians into Meleswin. On the eve of our attack, I will want the more popular of the leaders murdered, with blame falling to one of the others. I want them at each other's throats. You'll also make certain that the stores of *wyrlu* and rice beer are quite potent, so their troops will not be."

"Of course, my lord." She paused, drawing in a wheezing breath.

"I could arrange a plague as well, or a fungus in grain to drive them mad."

"No, it must be their own folly and factional disarray that allows us to smash them. It will weaken their alliances. And it needs to be a military victory, else Cyron will forget we are wolves."

"Yes, Highness. I have also had word of Keles Anturasi. He reached Asath and is bound for Gria. His party is quite visible and moving slowly."

"A deception."

"Unquestionably. At the same time he arrived, the local authorities lost a dozen or so men in a midnight battle. Four passengers did not continue to travel with the others from their riverboat. Two pairs. Keles and a Keru traveling as Helosundians, or Keles and a *xidantzu* traveling as a priest and his dowager aunt. We have lost track of them, but should find them again in Gria."

Pyrust nodded. "If Keles slipped away from his decoy, then he has no way to communicate with Moriande, save through his grandfather."

"And transmission of information that way is limited, and there is no telling how much Qiro will pass to the Prince. Were Keles to pass messages through agents on the river, we would know, Highness. He has not done this so far."

"Good. This means Cyron does not know precisely what his circumstance is, so cannot send support. That he is placing so valuable a person in jeopardy is curious, which means the gain he perceives is worth the risk."

The Desei Prince turned. "Dispatch a group of your finest operatives. I want Keles Anturasi alive and here in Felarati within the year."

"This is not what you wished for before."

"I know, but I need to have him more than just beholden to me. I wish him in my grasp. If the *Stormwolf* is successful in its mission and Keles can be ransomed for those charts, it will mean more to us than his willing cooperation. Moreover, the longer he spends with us, the more he will come to like us. He may never wish to leave."

"As you wish, my lord." Her voice lightened slightly. "Do you wish me to conduct a survey of the comeliest daughters of your nobility and find a half dozen to tend him and steal his heart?"

"That will do nicely, but only as a fallback plan." Pyrust smiled slowly. "Once I have him here I will show him that he can do more for us than his grandfather can do for Nalenyr. His grandfather is great, but I shall make him greater. Flattery, greed, and lust are the three weapons we shall use, and he *will* be won to our cause. That, or there will be one less Anturasi to plague me."

Chapter Thirty-one

36th day, Month of the Dog, Year of the Dog
9th Year of Imperial Prince Cyron's Court
162nd Year of the Komyr Dynasty
736th year since the Cataclysm
Stormwolf, Archurko
Ethgi

Jorim Anturasi watched as sailors in one of the *Stormwolf*'s boats pulled hard for the ship. As seen from the ship, the landing party and villagers met peacefully. However, the urgency with which the sailors returned suggested something unusual. The same breeze coming in from the ocean had prevented him from hearing anything said on the island, and would likewise have stolen the sailors' words, so they just rowed strongly.

The day after he'd been shown the copied chart at Nysant, he had been taken out to the site where the original drawing had appeared. His guide knew the way through the verdant rain forest intimately, and Jorim had a sneaking suspicion the fellow made his living searching out and looting old Viruk ruins. Several hundred years back there had been a strong market for such things in Erumvirine, but tastes had shifted away more recently. Still, the odd pieces often had magical powers attributed to them, despite all evidence to the contrary.

The last leg of the trek involved slithering through ruins until he came to a chamber that had survived the eons relatively intact. His guide, a slender, swarthy fellow with a nose which was much too large for his face, held a torch as Jorim studied the wall map. The chart he'd seen had just been an outline of the drawing, and not rendered terribly accurately, whereas the original had been painted as a mural in rich blues. Mildew had eaten away at the edges, but something in the white paint used to depict the Mountains of Ice resisted it. The chain of islands, likewise rendered in white, stood out against the blue of the ocean.

Jorim studied it carefully, then made a detailed drawing. He affected mild disinterest to counter his guide's growing enthusiasm. Retaining his composure was not easy, however, as things that had been poorly rendered on the chart still retained their clarity on the wall, and he had worked hard to re-create them accurately on his drawing. What the other chart maker had taken as lines to indicate mountains or squiggles that were rivers were in fact Soth symbols for Viruk words, and Jorim knew them well.

The island of Ethgi, off which they were anchored, had been the largest in the chain on the original chart and the only one to have indications of a settlement. On that chart it appeared to have mountains that ringed a bay. The mural showed something different—a flat atoll with a circular reef. The Soth symbol that had been taken for hastily drawn mountains really represented the old Viruk word *eshjii*. For the Viruk it meant the island was home to demons and a place to be avoided at all costs.

Sailing down to it had been relatively uneventful, save that breezes came only lightly. Captain Gryst exercised her crew endlessly, drilling them on raising and lowering sails, clearing the decks for battle, and conducting a host of minor repairs. She forbade Jorim from even using the word "demon" and from trying to explain to the sailors what they might face at Ethgi—no matter that the name they were using for it was the more recent pronunciation of the Viruk word.

What *eshjii* truly meant in the Viruk tongue was Fennych. In all his travels Jorim had never seen more than one or two, and that was good. Singly or in pairs, the Fennych could be intelligent, amusing, even charming—displaying skills at games, singing, dancing, and even small contests of strength or dexterity. They often featured as comical characters in the stories of heroes, and Men tended to look upon their appearance as a good sign.

For the Viruk, the Fenn were not comical. Though the tallest reached no more than three feet in height, their burly bodies boasted disproportionate strength. In their most humanoid form they had sharp teeth, keen-bladed retractable claws, acute vision and hearing, and a short bristle of hair on their heads, usually grey, with dark black stripes or spots running through it. The Fenn had the ability, however, to change shape into a variety of small and medium-sized animals—never quite looking like a dog, wolf, mountain cat, bear, or badger, but a mongrel mix of any two. More importantly to the Viruk, they had an insatiable taste for Viruk flesh, a hardiness that made killing them very difficult, and when in a pack they became feral, vicious, and all but unstoppable. While they would gladly burrow into graves to eat the dead, they were not beyond coursing and killing live prey—and it mattered not to them if it were male, female, adult, or child.

Jorim had little doubt, given the animosity between Men and Viruk, why Fennych were seen favorably by Men. When they got into a pack and changed to their more bestial forms, any affection they might have had for humanity also vanished. They just became part of a voracious horde that could chew a swath through a forest, devouring anything that couldn't get out of their way, be it plant, animal, or anything else.

The boat reached the *Stormwolf* and Lieutenant Geressa Toron came up on to the wheel deck to report to Captain Gryst. Though Anaeda's opposite in size and coloration, the two of them shared a devotion to the ship and the sea that made them seem more alike than not. Geressa glanced at Jorim as if she expected him to leave, but Anaeda shook her head.

"Report, Lieutenant. Master Anturasi has an interest in this."

The slender woman nodded, the sunlight flashing gold highlights into her light brown hair. "We were greeted warmly by the people, who are all half-starved. Most of them are fisherfolk who cast their nets outside the bay, but never beyond sight of the island. Others raise some crops at the edge of the jungle. They clear an area, farm until it produces no more, then clear another. They offer food and fish to the forest spirits. The last several years, the island and seas have produced a bounty, but this year they did not. Their fishing grounds yielded nothing, and the gardens did not get enough rain.

And now they say the forest spirits are angry and have killed people who have tried to clear more land.

"We were greeted warmly because the last time this cycle took place—I can't tell how long ago, but the oldest person there claimed to be a hundred and three, and it was before she was born—a priest prophesied that in the next time of terror, a ship would arrive to carry them away. They believe the *Stormwolf* is that ship."

Anaeda walked to the rail and stared at the island. "How many did they say they were?"

"Five hundred, but I think they were lying. I saw few children and fewer women of childbearing age."

Anaeda looked at Jorim. "What do you think?"

"I suspect the good years meant the Fennych population grew swiftly. If this is a cycle, they've been through it before. If the Fenn attack in a pack, the settlement could be wiped out." Jorim sighed. "Even if their reported numbers are correct, it's not a group the fleet can absorb. Malnourished, and not having any education or abilities beyond basic survival skills, means their chances elsewhere in the world would be small."

The captain raised an eyebrow. "Are you suggesting we just let them die?"

"I'm suggesting nothing of the sort, but we can't let a mythical prophecy create an obligation. If you think about it, Captain, the people there had to have sailed here—either by themselves or in the holds of Viruk ships. They know they can sail away, but they've not tried it. We're a week and a half out of Nysant under calm winds. They could have saved themselves already if they wanted to. Instead, they are waiting to be saved, and had we not chanced on this voyage and that chart, we'd never have come here."

Anaeda smiled slowly. "Your point is well-taken, but it does not solve the problem they face. We can't take them with us, nor can we send them north to Nysant on one of our tenders. If we did take them aboard, the crew would view them as bad omens. Worse yet, they might have diseases and, at the very least, would eat far more than we can spare. To leave them behind, however, would have the crew blaming any evil that befell us on their spirits. I need something I can do to help them. Have you a suggestion?"

Jorim nodded. "I do. I've never seen a Fenn pack in full rampage, but villages in Ummummorar tell stories of how they manage to keep the Fenn at bay. We'll use up some of our supplies, but I think the crew will understand."

He glanced at the sky. "We have enough time before dusk to make the plan work. Captain, if you'll order the *Seawolf* in to Ethgi's harbor, we'll have the problem solved in no time."

Jorim waited with a contingent of soldiers from the *Stormwolf* at the inland edges of Archurko. The settlement was little more than a collection of mud huts and longhouses built from native bamboo. The town had dug a trench and raised a breastwork long in the past, though new slivers of sharpened bamboo had been set in place. It would not have been enough to even slow the Fennych, since many could leap to the top of the mound with ease, but the wall's fierce appearance gave people heart.

He'd been overjoyed when Captain Gryst gave him leave to accompany the expeditionary force onto the island. While the soldiers and sailors went about their duty, he spoke with the village elders to learn more about the settlement's history. It did not surprise him that the headman also served as a priest of Quun, the Bear. Followers of that god valued steadfastness and continuity above all else, so would easily see themselves bound by traditions and as part of cycles.

Several things *did* surprise him, however. He asked for and was given samples of the fish they caught. He easily recognized them, but there were far fewer species than he would have expected. The total of varieties he saw available were a third of those sold in Nysant and when he asked why other fish were not eaten, his questions were answered with a simple, "It is against our way."

As he spoke to more people he discovered many things that were counter to their "way." Sailing beyond sight of the island was a violation of religious law. The manufacture and consumption of alcoholic beverages was similarly banned. Religious laws proscribed many things, narrowly focusing their lives on things that were important and would allow them to survive.

Jorim slowly began to form a picture in his mind of what must have happened down through the eons. The small settlement looked to its religious leaders for direction during times of crises. A priest, or a series of them, outlawed one thing and another. It could have been that during a particularly poor year for grain, he forbade brewing. Conversely a celebration where men drank to excess and started fighting might have resulted in the same ban. Similarly, cases of food poisoning linked to one type of fish might have resulted in its banning, and the fear of ships being lost in a storm when too far from the village might have caused the laws about that to be born.

Instead of expanding and growing as a society should, this one contracted. The whole idea of a society shrinking sent a chill down his spine. His entire life, his family's vocation was dedicated to *expanding* society and its horizons. Removing the people from Ethgi would not only be logistically impossible, it would destroy them. Nysant would be seen as a pit of vice and depravity—and he wasn't sure he disagreed wholly with that—and the Ethgisti would flee back to their island as fast as they could.

Darkness had fallen and silence stolen in save for the crackling of torch flames and the flutter of bats' wings in the night. All the soldiers remained still, their eyes and ears straining. The breeze easily carried their scent into the jungle, but it also carried another scent. And that scent drew the Fennych as fire draws insects.

The soldiers and sailors had not been happy when cask after cask of rice beer had been loaded into boats and rowed to shore. The villagers carried it through Archurko and to the forest edge, where the casks were buried to within a foot of their tops, then broken open. Jorim had no idea how many Fenn there might be, so he'd had twenty casks shipped out, and the expedition's personnel mourned each one as if it were a sweetheart.

He had hoped rice beer would work, for in Ummummorar a variety of fruits and roots were mashed up and allowed to ferment in preparation for what was known to be prime Fennych season. When it passed without danger, the villagers consumed the mixture in an orgy of drunken joy. If danger did present itself, the potent liquor was poured into troughs made from split and hollowed logs.

True to the Ummummoraran tales, the island Fennych approached the alcohol cautiously. Jorim could barely make out the single individual crawling forward to reach the first cask. About the size of a small bear, but with a long tail and tufted ears, it dipped a paw into the rice beer, then licked. It growled, then tried a bit more, before grabbing the edge of the cask with both paws and plunging its head fully into it.

In less time than it took for bubbles to rise from the first Fennych's splash, others poured from the forest and went for the beer. Some dived in and splashed, others crowded around, muzzles sunk deep, while yet others jostled and pushed like puppies searching for a teat. A few fought for possession of a cask, then broke apart, little harm done, to chase other interlopers away from their prize.

Snaps and snarls filled the air, followed by long howls that sounded mournful. As the din died down and the owl-moon's face shone over the scene, furry, barrel-chested creatures lay all around the casks, twitching and snoring, staggering a few steps and falling. Several poked their unconscious comrades, prodding them to get up, but gradually succumbed to drink and gravity.

When Captain Gryst deemed all to be safe, the people of the *Stormwolf* left the breastworks and approached the horde of drunken monsters. Jorim made certain he was out in front and reached them first. They'd not begun to revert to their more docile form, but they hardly seemed threatening. He checked first one, then another, looking at their teeth and paws, and after looking over a half dozen, settled on the third one he'd inspected.

He rolled the young male onto his stomach, then lifted him by the scruff of his neck. "This one will do, Captain."

Anaeda nodded. "Slaughter the rest of them, then report back to the ship."

A sergeant with the Sea Dragons looked at her. "Begging your pardon, Captain—"

"Yes, Sergeant Solok?"

"This killing is likely to be thirsty work, Captain." The man smiled as his men fell to butchering the sleeping Fenns. "Be a shame to waste what's left of the beer."

Chapter Thirty-two

4th day, Month of the Rat, Year of the Dog
9th Year of Imperial Prince Cyron's Court
162nd Year of the Komyr Dynasty
736th year since the Cataclysm
Telarunde, Solaeth

Had the situation they'd discovered in the small town of Telarunde not been so potentially explosive, Moraven Tolo might have laughed. As it was, he shot a hand out to restrain Ciras. Tyressa had the good grace to look at him before she chose to do anything. Keles Anturasi just reined his horse to a stop, then squinted and studied the town square as if trying to clear his mind of the fog that sometimes consumed him.

The journey from Asath to the coast of the Dark Sea had gone quickly. They decided to avoid Gria, so Moraven led them northeast to a cove where smugglers plied their trade. The smugglers were not choosy about cargo, and accepted their horses as partial payment of passage. They'd often transported *xidantzu* and did not mind having one in their debt. Moraven had employed this family before and found one of their virtues was that they had a very short memory span, save for good friends.

The passage to Eoloth went quickly and uncharacteristically smoothly. They saw no pirates and had no foul weather. The food, which was served very salty and cold, made them long for the rancid rations on the *Catfish,* but within three days they'd quit the ship and entered Solaeth's largest city.

Eoloth's buildings rose to three and four stories, despite being made of mud bricks that were then stuccoed over and whitewashed. The people actually took pride in their homes and regularly decorated them with verses scripted in bright paint surrounding doors and windows, or with painted-on ivy that could never have survived in the cool, dry climate. The brightest colors and most exotic images adorned the wealthier homes, though neither Keles nor Ciras thought much of what the Eolothans counted as wealth.

The two of them shared many characteristics born of an early life of privilege. Ciras remained very precise in action and ritual. He even continued to be well-mannered despite being hot, tired, and hungry—a state that was nearly constant in the ship's cramped, damp quarters. Moraven admired his stubbornness and unwillingness to compromise unless there was a tactical advantage.

Keles likewise found the hardships trying, but remained game and made the best of things. Moraven had been led to believe Keles was smart, but the young man did make a number of errors. They were not consistent, but similar in nature. Part of the time he seemed to be in a fog, and several days complained of waking with a headache as if he'd spent the previous night drinking.

Tyressa intrigued Moraven because she possessed a discipline that belied her age and clearly had been well trained, but was more than willing to listen to his ideas about how they might accomplish their missions. Usually warriors associated with a nation or particular noble house looked down on *xidantzu*—thinking them too independent to be worthy of hire. Tyressa seemed to put that all aside, save where Keles' safety might be jeopardized.

Once they'd bypassed Gria, Tyressa had opened the sealed orders she'd been carrying. She passed a message to Moraven, then read through the remaining documents. After a second read, she turned them over to Keles. He read them, frowned, and slumped back against the boat's hull. "This is going to be difficult."

Moraven had smiled. "That would be true of any mission out here. This just makes it more curious."

The Prince's message had expanded Keles' mission by adding

two additional tasks. First, he was to help Moraven in locating possible caches of weapons from the time before the Cataclysm. He was to make exact maps of their locations and not communicate any of that information to anyone, even his grandfather. That latter instruction had confused Keles, but he agreed to it, noting, "It just means I'll have to have lots more things to give him, so he won't go looking for stuff."

The second thing the Prince asked him to do was to help find Borosan Gryst. Keles knew who that was and brightened at the prospect of meeting him. Keles started to explain about something Gryst might be carrying, but then grew quiet. Everyone in the group noticed his reluctance to explain further, but no one cared, since they'd undoubtedly learn what it was if they ever found Gryst.

The message to Moraven, penned by the Prince himself, had been separately sealed. "Gryst is paramount. All else matters not." Moraven had read it, then burned it saying, "The Prince wishes us luck. I'll let the gods read the message of luck in the smoke, and we shall have help on our journey."

The others accepted his not having let them read the message themselves. He didn't like Prince Cyron's subordinating their efforts to the locating of one man, but leaders always put their concerns first. The implication in the message had not been subtle at all: the others could die or be murdered as long as Borosan Gryst was returned to Moriande.

Moraven felt a chill ripple down his back. There had once been a time when he'd thought of lives in such a casual manner and he was glad he had changed. Killing the men at Asath had been necessitated by the fact that survivors would have summoned more help. Their pursuit might have continued even into Solaeth or, more likely, would have drawn unwanted attention to the four of them.

The deaths in Asath will barely merit a mention to the Prince. Moraven wished Cyron would have the chance to see the true value of an individual life, but he doubted it. The scale of the problems the Prince had to deal with, and the fact that his ministers insulated him from the gory realities of life, meant he never would have that chance. It was a pity, but was also likely the only way the Prince could acquit his responsibilities to the nation.

Moraven considered this and other things as they rode. *Thank the gods I've not been placed in those same straits.* Even as that idea occurred to him, a carrion crow's piercing cry mocked him.

Solaeth had only ever been a frontier province and never truly a full part of the Empire. Very little in the way of Imperial influence could be seen in the architecture or the tangle of alleys and roads that threaded through the city. Warlords had long since divided the nation, though they sent representatives to a ruling council in Eoloth, keeping up the pretense that it was a nation and that the High Governor actually ruled it.

What struck Moraven as the greatest departure from Imperial influence was the preponderance of devices created through *gyanri*. He had seen the blue lights that glowed at night in the larger cities and knew them to be very expensive, but here the same blue light glowed from brooches or the pommels of decorative swords. He had no doubt that the light would not last very long, for the *thaumston* to power it came dear, but these people used as trinkets what the finest people of Moriande could only dream of owning.

The sheer volume of *gyanri* product did make entering a discussion about it easy. Moraven and the others had no trouble appearing wide-eyed with amazement at the things they saw. Carefully they were able to turn the resulting discussions toward Gryst, and after a day had been pointed in the right direction. They traveled almost due north out of Eoloth, bound for the small town of Telarunde.

Telarunde had sent people to the capital to seek help. The village lay at the foot of a mountain containing the ruins of an old citadel. A creature, said to be of the Ixae Yllae, had taken up residence in the ruins and regularly preyed on cows, goats, sheep, and the occasional shepherd. It had become more emboldened in the dry summer, and carried off far more than it had before. The villagers were afraid that it might be feeding a brood.

Borosan Gryst, with a wagonful of his *gyanri* inventions, had headed off to destroy the beast. He'd said it was on his way to Dolosan anyway, and he would be happy to help. He'd gone with the town's representatives, and everyone who had related the story to them in Eoloth was pretty certain it would not have a bard's-tale ending where everyone lived happily ever after.

How true their predictions were. Moraven smiled in spite of himself as he watched the villagers working hard in the town square. They were piling bundles of sticks, bales of straw, and even the occasional broken piece of furniture onto a heap. They muttered as they worked, with an occasional sharp outburst shocking everyone to silence—a silence that was then filled with murmurs of agreement.

At the center of this pile, bound to a thick stake with thick ropes, was Borosan Gryst. At least Moraven took him to be Gryst, for he had the man's reddish-brown hair, and his eyes did appear to be mismatched blue and hazel. He'd not been described as being too tall, and the ropes, despite being snug, did allow his paunch to show. The match to the description was enough for Moraven to feel confident in his identification, but when the man spoke, that cinched it.

Exasperation colored his every word. "No, no, why won't you listen to me? The *bundles* of sticks should be closest to the stake and angled up. Point them at my knees. The kindling goes under them. You hold that other, bigger wood back because it will take much longer to burn, and it's mostly hardwood. It will burn slowly. You want softer wood, so it will burn hotter. Listen to me. Do you want your fire to be efficient or not?"

The response from the crowd indicated their wishes ran to the contrary. His exhortations just made them work harder, piling things higher and in a most haphazard manner. Plead though he might with them, they refused to pay him any heed. "Save your breath for screaming, you fool!" one man shouted.

"Told you we should have gagged him first," remonstrated another.

Moraven spurred his horse forward and raised his voice. "Good people of Telarunde, my companions and I are curious. What are you doing?"

"They're building a wholly inefficient fire. This will take an hour to do what could be accomplished in tens of minutes, with less wood wasted!"

The swordsman held a hand up. "If you don't mind, Master Gryst, I understand your thoughts in this matter. My wish is to learn how you came to be lecturing these good people on how to build a fire."

An older man, the one who had extolled the virtue of a gag,

squinted up at Moraven. "I'll tell you and gladly. He come here and said he'd kill the monster in the mountain. He put one thing here, another there, and another until he had things all over, then he put them together into something round as a cookpot and pointed it at the fortress and sent it rolling off like it was a hound after a fox. He said that would take care of it and we all celebrated."

He pointed at a longhouse toward the north edge of town. The northernmost third of the thatched roof was missing, and Moraven guessed much of the back wall was gone as well. "We were sitting in there, thanking him and praising the gods for our good fortune, when the monster came and ripped the longhouse open. It grabbed a man or three—full-growed men, not boys like in the fields—and hied off for its lair. Now he said it would take time, and we gave him time, but a deadline was set, and now this fire will be set."

Moraven shook his head. "I would not light the fire yet, were I you, for Borosan Gryst kept faith with you."

The old man's face screwed up sourly. "You're not from around here, and we don't like being tricked by strangers. We already have been tricked once. Speak plain. We've wood aplenty."

The swordsman gave Gryst a hard stare that silenced him. "The device he employed works in many ways. It went to the fortress. It found the beast. It realized the beast was more than it could deal with, so a message went out to me. I have come with my companions to help it complete its work."

The villagers around the old man watched as he tried to figure out whether to believe Moraven or not. Flickers of emotion stole over his face, and for a second Moraven thought he'd won. Then the man's expression darkened and he opened his mouth to speak.

He never said a word, however, for Keles Anturasi slid from the saddle and pointed toward the fortress. "Without a doubt, that's the Fortress of Xoncyr. It's just like the other one said. That's where his sister is."

The old man blinked. "What other one?"

Tyressa rode up and leaned forward in the saddle. "The other creature we destroyed. Borosan here is our scout. You can't imagine we'd have come without a scout, can you? We'd have been here faster, but the last one was her older brother, and his bride had just laid a clutch of a dozen eggs, so both were very determined."

The villagers began to murmur among themselves, but the old man refused to be fooled. "You don't look like you've been in no fight."

Ciras spoke softly. "It was not the fight that delayed us. It was laying to rest the five of our comrades who were slain. We were once nine."

The invocation of nine had the desired effect. Some people grabbed the old man and others started tearing apart the bonfire. One even asked Borosan if there was an efficient way to remove wood, and he happily offered advice.

Moraven looked down at the village's leader. "If you would show us the destruction done and let us confer with our comrade, we will determine how best to proceed."

"Yes, of course." The old man held his hands up. "You wait right here. I'll get everything ready for you."

As the old man ran off, Keles came closer and looked up. "We get Gryst and go, right?"

Moraven shook his head. "We bought Master Gryst's freedom with a promise."

Keles' eyes grew wide. "You're not joking, are you? You're going to go up there and kill whatever that monster is?"

"Me, no."

The cartographer smiled. "Good to hear that."

"No, I'm not going to do it, Keles." Moraven smiled. "We're *all* going to do it."

Chapter Thirty-three

5th day, Month of the Rat, Year of the Dog
9th Year of Imperial Prince Cyron's Court
162nd Year of the Komyr Dynasty
736th year since the Cataclysm
Wentokikun, Moriande
Nalenyr

Prince Cyron sat on his throne, again encumbered by the suffocating robes of state. Between him and the doorway ran a red carpet, edged in purple, but barely wide enough this time for one man to walk down it. A stretch of blond wood remained visible between its edges and the pillars, which was why the two ministers who knelt on either side of it, at his feet, were allowed to be in the center of the chamber. Had either of them or their robes even accidentally touched the carpet, he could have ordered their deaths.

He did not smile as he recalled the story of an emperor who had once combed a hated and grasping minister's robe to find purple fibers on it. Whether or not they had been there or planted by the Emperor himself in the bristles of the brush used, no one knew. Cyron doubted he would ever go to those lengths to rid himself of an annoyance, but some days he found himself sorely tempted.

His own Minister of Harmony, Pelut Vniel, knelt at his right hand. As befitted the man's lineage and station, his blue robe had studious dragons coiled back and breast, while purple trimmed each hem. Vniel was not his most senior minister, but had risen to the powerful position of Harmony through his wiles and the fact that he seldom remonstrated with the Prince about matters of form over substance. This meeting, however, had been one of those times and had set Cyron's temper slowly boiling.

Across from him knelt Helosunde's Minister of Foreign Relations, Koir Yoram. Even younger than the Prince himself, Koir had the fiery spirit of a refugee who wished nothing more than the complete liberation of his homeland and the restoration of his nation. The fervency with which he wished this left him trembling whenever he was given news he did not like hearing. Much had happened since the Festival that did not please him and, Cyron was certain, he'd badgered his Master into letting him approach the throne with demands.

Pelut had given vent to his irritation in explaining things to Cyron—less to reveal his true feelings than to show Cyron why this audience was necessary. Bureaucrats evidenced odd patriotism because they fought more to protect the structures that kept them in place than they did to defend their nation against predation or outrage. Koir's request for an audience had come far too abruptly and on too high a level to be tolerated.

Cyron had finally consented to the audience because it was expedient. He was more than happy to fund Helosundian military options, for it was better to shed the blood of mercenaries than that of his own people. The difficulty was that these mercenaries didn't think of themselves as such. They actually thought they were a nation and should have a say in their own affairs. Moreover, they saw themselves as full allies of Nalenyr, not paupers begging alms, and therefore entitled to advise the Prince and consent on any policies that affected them.

Pelut Vniel's hands pressed flat against his thighs. "You will find, Minister, we never intended to keep news of rice shipments to Deseirion hidden from you. Reports were communicated to your subordinates. We apologize that the incorrect cover obscured their true nature, causing them to be set aside. New reports, updated reports, have since been sent, with the correct covers and under my seal."

Koir bowed his head. The man's green robe had gold hounds embroidered on it, but nothing to indicate that these dogs lived at the sufferance of the Naleni Dragon. *And to think that purple fibers would show up so brightly against that emerald silk.* Koir had dressed to show disrespect and all three of them knew it, but they also knew that to take notice and react would be a victory for him.

"Minister, your attention to detail pleases us. The question we have concerns this aid being given to our mutual enemy, at a time when he is most weak. For the first time in enneads we are poised to drive him from Helosunde. The grain makes his soldiers stronger. And at the same time you have slowed delivery of supplies to us. We do not understand this strategy."

Cyron consciously controlled his breathing. The Helosundians had yet to agree on an heir to the last Prince—whose only talent, it seemed, was siring children on everyone but his wife. *Then again, I've met his widow and found her so disagreeable that I would sooner become a monk than lie with her.* The bureaucrats had formed a committee to decide which of the Prince's bastards should lead Helosunde, as much to preserve their positions as to remove any claim to legitimate rule on her part. This embittered the widow even more, making a political marriage to her yet more unthinkable in Cyron's mind.

The Naleni Minister of State kept his voice low. "The shipments of grain are not to the Desei troops. They go to the people."

"But, Minister, you would acknowledge that Pyrust draws from his people's stores to feed his troops."

"Of course. We assumed this would happen. Pallid Desei rice fills the bellies of troops, while our golden rice goes to the Desei people. Do you suppose they do not know where it comes from? They do, and they know whom to thank when their elders and their children survive. They will see Nalenyr as the land of gold."

"Which will prompt them to join Pyrust when he commands them to move south to take what you give. They will pour through Helosunde to get it. We will be unable to stop them, for our warriors are hobbled. Our requests have been reasonable."

Pelut nodded thoughtfully. "Reasonable, yes, but for offense, not defense. You are planning an attack against Meleswin."

Koir's lower lip trembled, betraying his surprise at both the information Pelut possessed and his willingness to deliver it bluntly. By rights there should have been much more time wasted peeling back layer after layer of motivation until Koir expressed his desire to drive the Desei from what had been Helosunde's third largest city.

"Our agents have learned that, in response to demands made upon him by your own Prince Cyron, Pyrust will withdraw his troops from Meleswin. We plan to take the city back, freeing our people."

Cyron knew that for a lie. Meleswin had long ago spawned a twin Desei city on the north bank of the Black River. Since its conquest, the Helosundian population had been driven from it and the Desei leaders had transplanted their own people. Meleswin was now more a Desei city than a Helosundian one. Any conquest of it would result in a bloodletting that Pyrust could not help but respond to.

"Minister Yoram, the court has given as much study as possible to this situation." Pelut pressed his hands together. "It is believed that any strike against Meleswin is ill-advised. We cannot support it."

Koir did not even attempt to control his outrage. "You mean to say you will not *permit* it."

"That is your choice of words. Mine were chosen with care to their meaning."

"Might I remind the minister that Helosunde is a sovereign state with every right of self-defense and every right to pursue its national self-interest. Reestablishing its power over territory stolen by greedy interlopers is but one of the ways in which we defend ourselves. Moreover, the stronger we are, the less of a threat the Desei pose to you."

With a flick of his wrist, Cyron snapped open the fan in his right hand. A golden dragon on a field of purple unfurled on the crescent and hid his face from his eyes down. " 'And the Master said, "The dog awaits his master's pleasure and is rewarded. Impotent barks breed only displeasure.' "

Koir stiffened sharply, and Pelut covered his shock as well. Had the meeting gone as scripted, Cyron would have said nothing, remaining impassive and unmoved throughout. By hiding behind his fan he was not to be noticed, and though they both heard his Urmyrian quote, manners demanded they had to deny he had spoken. At the same time they were required to heed him.

The Helosundian's blue eyes blazed furiously, but he said nothing for as long as it took Cyron to close the fan. "Helosunde sees its duty to Nalenyr to be as sacred as it is to its own people. We have not forgotten the many kindnesses of the Naleni people. We are willing to interpose ourselves between the noble Naleni and the vile Desei, even as the Keru impose themselves between Prince Cyron and his enemies."

Pelut allowed his eyes to half close. "Nalenyr would never forbid Helosunde from any action Helosunde's prince deemed necessary, but this matter of Meleswin is one in which we urge extreme caution and deliberation."

The flicker of Koir's eyes betrayed his thoughts. Pelut had told him that Nalenyr would back the decision of a Helosundian prince. This would force the bureaucracy to come to a decision about an heir before they would authorize the attack. The wrangling over the heir might take months if not years, and the urgency of the attack would pass.

That, or all will be done in haste and disaster will result.

Cyron smothered the desire to shake his head. Had Pyrust been in his place, he'd have exploded off the throne and likely kicked the insolence out of Koir. *Probably have to kick him to death to do that.* While a kick or two would be gratifying, Cyron would have just as soon bribed Koir and his fellow ministers to do nothing. Unfortunately, they would have taken his gold, then used it to fund their plan, the whole time conspiring with his own ministers to keep the results of any disaster secret.

Koir bowed, but not low enough for his head to touch the carpet. "The dragon's wisdom and friendship is the greatest treasure of the Helosundian people. I shall withdraw and share it with my leaders. May the Strength of the Nine continue to enrich the Komyr House."

The Helosundian minister rose and backed from the room. Pelut watched him go. He then turned to Cyron and bowed. "He is where we desire him to be."

Cyron snorted. "Committed to doing nothing, or speeding forward on a course that will create more problems? Meleswin is a disaster in the offing. If they cannot see it is a Desei trap, they are stupid. I can only hope Koir leads the horde into the city."

"Unlikely, Highness."

"I know, which means their brave die and their idiots remain." Cyron again snapped open his fan, cutting off any further discussion. "A dragon weeps, not of disgust, but pity for courage spent worthlessly."

Chapter Thirty-four

5th day, Month of the Rat, Year of the Dog
9th Year of Imperial Prince Cyron's Court
162nd Year of the Komyr Dynasty
736th year since the Cataclysm
Stormwolf, in the South Seas

Only two-thirds of a week out of Archurko and Jorim realized he'd learned far more about the Fennych than any other source in the world—at least, any human source. He had no doubt the Viruk knew a lot about them, but he hardly expected their reports to be without bias. He watched the creature carefully, keeping it with him constantly for the first three days, then letting it wander from his side once Captain Gryst became convinced it would cause no mayhem.

Jorim had encountered creatures, like the rainbow-lizard, which would shift color so it could fit in with its background. The Fenn seemed able to do so with his shape and even personality. Isolated from his species, the Fenn immediately began to adapt to life among humans. He took on more human proportions, though his head, eyes, and ears remained large. In fact, according to measurements Jorim took, his head, orbital cavities, and eyes actually grew larger.

Jorim had explained it to Iesol rather simply. "He exhibits a marked degree of neoteny—he's modeling himself after a human child because that's what invokes our most protective instincts."

"But we have no children on board."

"That's true, but the overlarge head and large eyes are common for infants of most species." Jorim nodded as the Fenn leaped from a squat and swatted at a cable-end being dangled playfully by a sailor. "Likewise such play behavior is common. He's slowly being socialized in the ways of Men, and being cute means he gets attention, avoids harm, and gets fed."

It came down to much more than simple imitative behavior, however, for fairly quickly the Fenn began to speak. He showed a preternatural ability for discerning and discriminating sounds—and Jorim thought this might have been one of the reasons his ears actually got bigger even though they were decidedly not human. Syntax seemed irrelevant to him, but he developed an insatiable desire to know the "nama" of everything and everyone. "Jrima nama," followed by the sound of a paw patting something, became so common that Jorim found himself answering in his sleep.

The learning of language clearly was an adaptive skill, and the fact that the Fenn was able to attach meaning to more conceptual words provided a big clue as to his level of intelligence. After several days, the Fenn provided his own "nama," by patting his chest and announcing "Shimik." Shimik often mumbled to himself in a melodious language, but resisted any of Jorim's entreaties to share words.

Shimik did learn very quickly what behavior was and was not allowed, such as waking folks from a sound sleep or interfering with people at work. He likewise picked up language from belowdecks and incorporated it into his vocabulary. Thus anything broken or bad became "dunga." Being able to provoke laughter was quickly rewarded, so he became something of a clown, though he turned those antics off when he joined Jorim in his cabin and Jorim needed silence to take measurements, record data, or communicate with Qiro.

Despite having had less than a week to study Shimik, Jorim drew conclusions about the creature that explained how it could be so docile away from others of its kind, so intelligent, and yet become bestial in a community. While alone, Shimik remained so compliant that Jorim could force his mouth open, study his teeth, or expose his claws without so much as a growl. The offensive weapons that made the Fenn capable of attacking and killing a Viruk warrior were still present, just not used.

What he decided was that the Fenn were inordinately intelligent and creatures well suited to living in a society. When away from their own kind they felt extremely vulnerable, and with good cause, since a lone Fenn was unlikely to be able to defeat a lot of creatures—and certainly not a Viruk. In a Fennych mob, however, they had little to fear. Their numbers could overwhelm almost anything, and the chances of any one of them being singled out and killed dropped with each new Fenn added to the group. When a bunch of them came together, the need for intelligence fled and they just acted and reacted together.

What he assumed happened on Ethgi was simple. Under normal circumstances, Fennych probably had their own separate ranges and remained relatively solitary. They obviously found members of the opposite sex for breeding, and he wondered a great deal about the size of litters and the like. The kits, when old enough, would spread out and find their own ranges, but as more of them grew up, the population expanded and forced them into closer company with each other. A mob would form and go rambling off, killing things and pushing into a new area where they could spread out again. The whole process would begin anew, with the time between mobbing determined by food supplies, local predators, and other factors that would limit population growth. On Ethgi there was no place to go save into the village, and no prey to be had but villagers, which resulted in the situation in which the *Stormwolf* had intervened.

Studying Shimik and taking navigational readings provided Jorim with something to do. Had he not had the Fenn to watch, he likely would have gone mad, for there was little else for him to do. The *Stormwolf* sailed south, looking to catch a current running east. As they went, they looked for the islands in the chain, but had little success. This frustrated him because the Soth chart had seemed promising. They'd found Ethgi with it, after all.

Captain Gryst was more inclined to dismiss the absence of islands. She stood with Jorim at the aft rail on the wheel deck, studying the faintly luminescent wake of the ship as the sun slowly set. "There are various explanations for why the islands aren't here, Jorim. That map was over three thousand years old. What were indicated as islands may have been atolls exposed at a time when the sea was at a lower level. And we have no indication the Viruk understood more about longitude than we do, so they could be leagues away from where we expect to find them."

Jorim shook his head. "You might as well say some god reached down, scooped them up, and moved them somewhere else. They should be there. The arc was right on the map for a chain of islands. Maybe they were old volcanoes or something."

"Maybe they were just legends to the Viruk, much as the Mountains of Ice are legends to us."

"You don't mean that." Jorim cocked an eyebrow at her and turned to look south past the prow. "They're there."

"How do you know, Master Anturasi?"

"It stands to reason. If one goes north, through the Turca Wastes and beyond, you come to a land of ice. It makes sense that the same conditions would exist south. That, coupled with the legends, indicate the Mountains of Ice will be there."

Shimik, whose fur had grown shorter and had taken on the honey-gold hue of the oak deck, loped over, then held his paws up to Jorim. "Jrima uppa uppa." The little fingers twitched and Jorim lifted him up lest claws appear and he start to climb.

Anaeda smiled as the Fenn waved a hand at her. "I find you quite curious, Master Anturasi. You are here taking measurements so we can define the world and know it better. You are studying this Fenn very carefully and recording what you learn. You similarly sketch the fish we catch, draw birds we see, map out the constellations that are not visible from Moriande, yet you allow yourself to believe in a land where the mountains are made of ice based on nothing more than fanciful stories from a time of heroes. How do you reconcile such things?"

The sea breeze made his braids float and Shimik tried to catch one in his paws. "I'm not certain, Captain, that I need to reconcile those things. There are plenty of people who live in mountain valleys who are certain the world is flat and the sky a bowl over it. They are doubtlessly convinced that we've already sailed off the edge of the earth.

"But I believe the mountains are there, and I know why. In part it's the stories I've heard. All the ancient maps show them. As I said before, if we have a land of ice in the north, why not the south? And the measurements I've taken show it's getting colder. Many of the birds and fish I've seen resemble those in the colder climes to the north. It stands to reason that the Mountains of Ice exist."

"I accept your reasoning, but where do you draw the line?" A smile twisted her lips. "There are those who believe that, beyond the mountains, there is a hole that is the entrance to the Underworld. If you venture in there, you can find all the wealth that is sacrificed and sent to our ancestors. You can bet that if we find the mountains, there will be those who want to make the trek beyond them."

Jorim shook his head. "I know the legend, but I put as much faith in that as I do the idea that Empress Cyrsa will return from the west when the Land of Nine Princes is threatened. The idea that she and her surviving heroes are just sleeping makes no sense. There's no information to support it. When she didn't come back, folks started that story to make themselves feel good. Times were so bad they wanted a little hope, so they made up a savior who would return if things got worse."

She nodded. "That very well could be what happened. Or, she *is* out there, waiting."

"Why, Captain, I'd not thought you would allow yourself to believe in such superstition."

Anaeda's eyes narrowed. "Don't limit yourself for the sake of making a point. You were quite clear in amassing the evidence that leads you to conclude that the Mountains of Ice exist. There is more to suggest that Empress Cyrsa existed and might yet exist. We both know that the *jaecai* are said to live longer lives. We know she and her warriors were present at the spawning of the Cataclysm, in which great amounts of magical energy were released. You've seen the changes it made in the world.

"Think about it, Master Anturasi. Outside many villages there are circles in which swordsmen engage in their duels, and where two *jaecai* have met, magical energy is released. In some of those circles, the ravages of winter are never seen, and in others the snow that falls never melts even in the heat of the summer. Thus magic can clearly preserve as well as destroy, so why is it not acceptable to believe she is preserved as well?"

"That's a very good point, Captain." Jorim looked at Shimik. "You are very heavy, and the evidence points to your needing exercise. Earn keepa, Shimik."

With a shriek of delight, the Fenn leaped from his arms and scampered off, leaping the rail to the main deck and disappearing down the nearest hatch, bound for the bowels of the ship. One of the few reasons Captain Gryst had allowed him to travel alone was because he took pleasure in ratting, and proved far better at it than any of the dogs brought on board for that purpose.

"Again, you make a very good point. She *could* be out there." He folded his arms across his chest. "Why are you bringing this up?"

She leaned against the railing and kept her voice low. "I read your reports and add bits and pieces of them to the log. I read the measurements you're taking and compare them to my own. We agree, for the most part, on things. As much as I tell you our inability to find the islands means nothing, I find something disquieting about it."

"Meaning?"

Anaeda exhaled slowly. "Islands don't just vanish. We could have missed them—just sailed past in the night—but we're not traveling so fast that we would have missed all signs of them. We'd see clouds over them, or bits of wood drifting. Something would be out here."

"So we have no empirical evidence for having missed them, but that means nothing." Jorim kept his voice low. "It's something else, isn't it? Something that isn't as substantial."

"I have been on a ship for over eighteen years, almost twenty-seven. I've seen a lot, and something odd is on the wind. There is something out there that isn't right. It could be your Mountains of Ice, but it could be something else."

Jorim frowned. "Do you think we've sailed into an area, say, where some huge, prehistoric naval engagement was fought and magic lingers?"

"I don't know. That could be one explanation. Just as easy is that magic flows in currents just like water, and we are caught in a cross-current of it." She shrugged. "It could be something else entirely. I am seeing no ill effects on the crew, and we have plenty of supplies, and our measurements indicate we are moving south steadily. It is just something I can't explain, and, as such, it does pose a threat to the fleet. And I don't like threats to my fleet."

"I don't blame you." Jorim thought for a moment, then nodded. "I don't think my grandfather would be much help if I asked him about this. It's too bad my brother isn't here. He's the one who remembers all the folklore of old. He'd know if something had happened."

"See what you can remember. I would appreciate any insights possible." She straightened up and looked him in the eyes. "Needless to say, you speak to no one about this. Not even Iesol."

Jorim smiled. "You don't want the benefits of Urmyr's wisdom on this point?"

"I'm not that desperate yet. We'll see what we can come up with before widening the circle of people involved in this. Anything odd could upset the crew, and if we *are* looking at trouble, I want them with us."

Jorim smiled ever so slightly. "That's why you're letting Shimik run around? As a distraction?"

"No, actually I like that he kills rats. And I like that the crew sees him as a good omen. They believe in these talismans of good luck and, before this journey is ended, that belief will be seriously tested."

Chapter Thirty-five

5th day, Month of the Rat, Year of the Dog
9th Year of Imperial Prince Cyron's Court
162nd Year of the Komyr Dynasty
736th year since the Cataclysm
Telarunde, Solaeth

As they made their way up the mountainside to the shattered Fortress of Xoncyr, the irony that his brother would have gladly been trooping off to destroy this monster was not lost on Keles Anturasi. Jorim wouldn't have needed anyone else to accompany him, and he'd come back having slain the creature as easily as a leaf falls from a tree. *It would be another of his grand adventures, which would enrage Grandfather and earn him the admiration of the flower of the nobility.*

He smiled, trudging behind Ciras. That he was unsuited to such an adventure was a point Tyressa had made to Moraven Tolo earlier in the morning. She'd pointed to Keles and Borosan and said, "The two of them should remain here while we take care of the creature."

Borosan, who had spent most of the morning tinkering with a small metal ball that had been pieced together from bits and pieces in a big leather satchel, raised his head and blinked. "Under no circumstances."

The Keru had smiled and squatted. "I appreciate that you came out here to try to rid Telarunde of this creature, but your effort failed."

"No it didn't." Borosan set his handwork down and pointed to the ruins of what the locals called Dorunkun. "My *thanaton* is up there already. If it has not killed the creature yet, it is because it has not figured out how to do it."

Before anyone could ask what a *thanaton* was, Borosan took up his ball again, pushed one panel aside, twisted something inside, and tossed the ball underhanded toward the center of their hut's dirt floor. It bounced once, then four metal legs popped out. It scuttled to the left, turned, then a circle irised open. A high-pitched thrum sounded, then a rat squealed, stuck to the wall with a finger-length metal dart impaling it.

Ciras leaped up and half drew his sword. The small device retracted its legs and lay there, inert and unthreatening. Moraven studied the ball for a moment or two, exchanged glances with Tyressa, then bowed his head toward the *gyanridin*. "The *thanaton* you sent up there is larger?"

"Much. I built it out of parts I had in my wagon. This mouser is just a model. The real one is up there studying the creature and figuring out how best to kill it."

The Keru slid a whetstone along the edge of a spear she'd appropriated from a local. "That certainly works well on a rodent, but that's not what's up there waiting for us."

Silence greeted her grim comment. Keles again felt his brother would have been better at determining what it was they faced. In an effort to get as much information as possible, Keles had interviewed everyone who had seen the creature or had ever been in the fortress. Far more of the latter existed than the former, and he didn't believe but one or two of those who said they'd seen it. The best description made it out to be a giant serpent that could project a poisonous vapor. It had fur and a mane and had been able to drag off three strong men the night it attacked the village.

Keles had never heard of such a creature, but if it were coming out of the Ixyll Wastes or Dolosan, it would have been bred in the wild magic. As Borosan pointed out, the creature could have a very thick hide or only be vulnerable when its mouth was open, exposing a soft palate. His *thanaton,* they were assured, would figure things out, but it might take some time.

Time was not something they had. No one even suggested wandering off without killing the monster—even though dying in the process was a distinct possibility. Moraven was determined to fulfill his promise to them and perhaps add to the tales of the *xidantzu*.

Kelcs had helped as much as he could with the preparations. From the initial interviews concerning the fortress he was able to sketch out a fairly complete floor plan. He actually believed it was the Xoncyrkun mentioned in Amenis Dukao's memoirs, for the general shape and tall tower at the heart matched the description very closely. The locals called it Dorunkun after a warlord who had occupied it more recently and from whom several of them claimed descent. They denied ever having heard of Amenis Dukao, which made them somewhat more ignorant than the sheep they herded, as far as Keles was concerned.

Even so, they knew the fortress well, and shared with him a wealth of detail. The ruins certainly dated from the late Imperial period, and had been part of the chain of strongholds used to discourage the Turasyndi from attacking. Built to encompass a hilltop and use a natural outcropping as the final stronghold, the entire fortress included tunnels and rooms hacked out of the stone. The monster lurked in these dark warrens.

Moraven said Borosan would accompany the group, but Tyressa still wished Keles to stay behind. Though Keles really had no desire to be anywhere near a monster that could drag strong men off, he refused. He pointed to one of the floor plans he'd drawn. "Look, during this period there were several basic designs for fortresses. Once I'm inside, I can determine where the garbage chutes will come out, as well as other alternate routes for getting down to the stables where this thing is lairing."

Tyressa shook her head. "It is too risky."

"It's too risky without me. I have a bow and I can shoot pretty well. Besides, even if you leave me here, I won't be safe." He jerked a thumb toward the hut's closed door. "I'll be taking Borosan's place if you fail."

Tyressa did not like that argument, but agreed it was probably right. Keles didn't like it, either, but was happy they were going to allow him to go along. "I'll be fine. A Viruk couldn't kill me, so I don't imagine this thing will either."

After a night of too little sleep they awoke to a breakfast that was well shy of generous. The illogic of wasting food on dead men was not lost on the village. Keles didn't mind getting a tiny serving of gruel, since it was very watery and made out of some purple-blue grain he couldn't identify. It and the fact that several of the village cats had spare toes and even an extra set of legs reminded him they were in the land wild magic had corrupted.

His stomach soured, and it wasn't just the gruel that did it.

The five of them set out. Keles had hoped for bright sun to warm them as they trekked two miles through golden fields to the stronghold, but instead the day started grey, and a cold rain began to fall as they marched along. Moraven welcomed the rain, noting it kept the dust down, but Keles considered that a minor benefit.

Xoncyrkun had a ribbon wall that surrounded the top of the hill in an oval just over fifty yards from end to end. The wall, which once had been a dozen feet high in places, had fallen into disrepair, and the people of Telarunde had used it as a quarry for years. The squat outbuilding in which most of the garrison would have been housed survived save for the roofs. The main keep, which crested the hill and rose another thirty feet, had once had carrion crows roosting in it. Their guano stained the grey stone white and black in streaks, but Keles saw no evidence of current occupancy. He assumed the monster had frightened them off because, even if it were twice as big as described, it couldn't have slithered high enough to eat the birds.

A dark hole in the wall about halfway between the main gate and the keep marked where the creature came and went. Low clouds soon descended to shroud the fortress, and Keles thought this was a good thing. Every step closer emphasized just how big the hole was, and that meant the monster was bigger than any of them wanted to think about.

The clouds dropped visibility to a dozen feet. Tyressa led the way through a breach in the wall and into the central courtyard. They all moved as quietly as they could. Keles studied the interior of the ruins, then crouched and pointed to the nearest of the blockhouses. "That would have been the storehouse. There are passages down to the stables there, and over there, past the garrison, just to the left of that stone spur. That would be the main ramp down, from which warriors could ride up and out. The opening is probably as wide as the hole in the wall."

Ciras rose and began to move toward the storehouse. As he circled left around a large block that had tumbled from the wall, a black serpent rose from behind it. Its maned head swayed easily nine feet above the ground and its body was as thick around as Keles' thigh. The snake hissed and reared back, but before it could strike, Ciras' sword cleared the scabbard and came around in a flat arc. The silver blur bisected the serpent as if it were no more than the fog that had helped hide it. The upper half toppled back to the stones, while the main body writhed in a gush of blood.

Ciras spun away with a greasy grey vapor rising from his blade and his overshirt where both had been splashed with blood. Keles felt a burning on his own right cheek and smeared serpent's blood away with his fingers. They began to tingle as a result, but he resisted the temptation to put them into his mouth and suck.

Ciras yanked his overshirt off and used a corner to wipe his blade before tossing the garment away. He slid his blade back home, then allowed himself a laugh. "Well, Master Gryst, what trouble would your *thanaton* have had in killing that?"

Borosan frowned. "It should have had none. And it should be out here now, if that's what it was tracking."

The young swordsman snorted. "You should save your magic for mousing. The monster is slain; our duty is done."

Ciras' master dropped to one knee. "You are mistaken."

"How? It is exactly as the peasants described it to Keles—though they exaggerated mightily. It was strong enough to carry off sheep and men."

"Yes, but look at where you cut it." Moraven pointed at the severed spine and, beside it, a slender tube ringed with cartilage. "It might have been able to carry men off, but it never could have swallowed them."

Ciras frowned. "Perhaps it feeds as a spider does. It injects poison into prey and when they dissolve, it drinks."

"Or," Moraven said quietly as he stood, "it suckles at the breast of something a good bit larger."

A low vibration ran through the ground, as if a big rock had plummeted from the top of the tower and struck the courtyard. Another vibration shook the stone, and another, coming faster and stronger. Unbidden, the image of something *much* larger slithering up a narrow passage, its coils slamming into the walls, came to Keles' mind. He looked toward where the ramp should have come out and dug for an arrow at his right hip.

Time slowed, and every sensation registered with indelible clarity. Fingers still tingling from serpent blood brushed soft feathers and closed on hard wood. The jade thumbring refused to warm. The silver broadhead rasped against the quiver's hide, then the bow groaned as he nocked and drew the arrow. His right shoulder began to burn, and the tip of the arrow quivered as Moraven's blade hissed from its scabbard and Ciras sprang to his feet.

Borosan's *thanaton* came rolling out of the fog first, striking sparks from the garrison building and the outcropping. Just beyond the narrowest point, its four legs sprang out with loud clicks. A curved panel slid from front to back over its dome, and a heavy crossbow emerged, twisting and locking down. Two delicate arms set a quarrel in place, while another heavy arm cocked the bow. The *thanaton* crouched, its knees rising above the dome.

The monster came on quickly, a black shadow undulating through the mist. It reared up as the fog parted, giving Keles a good view of a golden-scaled, blunted, wedge-shaped head. He saw no eyes and only slit nostrils in its face. The creature's lower jaw dropped, revealing serrated ivory teeth. It hissed, and panic froze Keles in place.

The *thanaton* did not register fear. It shot, hitting the snake in the throat at close range. The bolt pierced the creature's flesh, muting the hiss for a heartbeat, but clearly it was more from surprise than damage. The bolt might as well have been a wasp's sting to an elephant.

The snake's head darted forward and the rising hiss cut off abruptly. Crystal-clear venom streamed from within its mouth and splashed over the *thanaton*. The crossbow's wooden stock immediately burst into flame and the stones beneath the mechanical hunter began to smoke. Pieces of the *thanaton* began to melt, with springs and wires pinging as they snapped. First one leg then another twisted and rotted away, with Borosan's agonized screech giving voice to what his creation might have been feeling.

Keles loosed his arrow, and the shot went far better than he would have expected. He allowed himself a flash of pleasure at how well his brother's gift worked, because the shaft flew directly where he'd aimed. His joy vanished, however, as it skipped off the snake's flat head and raked back through the black mane. It hadn't so much as dented a scale and, with a sinking feeling in his guts, he realized that even it if had, it would have hurt the snake less than the *thanaton*'s bolt.

His arrow did have one unexpected result, however. As it sped through the mane, it transfixed a snake the size of the one Ciras had killed. Two more, then three and four, then up to a dozen of them emerged from that thicket of fur, all of them hissing madly and spitting venom as their mother had. To make things worse, his arrow had not actually killed the snake he'd hit, and the way they were writhing and springing free, he doubted he could hit another.

Keles suddenly found himself detached, as if he were standing back, watching himself draw another arrow and letting fly. The observer cataloged all the details of the beast, drawing conclusions and, he hoped, somehow communicating them to his grandfather or brother, even as he died. The snake's young clearly nested in the mane and likely took nourishment there. The mother, blind—by design he assumed, since he could see no scarring—relied on them for gathering food, which she then devoured and fed to them. He could only hope the snakes had some sort of natural predator, for if that clutch grew and reproduced, stemming the tide of their expansion would be difficult.

Moraven, Ciras, and Tyressa flew into battle. The Keru hurled her spear and stuck the mother through the lower jaw. The spear's head lodged in the snake's upper palate and clearly caused her pain. The viscous venom already had the spear smoking, mixing with the black blood dripping from the shaft. Drawing her sword, the Keru closed fearlessly, intent on wounding the beast even more.

The two *xidantzu* attacked with a spare economy of effort that should not have surprised Keles. Their command of their bodies and weapons so surpassed anything he had seen before—including Moraven's fight in Asath—that he could do little but marvel. Swords beheaded several of the smaller vipers, then warriors leaped past writhing bodies to strike at others.

For the barest of moments, Keles believed they might actually win the fight. The smaller snakes had begun to fall and all three of the attackers had drawn within range of the largest snake's belly. His own second arrow had stuck it in the mouth. It had not done nearly the damage of Tyressa's spear, but the viper had reacted to the pain.

Then one of the smaller snakes whipped its tail around, sweeping Tyressa's legs from beneath her. As she went down, Moraven leaped to her side and slew the snake that had dropped her. To his right, however, another of the small vipers breathed venom in a vapor that sent Ciras reeling back. His sword clattered to the ground as he spun away, hands over his face, coughing heavily. Keles loosed a third arrow at the snake chasing Ciras and missed, dooming the young swordsman.

Then Borosan stepped up and whipped his arm forward. The mouser spun through the air. The small snake struck at it, catching the ball in its mouth. Suddenly the legs sprang out, thrusting up through its skull. The snake flopped, writhing, but that proved to be only a momentary benefit, as the small snakes were truly the least of their worries.

Moraven stooped to help Tyressa up. The mother rose above him as the undissolved pieces of the spear fell away. Whether the snake intended to spit venom or just lunge to devour them, Moraven Tolo and Tyressa were dead.

Then a keening screech of contempt and ecstasy filled the fog and echoed from the fortress walls. Something angular and dark descended through the mist and slammed into the back of the viper's head, jolting the creature. The attacker disappeared immediately into the mane. The viper's head rose, nose high in the fog, to smash into the tower. It wriggled side to side as if trying to scrape off whatever had landed. It hissed furiously for a moment, then squeaked piteously. A shudder rippled through its entire length, cracking its tail against the tower's base. The body slackened for a second, then, as if it were a piece of cable falling, it crashed to the courtyard, cracking ages-old mortar.

Keles went down, groaning inwardly as his arrows clattered onto the stone. Rising to his knees, he grabbed one and tried to fit it to the bow. His hands trembled and his stomach began to roil. The arrow fought him, refusing to be nocked. He glanced down, guiding it into place, then looked back at the head of the viper, five yards distant and twice his height.

Something rustled in the mane, then stood. Steaming viper blood drenched it and ran from elbows and hunched shoulders. A hot light burned in its eyes, then it raised clawed fingers to the sky. It shrieked again, this time triumphant, then lowered its hands. It moved forward, then crouched on the viper's golden brow.

"Keles Anturasi. Very good." The scars on Keles' back began to burn as he recognized the Viruk. "The journey has been long. I have come for you."

Chapter Thirty-six

14th day, Month of the Rat, Year of the Dog
9th Year of Imperial Prince Cyron's Court
162nd Year of the Komyr Dynasty
736th year since the Cataclysm
Anturasikun, Moriande
Nalenyr

Even though Nirati had not liked Majiata, she hated seeing the hopeful look on Lord Marutsar Phoesel's face. A small, slender man, he wore a nicely trimmed moustache and goatee which, like his hair, had been dyed to hide signs of age. His black robe had gold cranes embroidered on breast and back, and a narrow gold sash had been wrapped twice around his middle to keep it closed. Many people considered him handsome and charming—stories abounded about his legion of mistresses—but knowing Majiata had sprung from his loins killed any appeal as far as Nirati was concerned.

She quickly amended that thought. *That she had come after Keles at her father's prompting is what makes him hideous in my eyes.*

Lord Phoesel's only concession to mourning was the white undertunic he wore. It was visible at throat and cuff, and suggested to many that he was holding his grief deep inside. Nirati felt the man just thought he did not look particularly good in white. And while she did not really mourn Majiata, she would have thought her father might make more of a show of it.

The man hesitated for a moment as he came into the antechamber to Qiro Anturasi's receiving room. When Marutsar met with

Qiro before, Qiro had received him in a different room—one much lower in the tower and less intimate. This room, with its stark white walls and bare wooden floor, mocked the finery of the halls leading to it.

The room had only two adornments, and neither seemed appropriate. Most notable was the semicircular cage of golden bars that ran from floor to ceiling. It extended to the middle of the room and covered the far wall from corner to corner. Built into that wall was a doorway, similarly barred with gold, only four feet in height.

Nirati, waiting inside the cage, welcomed Lord Phoesel through the door. "If you please, enter and wait over there by the other door."

The man nodded and looked around as he entered. "I have not been here before."

"Few have." Nirati moved behind him and pulled the cage door shut. It closed with a click. Another click echoed it, and the small golden door slid up into the wall. "My grandfather will see you now."

Lord Phoesel approached the low doorway and stooped. He peered in, then glanced back at her, consternation on his face. She said nothing, so he started forward in a crouch, then yelped as his forward foot missed the step down. He sprawled forward on his belly.

As my grandfather intended.

Nirati sank to her hands and knees and crawled through, then rose inside the far room. The circular cage extended out on this side of the wall, the circle trapping visitors. She bowed to Qiro, then waved a hand toward Majiata's father, who had risen no further than his knees. "You know Lord Phoesel."

Qiro, who was studying a gold-plated human skull he'd brought back with him from the Wastes, nodded. "We have met before." The old man stared into the skull's empty eye sockets, then returned it to the small pedestal upon which it normally resided. He smiled and looked down at the merchant, but said nothing.

Lord Phoesel remained on his knees, his head craning back to take in all the treasures displayed around him. While Nirati and he were the only things inside the cage, all around it, an arm's length past the bars, lay wooden casks and ironbound chests. Huge tapestries and paintings covered the walls. Weapons had been stacked in the corners. The scent of spices filled the room, wafting from dozens of containers piled high in pyramids. Jewels glinted from half-open boxes and split sacks had spilled out a glittering carpet of gold coins.

The skull, while a unique piece of art, was not the most unusual artifact. The heads of countless animals, from four-horned oryxes and sable tigers to the gaping jaws of a Dark Sea shark, had been mounted and hung. Hides of rich, thick fur covered the throne centered against the back wall, and plumage of unimaginable delicacy decorated ceremonial masks, armor, and fletched quivers of arrows.

The room contained items from the entire world, and if sold in the market could have ransomed a prince. But here they lay, piled haphazardly, languishing beneath a coat of dust as if they were nothing. More, Qiro was free to roam amid it all, while his visitor remained caged.

Lord Phoesel finally found his tongue. "Thank you for receiving me, Master Anturasi . . . Grandmaster Anturasi. You have no idea how much I appreciate this favor."

Qiro sat on the throne, and ran his fingers through striped monotreme fur. "I agreed to meet you as a favor to my granddaughter. Let us have no mistaking why and how you are here. Were it up to me, you would never have been admitted to my presence."

Majiata's father had started to stand, but quickly went to his knees again and bowed deeply. "I have offended you somehow, Grandmaster. What can I do to make amends?"

"You *have* offended me, and I don't know that you can make amends."

"Surely I can do something. What was it that earned your ire?"

Qiro smiled slowly and Nirati felt ice trickle through her belly. She'd intervened with her grandfather for Lord Phoesel as a favor to Junel. But Qiro did not like how Lord Phoesel had used Nirati to get to him, and the man would be made to pay.

"My dear Lord Phoesel, you made a contract with the House of Tilmir to supply charts for the *Gold Crane*. Your ship was bound to Nysant—following curiously close in the *Stormwolf*'s wake."

"Grandmaster, my ship was not following the expedition. *Gold Crane* will sail west to Aefret."

"Regardless, you made a contract with a house that rivals mine. A house of inferior cartography."

The man bowed deeply. "Yes, Grandmaster, I have discovered

this, and this is why I am here. I hoped I could obtain from you new charts and have them put aboard the *Swift*. It will sail after *Gold Crane*."

Qiro examined a fingernail. "That might be possible. There will be the matter of payment."

"Yes, Grandmaster. I will have to pay Tilmir something, but I will yet be able to pay you your customary rate."

The corners of Qiro's mouth curled up. "It will be thirty percent of your total return. Your expenses are not my concern."

"Th-thirty percent?" Lord Phoesel shook his head. "But you normally take only fifteen, and that after expenses."

"This is an emergency, Marutsar, and you know it. Your *Silver Gull* was using Tilmir charts and ran into a shoal off Miromil. If you can refloat the ship, it will not be before next spring. There are other hidden dangers out there, and you can't afford to lose *Gold Crane*."

"But this is extortion!"

"Hardly. I am doing you a favor."

"A favor?" Lord Phoesel came up on one knee, color darkening his face. "After all our families have meant to each other, *this* is a favor?"

Qiro shot to his feet, pale eyes blazing. "Do not attempt to manipulate me. I see so much more than you do, than you are capable of seeing. I see the world. I see beyond the trinkets here to what is true.

"You are a fool, Marutsar Phoesel, for you do not recognize a favor when I am doing you one. There are things out there, things not indicated on any Tilmir chart—nightmare things that will swallow your ships whole. I know that. I've known that for years. I knew you shipped without my charts. You've asked others and you know I have granted no one else an audience such as you have now. *That* is the favor. You have already made one mistake; do not compound it."

Lord Phoesel struggled. He clearly wanted to scream at Qiro, but merely clenched his fists in impotent rage. Fear started him trembling and his restless gaze darted around the room. So much of the world's riches lay there about him, and the lack of charts kept them from his grasp as effectively as the bars.

He came back down to his knees. "Thirty percent?"

"I feel generous, yes."

Lord Phoesel's head came up. "The *Crane* would be lost?"

Qiro canted his head to the left. "It might yet. Pray it remains becalmed at Nysant while your *Swift* sails south. There should be enough time."

The merchant nodded slowly. "I shall have the papers drawn up immediately for your signature. Once they are signed, I will have my charts?"

The Anturasi patriarch frowned. "My lord, please do not insult me. I trust you. Think of the association of our families, after all. The charts are already drawn up and await your departure. *Swift* can leave within the hour. The papers you may have here by week's end."

"You are most kind, Grandmaster Anturasi."

"I am, aren't I?" Qiro's eyes narrowed. "And, Marutsar, I *am* sorry about your loss."

The kneeling man nodded. "The *Gull,* yes, quite a tragedy."

"I meant your daughter."

Blood drained from the man's face and Nirati feared he'd be sick. He bowed deeply, pressing his forehead against the floor, then came back up, but not fully. "Thank you, Grandmaster. May prosperity continue to smile on the House of Anturasi."

"It will, my lord. It most definitely will."

Majiata's father slunk from the chamber on hands and knees. Nirati made to follow, but her grandfather raised a hand. She waited, and when Lord Phoesel opened the outer cage door, gold bars again slid down over the small doorway.

Nirati raised her chin. "Something you would have of me, Grandfather?"

The old man sat on the throne and smiled warmly this time. "You did this as a favor to your Desei friend. Is he worth it?"

The question surprised her. "I think so. We have become close."

"I understand he is working by brokering shipments, arranging transport, and administering trade agreements. He would find any connection to us of value."

"He would, Grandfather, but he has asked me for nothing for himself. He feels sorry for Lord Phoesel."

Qiro's eyes glittered. "And you risked my ire for him. He must be special, indeed. To have survived Pyrust's wrath and escaped south speaks well of him. Is he involved in intrigues?"

Nirati frowned. "He has met with some of the inland lords and has helped them invest in ships. I know he has warned them against trading with anyone using charts that are not of Anturasi manufacture. That is the extent of things."

"Does he please you, Nirati?"

She hesitated, trying to hide a smile, but then let it blossom fully. Junel had been charming and very well mannered, enjoying her company as much as she enjoyed his. He had not been insistent about anything, so when they had come together intimately, it felt natural. Their trysts had the quality of a romance story about them, and just remembering his caresses puckered her flesh.

"Yes, Grandfather, he does."

"Good. This pleases me as well." Qiro nodded slowly. "I will ask you only one thing, Nirati."

"What, Grandfather?"

"You are very dear to me. I know there are those who say you are not part of this family because you have no talent at cartography. But if you are happy, so am I, and so are your brothers. If you are ever unhappy, you will let me know, won't you?"

"If that is what you wish, Grandfather."

"It is." He opened his arms. "I sit here amid the treasures of the world, but that which I love most dearly stands there, behind those bars. I would tear the world asunder were someone to hurt you. Remember that you are the world's most precious treasure, Nirati. If someone is going to win you away from me, please let him be worthy of you."

She bowed deeply. "Yes, Grandfather. Thank you." She wanted to straighten up, run from the tower, and find Junel; but when she looked into her grandfather's eyes, that desire drained away. He watched her with the patience she'd not seen since she was a child.

"May I ask another favor from you, Grandfather?"

"Of course."

"Let me spend the day with you. I want to visit the workshop again. I want to see your work, and see where my brothers have gotten. It's been so long—too long—since I have done that."

"Yes, Nirati, I would like that." He stood, smiling proudly. "Come to the workshop and I will share my world with you."

Chapter Thirty-seven

25th day, Month of the Rat, Year of the Dog
9th Year of Imperial Prince Cyron's Court
162nd Year of the Komyr Dynasty
736th year since the Cataclysm
Stormwolf, in the South Seas

After two more weeks of sailing, the *Stormwolf* finally found one of the islands from the Soth chart. It had a small harbor into which they sailed—and none too soon, for a savage storm came whistling up out of the southwest. The island was an extinct volcano covered with jungle, barely more than three miles across, but it still protected the fleet. Only one of the smaller ships, the *Mistwolf*, broke her moorings and was driven aground.

In some ways the ship's grounding was a gift of the gods, for the crews quickly scavenged bits to repair storm damage done to the other ships in the fleet. The supplies it had carried were redistributed, and the ship refloated. With only one mast it could not continue the grand voyage, so Captain Gryst outfitted it with a skeleton crew and sent it back north toward Nalenyr, bearing word of what they had seen and done so far.

Jorim had been tempted to send Shimik back with the *Mistwolf* for the Prince's amusement, but the crew's attachment to the Fenn stopped him. At least that is what he recorded in his report on the matter, further noting that he would continue to study the creature and its adaptive capabilities. The truth of the matter was that he was quite fond of Shimik and had no desire to be parted from the little beast.

Shimik continued to develop in response to life on the ship. Since he spent so much time in the hold hunting rats, his fur darkened to a deep mahogany. His fingers lengthened and developed bony ridges along their length and the backs of his hands—where he had previously shown evidence of rat bites. He also became leaner and could ascend the ship's ratlines with the best of the sailors. He continued his comedic antics to the delight of all, but he also could have his grim moments—as if mimicking Captain Anaeda. Oddly enough, she did not seem to think he was mocking her, and more than once he'd found the two of them hunched over a chart, studying things.

While none of the other storms that blew up from the south were as savage as the one they'd weathered at what they called Byorang—Storm Island—the fleet found itself regularly lashed by strong winds and driving rain as they continued. The seas became heavy enough that even the *Stormwolf* rose and fell like a toy. At those times, Anaeda reminded him that he needed to use two hands—one for himself and one for the ship—lest he be lost overboard. For the most part he kept to his cabin, since the clouds and rain made attempting any positional reading of the stars impossible.

When he did venture out, he did not go far, and just watched the water in all its myriad forms. He witnessed an elemental struggle, with wind and water doing their best to destroy the vessel of wood. He watched other ships rise to the crest of waves, then disappear over them, never knowing if behind the curtain of water they had been shattered, or if they would reappear once more.

Sheets of rain assaulted the *Stormwolf*. Heavy droplets exploded against the deck, drumming loudly, opening holes in the rivers that washed over the deck. Waves crashed against the bow, dark water fragmenting into foam. The sails remained taut as the wind filled them. Masts creaked under the strain, and Anaeda was constantly bellowing orders to hoist one sail, or furl another. A good gust could have ripped them apart or snapped a mast, but to run without sails would be to surrender all ability to steer. The wind would blow the ship broadside to the towering waves and that would be the doom of any ship, even one as big as the *Stormwolf*.

Most of the crew handled the storm well, but the same could not be said of the passengers. Iesol spent most of the time frightfully sick. When calm did descend, he labored feverishly to get caught up with all his work, which left him exhausted and even less able to tolerate a lively sea. Others remained in seclusion, but kept the cooks busy preparing concoctions to fight seasickness.

The nastiest of the storms hit them on the twentieth day of the Month of the Rat and lasted for three long days. It broke around noon on the twenty-third, and the clouds vanished so quickly that one had to wonder if there had ever been a storm at all. As per orders, the fleet sailed south, cutting back and forth to the west and east every three hours, and pretty soon seven of the nine remaining tenders rejoined the *Stormwolf*.

Two ships had not rejoined the fleet by the twenty-fifth, and all aboard assumed the *Moondragon* and *Seastallion* had not survived the storm. But as dawn broke on the twenty-fifth, a lookout perched up among the starcombers saw a ship to the east. Anaeda ordered the *Stormwolf* to come about.

Jorim watched from the bow with a sinking feeling in his stomach. One of the crew had identified the ship as the *Moondragon,* and if he was right she had lost two of her four true masts. The remaining two only had scraps of tattered sails fluttering from yardarms, and cables snapped in the breeze. As they drew closer, he saw no signs of life on board and took as a good sign that none of the ship's boats remained on the deck.

He commented about that when Captain Gryst joined him, but she shook her head. "That's not really a hopeful sign. It's possible they thought the ship was going to sink. But putting out in boats in such a storm was as suicidal as remaining on a sinking ship. Yes, there; take a look at the aft, at the rudder."

Jorim squinted. "What rudder?"

"Exactly. It's gone. They survived the storm, then put the boats out with cables to help steer the ship."

"If that's true, then where are the boats and where are the crew?"

She sighed heavily. "I don't know." She turned and barked an order. "Lieutenant Minan, lower my boat. Master Anturasi and I will be crossing to the *Moondragon*. Give us a squad of soldiers and send over another boat with a crew that can get her cleaned up."

Minan started barking orders. By the time they crossed to midship, the captain's boat had already been lowered. Anaeda descended the netting first, then Jorim followed, with Shimik scrambling down headfirst after them like a squirrel. Anaeda noticed the Fennych's presence but did not comment on it, and Shimik remained quiet as the soldiers boarded and sailors began rowing them to the *Moondragon*.

Jorim saw no other significant damage to the smaller vessel as they approached. Anaeda had the sailors take them around the ship once, then come in close to where the boarding net hung on the ship's port side. Soldiers went up first, and once the nine of them signaled all was clear, Anaeda ascended. Shimik clung to Jorim's back for the trip, then leaped off and scampered across the deck and down into the bowels of the ship.

Captain Gryst strode across the deck and back into the cabin that belonged to Captain Calon, with Jorim only a step behind her. The cabin looked to be in order, showing no storm damage. "They got through the weather and were able to reorganize."

She went to the small desk against the port bulkhead and opened the logbook to the last page. "Heading, estimated speed, and continued damage reports on the morning of the twenty-fourth. Calon had the boats out, but only two of them. No indication the other two were lost in the storm. No sign of panic, and she'd not have left this log on board if she abandoned the ship."

Jorim glanced at the oil lamp swinging from a slender chain next to the captain's bunk. "The oil's all gone. It's cold, but probably was burning since yesterday."

"Yes, you can't get much more than a day's worth of oil in one of those, and it would have been filled in the morning watch." Anaeda closed the logbook and tucked it under her arm. "Let's go forward and check the galley."

Lieutenant Minan and the crew arrived as they were making their way to the galley. Captain Gryst assigned them to clearing the deck of debris and getting ready to hoist sails. They fell to the tasks with some muttering. Jorim gathered, based on half-heard comments and wide-eyed glances, that none of the sailors liked being on a ship where not one of their comrades remained.

"Captain, this ship had how big a crew?"

"Two hundred." She ducked her head and descended steps to the galley. The cooking fires had died, and a huge black kettle contained a congealed mass of rice with a wooden spoon stuck into it. She grabbed it and tried to wrench it free, but only managed to snap it in half.

She stared at the broken handle for a moment. "Whatever happened, it happened yesterday morning. Let's keep looking."

Jorim turned and moved past the stairs into the long area below the main deck. A hundred empty hammocks swayed there, as gently as they would have with sailors occupying them. Blankets hung from some; others had fallen to the floor. At first glance it looked as if the sailors had just been called to their stations and would soon be back to stow their bedding, set up tables, and enjoy a hot breakfast.

Jorim toed one of the blankets, but the fabric moved stiffly and clung to the floor. "I don't like this."

Anaeda turned. "Blood?"

"I think so."

She nodded. "I agree. You can smell it."

Anaeda threaded her way through the hammocks to the ship's aft. There she looked into one cabin after another. The wooden latches and doorjambs had splintered, and the cabins showed signs of a fierce struggle. The junior officers' cabins were liberally splashed with blood. The one that had been home to a priest of Wentiko had a bloody robe on the floor that had been clawed to pieces.

She crouched beside the robe and Jorim examined the hatch. "Look, right here about where a shoulder would hit if someone was forcing the door . . ." He reached up and tugged off a scale the size of his little finger's fingernail. "It's from a fish, but no fish I've ever seen."

Anaeda stood. "Not many fish I know of with claws. Let's keep looking."

The hatch to the ship's sick bay remained intact, but also had scales at about shoulder height. Anaeda slipped a knife from her belt and slid it between door slats, flipping the latch. They forced the hatch open, sliding a trunk away from behind it, and slipped in through the narrow opening.

The sick bay had been a fairly good-sized cabin, large enough for two patient bunks and a third for the physician. Chests of various sizes were stacked against the interior wall, and the doctor's desk was jammed back into the corner. The two far bunks remained unoccupied, but not so the physician's bed.

It had a body in it—the body of a corpulent man. His swollen tongue protruded from his mouth, and dried white traces of spittle foam flecked his lips. The remains of a small ceramic cup lay beside the bed, and a dark stain colored the deck amid the fragments.

Anaeda touched the back of her hand to his cheek. "Dead."

"By his own hand, it would seem."

She picked up a paper packet from his desk and read the characters inscribed on it. "Heartblossom."

"That could have been used for seasickness. That's what Iesol has been taking."

"Yes, but severely diluted. Half this packet is gone. He wanted to make sure he died, and quickly, too." She leafed open his medical log, then snapped it shut and growled. "He was terrified enough to kill himself, but recorded nothing."

A rapid drumbeat sounded outside the room, then Shimik leaped and caught the edge of the hatchway. His claws gouged curled splinters from the wood as he rooted himself there. "Comma comma, cappatana naeda comma. Jrima comma." He sprang away, twisting in midair, and scrabbled across the deck back toward the bow.

Jorim and Anaeda followed him as quickly as they could, but the hammocks slowed them. Shimik waited at the stairs heading down to the next deck and crouched there, watching them, then peered down. As they cleared the last hammock, the Fenn darted down the stairs and they thundered down after him. Casting one last glance at them, he bolted for the open armory hatch.

Anaeda reached it first and stopped in the hatchway. Shimik squatted at her feet, so that she would have tripped over him had she advanced. But she seemed quite content to grab the hatchway and hang on. She leaned slightly forward, then turned and looked at Jorim.

"I believe, Master Anturasi, you may have the advantage of me in explaining this."

She moved aside and he looked in. The only illumination came from a shaft of light poking through an open port. It clearly let him see two bodies stretched out on the floor. One, a bald man in a sailor's robe, had a smith's hammer clutched in his right hand. Most of his face had been slashed to ribbons and his left eye dangled from its stalk. Similarly his robe had been torn at the neck, and the congealed pool of blood in which he lay had pumped out through a torn carotid artery.

But it was the thing that killed him that stopped Jorim from going any further into the room. The creature appeared vaguely humanoid in that it had arms and legs, though they were more lozenge-shaped in cross section than rounded like a man's limbs. This also held true for the long tail and the body, which narrowed through the chest. The head's exact shape was difficult to discern because the hammer had clearly dented it. A number of the silvery scales that covered the creature's body had been knocked loose and flashed in the sunshine.

The creature's hands had webbing between its fingers. They ended in sharp claws, which had obviously killed the ship's smith. Also visible were sharp triangular teeth, a few of which had been scattered by a hammerblow.

Jorim pointed at the creature. "Scales match. It has characteristics of a fish. I think those are gill slits."

"I concur. So, what is it?"

He shook his head. "I have no idea. I don't even recall this from folktales or legends. They're suited to life in the sea, whatever they are. Could they be why ships that head south seldom make it back? Possibly, but I doubt it."

"Why would that be, Master Anturasi?"

He stood and met her stare very frankly. "If we're going to assume that a school of these sharkmen are what killed the crew and took their bodies away, we are required to make a few other assumptions. One is that for their hunt to go as successfully as it did, they've had practice. That means they've taken human prey before. They found harvesting ships an efficient and rewarding way to hunt."

Anaeda nodded. "Sound reasoning."

"So, if they've been doing this for a long time, they would have expanded their range. Taking a settlement like the one on Ethgi would be fairly simple. We would have seen them move into deltas in populated areas. We would have had stories and evidence of their existence before this."

"That could be, Master Anturasi, but perhaps they can only exist in cooler waters?"

"It was once said the Turasynd could only exist in their cold and dry plain, but when population pressures pushed them to expand, they did." Jorim shook his head. "It may well be we've never heard of these things before, but I'm willing to bet we'll be seeing a lot more of them in the future."

Anaeda rubbed a hand over her forehead. "Two hundred souls gone and we killed only one of them?"

Jorim shook his head. "We might have killed more, but they took the bodies."

"So they're cannibals, too?"

"I don't know. If we dissect the one left here, we might find out."

The captain posted her fists on her narrow hips. Her eyes narrowed. "Do it. I want to know what they are and what we've gotten ourselves into."

Shimik, rising from his crouch, aped her stance. He looked up at her, at the bodies, then shook his head. "Dungga. Bad Dungga."

Chapter Thirty-eight

17th day, Month of the Bear, Year of the Dog
9th Year of Imperial Prince Cyron's Court
162nd Year of the Komyr Dynasty
736th year since the Cataclysm
Dolosan

In the five and a half weeks since they killed the maned snake and its brood at Telarunde, the group made slow progress west. Keles Anturasi accepted full responsibility for their torpid pace, because he was unable to move very fast. Haste would have made his survey less than complete. Moraven agreed that while his mission to locate the source of trade in ancient weapons was urgent, the survey would be the key to his success. His agreement only slightly mollified Ciras, who clearly was in pain, but steadfastly refused to admit it.

The simple fact had been that after the battle, the six of them had needed time to recover. Though he had been physically unhurt, Borosan seemed to come out the worst. He mourned the *thanaton*'s destruction as if it had been a family dog. What hurt him most was that the *gyanrigot* had failed in its mission, and he apologized for the predicament its failure had created for everyone else. Even Moraven's suggestion that it might not have struck because the snake and brood constituted a multitude of targets and confused it did little to mollify him. He vowed he could make a better *thanaton*—and while the rest of them humored him, they hoped they'd not find another maned snake to test it on.

Also, the survey necessitated several steps that kept them moving very slowly. The first was to visit settlements in western Solaeth and Dolosan. They talked to the locals and gathered information about the surrounding area. If they were able, they engaged someone as a guide to the next settlement or other points of interest. As they traveled west, the settlements became fewer, and the points of interest greater, which cut their progress yet again.

Once they'd gathered some preliminary data about the area, they explored it carefully. Keles made best-guess estimates about rates of travel and distances covered. With a practiced eye, he could measure distance just by having Tyressa ride out ahead and seeing how much smaller she got. Every scrap of information, from the location of streams and caves to the sorts of fish to be found and estimates of lumber yield per acre got jotted down in Keles' books.

When Borosan Gryst came out of his funk, he made himself very useful in the survey. He tinkered with his mouser and put together a second, smaller *thanaton* about the size of a wolf. He measured their paces exactly, then would send them out to certain points and back, giving very precise measurements of distance. The *gyanrigot* could even scale trees and cliff faces, providing data on height.

Even the Viruk helped him. Rekarafi gave him names in Viruka of mountains and rivers. He pointed out places where what appeared to be piles of rocks had once been Viruk strongholds. He was even able to show how forests had been harvested and regrown after Viruk and human occupations of the area.

When Keles had first seen him rise over the maned snake's corpse—Rekarafi said the Viruka word for it was *"etharsaal"*—his heart had caught in his throat. He'd been certain the Viruk had come to kill him because of what had happened in the capital, or to avenge the Viruk his brother had killed. His stomach had knotted and he doubled over to vomit.

The warrior had indeed come for him, but not in the way Keles feared. He explained to Moraven and Tyressa that he had been sent by his consort to protect Keles. The Viruk ambassador had correctly discerned that Keles would not have been sent into the Wastes were it not for the incident at the party; therefore, his safety became a matter of honor for the Viruk. Rekarafi had anticipated their arrival at Eoloth and had been waiting there to follow them—though how he had gotten that far that quickly had never been explained. Keles assumed it was through Viruk magic, and that made him wonder how Men had ever thrown off their Viruk overlords.

But for all his helpfulness, Rekarafi was also the greatest impediment to progress. Keles could not remain in close proximity to him for more than a few minutes. One time he made the mistake of drinking water downstream from the Viruk. The water that had washed over Rekarafi made Keles violently ill—so much so that he could not be moved for two days, and remained sickly for the rest of the week. Nightmares haunted his dreams, and more and more frequently he woke unrested, with fierce headaches, his body feeling as if he'd been trampled beneath horses' hooves.

The headaches and illness affected the way he was able to send information back to his grandfather. Many days he could not concentrate enough to make contact, and when he did it remained insubstantial and vague. He was used to his grandfather's making demands on him, but the old man did that less and less. Keles put it down to the fact that when he did reach him, he was communicating so much information in a lump that his grandfather had all he could do to digest it. The other possibility, that his grandfather's mind was failing with age, was not something Keles even wanted to think about.

Instead of concentrating on his grandfather's aging and the problems it might cause, Keles grasped at the idea that the difficulty with sending him information might also have to do with the nature of Dolosan itself. Dolosan had caught the first blast of magic energy released by the battle in Ixyll. The evidence of it was undeniable. The land had broken and shifted, with vast plates of stone rising out of the earth and stabbing toward the sky. Beyond that, however, the upper edges were softened and rounded, as if melted. The magic wave had rolled out, coursing through valleys, washing over mountains, eroding stone, and changing everything it touched.

Some of the sights he would not have believed were he not taking exact measurements. In places huge boulders moved between dusk and dawn, slipping out of alignments he'd drawn the day before. When he went to see if they'd been rolled aside—by what he couldn't imagine—he found no evidence of disturbance. He marked one of these stones with chalk on the north side, and the next morning found the mark all the way around to the south. The mark itself had migrated, but the feature he'd drawn the mark around had not.

Dolosan had been steeped in virulent magic, and even though it had retreated over the years, its effect was inescapable. In one valley a whole copse of trees had been transformed into a living copper forest. More strangely, they swayed with the languid motion of seaweed undulating beneath the waves. The party paused on the valley's rim, uncertain if they should go down or if they would drown in some unseen liquid. When they did enter, they felt increased pressure and were forced to move more slowly. Their words came more thickly, and Keles felt the tug of currents on his clothes and hair.

Keles looked for plants and animals to see what effect living in that sort of place would have on them. Did birds breathe fire so they could mold leaves into nests? Or would they have to become more like fish to swim through the air? And would fish be able to swim around out of water? He didn't see anything that answered his questions, but in looking for them he began to understand his brother's curiosity about the world. For Keles, those things had always been *on* the land; but for Jorim, they were *of* the land.

As they went further west, they truly entered the Wastes. In the day, the land visibly shimmered as if heat rose off it—yet one valley would be frigid enough to frost their breath, and the next would make metal hot to the touch. Hills shifted—albeit slowly, but they shifted—as if made of blankets beneath which children crept. In places, Keles could recognize many plants, but they appeared larger or smaller than normal, and often their blossoms were out of proportion to the plant and boasted colors he'd never seen in nature.

Entering the Wastes made Borosan Gryst happier, and Rekarafi and Ciras more morose. For the *gyanridin,* the Wastes were a land alive with magic energy, where *thaumston* could be found to make his creations live. But Rekarafi looked on a land his people had once ruled, and found it unrecognizable. For Ciras, it was the womb of a new magic that threatened the art he struggled to perfect.

One evening, Ciras' irritability increased because the day's sun had reddened venom-stung flesh. Ciras nudged the mouser aside with his foot. "Keep that abomination away from me."

Borosan blinked his wide eyes. "Abomination? It slew one of the maned snakes as easily as you did."

The swordsman shook his head. "It killed with no honor, no sense of what it was doing. It is an abomination because it does what it does without consideration."

Moraven poked a stick into their fire. "Is it not true, *Lirserrdin* Dejote, that the consideration is that of Master Gryst in his creation of the *gyanrigot*?"

"To agree to that, Master, I would have to weigh the consideration of the swordmaker as being greater than my own in using his tool. The swordmaker may have intended his blade to slay indiscriminately, but I choose when and where to employ it. I accept the responsibility for the consequences of actions."

"And do you not think Master Gryst does that as well? Remember, he did apologize for the *thanaton*'s failure."

Ciras pressed a cool cloth to the right side of his face. The venom had burned him, twisting the flesh near the corner of his mouth and his eye as if they had been touched by fire. "I remember, Master. Master Gryst takes responsibility, but there are those who would not. You have seen the *thanaton*. Imagine a company of them patrolling a castle or, worse yet, being sent to drive villagers from their homes. They would do this regardless of reason. They would not listen, could not be convinced that the lord who gave them orders was wrong and evil."

Tyressa rolled out her blanket. "So you fear these *gyanrigot* will replace the *xidantzu*?"

"No. That could never happen."

"Then what do you fear?"

"I fear nothing. The problem with *gyanri* is that it confers on the untrained skills that ordinarily require years of study. It will erode respect for those who have developed skills. Hard work will become a thing of the past. People will no longer respect or fear magic, and that will pave the way for the return of the *vanyesh*."

Keles, relishing the sorts of discussions he used to have with his brother and sister, raised a hand. "Forgive me, Ciras, but you make quite a leap. Having *gyanrigot* work for someone does not make them want to become a magician."

"I said nothing of the sort."

"But you implied it. Freed of the need to till the earth and plant and harvest, a peasant might learn many things. He might become a great poet or artist or a skilled potter or even a swordsman."

Ciras' eyes shrank. "Or a magician?"

Keles shrugged. "He could be anything. You should credit him with enough sense not to be a magician."

"You have greater faith in common sense than I do, Master Anturasi." Ciras pointed at the mouser. "It travels and measures for you now, but could it not do that for anyone? Training is not required. The link between self-discipline and the ability to control magic is broken. If they see magic as simple in one area, they will see it that way in another. Just as the *gyanrigot* scout paths out for you, they will lead others to the madness that destroyed the world."

Moraven Tolo frowned. "Your thoughts are interesting, but your reasoning unsound."

Ciras sat up straight. "How so, Master?"

"You see the *vanyesh* as purely evil, for this is how you have been taught to see them. They rode with Nelesquin, but so did many *serrdin*. Were the swordsmen evil for fighting in Nelesquin's cause?"

"They must have been."

"Or might they have been deceived?"

"That, too, is possible."

"Which would mean, Ciras, that some of the *vanyesh* may not have been evil, but just deceived." Moraven pointed at the mouser. "Just as that is a tool, so can men be. The difference is that men have a chance to control their behavior. Your concern should not be for which behaviors to allow or not, but how to encourage people to be responsible for their behaviors. Prohibition will always fail at some point. Responsibility does not have to."

Ciras hesitated, then bowed his head. "I beg forgiveness for my lack of sufficient thought."

Moraven, the firelight shimmering through his black hair, hardened his eyes. "The lack of thought will be forgiven this time. You allowed yourself to become as mindless as the *gyanrigot*. That makes you as dangerous as you claim they are. The only way you show restraint is if you actually think. All too often people confuse their being *able* to think with their actually having done so. A more pernicious mistake does not exist."

Their journey took them into the very heart of Dolosan, entering the southern edge of a giant basin roughly two hundred miles from southwest to northeast, and a hundred and fifty miles wide east to west. Scrub vegetation provided sparse if colorful cover. Each of the countless gullies etched into the landscape was home to rainbow streaks of plants.

Rekarafi remained silent for several miles as they descended the gradual slope. "This was Isdazar."

Keles spat sour saliva. "Shining waters?"

The Viruk warrior nodded. "A vast lake. I sailed here with my Ierariach in the times before."

Moraven turned in the saddle and looked back at the loping Viruk. "Was there a large Viruk population here?"

"Once, yes." He pointed a clawed finger toward the north. "Tavliarch was home to many. When the *tavam alfel* came, the water boiled. It rose in a scalded cloud that fell in black rain. What it touched died. It melted Tavliarch. The waters flowed back into the basin and boiled again and again. Finally, they drained into the land."

Borosan nodded. "The continual process of draining and raining allowed minerals to collect in deposits. Some are simple geodes, while others are full layers. It is here that deposits of *thaumston* are found in abundance, though the magic in them often is weak."

"How can it be weak?" Keles stood in the stirrups and pointed to a plant with a cluster of feathered berries. "We're on Ixyll's doorstep. Things should be stronger here."

"No, Keles. You see, the water here, perhaps because of trace minerals, was a poor conductor of magic. It collected it, but transferred little of the magic to other things. What we have seen before are signs of the magic *itself* having touched things. Here it touched the water, which insulated the underlying area. West of here, heading to the uplands, you will see more and stranger things, especially where magic had continued to stream, but here there is only residue.

"The advantage to this *thaumston* is that it is concentrated and capable of absorbing a great deal of magical energy. People dig it up and set it in places where it can be charged. Once it is energized, the possibilities are limitless."

Keles frowned. "How is it charged?"

"It's relatively simple. You put the samples in a metal box and raise a mast above it, or spread leader lines around it; techniques differ. Then you wait."

"For?"

"For a very special storm. You want a moderate chaos-storm. Enough to charge the *thaumston,* but not much more. Luckily, the basin tends to contain the storms."

Moraven raised an eyebrow. "What if the storm is too large?"

"It would kill us." Borosan smiled. "But don't worry. I'm sure it would be a most spectacular way to die."

Chapter Thirty-nine

3rd day, New Year's Festival, Year of the Rat
9th Year of Imperial Prince Cyron's Court
163rd Year of the Komyr Dynasty
737th year since the Cataclysm
Meleswin (Helosunde)
Deseirion

Prince Pyrust smashed the iron edge of his shield into the Helosundian's face, spinning him away. The man's weapon went flying, and the Desei Prince advanced, thrusting deep into another man's vitals. The sword came free with a wet sucking sound. Pyrust kicked the thrashing man away from his feet, then moved on.

Around him, the Golden Hawks moved through Meleswin's main street, slashing and stabbing anything that moved. Most of the Helosundians in the city were drunk and exhausted. When they'd taken Meleswin, they had spared none of those left behind. The men died, the women were raped, and the children sent away as chattel. Delasonsa had accurately predicted what would happen, but even Pyrust had not expected to see streets littered with bodies. Rats and dogs fed on them even as raucous laughter came from windows shuttered against the cold.

The plan to divide and slay the Helosundian leadership had needed little encouragement. The Council of Ministers had been split sharply over who should be chosen prince and settled on Eiran—a minor noble with modest ambition and a comely sister to whom many looked as an avenue to power. Eiran fancied himself a military genius, having waged many wars with toy soldiers. The retreating Desei troops had offered less resistance than his fantasy armies ever did, so he and a horde of undisciplined troops had poured into the city.

Pyrust had planned to counterattack later in the Festival, but stories of fights between the factions provided the impetus to strike sooner. General Pades, who had been passed over as prince, had laid claim to the warehouse district on the river, locking up the storehouses of goods. Eiran had sent troops to open them back up, drawing them from the garrison at South Gate.

The half-trained boys and cripples left there had not even been able to raise an alarm. The Shadow Hawks slew them, then moved into the southern quarter. They went from house to house, slitting throats until there was no resistance left. The Golden Hawks, Mountain Hawks, and Silver Hawks then entered the city and spread out. The Golden Hawks, with the Shadow Hawks moving through the city on both flanks, drove straight to the city center and the mayor's palace, while the other two units swept around east and west to contain Pades and his people in the north.

Fighters began to appear as the Desei closed with the palace. Most, it seemed, had barely enough time or sense to pull on some clothing and draw their swords. They had no idea who they were fighting or why, and some screamed that they had been betrayed by Pades. Others, limping back from the fighting in the north, laid down their arms expecting mercy.

They got none.

Pyrust strode through the streets. His shield had been strapped to his half hand so firmly that he'd lose the limb before it would come off. His black armor had a Golden Hawk emblazoned over the breastplate, and he'd even instructed that it be rendered with the two clipped feathers. His advisors thought that rather unwise, but he knew the Helosundians were unlikely to understand the significance of the ensign. But still, it gratified him to see that a number of the Golden Hawks had defaced their armor to hide those same feathers, providing the enemy with a multitude of targets.

More warriors appeared in the streets, half-naked and bleary-eyed. The wisest of them took one look at the battalion of armored Desei filling the street and fled. The Shadow Hawks would get them.

The rest, with typical Helosundian belief in the virtue of their cause, shrieked out a war cry and charged.

Their cries became whimpers, then rattles and silence.

A knot of them stood on the palace steps, brandishing spears and swords. They'd set themselves for battle, but shivered like the curs feeding on corpses. If they'd had tails, they'd have been tucked firmly over their genitals and bellies.

For a moment or two, Pyrust pitied them. Prince Cyron was responsible for their deaths. And perhaps, as they faced his men, they realized it. The soldiers Cyron brought remained in Nalenyr. The best of them, the Keru, never ventured into combat. Had the Naleni Prince freed them to fight, there would have been a true battle for Meleswin.

And I might even fear what I face.

Pyrust clanged his sword off his shield's rim. "No quarter." He gave the order in a low voice, and word passed quickly back through the ranks. Another clang set his sword to shivering, then he took off at a sprint.

As he raced in, Helosundian spears arced out. A few, thrown weakly, landed in front of him. One spitted a warrior running beside him. The rest passed over him harmlessly. Those who had thrown them slowly began to realize, as the Hawks came on undiminished, that their spears would have been more effective had they been used to stab.

Pyrust raised his shield to intercept an overhand blow. It shivered his arm and splintered part of the shield, but the rim blunted the blow. The warrior wrenched his sword free, but by the time he had, Pyrust's blade had cloven his left shin in two. The man screamed and fell, knocking another man down. Quick thrusts finished both of them. Their limp bodies slid down the marble steps, painting a red carpet for Pyrust's advance.

Soldiers who had flanked the knot of Helosundians ripped the palace doors open. Bows twanged from within and men spun away, arrows through throats, arms, and legs. More poured into the building, and by the time Pyrust fought his way to the entrance, the half dozen archers lay dead.

Pyrust helped a leg-stuck man to his feet. The warrior reached down and snapped the shaft off, casting it contemptuously aside. "It is nothing, my lord."

"It is a blazon of honor." Pyrust mounted the stairs and marched up slowly, matching his pace to that of the wounded man. Other Golden Hawks streamed up the white marble stairs before him and spread out on either side of the brass doors to the main audience chamber. The Prince held a hand up, and the men who were preparing to draw the door open relaxed.

Pyrust approached and hammered the doors with the hilt of his sword. "Prince Eiran, I am Pyrust, come for my city. Open this door and no harm shall befall you."

He heard no response and frowned. He spun, then waved his sword to clear the soldiers from the direct line of the door. "Do nothing for the moment." Turning back to the door, he got out of the way, sheathed his sword, then nodded to the soldiers waiting there. "Open, now."

They tugged on the ropes they'd attached to the handles, and the doors slowly opened like theater curtains drawing back. A rattle of arrows skipped off the doors and floor. Pyrust stooped and picked up one of the arrows, then laughed. Holding it in his right hand, he stepped into the doorway and through.

The audience chamber was too small to have ever been considered grand, but the marble and granite inlaid in the floors and forming the dais at the far end had been imported. They had been fitted together in the Helosundian dog crest, which Pyrust's father had left intact, since the artistry did give the room some majesty. The murals on the walls had been repainted to depict glorious scenes from Desei history, and it amused Pyrust to see that the portrait of himself on the east wall had been defiled. His face had been obliterated by repeated pounding with a dented brass urn.

The sprawl of young and very drunk Helosundian nobles between the crest and the dais echoed the corpse-strewn streets outside. Out there, bodies lay in pools of blood, urine, and excrement; inside, the nobles lay in spilled wine and their own vomit. Their armor—none of it showing battle wear—had been cast aside. Whatever robes they had worn beneath now gave thin shelter to cowering women who looked up at Pyrust with haunted eyes. A half dozen of the nobles, including the new Prince, had managed to stand and shoot, but none of them had nocked a fresh arrow, and only two fingered shafts in their quivers.

Pyrust lifted the arrow he'd plucked from the ground. "Care to try again?"

Bows clattered to the ground in reply. Archers soon followed, their ashen pallor deepening. Only Eiran remained on his feet, but he wavered and swallowed. Pyrust stared at him as he advanced, slowly spinning the arrow between his fingers. With each step he took, the Helosundian's trembling increased.

Pyrust looked past him to the woman sitting in the mayor's chair. She could have been a Keru, were she taller and heavier, for she had the blonde hair and the icy eyes and the hardness that came with pure hatred. He quickened his pace, sweeping past the Prince and up the three steps to the throne. He threw the arrow aside and grabbed her by the throat, lifting her roughly, but she did not cry out.

Blood from his glove streaked her neck. She swallowed, and he felt it. He felt her life in his hands, the thrumming of her heart. Only the shrinking of her pupils and the slight flair of delicate nostrils betrayed her feelings.

She spat in his face.

Pyrust released her and wiped the spittle from his cheek, then flicked his hand out in a backhanded slap. It snapped her head around and rocked her back against the throne, but she did not go down. Rising redness marked her right cheek. She straightened and her eyes narrowed.

Pyrust held his hand before her face. "Don't spit again. I would be disappointed if you could think of no new outrage."

He turned, deliberately presenting his back to her, then stalked down the steps to where her brother still stood. Pyrust let his hand fall heavily on the Prince's shoulder. With the slightest pressure, he could have driven him to his knees. Instead, he tightened his grip and kept Eiran upright.

He whispered in the Helosundian's ear. "Your sister has bought your life. That is who she is, isn't it? You could never attract someone with that much spirit, no matter the crown you wore."

"And you, Jasai." Pyrust spun and looked back up at the girl.

"When they made your brother a prince, did they make you a princess?"

She glared at him. "No."

"Then I shall."

Eiran shook off his hand. "No."

Pyrust hooked his shield arm out and turned the young Prince around. He kept his voice low and cold. "Understand something, Eiran. You are a fool and a coward. You say no, but you can do nothing to enforce it. In fact, if I chose to take your sister right now, right there, on that throne, you would hold her for me. Look, she knows it."

Eiran's head came up and his sister's stare impaled him. He sank to his knees and vomited over Pyrust's boots.

The Desei Prince nudged him onto his side, less to move him from the puddle than to wipe his boots clean. He again mounted the steps to the throne. "You, Jasai—duchess, countess, whatever they in their foolishness made you—shall now be a Princess of Deseirion. You purchase one thing immediately: your brother's life. I'll have his court sobered, saddled, and escorted south to where they can reach Nalenyr without incident. A second thing you purchase when we wed: a truce in this province. No more raiding against your people. No more forced resettlement."

Jasai shifted her incendiary gaze to him and he hesitated for a moment. There could be no mistaking the fury on her face, but flickers of ambition also flashed there. Her foolish brother had become drunk with his success and the spoils of battle, but she'd remained sober. She had positioned herself to rise to power.

"You don't think you can trust me. You're wise in that, but you will learn you can." Pyrust reached up and took her hand in his. "You will buy one more thing. Give me a son, and he shall rule Helosunde as your brother should have. You will be his regent."

Her brow furrowed for a moment. "Why would you offer me Helosunde?"

"If I do not, you will hate me forever."

"I assure you, my lord, I *will* always hate you."

"But you will tolerate me to save your people. Life will be better for my people. It is not much of a dowry, but I shall accept it."

Jasai raised her chin. "I think, my lord, you leave unnamed the greatest gift I will give you."

"Do tell me."

"My rule of Helosunde will free you to pursue other ambitions." She smiled. "You make me a princess, you give me Helosunde, but I will make you an Emperor."

Pyrust bit the inside of his cheek to kill his smile. "In a Festival of new beginnings, this may be the best beginning of all. The new year will be full of portent, indeed."

Chapter Forty

3rd day, Month of the Tiger, Year of the Rat
9th Year of Imperial Prince Cyron's Court
163rd Year of the Komyr Dynasty
737th year since the Cataclysm
Stormwolf, in the South Seas

Since finding the *Moondragon* and the odd creature aboard it, the expedition had known little joy. In part that could be blamed on their traveling further south with the prevailing current. The seas became more hostile and the weather significantly cooler. Shimik began to grow a thick coat in response, and the treachery of ice on the decks added to the dangers of shipboard life.

Though Captain Gryst was content to leave the sea devil to Jorim for study, he quickly brought the scholars on the *Stormwolf* in to study the thing. They all dissected it and preserved pieces in various jars. Drawings were rendered of its overall physiology from flesh in. The claws were tested and found to contain a venom thought to be similar to a Viruk warrior's. It caused paralysis in small animals, and the investigators suggested that many of the crew had been felled by it before they had a chance to fight.

A study of its stomach contents yielded fishbones and fingers, suggesting strongly that the rest of the *Moondragon*'s crew would never be found. Bits and pieces of its flesh were fed to cats and a few rats with no ill effect. The fact that cats ate it with relish did nothing to make any of the men want to partake.

But the effect of all the study proved less than satisfactory. The only thing the scholars could agree on was that they'd never seen anything like it. The reasons for that abounded, as well as stories of how the creature could have come to exist. Some decided the gods were upset with Men in general and created these things to supplant them. Others spoke of more sinister and salacious situations, in which lost sailors had committed unspeakable acts with fishwomen. Jorim still favored the theory he had advanced to Anaeda; that they were just a heretofore undiscovered race of creature. The utter lack of stories about them did worry him, but since the only logical alternative was that they were a spontaneous creation of the gods, he stuck with his theory. Divine intervention just did not sit well with him.

He did remember his conversation with Keles before they both departed. Keles had suggested Empress Cyrsa still existed in Ixyll and was out there fighting something that still threatened the old Empire. Keles had advanced the theory that perhaps the Cataclysm had opened a rift to another world, letting in forces as yet unseen by man. While Jorim considered that highly unlikely, it did serve to explain why there was no long-standing tradition of these sea devils in folktales.

In the end, he just accepted that they were what they were. It wasn't so important to know where they had come from as it was to spot where they were and to determine where they might be going. The fact that they had been able to attack a ship and denude it of crew, leaving only the barest of signs of their passing, frightened him. He wasn't so much worried for the *Stormwolf* as he was for a small island, or what would happen if the creatures passed up a river delta and began to devour villages.

In the month of the Bear, the fleet located more of the islands from the Soth chart and landed crews to examine them. They did find some signs of human habitation, but it had been years since the villages were populated. On one island they were able to harvest a lot of feral pigs to replenish their supply of fresh meat, and it provided ample feasting for the New Year's Festival. Even better, the pigs' presence suggested the sea devils hadn't visited the islands, which made everyone feel somewhat at ease.

The New Year's Festival passed without so much as a storm,

which they all found welcome yet unusual. No one complained, however, and the Festival carried on with an exchange of gifts among the people of the fleet: nothing extravagant, and all of it the product of labors undertaken in spare minutes here and there. Clothes newly decorated with embroidery were exchanged, serenades were sung for the enjoyment of all, and even the cooks outdid themselves by making the normal fare extraordinary through use of spices that had been hoarded against such a time.

Shimik even provided a present to those on the *Stormwolf*. Alotia, one of the concubines who had been apprenticed to the Lady of Jet and Jade, spent hours teaching the Fennych a dance. Jorim had not quibbled over her constant requests for the Fenn's company since she kept him occupied during the dissections. It was only when she dressed the small creature in a blue robe embroidered with golden tigers that he wondered what she'd been doing with him all that time.

The traditional dance, which went by the formal name *Chado-ong-dae,* was usually performed to greet the new year by a young woman of marriageable age who sought a mate. It had long been seen as dance of seduction, with the lithe and fluid movements reflecting the dancer's grace and sensuous nature. Jorim had seen it performed a number of times through the years, in a variety of forms, all over the Nine Principalities and beyond.

But never had he seen it done the way Shimik did it. What for a girl were graceful and delicate motions became strong and stalking. Where she was a tigress slipping through the jungle eluding all those save for the mate she chose, Shimik became the hunting tiger. His leaps tucked into rolls from which he emerged with a flash of claw and fang. He became all muscle and sinew, his movements deliberate and menacing, his hunting turns fearsome enough to make sailors scoot back and give him room.

And then, the music and dance would end and his demeanor would shift. He'd run to Alotia and leap into her arms as people cheered. The vestiges of feline nature would vanish into an infantile hug the concubine returned heartily, and growls became delighted coos. The transformation brought another round of applause from the spectators, prompting both performer and teacher to bow most humbly and wish the joy of the Festival to all.

So well received was the performance that Captain Gryst ordered Shimik sent around the fleet to entertain all the ships. Parties from each ship visited the *Stormwolf* in the wake of his performances. Before the month of the Tiger dawned, Shimik had uniforms from each ship as well as a variety of trinkets with which he filled a wooden box and gleefully pawed whenever foul weather kept him in the cabin.

But where the Festival had given them respite from foul weather and ill omens, the month of the Tiger lived up to its worst potential. Chado, the tiger god, moved through shadows and visited misfortune on those who displeased him. Clouds and fog closed in with the turn of the year, making it all but impossible to discern even the lamps burning fore and aft on the nearest ships.

Information passed between ships through a laborious process of lantern signaling. Not only did it take a long time to pass any messages, but many on the ships could read the signals. Rumors based on these messages abounded, and the last remnants of joy from the Festival evaporated.

The fleet was being stalked.

Everyone knew about the sea devil; there had been no keeping that news quiet. To counteract the fear, the scholars had been charged to try to figure out what the thing actually was. Captain Gryst had labored under the vain hope that someone might have known, thereby ending all speculation. Absent that sort of victory, the plethora of explanations could have split opinions and directed folks away from worrying too much. Unfortunately, the sailors uniformly dismissed any scholarly speculation, assuming that since the sea was their home, they knew best. And what they knew was that the sea devils were nasty and had attacked a ship, hauling the crew away. This meant they would be out there waiting to take the next ship that got careless, and would continue to do so until they were all gone.

Jorim realized that, given the sailors and their opinions, there would have been stories about the fleet being stalked whether or not there was anything to it. While he didn't want to believe in what they were saying, there was no way the stories couldn't get into his head. He felt ashamed of falling prey to superstitions, and said as much to Captain Gryst as they sat over a game of chess in her cabin one evening.

She looked up from the board and frowned at him. "I need not lecture you on how strange the ocean can be. If you think about it, water is but a thick fog over an incredible landmass. As the air has birds, so the ocean has fish. What is down below the fish, though, we have no way of knowing—any more than we can determine what is above the clouds. If you think about it just for a moment, you might see that the sea devils have their own empires down there, on the bottom of the ocean, and they have found a way to rise into their sky, to find out what is skimming their clouds. What they have found is us."

Jorim shifted his shoulders as a chill trickled down his spine. "You don't actually believe that, do you?"

"Believe? No." She moved her Master of Shadows. "I would not waste the time or energy believing in that. But I accept it is possible. What I want is an answer, because this not-knowing is harming my crew."

From somewhere on deck, a voice raised an alarm. Before the two of them had slid their chairs back from the table, Lieutenant Minan opened the door to her cabin. "Begging your pardon, Captain. Green lanterns off the port bow."

"Out of the way, Lieutenant." Anaeda pushed past him and led the way to the deck. "Keep to your duties, all of you. Helm, steady the course."

They raced along the deck and Jorim went down once on an icy patch. He got up and sprinted up the ladder to join the captain in the bow. Cold wind cut at him, but it really didn't matter because nothing could have warmed him.

Above, a thin crack opened in the clouds and bled silver into the mist. The moon's light silhouetted a huge ship—one not nearly the length and breadth of the *Stormwolf,* but equally suited to long voyages over deep ocean. It bore the customary nine masts, but from them hung tattered sheets. Jorim could make out the crest on one of them and knew it to be Naleni, but from a time before Prince Cyron ruled.

One of the older sailors in the bow pointed. "That's the *Wavewolf.*"

Jorim's flesh tightened. "The *Wavewolf* was lost eighteen years ago. My father was on it."

"No longer, Master Anturasi."

The moonlight illuminated the creatures capering on the deck and clinging to the ratlines. Sea devils, each and every one of them. The one they'd found on the *Moondragon* had been a runt, for these creatures were half again the size of a normal man. The lanterns fore, aft, and hanging from masts burned with a green light that shimmered from scales as creatures spun through dances that had no accompaniment.

A million thoughts rioted through Jorim's mind. He tried to recall what his father looked like and could not. The image of the man he'd held in his mind had been created from dozens of stories, but they all evaporated as he watched the shadowship keep pace with them. His father had filled how many bellies over there? He couldn't imagine what he would tell his mother or grandfather, sister or brother. *Will I get the chance, or will I feed them as he did?*

An urgent tug on his trousers brought him back to reality. He glanced down.

Shimik raised his bow. "Twanga twanga!"

Jorim wondered for a moment how the Fenn had managed to string the bow, but didn't let that stop him from bringing it to hand and pulling an arrow from the quiver Shimik had dragged on deck. He drew, aimed, and let fly.

The arrow disappeared in the darkness. Jorim thought he'd missed his mark, then one of the sea devils spasmed and fell from the rigging. The other sea devils paused in their dancing as he flopped to the deck, then fell on him, clawing and biting. They tore limbs free and several led merry chases over the deck as others sought to steal part of their bounty.

Jorim nocked another arrow, but Anaeda held a hand up. "It will do no good."

"One more, Captain, please." Jorim swallowed hard. "For my father?"

She nodded and stood back. He drew and aimed. He held his shot, measuring the distance, letting the ships rise and fall. He let the rhythm move through him, and finally shot.

The arrow hit its mark. A green lantern high on the main mast fell like a streaking star to the main deck. It exploded when it hit, spraying burning oil over the decking and back up the mast. Several of the capering sea devils became spinning torches. They careened over the deck, igniting cable and sail while the ship's rolling spread the liquid fire further. Another lantern exploded, and another.

Whatever had been propelling the *Wavewolf* forward stopped. The burning ship fell off the wind and the clouds closed. But even without moonlight, the ship remained visible. It turned broadside to the ocean's swells, rising and falling. One moment they could see the whole of it ablaze, and the next the masts showed as distant candle flames. And then even the candles went out and the *Wavewolf* disappeared.

Anaeda Gryst turned to him. "Shall I congratulate you on your shooting?"

Jorim shook his head. "If I thought that was the last we'd see of the sea devils, I would welcome it. I don't think it is."

"Nor do I." She sighed. "In fact, I think it is highly likely that you've only made them angrier."

Chapter Forty-one

3rd day, Month of the Tiger, Year of the Rat
9th Year of Imperial Prince Cyron's Court
163rd Year of the Komyr Dynasty
737th year since the Cataclysm
Dolosan

The disharmonious nature of Dolosan's western reaches—including the approaches to Ixyll—disturbed Moraven in ways he had not expected. In his life he had seen many things, but nothing quite matched the Wastes. He found all of it hauntingly familiar, as if he were half-remembering dreams.

The western reaches seemed to be full of places apart from the world. It took them a day to get through a lush valley carpeted with maroon plants that bore massive blue blossoms. The stems and roots throbbed, and none of the horses would eat them or the flowers. Tyressa had picked one blossom, and a whole swath of flowers had snapped shut in a rippling wave. Keles had dug into the ground and, as nearly as any of them could make out, the plants shared a network of roots.

Even more interestingly, the valley began to shift. The land itself moved, deepening the valley and urging them forward. Things never got to the point where they were in danger of being crushed, for the land's swelling came gently. Moraven just felt as though the valley was nudging them along the way a finger might nudge a caterpillar off a leaf.

He'd looked over at the Viruk trotting alongside them. "This valley can't possibly be alive."

"No more so than the *gyanrigot,* but that does not prevent them from moving."

Things continued to get more strange, as if each valley or plain had been shaped according to a plan. One meadow they rode through caused Rekarafi to stop dead and just crouch amid the flowers. Moraven wasn't sure why, but Ciras offered a quiet answer.

"On Tirat there are scrolls. They are very old and on them are pictures of plants that no longer exist." He looked around. "They look like these."

The swordmaster rode over to the Viruk. "We can linger here, if you wish."

"And allow me to wallow in a past that will never return?"

"Let you refresh memories that once brought you joy."

Rekarafi looked at him carefully. "Even happy memories hurt. It's the separation."

Moraven had ridden off to allow the Viruk some peace. The ancient one's words had found resonance in him. There was something about the Wastes he did not like. He wanted to ascribe it to constantly feeling the tingle of magic, but that had never been an unpleasant experience before. Still, he was so used to controlling magic that the sensation had him constantly on guard, and that did wear him down.

But as unsettling as he found the land of wild magic, Ciras clearly found it more so, and this bothered Moraven. He had not been as young as Ciras when he first felt the tingle of *jaedunto,* and had been more fortunate in having had training in a variety of schools prior to that. He couldn't remember that training, but it had existed and Master Jatan's instruction brought the skills back to him, even if he could not recover the memories.

The *serrian* experience had given him discipline and had trained him how to evaluate experiences so he could learn from them. This he had done immediately, and learned how to expand his access to the magic of swordsmanship. Phoyn Jatan had recognized his potential and position. He also took measure of Moraven's maturity and explained very simply that he was at a crossroads in his life. If he were to view *jaedunto* as power, as some sort of right that allowed him to do as he willed, the power would twist him. Though he would live for generation after generation, his existence would be an eternity of torment. He would never know peace.

Taking to heart Master Jatan's teaching, Moraven slowly learned how to harness his power. His lessons did come slowly, however, mastered only over time. He could never forget the haunted look in the eyes of young Matut when he'd slaughtered bandits without a thought on the road to Moriande. From that day forward, if it were possible to avoid combat, he did. If it were possible to avoid killing, he did. Where he had to kill, he made it clean and quick.

Ciras had not yet reached the point where he could separate the desire to perfect his skill from the consequences of employing that skill. Ciras did argue that the slaying of ruffians in Asath really mattered little and, in fact, had been necessary to prevent any alarm about Keles' escape. Moraven agreed with both points. Had he not agreed with the latter, he would not have slain those he faced. The former point, however, was not as clear-cut. While the death of a ruffian had limited consequences—grief to those who loved him being the most likely—that view failed to take into account the effect on the swordsman.

Moraven could not remember every person he'd ever slain, and believed the peace of *jaedunto* insulated him from many of those memories. It did not save him from all of them, however. He'd killed in battles, in roadside encounters, and in duels. He recalled how it felt when a sword stroked a belly open, or the scream when a limb parted company with the body. Each time he took a life, it weighed his spirit down. *In realizing my full potential, I block others from realizing theirs.*

Moraven was fully aware that one school of thought about *jaedunto* suggested this was entirely necessary. It suggested that the way one reached that lofty position was by assuming the potential of those slain along the way. The obvious contradiction of this was a skilled cobbler whose skill slew no one, yet grew daily and carried him ever closer to *jaedunto*. Perhaps there was more than one path to *jaedunto,* or just that with each masterpiece made, someone else was robbed of the chance to have created it.

Regardless of the theoretical source of the power, hard work, discipline, and patience were all seen as vital. In their wanderings, Ciras Dejote had developed a certain impatience which, while it had not yet entered the realm of swordplay, did bring with it a disturbing contempt. He had no use for Borosan Gryst and his *gyanrigot*. While Moraven had been impressed with the Naleni's skill at creating and re-creating the devices, Ciras harped on how quickly they broke, or how other, more simple methods could accomplish what they did.

Moraven had tried to deflect Ciras by giving him a simple duty. In their survey they cut across signs of a bandit company scouring the landscape. They found evidence of raids at several small encampments. *Thaumston* prospectors had been murdered and any store of the precious mineral stolen. Likewise they'd discovered a number of small tombs—things from ancient cairns to tiny caves that had been walled shut—which had been opened and the contents rifled.

To Ciras fell the duty of recording all evidence of the band's predation. This kept him focused. The idea of meeting and dealing with cutthroats, murderers, and defilers of the dead fueled him. It sharpened his powers of observation and even sparked his imagination. He watched the tracks so closely he could identify individuals based on their horses and footprints. He gave them names and would report back on their current states of existence.

Unfortunately, this duty also fed his impatience. Whenever they would find fresh tracks, he would want to set off immediately in pursuit. Moraven always forbade it, citing the need to help Keles. Ciras argued that their mission from Master Jatan demanded they intercept the raiders and should take precedence. Moraven reminded him that the mission had been given to *him,* not Ciras, and he would decide when the time to strike was at hand.

Finally, they had run across tracks that told a story that required investigation. Moving through lowlands, they came to a canyon splitting the face of an escarpment. The bandits had ridden into it, then most of them had come back and continued along the escarpment toward the northeast. Yet three of them had not returned, and Moraven found his curiosity piqued.

He chose to ride in the lead and studied the rock walls rising up so high the sky became but a thin ribbon of blue. He saw no one up there, nor any signs of climbing, but he remained alert. Moraven was fairly certain that the bandits had no idea they were being trailed, so the chances of their setting up an ambush were minimal—and using only three men to do so was foolish. Assuming, however, that the missing members of the group might be dead meant that something had killed them. *Whatever or whoever that was will present a similar threat to us.*

Three miles in, the canyon opened onto a narrow valley that continued for another couple of miles before closing in again. Moraven could not see to the far end, but found it easy to imagine that the trail led to the top of the escarpment. It looked to be a fairly convenient way to move to the highlands, and doubtless was used by people and animals alike.

It was not without its perils, however. Three hundred yards into the valley sat a small pool of water roughly thirty feet in diameter. Not a ripple showed on its surface, and the sun reflected brightly from it. Given that much of the water in the Dolosan lowlands had a brackish quality to it, this pool looked quite inviting.

The only thing that spoiled the image was the circle of bleached skeletons and fresh bodies around it. Most lay with their heads facing the pool but a few, including one of the bandits, had been running from it. The circle touched the valley's east and west walls, and several skeletons huddled against the stone—including a couple of warriors in armor.

Moraven reined up, and the others spread out in the small safe zone nearest the canyon, with the Viruk squatting in a thin slice of shadow to the east. The horses stamped and shied, not wanting to linger in this place of death.

Keles patted his horse's neck. "I don't blame you for not liking it here."

Ciras rode up beside Moraven and pointed his quirt at one of the bandits. "That is Pegleg and the dead bay is his horse. The other two are Cutheel and Solehole. Pegleg went down first, and Cutheel next, knocked out of his saddle. Solehole went down with his horse and tried to run. He may have even dived for Cutheel's horse—that, or fell—then tried to crawl away before dying."

"I think your reading is correct." Moraven used a hand to shield his eyes from the sun and peered more closely at the bandits. From where he sat, he couldn't see what had killed the horses, but Solehole had a hole in his overshirt right over his spine. It appeared to be a burn mark, with considerable scorching around it. One of the armored skeletons also seemed to have a hole in his breastplate, but it was too far distant for Moraven to figure out what had caused it.

He slid from the saddle. "There definitely seems to be a perimeter. Stay back. I want to see what happens when—"

"If I might make a suggestion, Master Tolo?"

Ciras spitted Borosan with a harsh stare. "Quiet, *gyanridin*. My Master knows what he is doing."

Moraven laughed. "Actually, I don't. I would welcome a suggestion."

"It would have been easier had we not abandoned my wagon at Telarunde, but I'll make do." Borosan climbed down off his horse and walked back to the packhorse he'd been leading. He opened a pouch and pulled out the mouser. "We can use this to see what is out there."

The swordsman nodded. "Excellent idea."

The *gyanridin* bowled the mouser into the circle and it snapped its legs out the instant it stopped rolling. The little metal ball scuttled forward, then left and right, slowly closing with the dead bay.

The pool reacted. As if a rock had dropped at its heart, a ripple spread out in a perfect ring. It hit the edges, but instead of lapping over, it reversed and sped back in. It picked up speed, and when it converged at the center, a column of water shot ten feet into the air. A spherical drop leaped up and hung there, glistening in the sunlight as the column flowed down again.

The sphere throbbed and altered its shape. It flattened into a disk, then thickened in the middle. Sunlight flashed through it, and suddenly the mouser began to smoke. The little *gyanrigot* continued its dash toward the dead horse and the zigzagging course forced the disk to shift shape and reposition itself. Several black char marks dappled the mouser's shell, but it reached the dead horse and hid between haunch and tail.

A final puff of smoke matched the curling of tail hair. The disk became a sphere again and floated there. Light played through it slowly and languidly. It appeared almost inviting and certainly benign.

And had I not seen what I have just seen, my thirst might have driven me to accept the pool's hospitality.

The Keru crouched at the edge of the death circle. "I don't know what it is. I don't know if it is alive, so I don't know if we can kill it. I don't know if we should even try, but I've grown to be fond of that little mouser."

"It would be a pity to lose it." Moraven ran a hand over his jaw, then glanced right at Ciras. "What are you doing?"

His apprentice neatly folded his overshirt and began to draw off his shirt, despite the chill air. "I am the swiftest among us. I will run to the mouser and retrieve it. If I dodge as it did, the sphere will be unable to kill me."

Sacrificing yourself for something you despise? Perhaps there is hope for you, Ciras. Moraven held a hand up. "That may be a bit premature. Master Gryst, can you not recall your mouser?"

Borosan frowned. "I'm afraid I can't. The last thing I used it for, if you will recall, was going into a hole to see if there was any *thaumston* secreted there. It went for the horse because, I would imagine, the saddle pack has some *thaumston*. Once it has detected it, it will keep going for it and I've not enough here to bring it back in this direction."

The clatter of armor and bones sounded over by Rekarafi. The Viruk tossed a helmeted skull at the sphere, but missed. As the missile flew past, the water flowed into a disk and concentrated sunlight melted the helmet.

"No matter you are faster than *us,* Master Dejote, you need to be faster than *it*." The Viruk shook his shaggy head. "You are not that fast."

Ciras ignored him and began to stretch. "I will not fail, Master."

"Wait, I have an idea." Keles started to rummage around in his saddlebag, then dismounted. "Borosan, that thing was focusing sunlight to burn the mouser, right?"

"I believe it was." The *gyanridin* smiled broadly. "Yes, how incredibly efficient. As long as the sun is shining, it has a limitless source of power, and if it can do the same with moonlight and starlight, which it must do since some of those skeletons are of purely nocturnal animals, then . . ."

Ciras shook his head. "There isn't a cloud in the sky. Speed will be the key."

Keles shrugged his shoulders. "You could be right. Let me look at something here, though." He tossed his horse's reins to Tyressa, then jogged around to the west along the perimeter of the circle. Almost opposite where the Viruk crouched, he dropped to a knee and studied the pool. He weighed the leather pouch in his left hand, then undid the thongs tying it tight. He clearly measured the distance to the pool, and Moraven had no doubt the cartographer could estimate it down to the inch.

Then, instead of coming back to tell them how far it was and calculating how fast Ciras would have to run, Keles sprang to his feet and sprinted. He drove straight at the pool, leaping over piles of bleached bones and cutting around the half-melted helmet. His legs pumped and sand flew with every step. With his head down and arms swinging, he ran faster than Moraven would have thought possible.

His speed really didn't matter, though.

The motion in the sphere quickened. Ripples formed on its surface and the light swirled through it. The disk flattened as it had before. The center swelled. Sunlight silvered the edges. Because Keles charged straight at it, the disk didn't have to swivel to aim. It just tipped down effortlessly, tracking him with all the cold deliberation of a raptor soaring above a rabbit.

Moraven would have shouted a warning, but a cry of "Brilliant!" from Borosan stopped him. For a heartbeat the swordsman thought the *gyanridin* was describing the disk's performance, but then he saw what Borosan was seeing.

"Faster, Keles, you're almost there!"

Keles laughed in triumphant panic. His chosen path started in sunlight, but carried him into a narrow wedge of darkness. An outcropping of stone high up on the canyon's wall cast a slender shadow into the pool's heart. Another minute or two and the sun would have shifted enough to rob him of this passage, but Keles had seen it and acted instantly.

But what will he do when he reaches the pool?

Chest heaving, the cartographer dropped to his knees, powdering an ancient skull at the pool's edge. He flicked the leather pouch skyward. A black jet of powder shot out and peppered the disk. The disk boiled and darkened as Keles upended the bag and emptied its remaining contents into the pool. The same inky blackness that had flooded the disk flowed through the pool, rendering both opaque.

Tyressa clapped her hands. "Of course, ground inkstone."

Keles, his face blackened by ink dust save for his teeth and eyes, laughed aloud. "If light can't move through it, it can't burn anything."

Moraven applauded. "Well done, Master Keles."

The swordmaster's companion scowled. "How did you know that would work?"

Keles shook his head. "Running into the shadow just made sense."

Ciras nodded. "I know. I had seen it, but it was not near the mouser. I meant the inkstone."

The cartographer sat back on his haunches. "I didn't think if it would work or not."

"Perhaps we need to consider how long it will continue to work." Moraven climbed into the saddle again and reined his horse around. "If it is alive, it might purge itself of the ink. If it is just magic, it may do so faster. I would suggest haste."

Nodding, Keles scrambled to his feet and retrieved the mouser. "Do you want the *thaumston,* too?"

"Please, yes. Never can have too much."

"Ciras, get what you can from the bandit bodies, including any other *thaumston*. Maybe there will be clues to let us learn who they are." Moraven took the reins of Ciras' horse. "Be quick about it. If this canyon does go through, we'll be in the uplands ahead of them. Knowing where they are going and what they are planning will make our journey much easier."

Chapter Forty-two

10th day, Month of the Tiger, Year of the Rat
9th Year of Imperial Prince Cyron's Court
163rd Year of the Komyr Dynasty
737th year since the Cataclysm
Wentokikun, Moriande
Nalenyr

Prince Cyron read Prince Eiran's ire as if it were written in the blackest of ink on the most pristine of papers, but he did not care. Snow had fallen during the day—fallen pure and white, no longer something to scare children. Cyron could see it as a thing of beauty, not a harbinger of evil times, and greatly enjoyed walking in it in his garden sanctuary.

The rising moon made the snow glow, and provided enough light for him to see the nocturnal animals begin to stir in their enclosures. Some of them did not tolerate the cold well and remained nestled in their burrows until their keepers came to feed them, but his favorites heard his tread and his voice, emerging to watch him pass in hopes of a treat.

Cyron paused before one small cage and smiled. In it, a clouded linsang had crawled into a wooden branch. Tan-furred with thick black stripes and dots running the length of its sinuous body, it struck the Prince as a cross between a cat and a weasel. *Much like you, Eiran, save you lack its grace, poise, and charm.* Cyron clicked his tongue at it and the creature's narrow head came up.

"This one, Prince Eiran, came from the southernmost reaches of

Ummummorar. Jorim Anturasi brought it and its mate back for me. Though it tolerates being caged, it would much prefer I give it the run of the garden. I can't, however, because it likes to eat eggs and that disturbs the birds I have."

Eiran, looking poorly for his fast ride to Moriande and the fact that he'd not been received the night before, did not even attempt to feign interest. "It has something in common with my sister, then."

"Your sister sucks eggs, does she?" Cyron opened his cloak and brought out a small basket that held a clutch of tiny blue eggs. He lifted one to the bars of the cage and the linsang sat up. The creature accepted the egg in its forepaws, then cracked it and began to lick at the oozing albumen.

"No, Prince Cyron, she, too, is a captive. Prince Pyrust has her. They are probably back in Felarati, living as husband and wife."

"Thank you for reminding me. I shall have to send them a gift."

Eiran began to tremble with rage, his pale face purpling. Had Cyron not long since mastered his own anger, his face would have been similarly contorted. He had not anticipated that the Council of Ministers for Helosunde would choose a prince to lead them so quickly, and he certainly never would have thought Eiran would be their choice. Jasai would have been a better choice than Eiran; but Helosundians only seemed to revere women as mothers, concubines, or the Keru, and she fit none of those categories. He had no doubt that Eiran had been advanced so someone else could move into the succession through marrying her, and Pyrust was doing just that. And the only way to blunt his claim on the Helosundian throne would be to keep Eiran alive, when he wanted nothing more than to toss the idiot and those who elected him to the tigers.

Cyron had thought that if the ministers were going to make a quick choice, they would pick General Pades. He had the military background to make him the logical choice. Pyrust had seen how dangerous he was, and had doubtlessly taken great delight in charging Eiran with bringing Pades' severed head to Cyron.

The retaking of Meleswin had killed the most able military leaders outside the Keru, and had harvested the most able-bodied of the Helosundians. The mercenaries—termed Honor Guards to assuage the gods and appease human vanities—remained in their fortresses in the mountain passes. Pyrust still would be neither strong nor foolish enough to venture south, especially with snow falling, so the situation in the north would remain static until the spring.

I could but hope for a long and deep winter. Not only would it keep him home, but would give me an excuse to skip a shipment of rice. Cyron sighed as he dismissed that thought. The Desei people were as much captives as the linsang, and if Cyron did not feed them, they would starve. He did not want that happening.

He shook his head and moved on, hearing Eiran crunch snow beneath his feet as he followed. In the songs of heroes there usually was a verse or two about some great hardship a hero witnessed that prompted him to do great good later in life. Were he worthy of such a song, a bard somewhere would manufacture some incident that explained why Cyron did not let the Desei starve. Perhaps it would be his having rescued some exotic animal from the Moriande bazaar and nursed it back to health. He would have seen it as his calling to do that for the Desei and, perhaps, eventually, the whole Empire.

Cyron would have found it a comfort if such a thing had actually happened. If it had, he could have put it in perspective, defined it, and seen its limitations. He could work around it when necessary. Having his enemy weakened by starvation would be a benefit, but he could not bring himself to do that.

His father or grandfather could have, without batting an eye; but they'd grown up in a more difficult time, when ruthlessness was a virtue. For him, with his father's program of exploration, he saw the world as one of expanding resources, not a limited supply that necessitated rationing. Trade was making his nation strong and providing benefits to all, which made most of his people happy—and those who were not were just impatient because wealth was taking its time in trickling down to them. Even they, however, had to admit that he was spending money on projects that benefited them, like dredging the Gold River.

Because his nation was master of a growing world, he had the time to look past the divisions that had separated the parts of the old Empire. During the Time of Black Ice, the Principalities had become fiercely nationalistic. They needed that sense of self to give them purpose and unite them in common adversity. The snows that fell all but isolated them, so they really had little news of and contact with the rest of the world. People barely had enough to survive, so trade was seen as a luxury, and wood more useful for heat than for building ships to explore.

The other Princes, when they did give thought to the old Empire, saw it as a place split up by a warrior-Empress and one that, therefore, would have to be reunited by the sword. There was no doubt that Cyrsa had divided the Empire among families that would compete with each other for power. She had done that because she assumed none of them would become ascendant and be able to oppose her on her return. What was expedient for a year or two, however, had become entrenched and unworkable after the Cataclysm.

Cyron didn't see the need for conquest by the sword. The Helosundians seemed content to remain bought. Erumvirine enjoyed the expansion of trade and didn't seem to mind that their access to the rest of the world came through Nalenyr. Their more moderate climate lent itself to a lifestyle that rewarded lazy indolence. The Virine slumbered like the Bear that represented them and, at this point, Cyron doubted the Bear would be much of a threat were it ever roused.

In another generation I could join the houses through marriage and merge our nations.

"My brother, you have heard nothing of what I have said."

Cyron stopped and regarded Eiran coldly. "Look about you, my *brother*. What do you see?"

"Snow. A garden. Cages. Animals."

"Now really look."

Eiran slumped his shoulders beneath a snow-flecked cloak. "I see what I have told you."

Cyron nodded. "Then tell me what you don't see."

"I don't follow."

"No, you don't, which is why you are in the muddle you are in now, and why your nephews and nieces will have a half-handed man as their father." Cyron waved a hand along the row of cages. "Do you know what you will not see here, Eiran? You won't see a dragon. Everything else, you will see. A Desei hawk, a Helosundian dog. Do you know why you won't see a dragon?"

The Helosundian snorted. "Because your vaunted Anturasi hasn't found one?"

"Oh, I daresay that if I asked Jorim to find me one, he would. He would find me a dozen and bring them all." Cyron lowered his hand and let his cloak close about him. "It is because I would not cage a dragon. A dragon would wither and die in a cage. A dragon cannot be caged, for a dragon has larger concerns."

"So does the dog!"

"Ha." Cyron reached out and grabbed Eiran by the front of his cloak. He dragged him forward a dozen stumbling steps, then tossed him against a cage. "There's your Helosundian dog. He's magnificent. *My* Keru take very good care of him. He is their pet."

The dog, which had been huddled with his tail curled up to warm his nose, stood and shook his thick winter coat. Black with a white band around the eyes and white stockings, the long-haired animal had enough size and bulk to take a wolf. The Keru, when entering combat, painted a white mask around their eyes to honor their nation's emblem.

The dog sniffed at Eiran, then backed, baring his teeth.

"The only thing a Helosundian dog cannot tolerate is cowardice, Eiran." Cyron let his voice drop into a deep whisper. "If what you reported as passing between Jasai and Pyrust in Meleswin is true, then she accepted him as her husband without duress. Some would dispute that, saying she bought your life so you will be able to succor her. They would make her captivity a cause around which to rally support and send an invasion force north."

"That is exactly why she agreed."

"Look at him, Eiran; he still growls at you. He knows you are terrified of Pyrust. Your sister knew it, too. She knew you would never come for her. She knew you would use any excuse possible to avoid that. She'd seen your army slaughtered.

"No, she accepted Pyrust's offer knowing exactly what it was. It affords Helosunde a degree of autonomy and relieves it of oppression. There will be no more war in Helosunde. I will continue to maintain the Keru and the other Honor Guards, and I shall even allow you to parade some of them about, but fear not. You are a hound that shall never go to war."

Eiran levered himself away from the bars of the cage. "You will keep my people caged as you keep this dog, then?"

"In a cage you will be safe. Like this beast here, I shall find you a cousin of mine to marry and you shall produce children. One of my children by whomever I choose will marry one of your nieces, linking our houses. Your children I will have married into the Five Princes. I will make you useful, but not a threat, so Pyrust will not feel the need to have you murdered."

The Helosundian stared at him, shock widening his eyes. "You can't do that. I am not in a cage. I am not a pet."

"No, you are not. You are just someone who is walking after he should be dead." From deeper in the sanctuary came the piercing cry of the Desei hawk demanding to be fed. "Even it knows you should have died in Meleswin, and you likely would have died save that you cause me more trouble alive than dead. If Pyrust had slain you, I could have countered by forcing the Council of Ministers to make a new choice—someone who was tractable—or to make no choice at all. By sending you back, he gives me the choice of killing you or not. Which reminds me, when we see the tigers, try not to stand too close to the edge of their pit."

Eiran shivered. "You wouldn't!"

If he had any intelligence at all, he'd know he just saw past your bluff. "Not today, for the tigers have already been fed. You would do well to make certain you do the things I desire in the future, lest I invite you to walk again in my sanctuary."

The Helosundian Prince's face closed and he looked down. Little puffs of vapor were the only sign he lived. Then his head came back up, his eyes dull. "My life is over, then?"

Cyron shrugged. "Tell me, what was it you thought when they elected you Prince?"

"I thought . . . I thought I would look very heroic in the robes of state." He sighed, exhaling two plumes of steam.

"Even the most resplendent robes will not a prince make, nor will mud-spattered rags unmake a prince. You were chosen, Eiran, to be manipulated and controlled. Those who followed you to Meleswin did not know that. They accepted your authority." Cyron's eyes tightened. "I am going to give you a chance—less because it will benefit me than because it will give Pyrust something else to worry about."

The young man's spine straightened. "What?"

"I am going to budget for you enough gold to buy a hundred thousand *quor* of rice. I want you to spend it on things to benefit the people who expect you to lead them. I want you to live with them, learn from them, determine what they need—not what they say they want, but what they *need*. I want you then to provide them the means necessary to attain those ends."

"I don't understand."

"If that is the case in a year, I will find you a tower that will become a gilded cage. You will never need, want, nor fear in that cage, but you will never be allowed out of it." Cyron reached a hand through the cage bars and scratched the Helosundian dog behind his ear. "Learn your duty, do your duty, then we will truly be brothers. Make yourself useful to me, and you will find that my resources and gratitude know no limits."

Chapter Forty-three

13th day, Month of the Tiger, Year of the Rat
9th Year of Imperial Prince Cyron's Court
163rd Year of the Komyr Dynasty
737th year since the Cataclysm
Stormwolf, off the Mountains of Ice

"Thank you for making the time to see me, Captain." Jorim bowed in her direction. "I asked Iesol to confirm what I have discovered."

Anaeda cleared her desk. "You've brought charts, so this is a problem of navigation?"

"Yes and no." Jorim set the rolled charts on her desk and unfurled the first one. "This is a map of our progress. I've been incorporating data as best I can, from what we have learned and from the Soth map. I've already drawn in the coast of the Mountains of Ice, at least as much of it as we have been able to survey."

Anaeda studied the chart for a moment, tracing a finger along the line the fleet had traveled. Their course had come down south and curved to the east, skirting the empty vastness of the ocean to discover the islands and to confirm the existence of the Mountains of Ice. "This looks accurate to me. What is the problem?"

Jorim drew in a deep breath and attempted to quell the fluttering of butterflies in his stomach. "You'll recall how the islands on the Soth map were further apart than we expected? And you'll remember me telling you that they'd drawn Cartayne smaller than it should be?"

"Something to flatter the Viruk, wasn't it?"

"Yes. That bit of lore about the Soth is wisdom handed down to me from my grandfather, and I have no clue as to where he got it, but I know he believes it. He's worked with Soth charts and, based on measurements, he's made some determinations. He knows the world is a globe. Based on the measurements he's been given, he's even managed to calculate the diameter of the world."

The captain nodded. "I am well aware of the hopes that by sailing east we could reach the western shore of Aefret. The logic of such a passage is inescapable, and the question is which path is shorter, sailing east or west? When you are on the sea enough, you also hear stories of those who claim to have found the place from which True Men sailed—the land of light eyes. Some think we came from another world, sent here after fulfilling some destiny. Others think we were just blown off course. Given the storms down here, I think that's most likely." She folded her arms. "I still fail to see what the difficulty is."

"The difficulty is, captain, that my grandfather's calculations were wrong." He unrolled the second chart. "The art of measurement is not wholly accurate. Nautical miles and statute miles are not the same. Each of the Principalities uses a slightly different distance to define miles, and most people don't worry about it. Other towns are a day's travel, or a week's, or just too far. Even the surveys my brother and I have undertaken are flawed. The further we go from Moriande, the greater the error, and it compounds.

"Now, the device your cousin created has allowed for more accurate measurements, but I realized I was making a mistake in calculating based on statute miles, not nautical miles. I communicated erroneous things to my grandfather, and when I corrected, suddenly the Soth scale for Cartayne made sense." He turned and rested a hand on Iesol's shoulder. "I asked the minister to check my math, and he put his students on it as well."

Anaeda's eyes narrowed as she studied the new chart. "How big a mistake?"

"Twenty-five percent."

Her head came up fast. "A quarter of the world unaccounted for?"

"Yes."

She sat down hard and rubbed a hand over her eyes. "So sailing east will bring us to Aefret, but it will take far longer than we expected."

Jorim leaned with both hands on the desk. "That's if we ever get there."

Anaeda sat back in her chair, steepling her fingers. "Explain."

"Currents. We're south of the equator, and the current is running from right to left. Water warmed flows toward the south pole. North of the equator it goes in the opposite direction. If the world were of the size we thought it was, then the southern circle would carry us to Aefret. The upper current would have carried us to lands at the other end of the Spice Route. The difficulty we have is that the world is much bigger than we thought. We know water is cooler away from land and hotter close to it. I think if there were nothing in the unknown quarter, the current coming across the equator would have cooled too much to have the force it does coming in to our coast."

The ship's captain smiled slightly. "I am pleased your time aboard the *Stormwolf* has conferred upon you the information you now possess. Your knowledge of currents is admirable, but faulty. All that is required is for the west coast of Aefret to be shaped so that it intercepts this polar current, warms it, and directs it back west along the equator."

She leaned forward and studied the vast expanse of ocean to the east of the Principalities. "Even as I tell you all that is required to invalidate your idea, I don't believe it. In every quarter of the world—every quarter up to this point at least—earth and water are in balance. To assume nothing but water exists out here is as absurd as to think it could be a solid wall of stone reaching to the stars. And then there is the mystery of the land from which True Men came. We also might well wonder after the sea devils and what they call home. Is it possible some new world lies in the heart of this emptiness? Of course, but this leaves us another question."

Jorim cocked an eyebrow. "And that would be?"

"Why didn't this emptiness or whatever is there appear on Soth charts?"

Iesol bowed his head apologetically. "Permission to speak, Captain?"

"Please, Minister."

"The Soth were subject to the Viruk. They served them in all ways, including as educators and keepers of information. Perhaps they chose to hide this knowledge so that any peoples in this place would remain out of Viruk hands."

"That is certainly possible, Minister, but the Viruk were capable sailors and explored much of the world. The idea that the Soth bureaucracy could keep knowledge of a quarter of the world from them is unsatisfactory."

Jorim straightened up. "I have another idea, Captain."

"What would that be?"

"Perhaps this quarter of the world did not exist when the Viruk Empire was its most powerful."

Anaeda frowned. "The idea of bureaucracy sounds better at the moment."

"No, think of it for a moment. We know how much the Cataclysm changed our world, but it really was very little compared to what happened when Virukadeen sank into the Dark Sea. The Viruk fought a war with magic—magic so powerful even our greatest legendary magicians could not begin to match it. Imagine, if you will, that the war changed what sank into something akin to *thaumston*. Anything could happen. We've seen volcanoes add to coastlines, so perhaps hundreds of volcanoes were triggered and were able to expand the world."

"And you would then suggest, Master Anturasi, that the Soth chart you saw on Cartayne made the island smaller than it really is to reflect the fact that the Soth had determined the world had expanded?"

Jorim shook his head. "I don't know, Captain Gryst. I make maps, I find animals. I am, as you said at our first meeting, an adventurer. I don't care what would have put a landmass here. It could be the gods. It could be Viruk magic, it could have been hidden by sloppy Soth cartographers. All of that is immaterial. I would just like to get there and see what we find."

Anaeda stood, then bowed to him. "I appreciate your scholarly approach to this problem. We have one duty for certain, and that is to survey the Mountains of Ice. I mean to continue that part of our journey. Where we go from there will depend on the answer to a question. Consider your answer before you speak."

"Yes, Captain."

"Knowing the nature of your relationship with your grandfather, I assume you have not told him of your errors in measurement."

"No, Captain."

"I also assume you would have avoided it until our return. Discovering something out here—a new landmass, the home of True Men, anything monumental—might distract him enough that he'd overlook your error. It would save you a great deal of pain."

"That's true."

"So, here is my question." She watched him closely. "Are you willing and able to deceive your grandfather about what we discover?"

A jolt ran through him. Jorim had no qualms about deceiving his grandfather; he had lied to him about countless little things—errors of omission mostly—all of his life. Qiro knew nothing of the Fenn or the sighting of the *Wavewolf.* His grandfather had been abrupt enough that he didn't probe, so Jorim had not needed to work hard to conceal information from him. He knew he could, but also that his own enthusiasm would make it difficult if such a momentous discovery were made.

"The duties I perform are not just for the Anturasi family, Captain, but at the order of Prince Cyron. If I deceive my grandfather, I deceive the Prince. You can see my reluctance to do that."

"I can, but we have a larger responsibility to the Crown, and to Nalenyr. The other Principalities believe that *if* we are fortunate enough to return, at the very most we will have found another route to Aefret. This threatens them because it means more trade for Nalenyr, but it is a threat they are already learning to deal with. If we find a whole new continent, we open not just the wealth of Aefret, but that of an unimagined world. Nalenyr will instantly be able to beggar any other nation. That means they will all be folded into a Naleni Empire. Deseirion won't stand for that, and likely even the Virine would have to react."

Jorim slowly nodded. "We could sail back to a nation devastated by war. Nalenyr might not even exist when we get home."

"If you will permit me?" Iesol looked up sheepishly from his chair. " 'As the Master said, "The danger of dreams comes when one acts on them as if they are prophecy." ' "

The cartographer frowned. "Elucidate, please."

"You touched on external threats, but with Nalenyr you have two other threats, both based in dreams of avarice. One is internal, for the inland lords will not allow themselves to be done out of whatever treasures might be found. They will spend great amounts to send out ships that will not return. It will ruin them. Peasants will leave the land and flock to the cities in hopes of crewing a ship, or working in a shipyard, so harvests will suffer and the nation will face famine. The whole fabric of society will be rent."

The little man shivered. As a member of the bureaucracy he could have no love for the chaos of such upheaval. Jorim saw fear on his face and heard it in his voice as he spoke, then his voice shifted. Fear ebbed, and anger rose.

"The second threat is that of the Ministers. You, Captain, and you, Master Anturasi, have shown me more kindness and respect than anyone in the bureaucracy. The Ministers do cherish order above all else, and already resent the fact that great wealth provides power they cannot control. They are capable of anything to maintain order."

Anaeda's eyes narrowed. "Even treason?"

"More, though they would never define it as such. If Prince Cyron were seen to be allowing power to flow to those who are not worthy, it would be a simple task for them to find a noble who thought as they did, or who could be controlled. By falsifying reports, they could blind the Prince to a growing revolt, and they could even deliver him into the hands of his enemies—if they did not decide to kill him outright themselves."

Jorim frowned. "That's overreaching."

"Consider history, Master Anturasi. The Council of Ministers for Helosunde has shown no desire to relinquish power, and their betrayal of the Helosundian Prince is accepted by many as fact. Establishing such a Council for Nalenyr might well seem a solution to a problem the ministers have not had to deal with before."

And I am the only link back to Nalenyr. Jorim wondered if that were actually true, since a number of the scholars with the ship might well be able to establish a link back to blood kin in Nalenyr. *Then again, none of them know where we are, so if we do find something and tell them it is West Aefret, that is what they would tell people back home.*

Jorim looked at his two companions. "You realize that we are entering a treasonous conspiracy? When we return, the Prince might listen to reason and sanction what we have done. Or he might decide that the time wasted in our return has hurt Nalenyr and have us hanged for traitors."

"I think, Master Anturasi, that you will be able to convince him it was all for the best. You know he loves the animals you bring for his sanctuary." Anaeda Gryst smiled. "We'll keep this secret so your gifts will be a surprise. How can he complain about that?"

"He's not that simple."

"No, but he's reasonable. After all, it's one thing for us to sail east. The trade route is only viable if we can make it back." She tapped the new world map with a finger. "Let's see what's there. Then we'll see if we can return before anyone gets excited enough to start killing over what we have found."

Chapter Forty-four

17th day, Month of the Tiger, Year of the Rat
9th Year of Imperial Prince Cyron's Court
163rd Year of the Komyr Dynasty
737th year since the Cataclysm
Dolosan

Keles Anturasi woke slowly, in the vain hope that doing so would make his head feel better. He didn't want to open his eyes, because even the slightest bit of light would start his head pounding. He knew Rekarafi did not mean to cause him discomfort, and the nausea that he had first experienced around him had long since passed, but the headaches would not abate. They arrived as the sun went down and remained, disturbing his sleep, leaving him achy for the rest of the day.

He hoped the last of the venom would finally work itself out of his system. He had done everything the others could suggest to help him get rid of it, from eating the sort of odd foods they found growing around them to exercise. The feathered berries, once they were plucked, had been the most effective. They had a sharp sour taste which, if it didn't actually cure the headaches, certainly distracted him from the pain.

Ciras had made it his personal duty to show Keles how to use a sword. The cartographer was fairly certain this was mostly because the Tirati was still embarrassed over his simple solution to the problem of the pool. Moraven had used Keles' action at the pool as an example of the employment of intelligence over thoughtless action, and Ciras seemed to take it to heart. Sword instruction was a means of paying off a debt, and it did force Keles to focus on something other than how he felt.

Tyressa adopted a different approach, which entailed taking Keles off on little side journeys. These had the advantage of distancing him from Rekarafi as well as removing him from his logbooks and maps. She showed great patience in educating him about animals, the tracks they left behind, plants, their seeds and flowers, and how to determine if they were edible or not. She took great pains to separate fact from speculation, though later observations of creatures often confirmed what she'd assumed based on their tracks and scat.

He'd listened carefully and had begun to understand some more of what his brother found so engaging about his surveys. He could measure the land and draw it, but that didn't convey a full knowledge of it. It felt good to fill his lungs with fresh air, and to feel delicate flowers, or spot a tuft of fur hanging from a thorn and know what it came from.

"It is odd, Tyressa, but I have always thought of the Keru as creatures of the city. This knowledge you have isn't something you could learn in Moriande."

She laughed and crouched beside some uplands heather, brushing a thumb over the purple blossom. "For the Naleni, we *are* of the city, but you only see us as a uniform company. I'm ten years your senior, but have only been in Moriande for seven years."

"And before that?"

She frowned. "I was not in Moriande."

Keles walked over and knelt beside her. "Tyressa, I remember your telling me that first night, on the *Catfish,* there were things I didn't need to know. I want to respect that. I *will* respect that, but I am curious. I assume you learned a lot of what you're teaching me in Helosunde. I'm not seeking to pry, but simply to find a frame of reference."

The blonde woman turned her head and regarded him. Her glance cut at him more coldly than the winds, but only for a heartbeat. Then it warmed—fractionally. "Keles, I have come to respect you for your dedication to duty and even your inventiveness. You believe you only want a frame of reference, but past experience tells me that is not entirely so. I know what Naleni men grow up thinking about the Keru. I even recall you and your brother passing into your grandfather's celebration—yes, I was at the door that night."

Keles blushed. "I didn't—"

"Don't worry. You didn't look at us any differently than any man, and your glances were far kinder than those of most women. The rumors you've heard shape what you think of us. We hold ourselves apart, you're told. We take no lovers, bear no children, and have undergone secret rituals that allow us to draw strength from Helosunde. You also hear we only love women, or that the Prince is the only man we will accept in our beds. Some even think we have seduced this Prince and his father before him, and are raising an heir to the Naleni throne that we can use to replace him when we decide he no longer serves the cause of Helosunde."

"I've heard those stories, but I've never believed them."

She stopped, then lowered her eyes and nodded. "You probably haven't, have you? Once you left behind adolescent fantasies, you didn't contemplate any of that. Not much of a surprise, in fact; just a pity."

He stood and brushed red dust off his knees. "A pity? How is it a pity?"

"It shows how insulated you are from life." She turned and looked up at him. "Did you love the woman you took the scars for?"

"Yes, of course."

"Why?"

Keles folded his arms over his chest. "Well, because she was pretty and she was from a good family and . . ." His voice trailed off. "My father married a woman from a merchant house, his father before him. It was expected."

"Expected." Tyressa snapped off a sprig of heather and tucked it behind her left ear. "You loved her because you thought you were supposed to love her. It fit into your conception of the world—just the way the numbers and distances allow you to quantify the world. You seek order, and she was part of that. She was the piece that would fit well into the mosaic you think your life should become."

"That's not true." Yet he found no reason to back up his denial.

He'd allowed himself to believe he loved Majiata because he wanted to love her. *I needed to, because I needed someone to love me just as my mother loved my father.*

She opened her arms and slowly turned a circle. "Look at this place, Keles. It existed before you ever thought of measuring and defining it. It will continue to be what it is long after your map has moldered to nothing."

He shivered. "Great. Thanks. I get the idea. What I do out here won't matter."

She shook her head. "No, you fool, you have it all backward. It's not what you do out here that matters. It's what being out here does to *you* that matters. Right now, you're nothing but a puppet performing for your grandfather. Worse, he's trained you so well that even after he dies you will continue to perform the same way. A puppeteer could not wish for more of the dolls he leaves behind.

"You don't seem to understand that everything you do out here will matter. Your maps will open this land to exploration. People will come—but unless you understand that the land is more than distances and elevations, you won't be able to guide them where they should go, or show them how they should prepare for things."

"This place, Tyressa, is a long way from colonization. Yes, there are scroungers and bonediggers who live here, but the land changes them. There is still wild magic."

"Yes, Keles, but will it change you?"

"I don't understand."

Tyressa sighed. "I don't suppose you do. Look, my world has been very small. Yes, I come from Helosunde; I grew up there. I killed a few Desei, which is why I was chosen to be one of the Keru. From there my world expanded to include Moriande. But now I'm here, seeing things I've never seen before, and I realize the whole of the world is not a captive nation. My people keep hungering for a tiny portion of the world that will cost them more than it is worth. Don't look at me with that sort of shock—you know what I am saying is true. If instead of spending time plotting raids and complaining about how the gods have hidden their faces from us, were we to pick up lock, stock, and barrel to head out to Solaeth or Dolosan, or even up the Gold River, we could build ourselves a new nation. As it is, we let our past and duty to it define us. It limits what we can become."

Keles slowly nodded. "And you are saying that my slavish adherence to my training and my grandfather's wishes limits me in the same way?"

"Only in that they stop you from seeing the world as it is." She smiled. "How can you think to define the world when you have a haze of numbers and an avalanche of scrolls to separate you from it?"

"I can't, really." He frowned for a moment, then looked up into her eyes. "What you've just said . . . It isn't the sole result of your having come on this trip, is it? You were thinking these things before, which is why you were chosen."

Tyressa turned and began to walk back to where their horses cropped heather. "That might have been a factor."

"It makes for a lonely life, doesn't it?"

The glance she gave him was daunting. "You'll offer to relieve me of that burden?"

"No, that's not what I was thinking." He looked down. "You feel lonely because your thoughts are spreading wider than those of your companions. For me, it was the opposite. I kept my world small, and others were content to let me go my way. Even here, you were all ready not to bother me—and bother with me."

"We might have, but then you dealt with the pool." She smiled. "You didn't tell someone else how to do it; you just did it. You did something for our common good. You joined us. You let us know we're more than just *gyanrigot*."

Keles joined her at the horses and hauled himself into the saddle. "If that's what you thought, I'm sorry. I wasn't . . . I was not thinking about the world; I was just thinking about what I was supposed to be doing."

She nodded. "We understand. Most of us, anyway. Borosan is worse than you, and I've no idea what the Viruk is thinking."

"Worse than me? Is that possible?" He smiled. "And, Tyressa, I'm sorry for thinking what everyone does about the Keru. I didn't mean to insult you."

The Keru slowly turned to regard him. "You mean you don't find us alluring in the way no pillow-bred Naleni waif could ever be?"

"Yes. I mean . . . No, I mean . . ." Keles' shoulders slumped. "Kill me now. It will save trouble later."

Tyressa laughed. "The sleeping dragon has awakened. Slowly, slowly, but awakened nonetheless."

She pointed out a multitude of things on their ride back—including the opening to a small cave that appeared to be breathing—and Keles drank in every word. When they reached the campsite Moraven had chosen, they found three scroungers had joined them. One, a wizened old man swathed in animal furs of a color not seen in Moriande, sat off to the side with Moraven and Borosan. The *gyanridin* often served as something of a translator with the prospectors and bonediggers. The other two, younger and decidedly more hale, tended the fire and were roasting something over it. Keles would have taken it for a rabbit save that it had seven legs.

Ciras sat with them and traded pleasantries, but the conversation remained strained. Rekarafi perched himself on a rock downwind of the campsite. The cool breeze ruffled his hair. He'd closed his eyes and lifted his muzzle. His slit nostrils flared as if he could inhale whatever they were roasting. His hands rested on his knees, and firelight flashed from his claws.

Ciras bowed his head as the two of them reached the fire. "We have visitors. They have seen no signs of bandits, but the winds have blown rumors. They are going to head for Opaslynoti, at the foot of the pass into Ixyll."

Keles immediately wanted to ask them to describe the pass, but he refrained. "And Opaslynoti is?"

One of the bonediggers smiled, revealing a tangle of yellowed teeth. "A crossroads."

"Once a Viruk town." Rekarafi opened his eyes. "The *tavam alfel* melted it to human proportions."

"Thank you, Rekarafi." Keles smiled. "I look forward to seeing it."

The evening consisted of shared fare, and Borosan entertained the visitors with a duel between his mouser and the small *thanaton*. Ciras sang a ballad from Tirat, and Tyressa offered a lament for lost Helosunde. Their visitors repaid them with the ribald songs that warmed the nights throughout Dolosan. It concluded with an agreement to travel together to Opaslynoti, and Keles crawled into his tent without a single thought about reporting to his grandfather.

Morning came quickly enough, and when he finally did open his eyes, his head began throbbing. He acknowledged the pain, then smiled. In the past it had been an impediment to his mission, but now it was just pain. It was just a small part of his world, so he set about doing all he could to make it as small a part as he was able.

Chapter Forty-five

18th day, Month of the Tiger, Year of the Rat
9th Year of Imperial Prince Cyron's Court
163rd Year of the Komyr Dynasty
737th year since the Cataclysm
Moriande, Nalenyr

Nirati woke with a start. There had been no sound or movement, or even stray ray of sunshine to bring her from a dead sleep to consciousness. It was just the instant alert of one who had been long and fitfully asleep somehow realizing that the time for more sleep had ended.

She found herself facedown against her pillow. Dampness on the pillowcase felt cool against her cheek. It wasn't from tears, though she was certain she had cried during the night. Instead she'd drooled, sleeping gape-mouthed. Her exhaustion had not even allowed her the dignity of composing her features in some semblance of beauty.

She slowly gathered her hands under her shoulders, but this was not as simple as it should have been. She ached all over, but especially in her shoulders and elbows. The dull ache seemed familiar, having the quality of a strain from repetitive motion. When she helped her mother with spring or fall planting in their garden, she similarly felt it in her shoulders and lower back.

Slowly she levered herself over onto her back, then lay there, panting with exertion. She knew that having something so simple exhaust her was ridiculous, but she felt incredibly weak. Her blankets seemed so heavy they might as well have been woven from lead. Her nightclothes had twisted around her legs, and though she plucked at them, she could not free herself. Being trapped sent panic through her for an instant, then she forced herself to remain calm.

The panic revived dreams. She slowly reconstructed the night in hopes of sorting fact from fiction. Somewhere in there she sought what had robbed her of strength—though she doubted she would find it. But there was little else for her to do than think, and she needed that façade of control if she was ever going to rise from her bed.

The evening before had been quite pleasant. Count Aerynnor had conducted her to the theater to watch the production of Jaor Dirxi's *The Feather Sword*. It was the best of his satires, featuring a goosegirl who was so good at wielding a feather that she was able to defeat every swordsman she met. That the swordsmen wore costumes denoting their allegiance to Deseirion, or that her feather was gold and she was a fair maid of Nalenyr, added a degree of contemporary commentary that saved what was an otherwise mediocre production.

From there they had walked in public gardens, then returned to the apartments the count had rented once he had formally severed ties with the Phoesel family. There they had drunk wine and made love, then he had conducted her home. At least, she was certain he had, since she had no recollection of the trip, but here she was.

Her mother knew she was sleeping with the Desei noble. But aside from worrying about Nirati's heart getting broken, she had approached the whole affair with practical good sense. She'd prepared the tincture of clawfoot and administered it before each evening meal. She invited Nirati to confide anything in her, and even suggested they might pay a visit to the Lady of Jet and Jade for advice.

Nirati had resisted that latter suggestion. Her prior sexual encounters had been with lovers as inexperienced as she. She had not taken much pleasure in coupling, save a joy that her partners were pleased and that they clearly desired her. Her own satisfaction she subordinated to theirs, because until Junel she had not known the ecstasy that could come from sex.

Junel had been a kind and gentle lover. He looked to her pleasure first, taking his time to undress her, to study her, to caress and kiss her. The warmth of his breath against her skin, the tingle of his caresses—whether touching her with fingertips, the back of his hand, or even when he wore thin leather gloves—started a fire burning in her. He talked to her, telling her she was beautiful and desirable, then asked what it was she wanted, how she wanted it. Faster, slower, more heavily or gently; whatever she desired he provided, and the times he made suggestions he opened whole new worlds of desire to her.

She would have thought, after making passionate love with him, that her dreams would be languid or peaceful or even torrid, but they had been something else entirely. Her limbs ached as if the dream had been real. She'd felt helpless, with her arms trussed behind her, her legs folded under. Thick bands restrained her. At first she thought they were leather, but as she studied them they became the coils of a furred snake. She could hear its hisses, and the crush of its flesh chilled her. She struggled to get away, but the snake merely laughed, saying there was no escape, would never be an escape. She was trapped forever.

Then her grandfather came and woke her. She was convinced that was a dream as well, but she drew her arms from beneath the blankets and could see red marks on her wrists and other bruises on her arms. She had struggled against him, she knew, for she could still hear his voice commanding her to be still.

She'd stared up at him. "Grandfather?"

"Yes, child. Yes, my little Nirati. I had to come." He stared down at her, his eyes ablaze, then they softened. He sat on the edge of the bed and took her hands in his. "You had a bad dream."

"Yes, I did; very bad." She let him tug her up into a sitting position. "But how can you be here? It's not possible."

Qiro Anturasi shook his head. "The Prince thinks he has me locked away, but there are passages and paths of which he knows nothing. I know them all. Coming to you was not difficult. And that you needed me was reason enough to risk it."

Nirati squeezed his hands. "Is there something wrong, Grandfather?"

The old man raised his head as if, by posture alone, he could deny that possibility. Then he sighed. "Truth be told, Nirati, I, too, have unsettled slumbers. Demons and monsters haunt my sleep the same as yours."

She kept her voice quiet. "Is there something you've not told me about my brothers? Are they in danger?"

"Your brothers are as well as can be expected. They report to me as trained. Jorim is working hard at keeping his mind focused. Keles has always had that ability. I am learning much through them, which shall be to the benefit of all."

"You've not answered my question."

Qiro almost smiled. "No, I haven't. Both of them try to keep things from me. It is not out of spite; that I would know. They keep it from me so I will keep it from you and your mother, but I know things. Keles, as expected, is encountering difficulties. He is ill—not seriously, child, have no fear. But he does not sleep well. At times he slips and I see things. The Wastes are stranger than I remembered. It is a challenge for Keles.

"As for your brother Jorim, he is excited about what he sees, but the journey is not progressing as planned. He has made wonderful discoveries, but there is also mystery. He seeks answers to questions that may not have answers."

Nirati shivered. "You would know if something terrible happened, wouldn't you?"

"Yes, child, I would." He stared her straight in the face. "But fear not. I shall let nothing befall a grandson of mine if it is in my power. Your brothers have resources they do not know exist. They will do well."

She gave her grandfather's hands another squeeze, for she knew not what to say. His voice, though distant as his stare, carried with it warmth and respect that she had never heard when Keles or Jorim were around.

"You love them, don't you?"

Qiro shook himself, and his eyes refocused. "Of course. I drive them because I love them." His voice began to rise and a strident tone entered into it. "The world is cruel and cold and hard. It resists the Anturasi attempt to define it, to tame it. It defies us, but it will lose. Their effort will help see to its defeat."

He squeezed her hands, then let them drop to the coverlet as he stood. "But now you, my pet, are the heart of my concerns. I would not have your sleep troubled. Do you remember the game we used to play?"

Nirati smiled broadly in spite of herself. "Oh, yes. How could I forget?" When she was young and had shown no talent for cartography, she had been crushed. So during the times when Qiro gave Jorim and Keles little tasks to perform, he would sit and draw maps for her. They created the mythical land of Kunjiqui, and as she would describe it, Qiro would add symbols to the map, refining and defining the world of her creation.

Qiro had extended a hand to her and she had slipped from the bed. He led her to the wall and touched it. A section slid back silently, revealing a black corridor. "For you, Nirati, I have found a path to Kunjiqui. Come. It shall be your sanctuary from fear."

She'd followed him down the corridor and into a sunlit meadow, which couldn't possibly exist, since all the grass was silk and the birds singing in the trees were creatures of embroidery. The trees had limbs heavy with fruit, all mixed varieties, each huge and succulent. She smiled, seeing a pear with the rind of a lime, and knew that inside would be sweet flesh tasting of both.

Qiro released her hand and let her drift into the land they had created. "You are older now, so there are other things you may desire. The streams that now run with sweet tea may flow with wine. The stars will dance for your pleasure if you so desire. The fruit will be what you crave. The wind will always be gentle and warm. What rain falls will refresh. It will always be thus in Kunjiqui."

His voice faded and she turned around to see him, but he had vanished like a ghost. That surprised her, but did not make her fear, for she did feel safe here in this land of her imagining. She sat down on the silk grasses and laid her head down, listening to the soft lullabies sung by the birds.

And she slept.

Fully awake now, Nirati summoned the strength to throw off her bedclothes and walked to the wall. She touched the cool stones, then pushed, hoping they would yield, but of course they did not. Not only was that an external wall, but it was three stories above the ground. *I dreamed the whole thing. I dreamed his coming. I dreamed Kunjiqui.*

Then she looked at her wrists again. The red marks remained, as did the bruises. Why and how they were there, she could not explain. She began to shiver. She turned and, pressing her back to the wall, slid to the floor.

Something was very wrong, but she could not identify it. She knew then that the only peace she would have would be that of an imaginary land created by a young girl.

"I hope," she breathed, "that it will be enough."

Chapter Forty-six

27th day, Month of the Tiger, Year of the Rat
9th Year of Imperial Prince Cyron's Court
163rd Year of the Komyr Dynasty
737th year since the Cataclysm
Stormwolf, off the Forbidding Coast

The coastal survey of the Mountains of Ice had continued for two days when a storm boiled up from the west and blasted the fleet. The skies had darkened so quickly that even Jorim began to suspect that the gods hated them. Most sailors assumed they were close to the gate to the Underworld and that the storm was an effort to keep them away. That sort of idle speculation, however, only came in grumbles over cold meals. The shrieking winds and driving rains made thoughts of anything but survival a luxury.

For Jorim, the four days in which the ships were buffeted and blown eastward were times of sheer terror, relieved only by frustration. Having few skills that were of use in this situation, he was ordered to his cabin. Even his requests for data like speed and direction were rebuffed. He learned later that the device used to measure speed had been tossed into the sea once by a hapless young sailor. The knotted rope tied to it had been yanked so quickly from his hands that he had lost a finger.

The storm's howl, the rattle of rain against the hull, and the creaking of every joint on the ship reminded him just how fragile the vessel was. Though the *Stormwolf* was the largest ship any man had ever built, the raging sea was enough to crush it like a paper lantern beneath a wagon wheel. The only thing which prevented that was the skill of the crew and the strength of those on the tiller. They kept the ship moving with the wind and through the towering waves.

Shimik had not taken well to the storm, and hid himself in a swaddling of blanket in the corner of Jorim's cabin. The little creature mewed when thunder cracked close by and moaned in counterpoint to the ship's groaning. Jorim wished he could have joined the Fenn in huddling safely away, but his pride and fury at the weather prevented him from doing so.

His mission, reinforced by Captain Gryst's order, was to perform readings that would determine their position. He had the Gryst chronometer, which was keeping nearly perfect time—at least, by one clock measured against the other. He couldn't determine noon, nor midnight, nor take readings from the stars, since the storm kept him in his cabin and the clouds hid the sun as well as the stars.

As annoying as the inability to take readings was, the storm prevented him from confirming a discovery he'd made during the survey. Just as the northern pole star was a useful point for navigation in the northern hemisphere, so his grandfather had charged him with selecting its equivalent to the south. He had decided that the Eye of the Cock would suit, and had intended to relay that information to Qiro as soon as he had confirmed it. While the Eye could not be seen from Moriande, the tail of the constellation could, and was known from old Viruk and Soth texts. Once south of the equator it would serve nicely, and was a discovery that would mitigate his error in measurements.

In some ways, being the keeper of the clocks became his only purpose on the ship. Captain Gryst would send sailors to ask him what time it was. And, as the storm wore on, those intervals degraded—as did the manners of everyone on board. Sailors had said a storm that intense could not last more than a day or two but, as it stretched into the third and fourth day, some came to think his timekeeping was mistaken.

After four days, the storm broke and the ocean became as placid as they had ever seen it. Jorim peeked out of his cabin and took readings. He did the math as quickly as possible, then double-checked it.

His whistle of surprise had awakened Shimik, who sat up, rubbed his eyes, and awaited an explanation.

"We go longa longa." Jorim sat back and studied the line he'd drawn on his map. The storm had blown them east over a thousand miles, and a bit north. It had carried them right into the unknown quarter.

It took two days for the fleet to reunite. Two ships had gone down, and the fleet's survivors were uncertain if they hoped the ships had smashed into the Mountains of Ice or had just been dragged to the bottom of the ocean. The latter would have been a quicker way to die. Promises were made that they would look for survivors on their return trip, but everyone knew those promises were hollow. Currents had carried them further northeast, away from the Mountains of Ice, and getting back down there would be all but impossible.

For another two days the currents and light breezes continued, taking them to the northeast over featureless stretches of ocean. Jorim was about to despair of finding any land when a lookout spotted a line of clouds on the eastern horizon. By the time the sun was setting they saw a dark line beneath them which meant mountains, and the rumor rushed through the fleet that they had found Aefret. Fair winds and calm seas contributed to the buoyant attitude, and Captain Gryst allowed some celebration before she told the crew, "It's time you did some sailing instead of just waiting for a storm to push us along."

By dawn, the mountains had grown considerably—and everyone knew those mountains had to be very tall indeed. Jorim remembered Anaeda saying a wall of stone was as unlikely as open ocean in the unknown quarter, but for a day's sailing it looked as if a wall was exactly what they were heading for. The mountains just kept growing, and none of the coastline looked the least bit inviting.

The fleet turned north and sailed up the coast. After several days, they had their first bit of luck. A gap in the mountains showed the outflow of a river, leading into a natural harbor. More important than the idea of safe anchorage and the prospect of freshwater, the *Moondragon* lay on the beach. It had been believed lost in the storm, and the sailors had felt that tragedy had just been part of the ship's evident curse. It clearly had been brought up the beach for repairs. Its survival made many reconsider the curse.

But only as long as it took folks to realize that no people were actually on the ship. As the rest of the fleet came in, Jorim joined Captain Gryst on the wheel deck. He couldn't see any signs of habitation—no fires or tents. Like everyone else, he assumed the worst—that the sea devils had taken the crew and were even now feasting on them.

"You'll be thinking the sea devils mild compared to what I'll do to the lot of you," Captain Gryst barked. "Keep your eyes open for them and we won't have another problem. Lieutenant Linor, get together two squads of soldiers to reconnoiter the beach and secure it."

"Permission to join them, Captain."

She turned and spitted Jorim with a sharp gaze. "Are you hoping to be eaten by sea devils, Master Anturasi, or to kill sea devils?"

"Neither. If there are sea devils about, we'll find sign of them quickly. We know they use ships, so I'd imagine that if it were they, they'd be fixing the *Moondragon*. The reason I want to go is to take a look around. Exploring is exactly why you have me along."

"I would prefer our soldiers to secure the beach first."

"I don't mean to argue with you, but I ask you to consider one thing before you make a final decision. Of everyone on this ship, I have the best chance of determining what is going on. I've been outside the Principalities in places that didn't even have names."

Her lips flattened into a line, then she nodded. "If you leave my sight, if you leave the beach, don't come back. I'll be leaving you here."

"As ordered, Captain." Jorim bowed to her, then retreated to his cabin. He strapped on his sword, then joined the soldiers as they descended into two of the ship's boats. Captain Gryst watched from the wheel deck and Shimik peeked out from between her feet and the railings.

"Lieutenant Linor?"

The woman leading the soldiers looked up. "Yes, Captain?"

"Listen to Master Anturasi, but no one leaves the beach until I give the order."

"Understood."

Jorim took his customary place in the bow of the boat as the sailors rowed toward the shore. He studied the vegetation, which was lush, green, thick, and tall. The mountains, which jutted up into the clouds, surrendered less than a mile of land to the ocean, and trees had aggressively colonized that small crescent. He might have expected the ocean water to have killed everything off, but clearly storms dumped an incredible amount of water on the cliffs. That freshwater would have been enough to hydrate them.

And the river as well. The sailors cursed as they had to pull against its current. Jorim suspected the bay's water was more fresh than salt, and wondered what sort of fish he'd find in it. Would they be riverine, marine, or some curious mix?

The boat rode a breaker into the beach and Jorim was out before oars had been shipped. He sank to a knee and let a handful of sand drift through his fingers. It felt normal, and the pieces of shell and strands of seaweed were recognizable. Even the calls of the birds he heard were vaguely familiar.

He got up and joined Lieutenant Linor as she walked the perimeter of the shore near the ship. "No tracks of the sea devils."

She shook her head. "Nothing to show a fight." As they walked along the beach she pointed to a path leading into the interior. "They off-loaded as much as they could and carried it inland. Maybe they found a cave or a hilltop where they could raise a structure to shield them."

They paused at the river's edge. Silvery fish swam in the current and birds waded in to knife sharp beaks at them. Jorim crouched and scooped up a handful of the water. He sniffed it, then poured it out. He rubbed a bit against his lips, but felt no tingle there or on his hand. "I don't think there is anything wrong with the water. Save for the blue plumage, that bird could be an Emperor stork. If it's drinking and eating, this place is probably safe."

He stood and looked back at the beached ship. "They made it into this harbor four or five days ago. They off-loaded the ship, dragged it in, began to make repairs. Let's say that took two days. Then something happened. Something that stopped them working and prevented the lot of them from returning. What could that be?"

Lieutenant Linor looked past him and her face drained of blood. Jorim spun and had the answer to his question.

A copper-skinned man stood at the entrance to the path. He was impossibly tall, and muscled as thickly as anyone Jorim had ever seen. He wore upper body armor woven from thick fibers, and a loincloth of finer weaving. Both had been decorated with geometric designs rendered in bright yellows, greens, and blues. Beaten copper greaves and bracers protected his shins and forearms. He had a small round shield in his left hand and an odd war club in his right. As near as Jorim could tell from a quick glance, black stone blades had been set in the club.

He made a mental note to study the weapon later, but that was only because the giant's mask demanded immediate attention. It did nothing to restrain the man's long black hair, which fell over his shoulders. The mask was made of gold, and had been inset with jade over all; jet likewise surrounded the open mouth and the eyes. A trio of long, gaudy green feathers with yellow eyes rose another three feet above his head, making him a full ten feet tall.

Jorim held a hand out, freezing Lieutenant Linor's attempt to draw her sword. Realizing he might be committing the final and most foolish act of his life, Jorim bowed and held it, then tugged on her arm to draw her down, too. Straightening up, he smiled with far more serenity than he felt.

"Peace of the gods be upon you."

The giant bowed his head, then his voice echoed from the mask. "May their smiles grace your life."

Jorim blinked. "You have a Naleni accent."

The man nodded. "Come. Your friends await."

Chapter Forty-seven

27th day, Month of the Tiger, Year of the Rat
9th Year of Imperial Prince Cyron's Court
163rd Year of the Komyr Dynasty
737th year since the Cataclysm
Opaslynoti, Dolosan

On the road to Opaslynoti, Keles Anturasi decided the place's name was sufficient to be the foundation for any number of romantic poems. It was far enough from Moriande that poets didn't need to care about the reality of it. The wild magics that raged through the area could have allowed it to be anything, and the name itself was a blend of Viruk and Imperial terminology that hinted at a grand history buried beneath layers of mystery.

But any romantic notions began to wither with the realization that there really was no road to Opaslynoti. A trade route did run from the seaport of Sylumak north-northwest to the city, but the shifting landscape of Dolosan's western reaches meant the route seldom appeared the same twice. Whole hillsides might melt beneath black rain, turning valleys into plains on which would grow forests of thorn trees. The branches would sweep flocks of birds from the sky and the plants would devour them. Those who chose to enter such places on foot fared no better, and Borosan's *thanaton* bore bright scars on its carapace from an aborted survey of such a thicket.

Travelers in the land remained few, with most coming up from

Sylumak or overland from Dolosan, as they themselves had. To the south lay Irusviruk, but the Viruk wanted little to do with Men, especially those mad enough to dwell in Dolosan. If anyone came out of Ixyll, none of the scroungers talked about it, suggesting that way was as closed today as it had been when his grandfather had tried to visit years ago.

Rekarafi watched the scroungers carefully, not trusting them at all. They preferred to be known as thaumstoners or thaumstoneers—a generational split, it appeared—but he referred to them as *talkiegio*. He said it meant scroungers, but he seemed to inflect it the way Keles would *lice,* and the thaumstoners didn't like it. They shot back that he must have been an outlaw, since outlaws were the only Viruk found in Dolosan.

Keles had quelled any dispute by simply noting that Rekarafi had been sent to see to his safety. Such a thing was unprecedented and gave the scroungers something else to talk about. This they did in mumbles and cant that made Keles wish for his brother's facility with languages.

The path to Opaslynoti led them to the western corner of Dolosan, to the base of the uplift that marked the edge of the Ixyll plateau. As they grew closer and night fell, it was easy to see the magic curtain that shimmered along the heights, though the purples and deep blues did not shine that brightly. Mostly it obscured stars and colored the moons as they sailed through it, but sight of it sent a thrill through Keles anyway. To enter Ixyll, they would have to slip through that curtain and the gods alone knew what lay *beyond*.

One evening he'd stood apart, on a small hill, watching the curtain lights shift as if teased by night breezes. How long he watched he didn't know, but he suddenly realized he was shivering. Yet even as he made that discovery, his rolled blanket hit him across the small of his back.

He turned and saw the Viruk crouched behind him, downwind. That sent a different shiver through him. "How long have you been there?"

Rekarafi, little more than a silhouette, shrugged. "Long enough to know you would be cold."

"Were you watching me?"

"You mean was I stalking you? I noticed you begin to shiver. I fetched your blanket." He reached out and pointed toward Ixyll. "I was watching that. *Tavam eyzar.*"

Keles untied the leather strips holding his bedroll closed, then wrapped himself in the woolen blanket. "*Tavam* is magic. *Eyzar* I do not know."

"Veil in your tongue, but more than garment. A veil obscures." He lowered his hand to his knee. "This veil has died quickly. You reckon things by nine, for your gods, and we reckon by ten."

"You have ten gods?" Keles looked to the sky to pick out a tenth constellation.

"No. Our slaves had ten fingers. We did not want them confused when they were counting." The Viruk came forward, still keeping himself downwind. "Seventy decades ago, the battle that hung this *tavam eyzar* was fought. In those days, it could be seen in the sunlight. It outshone the sun—for there was little sunlight in the Time of Black Ice. In your Principalities you could not see it, but it lit Irusviruk so brightly we had no night. Reds and yellows, gold, silver, green and blue, the light would roil and boil, then magic would pour from the heights and wreak havoc."

The Viruk's shoulders rose in a hunch. "You are incapable of understanding what that was like, Keles. What you have seen so far has been incredible—so many things, all different. When the magic flowed out it dissolved everything, but also *made* everything. All the places you have seen, and more than you could imagine, all existed here at the same time. Past and future merged, realities merged, plants and animals merged, everything that was not somehow protected was remade."

The cartographer closed his eyes and tried to make sense of his words. "You're right, I can't imagine."

"Think of a pool, Keles, and what you can see when the water is still. That was the world. Then think of the water churned to a froth. What you see changes. Here, where the water was magic, reality was distorted. All things existed at the same time, but none *persisted,* for the magic was too wild."

"It kept churning."

"Yes, and could only be contained by a *tavam eyzar*."

Opening his eyes again, Keles crouched. Though the Viruk had drawn close, his headache did not build. He expected it would, but did not mind. Rekarafi had maintained distance throughout the journey, and while Keles did fear him, the Viruk's attempt at bridging that distance prompted him to honor it.

"You refer to this veil in a way that makes me think there was another."

Rekarafi's head swiveled toward him and cold pinpoints of reflected starlight glistened in his dark eyes. "Virukadeen was consumed in a conflagration of magic you could not comprehend. Your Cataclysm changed land and boiled an inland sea. Virukadeen's death *devoured* land.

"Where your Dark Sea sits today, Keles, was once a range of mountains that caught at the stars. We lived there, and no matter how far we traveled from our home, we could still see it. The tallest peak should have always been buried in snow, for it existed above the clouds, but *tavamazari* bent the winds to their will and tamed the sun. Our home was as lush as Ummummorar, as warm as Miromil. It was paradise."

Keles shook his head. "How could they destroy it?"

The Viruk make a crackling sound in his throat that sounded as if he were gargling bones. "We sit in a place your people destroyed and you can ask this? Do motives matter after three thousand years? Those who had power wanted more and jealously guarded what they had. Those who had none wanted some and would stoop at nothing to get it. Hardly noble or lofty, though each side crafted stories to cast their actions as both.

"As things unfolded, there were those who saw the result. They gathered *tavamazari* who remained outside the conflagration and raised a *tavam eyzar* to contain it. Virukadeen sank, and the Black Pearl rose into the heavens."

The cartographer looked up. Gol'dun, the second largest moon, hung in the sky: a black ball with a silver-grey sheen to it. "Gol'dun is the treasure of the gods. It passes slowly among them because they cannot bear its being taken from them."

Again the rattling sounded from the Viruk's throat. "I could tell you of the true origin of your gods, Keles Anturasi. You would refuse to believe me. The Black Pearl did not float through the sky in my youth. Your name for it is a bastardization of ours. We call it *ghoal nuan*. The nearest translation for you would be soulstone. As with 'veil,' it does not contain the nuances."

"Tell me, please."

Rekarafi slowly closed his eyes. "It will not help you to map your world."

"But it will help me understand the world I am mapping."

The Viruk remained still, his eyes closed, then he lifted his chin. Keles wondered what Rekarafi was thinking. He almost allowed himself to believe the Viruk was listening to ghosts and seeking their counsel before speaking. *Perhaps he speaks with the ambassador as I do my grandfather.*

Finally, he opened his eyes again. "It is our belief that upon death we are judged. Every evil we commit creates a black stone in our soul, a *ghoal nuan*. Every kindness creates a white stone, a *ghoal saam*. The judge collects these stones and weighs them. More black than white, a soul enters eternal torment. If the reverse, the soul passes to paradise."

"If there is a balance?"

Rekarafi nodded. "The *ghoal* are discarded and the soul returns to the world anew."

"So you believe—" Keles stopped as the Viruk's hand rose and talons flashed. The faint scent of venom made him dizzy and he fell back. "What is it?"

"I tell you this for two reasons, Keles. The first is that we might find Viruk graves and if they are opened, you will see white stones and black. When a body is buried, often friends or enemies will throw stones into the grave to tip the balance. This lets you understand."

Keles nodded silently, but hoped they would find a grave so he could see evidence of what Rekarafi had described.

"The second reason is that when I struck you, I created a *ghoal nuan* for myself. I came to balance it by serving you. I may do many things, like the slaying of the *etharsaal,* which grant me *ghoal saam,* but my service shall not end until you grant me *ghoal saam*."

Keles frowned. "I think I understand. Thank you."

"It is my duty to serve and protect you." The Viruk cocked his head to the side. "Perhaps it will not be onerous."

They left the hill and returned to the camp, guided by the glow of a blue *thaumston* lantern. Keles crawled into his tent considering all that the Viruk had said. There was much there he understood, and a great deal he did not. Paramount among them was exactly *why* Rekarafi had chosen to speak to him. Pondering that conundrum carried him into sleep.

The next morning came early and with it a headache as usual, but Keles worked around it. The travelers broke camp quickly and made their way across a flat plain whose thin coat of black snow kept the dust buried. Everyone in the group took the snow's color as a bad omen, and the thaumstoners urged them on as quickly as possible. When Keles' mapping efforts slowed them too much, the scroungers left them behind.

Following the tracks in the snow, the six of them moved into a canyon which, while much wider than the one with the pool, still reminded them of it. The glassy sheen of the striated walls suggested to Keles that a river of magic had carved the canyon, and that periodic floods kept the stones well polished. He even saw himself reflected in their surface, but as he rode he caught different images. Most often he appeared as a child, but an unhappy one, and a few times he saw himself bowed and beaten like his uncle Ulan.

Worst of all there were times his eyes stared back at him out of his grandfather's face. Even the reflection of a skeleton wearing his clothes and riding a skeletal horse did not make him feel as uncomfortable as seeing himself as his grandfather. *Past and future may no longer coexist, but these reflections show them.*

No one else made any comment, but their pace did slow as they all studied the reflections. Keles only saw the others as they were now, but the expressions they wore, shifting from horror to delight, suggested they saw themselves as changed as he did. Only Rekarafi viewed it with disdain, though he did claw furrows across one flat surface.

They followed the twisting canyon down into a valley that spread out north and south as well as further west to Ixyll. Signs of human habitation began to appear, mostly in the form of discarded rubbish. Here and there pickaxes had chipped rock and shovels had turned soil. At one point Keles caught the reflection of someone digging, but in the real world all that existed was an old hole and the broken haft of the shovel.

Finally, cresting a small rise, they saw Opaslynoti. Borosan rested both hands on his saddle horn and smiled. "It's grown."

The last vestige of romance died in Keles' heart. Opaslynoti was a city, but unlike any *city* he'd ever seen before. Nothing even hinted at its Viruk roots. He wondered what Rekarafi was seeing. *Were Moriande reduced to this, I would wish to die.*

Opaslynoti most closely resembled a trash midden, with people wriggling through it like maggots. Nestled there at an intersection of canyons two miles wide, it had been built against the southwest wall. In the days of its Viruk glory it would have occupied land at the conjunction of two rivers. Keles could easily imagine ships sailing down them and towers soaring, but then the truth of Opaslynoti reasserted itself.

When human settlement was small, the rock outcropping likely would have provided some safety against magic storms. Were water to run through the canyon, its location would contain nothing more than a gentle eddy. From there it had grown downward. The earth removed had been piled to the north, extending the outcropping to create a dike. The way sunlight reflected from parts of the midden revealed it had weathered some magic storms, but the fact that the downstream side also had been polished suggested the magic had slopped over, and the sunken pit of Opaslynoti would have been a perfect catch basin for it.

A closer approach did not make Keles feel any better. The diggings had been organized into terraces, so dwellings sank back into the stone. Up around the perimeter of the pit, looking like the caps of countless toadstools, domed buildings large and small provided shelter. Camels and horses stood in paddocks around some of the larger domes, and he assumed the animals would be driven inside to protect them from storms.

The odd thing about the domes was that they all had clearly been constructed of mud and straw, but had flat grey stone plates set over them. "Borosan, what are the stones for?"

The *gyanridin* rested his hands on his saddlehorn. "The stones are dug from deeper in the pits. They contain some *thaumston* and will absorb magic. After a storm, people take the dome shields down and sell the *thaumston,* but it is very low grade and not terribly useful."

He gave his horse a touch of spur. "Come on. I have friends in the lower reaches. We will stable our mounts and they will take us in."

Moraven cleared his throat. "Down is best?"

Borosan nodded. "Storms will whip around the edges, but seldom fill the Well to overflowing. As long as we avoid the falls during a storm, deep is best. Opaslynoti, despite what you might think, is not a place where we will get into trouble."

Ciras, who had guided his horse off to the right to examine a separate set of tracks leading in toward the city, shook his head. "I do not think that will be necessarily true this time, Master Gryst."

Moraven frowned. "What is it?"

"These tracks run to the largest dome. I know them." Ciras dropped a hand to the hilt of his sword. "Somehow the raiders are here before us."

Chapter Forty-eight

27th day, Month of the Tiger, Year of the Rat
9th Year of Imperial Prince Cyron's Court
163rd Year of the Komyr Dynasty
737th year since the Cataclysm
Tocayan, Caxyan

Jorim was able to convince the warrior in the jet, jade, and gold mask to wait while they sent a boat back for Captain Gryst. The man seemed to understand the word Captain. Jorim dispatched Lieutenant Linor to the *Stormwolf*. The rest of the landing party took up a defensive position near the *Moondragon* and eyed the woods with suspicion.

Jorim crouched high up on the beach with the giant. Though he had rendered the greeting perfectly, his grasp of the Naleni tongue was spotty. He introduced himself as Tzihua and, at Jorim's request, began naming common items in his tongue. In short order, the cartographer learned that Tzihua's people called themselves the Amentzutl, their nation Caxyan, and that he was from a southern outpost called Tocayan. The *Moondragon*'s crew had been taken there for their protection since the Mozoyan—an enemy people—had scouts moving throughout the area.

Jorim began to pick up little bits and pieces of the language. The suffix "–yan," for example, denoted a place. The Mozoyan were from outside that place, which meant they were as much outsiders as the Turasynd were for the Empire. It pleased Jorim that the Amentzutl tongue had an orderly nature to it, since that made it so much easier for him to learn.

Within an hour Captain Gryst came ashore, bringing with her Iesol and Shimik, as well as the fleet's botanical scholar. Tzihua greeted her and was content to leave the fleet's people at the beach while he conducted a small party inland to the outpost. He communicated to Jorim that they should have little fear of the Mozoyan with such fine troops in evidence. He waved a hand and summoned a half dozen young men and women from the forest depths and left them behind to "help," but both sides knew they were hostages against the safety of those accompanying him.

Tzihua eyed Shimik carefully, but when the Fennych held his arms up and Iesol hefted him like a child, his concern lessened appreciably. He led Iesol, Anaeda, and Jorim into the forest, and within a half dozen paces the beach had disappeared in green gloom. Not much further on, other warriors joined them on the narrow trail that wound around past the boles of large trees. Golden monkeys and their smaller cousins screamed at them from the thick canopies above, rushing down, screeching, then darting away again to chatter with fellows.

Jorim and Anaeda said almost nothing, but Jorim was thinking what Iesol kept muttering. "Oh, my, oh, my," fell from his lips so often that Shimik started chanting "Omaiamaia." The Fenn wove into that some of the haunting, hooting tones of the monkeys and became loud enough that their arboreal stalkers would pause and cock their heads when Shimik returned their calls.

Jorim found the jungle to be a wondrous place, full of plants and animals the like of which he'd never seen. He was fairly certain he could spend a year or more and not even begin to dent the surface of all he could discover. Already he'd seen a dozen different varieties of brilliantly colored blossoms that were produced by plants growing on tree limbs, their roots hanging free in the air. The monkeys, as well as tracks of small deer and similar creatures on the trail, suggested there must be some larger predators around, but he saw nothing of them. This sent a trickle of fear through him, though he took heart that neither Tzihua nor his men appeared to be overly concerned with things lurking beyond the green walls that hemmed them in.

The trail moved parallel to the river. Jorim estimated that they traveled due east for three miles before the river curved south around a hill. The jungle made it impossible to see how tall the hill was, but the path broadened slightly as they climbed. Other paths fed into it, and suddenly the trail leveled out. They emerged from the jungle onto a broad green plain roughly five miles in diameter. The outer ring consisted of cleared fields up to the jungle edge. While Jorim did not recognize the crops being cultivated, other patches remained overgrown.

They practice crop rotation. He made that observation, realizing it set them apart from the people of Ethgi. The Amentzutl had enough science to realize that purposely letting fields rest one in five or seven seasons would mean it would never be played out. That observation occurred in a flash, suggesting to him a level of sophistication despite Tzihua's lack of steel weaponry. In the next moment, as Jorim's eyes focused beyond the fields and he realized that what he had taken for bare hills in the distance were not natural formations, his estimate of their sophistication expanded exponentially.

Tzihua had used the Naleni word "outpost" to describe Tocayan, but the word failed to encompass adequately what Tocayan truly was. In the distance he saw four stepped pyramids rising from the heart of the plain. It seemed quite obvious that the stones had been quarried from the nearby mountains, but that meant they'd been transported a minimum of three miles to where the pyramids were built. Moreover, the trail, which had become a full-fledged road, showed no signs of ruts made by wagon wheels. Nor did Jorim see any horses, though people working the fields did have with them beasts that looked like very small camels with no discernible humps.

In addition to the pyramids, which rose to a height of nearly one hundred feet, a number of circular buildings a third of that height dotted the landscape. They, too, had a solid stone construction. While they lacked the ornate nature of Imperial construction, they were clean and strong. What ornamentation they did have came in the form of carved stone blocks with serpent and bird imagery that reminded Jorim rather hauntingly of Naleni and Desei symbols.

"Tzihua, how many Amentzutl in Tocayan?"

The warrior held his right hand up, splaying out all five fingers. He closed that hand into a fist, chopped his left hand at his wrist, then again at his elbow. "Do you understand? Ten in hand. Ten more. Ten more."

Jorim knew thirty could not be the correct answer. "I am not sure."

Iesol spoke. "Master Anturasi, they use the Viruk system, counting by tens. The wrist would multiply by ten, and the elbow ten again. The shoulder another ten, perhaps? He is telling you there are a thousand people here."

"A thousand people in an outpost?" Jorim shook his head. "How long has Tocayan been here? Tocayan yan?"

Tzihua's fingers flashed and hand chopped.

A hundred and twenty years? Jorim glanced back at Anaeda. "Could they have done all this in a hundred and twenty years?"

"Not a thousand people, not unless they were far more industrious than even the Naleni are." Her dark eyes narrowed. "That, or Minister Iesol might have offered a solution?"

"What?"

"If they count in the Viruk manner, perhaps they used Viruk magic."

"That's not . . ." Jorim fell silent and tried to reconcile two ideas he thought of as mutually exclusive truths. First, he knew the Viruk used magic and could be very powerful. The Viruk ambassador had cured his brother, and no Naleni physician could have done what she did. While Men had once worked hard to refine skills that would give them access to magic, the Viruk just played with magic all by itself.

The *vanyesh* had sought use of Viruk-style magic. Their quest had proven to be a disaster. Playing with magic had triggered the Cataclysm. That humans could practice magic and be productive with it—all without disastrous side effects—clearly was unthinkable.

But Jorim knew that magic was a skill that could be mastered. The *vanyesh* had some initial success. The Viruk likewise were skilled at it. Perhaps the Amentzutl had discovered a discipline that provided access to magic under controlled circumstances. If that were true, then their most powerful mages would be Mystics, and that would be a sight to behold.

Discovery of such a discipline would be worth more than all the gold and jewels we could possibly return to Nalenyr. The outpost and fields suggested that if magic were being employed, its harmful side effects were controlled. Just the ability to do that, to harness wild magic, would allow the opening of the Spice Routes to the west.

Jorim found himself becoming very excited by the prospect, so he quickly reined himself in. Speculation was all fine and good, but he still had no evidence that these people controlled any magic at all. Everything he saw could have been performed by massive armies of slaves, and their dead bodies could have been fertilizing the fields through which they walked. It could be that the Amentzutl didn't even consider slaves to be people, so they weren't included in Tzihua's accounting. But regardless of how Tocayan had been created, for it to have been done in a hundred and twenty years was remarkable, and Jorim meant to have the secret of its history.

As they drew closer to the city, Jorim watched for evidence of magic, but saw none. In fact, what he did see reminded him very much of the Ummummorari. Women and men alike wore loincloths and, save for those wearing armor, strode about bare-chested. They wore their black hair long and braided into a single queue with brightly colored threads and the occasional bead. Field hands' clothing had none of the colors worn by the soldiery or people encountered closer to the heart of the city. Certain colors seemed to denote caste, with green common to the soldiers, red to merchants, yellow to laborers, black to officials, and purple to individuals Jorim assumed were part of a priesthood. While a particular color would predominate, accent colors seemed to indicate other affiliations, and decorations woven into garments or beaten into armlets, anklets, bracelets, gorgets, and pectorals fell into the classes of Snake, Cat, and Eagle.

Tzihua led them to one of the large round buildings, which clearly was a dwelling complex, and into its heart. He took them to a central chamber and opened the door. "Here is your *Moondragon*."

Within they found the crew of the *Moondragon* looking a bit haggard, but fed and rested. The circular room had a pool in the center for washing and waste stations around the outer perimeter. The crew had been given woven mats upon which to sleep and enough food that some fruits and meal breads remained stacked in a corner.

Lieutenant Minan straightened his uniform, approached, and bowed to Captain Gryst. "I deliver myself into your custody, Captain, for whatever discipline you deem appropriate."

Anaeda returned the bow—along with Iesol, Shimik, and Jorim. She straightened first. "For what am I disciplining you?"

"The loss of my ship."

"I think you will find it is where you left it. Repairs should be well under way by the time you return." She looked around. "It looks as if your crew is all present."

"Save for four we lost in the storm, Captain." Minan looked down. "And two these people have housed elsewhere. We have seen one of them on occasion, but nothing of the other."

Anaeda turned to face Tzihua, then glanced at Jorim. "I wish to know where my missing people are."

Jorim began to relay her request to the Amentzutl warrior, but from behind him one of the two missing men slipped into the room. Dirhar Pelalan dropped to one knee before Captain Gryst and bowed deeply. "I have come, Captain, to be of help."

Jorim half turned back to Minan. "The other missing person is Lesis Osebor?"

"Yes. How did you know?"

Anaeda frowned. "You had two linguists with you, Lieutenant. They took Master Pelalan to teach them our tongue. Master Osebor has been sent north, I assume."

Tzihua bowed his head. "Nemehyan."

She looked at Dirhar. "Meaning?"

"Master Osebor has been sent to the Amentzutl capital, Nemehyan. His task is to teach our tongue to the Witch-King."

Jorim raised an eyebrow. "Witch-King?"

"The title in Amentzutl is *maicana-netl*. The *maicana* are the ruling caste, inheritors of a magic tradition of great antiquity and power. The King is the strongest among them. It is said he can freeze the sun in the sky and shatter mountains with a word."

Jorim smiled. "That I would like to see."

"And you shall." Tzihua nodded slowly. "Now that your sea princess has come, we shall all travel north and the *maicana-netl,* wise beyond all wisdom, can decide what to do with you."

Chapter Forty-nine

1st day, Month of the Wolf, Year of the Rat
9th Year of Imperial Prince Cyron's Court
163rd Year of the Komyr Dynasty
737th year since the Cataclysm
Opaslynoti, Dolosan

Moraven Tolo found himself no more at ease in the scavenger city after a week than he had been when they first rode into it. He realized that while he had lived a long time, his experiences had been largely confined to the old Imperial borders, and usually in Erumvirine, Nalenyr, or the Five Princes. He knew a great deal about people, and his experiences told him a lot about how they would react in certain situations. Those situations, however, had always been within the confines of what could have been described as a civilized area.

The very approach to the city alerted his sense of unease. He'd seen odd reflections of himself in the smooth stones. He appeared as a child at times, but he could not recognize himself. Another time he wore a complete suit of armor, trimmed in purple; but he'd never seen such a thin material, much less had it on. He saw himself with a full beard streaked with white and again as a moldering corpse with a gaping wound where his scar existed.

He wasn't certain what he was seeing, and had no way to determine if it had significance or not. He wanted to dismiss it, but part of him could not. Ever since the healing, he'd felt different in an almost imperceptible way. The visions resonated with that sensation and fed it.

If he needed a sense of the normal to quell his sense of the unusual, Opaslynoti was not the place he would find it. Those living there took great delight in being the antithesis of the civilized east.

The six of them stood out, and the people of Opaslynoti acknowledged this and wanted little to do with them. Had Borosan not been with them, they would have been driven back into the Wastes and no one would have cared had they never been seen again.

But Borosan's presence earned them some tolerance. While most said he was still too normal to really be one of the thaumstoneers, his skill at *gyanri* still earned him respect. And while his manner did fit in with Opaslynoti's denizens, even Moraven agreed that, at least physically, Borosan was more normal than any of them would ever be.

Borosan's friend Writiv Maos provided them accommodations in his home, which was on the third of the eight levels in the city. The ninth level was the Well, but no one dwelt there, to the best of anyone's knowledge. Level three was the second nicest level. Anything above it was given over to visitors and newcomers, all of whom were viewed with suspicion. Below level four lived longtime residents who had no luck or ambition. They were content to grind out a meager and difficult existence working in the Well or in the ancillary industries that had sprung up to serve the needs of the *gyanridin*.

The Well became the focal point of the city and was, at once, revered and feared. When magic storms poured down from Ixyll, a certain amount of the wild magic would flow down into the hole at the city's heart. No one knew how deep it was, and various stories suggested it opened into a vast underground complex of caverns, while others said the hole opened into another world. All Moraven knew was that the Well was filled with magic: a shimmering pool with shifting violets and blues that matched the curtain surrounding Ixyll itself.

The laborers of Opaslynoti performed three major jobs. The miners dug into the earth and produced raw *thaumston* ranging from chunks the size of a man's head to buckets of dust. Many of the miners worked in Opaslynoti itself, but a significant number also worked independent claims outside the city. Prospectors roamed about looking for places where the *thaumston* already had accumulated a charge or was relatively free of impurities.

A second class of laborers cleaned and crushed the raw ore, mixed it with water and sand to create a slurry, then packed it into molds. The sheets were then set out in the sun to bake. The molds turned out pieces from a finger length to slabs suitable for using in a surface building. Most often, however, they were shaped into bricks nine inches long, three wide, and two thick.

The ingots of *thaumston* would then be loaded onto pallets or into baskets and lowered by means of cranes and pulleys into the Well. Moraven watched men performing that part of the operation for two days. The chargers worried about the day's temperature, the depth to which they lowered the cargo, and seemed to constantly grouse about how this load would likely be the last until the storm season started.

The artisan laborers concerned themselves with fabricating a variety of devices that consumed the magic energy in *thaumston*. Many were simple things similar to the lights that glowed on some of the Nine's finest buildings. Also popular were small mechanical animals with tin flesh and gaudy paint. For some reason, when Moraven traveled with Rekarafi through the market, an inordinate number of people offered him these small amusements.

Rekarafi dismissed the offers with a flick of taloned fingers, but only once spoke. "Do you not realize the Viruk no longer have children who would be entranced by these things?"

The remark shook Moraven. He had been cut off from his past, but he still had a future. *If Viruk can no longer have children, they are cut off from any future.* He wondered if it was that the Viruk could no longer reproduce, or just chose not to. *Would I make that choice if my people had fallen from glory?*

The easily attainable supply of *thaumston* made artificial light widely available. This allowed much of Opaslynoti's life to take place deep in the earth. The marketplace, which had its surface opening beneath one of the domes, descended all the way to level five. Terraces provided permanent space for longtime merchants, while transient traders fought for space down on the central floor.

Many of the merchants even invested in brilliant displays to attract people to their stalls, displays that could be considered works of art.

Light was not always useful, for many of Opaslynoti's citizens had suffered horribly from years of exposure to the wild magic. It did things to them—occasionally subtle—but even voluminous robes and masks failed to conceal the grander changes. Worse, many of the people seemed to revel in these.

Yet others had clearly sought them. Just as the Turasynd had inserted feathers into his flesh so they would become part of him, some of the people here had done even more bizarre things. One family group had four arms, one pair set below the other. The story went that several generations earlier two brothers had been prospecting. One had broken his legs in a fall, and the other was carrying him on his back when a magical storm poured over them. The two men had merged into one and the change had bred true.

Others, it was said, had sewn the arms of corpses to their chests in hopes that the magic might affect them the same way. They had failed, but people with insect antennae sprouting from their foreheads or tiger-stripe pelts to keep them warm suggested that sometimes the experiments worked.

Moraven found these deliberate changes more difficult to accept than the random ones. That struck him as curious because he, too, through his discipline and study, sought to perfect himself. He thought back to Ciras' comment about the disaster that would result from magic being made simple. What he saw here suggested Ciras might be correct.

He searched for patterns in the wild magic's random effects. He saw many people who shambled along on legs that no longer bent in the normal fashion, or dragged an arm that had grown longer than its fellow. Some of them were barely recognizable as human. The most tragic cases were blamed upon being caught out in a magic storm, or a fall into the Well. Apparently some sought to commit suicide by diving into it. And while the Well never gave up its dead, it did let the living bob to the surface from time to time—though once they were rescued they undoubtedly wished they had not been.

He saw no formula to how people were changed, but he realized finding one might be impossible. As he had told Nirati and Dunos, a healing would take time. But here the magic would also use as its foundation who the person had been at the time of his change. In the case of the brothers, had it been their abiding love for each other, and the sacrifice of one for the other that enabled them to survive as they did? Did the man have one arm grow longer than the other because he was greedy and grasping?

And, more importantly, could the discipline of the swordsman's art allow Moraven to control the magic and the change it would make in him? The tingle had grown to a distraction. It felt as if he had been sunburned. He hated the sensation. When he could no longer bear it, he sought distraction—and Opaslynoti had much to offer in that regard.

As with most other towns, hard work and spare money meant many recreational occupations flourished. Plenty of taverns had been dug out of the earth. None of them approached the simple elegance of taverns in the Nine, but this did not seem to bother those who filled them all hours of the day and night. Two breweries served the city, transporting kegs of beer on the backs of *gyanrigot* the size of draft horses. Houses of carnal pleasure did not seem to rely on *gyanrigot,* though Moraven would not have ruled it out. Though he did not survey the houses, he assumed that each would cater to a certain clientele and really had no desire to visit the more venerable establishments.

The largest centers of recreation, however, were the arenas. They ranged in size from a small pit dug in the back of a tavern to large amphitheaters capable of seating hundreds. Their presence did not surprise Moraven, since duels between men had always attracted a crowd. When Ciras heard of them, he wished to be given leave to enter a fight, and Moraven was almost tempted to let him do so.

Yet here, the arenas were not meant as places where life could be lost. The only combatants accepted were *gyanrigot*. Large and small, rigidly classified by weight, the machines battled to the delight of spectators. *Gyanridin* throughout the city proudly displayed their creations. Arenas accepted bets, and vast sums of money changed hands among the spectators. The combatants and their creators won fame and small purses for their efforts.

And while it might have seemed natural for the misshapen to battle each other like beasts, that was precisely the reason they did not.

While the citizens might eschew civilization, they had no intention of abandoning their humanity. Their resolution not to kill one another united them, and murder was punished by staking the killer out where the storms could get him. The magic that changed them all would judge him guilty or innocent, and all would live with the result.

Borosan Gryst had created a new version of his largest *thanaton* and had lost little time in scouting out an arena where it could fight. Moraven, Ciras, and Rekarafi accompanied him to a medium-sized arena on the third level. Keles had been felled by one of his blinding headaches and Tyressa had remained behind to tend to him, but both bid them go and enjoy themselves. The quartet paid for admission in gold, which seemed to strike the ticket taker as unusual; most others bought their way in with nine grains of *thaumston* dust.

The quartet moved along the upper tier and finally found a place to watch the battle down in the arena. Centered in the reddish sand, a *gyanrigot* looking a lot like a scorpion scuttled around in a slow circle. Its six small legs held its belly a yard off the sand. The two larger forelegs ended in massive claws with serrated inner surfaces. A curved tail, complete with a wickedly sharp stinger, rose over its middle.

It battled a smaller *gyanrigot* that had a domed shape, the edges of which plowed the sand as it moved. The tracks it left revealed some sort of wheels that provided mobility, but it didn't move very fast. Spikes festooned the dome, and a number had tapered heads that spun. By some mechanism, it could extend some of those spikes if it got in close, piercing the enemy. Several of the spikes had been sheared off, presumably by the scorpion's claws.

Borosan kept his voice low. "Both of these battlers are built for close combat. But you've seen my *thanaton*. It is nimble enough to stay out of range, yet can still damage its foes. It's accurate enough not to miss at this range, which means I should win."

Moraven nodded. "You have spent time scouting these fighters?"

"I have. Skorpe should win and will be the tougher kill, but I can handle Quillbeast, too."

Ciras managed to strain most of the disgust out of his voice. "Curious names. What will you call your *thanaton*?"

The *gyanridin* blinked as if he did not understand the question. "Name?"

"So we can bet on the battle, Master Gryst."

"Bet?"

Moraven rested a hand on Ciras' shoulder. "Perhaps you should call it Serpentslayer."

"I-I suppose I could. I just call it *thanaton* Number Four. I mean, you know it is really the third one with modifications, but there were enough that I felt it had become a new *gyanrigot*."

The Viruk rested his hands on Gryst's shoulders. "Perhaps you would honor me by calling it *Nesrearck*."

Borosan smiled. "Is that Viruk for Serpentslayer?"

"Similar, and appropriate."

"*Nesrearck* it shall be." Borosan jerked his head toward the action. "I'd best get down there. *Nesrearck* is waiting, and I need to tinker so I can defeat the winner."

As he departed, Moraven looked over at the Viruk. "You will forgive me, Rekarafi, but I heard you use that word before, as a curse—or so I thought. You applied it to the things merchants offered you. Did I mistake its meaning?"

The Viruk laughter sounded like breaking bones. "Permit me a jest. It means 'bad toy.' "

Ciras snorted.

Moraven watched Skorpe feint left, then cut right and catch Quillbeast with a claw. Quickly the larger *gyanrigot* surged forward and flicked its claw upward. The domed *gyanrigot* flipped over, scattering sand, and landed heavily on its back. Its spikes dug into the earth and its little wheels spun madly.

Remorselessly, Skorpe shifted around and began to pick the wheels apart with its claws. The tail quivered and everyone in the arena seemed to hold their breath waiting for it to punch straight through Quillbeast's belly plate. Before that could happen, however, a clanking length of chain was tossed noisily into the arena, then bells sounded and Skorpe withdrew to the arena's far side.

Moraven's apprentice looked at him. "Master, it is obvious that these machines are a perversion of life. Master Gryst's *thanaton* had its uses; I will not deny this. The mouser aided in the survey. But this is wrong." Ciras waved his sword hand at the arena. "Do you not see that this is a mockery of what you and I seek to perfect in life? Look down there. You have two combatants in a circle. They fight, but for what? The pleasure of a rabble and a few ounces of magic dust?"

"There are those, Ciras, who enter the circle and fight for pleasure." Moraven smiled. "It is a common enough entertainment, sometimes fought to the death."

"But, Master, we fight to perfect our skills. If we succeed we become more than we were. If these succeed, they have the dents pounded out and return to fight again for no real purpose."

The Viruk lowered his head. "Would you say, Master Dejote, that it is better to have people shedding blood and dying than it is for metal to be twisted? It is easier to recast metal than to reanimate the dead. Would not wars fought between armies of these *gyanrigot* be preferable to the conflict that triggered the Cataclysm?"

"Can you imagine that these machines would not make war on people?" Ciras lowered his voice. "We know the men who have been raiding the area and we know they are in Opaslynoti. They must see these combats and realize the potential. With enough *thaumston,* would it not be possible to create a Skorpe large enough to carry men? Would the claws not be employed against houses, livestock, and people? If we wish to keep the world safe, we should slay every *gyanridin* we can find."

The Viruk leaned forward, resting his weight on his fists. "We have a saying: 'The ocean's water cannot return to the mountains.' *Gyanri* exists, and there will be no destroying it. Furthermore, I think you should welcome it."

Ciras' eyes grew wide. "How can you say that?"

"You complain that these machines do not have the ability to make decisions as do you. That is their weakness. Study them as you would any foe. Exploit that weakness."

Bells clanged, drawing their attention back to the arena. A man in red robes strode to the center and raised his voice for all to hear. "In this battle we have the challenger from far Nalenyr. Borosan Gryst brings us *Nesrearck* the Serpentslayer."

Scattered applause broke out, but Moraven was not surprised by how sparse it was. *Nesrearck* just sat in the sand like a featureless ball. He'd have thought Borosan didn't want to reveal anything about the *thanaton*'s capability to his foe, but Borosan was not that subtle. He simply had no sense of the theatrical.

Skorpe's owner, on the other hand, knew exactly what he was doing. As the announcer welcomed the champion, the scorpion dashed toward the center of the arena, claws raised and clanging loudly. It then backed away slowly, strutting, claws and tail up. The crowd began to chant "Skorpe! Skorpe!"

The announcer scrambled away through a door in the arena's wooden walls, then bells sounded. Skorpe again raced toward the arena's heart and for a moment Moraven feared *Nesrearck* had broken, for the sphere lay there inert. Then panels slid back, legs popped out, and the harpoon's barbed head appeared to point at the larger *gyanrigot*. Before Skorpe recognized any sort of a threat, the harpoon shot forward and pierced the scorpion's face, popping out just above the last set of legs.

Skorpe rocked back, then its legs collapsed beneath it. It flopped down in a clatter of metal, and a cloud of red dust rose to obscure it. The claws clicked at random, and the tail slackened. The left claw closed on the harpoon's shaft, but made little headway in tugging it loose.

Nesrearck circled Skorpe twice, moving laterally to keep the next projectile—a much smaller bolt—pointed at it. Aside from the claw's grinding at the haft, the champion gave no sign of even being aware of its foe. Legs twitched, but at random.

Nesrearck circled one more time, then the bolt withdrew. The panels that had concealed the crossbow mechanism slid shut with loud clicks. Moraven thought, just for a moment, that he'd heard an echo, then noticed that Skorpe had finally snapped the harpoon shaft.

Quickly, the champion rose. It darted forward and almost effortlessly caught two of *Nesrearck*'s legs in its claws. As if a *bhotcai* pruning a tree, it snipped the legs off, canting the spherical *gyanrigot* to the right.

Though severely wounded, *Nesrearck* did not give up. It pushed off with its left legs and tried to roll out of danger. But Skorpe closed too quickly, catching the severed stumps in its right claw and holding *Nesrearck* on its back. The crossbow panels again snapped open, and the shot should have ripped up through the larger *gyanrigot*. The only difficulty was that the crossbow relied on gravity to keep the bolt in place, so that while the mechanism functioned, the bolt spilled harmlessly onto the ground.

Skorpe's left claw rose and plunged deep into *Nesrearck*'s belly. The legs spasmed, then curled in. The chain clanked into the sand not far from where Borosan stood. Someone else had clearly tossed it, for Borosan's shock was all too evident on his face.

Moraven tapped Ciras on the shoulder. "Go to his aid. Gather his device and see him back to our home."

"As you wish, Master."

Applause thundered through the arena and Skorpe scuttled around in a circle as attendants gathered up *Nesrearck*'s broken parts and rolled it from the battleground. Skorpe returned to where its creators waited. They drew the harpoon from it with a screeching of metal. They tossed the harpoon into the crowd and one man raised it triumphantly in a clenched fist.

The announcer returned to the center of the arena. "Ladies and gentlemen, I am assured that Skorpe is yet battleworthy, but we have no more combatants registered this evening. If any of you would challenge our champion, please come forward now. If not, we shall move to the smaller class of *gyanrigot*."

Rekarafi rose to his full height. "I would challenge Skorpe."

Heads turned as the Viruk's bass buzz sliced through the hubbub. People shrank back, giving the announcer a clear line of sight up to the top tier. "It has been a long time since a Viruk has offered a combatant. Bring your *gyanrigot* here and we will—"

"I offered no *rearck*. *I* will challenge it."

The announcer hesitated. "We don't let men fight—"

"I am not a man."

Across the arena a chant of "Die, Viruk, die," began, and picked up volume as it spread. The announcer looked at Skorpe's creators, who nodded adamantly. The red-robed man waved a hand. "Come on down, Viruk."

Moraven grabbed Rekarafi's arm. "Why?"

The Viruk laughed. "Your apprentice fears toys. I do not." He turned and galloped on hands and feet down the narrow stairway and leaped the nine-foot wall. He landed in a crouch, red dust puffing lightly around his feet. Rekarafi extended one hand and crooked a finger.

The announcer fled the arena. The champion *gyanrigot* approached, but slowly and cautiously. The Viruk clearly did not appear to be its normal sort of foe. The fact that it *did* orient on him, claws wide, tail high, confirmed Ciras' prediction that these machines could and likely would be used against people.

Ciras appeared at Moraven's left shoulder. "What is he doing?"

"He is proving to you what he suggested. He has found a weakness and will exploit it."

"What if he is wrong?"

"Then you will see what color a Viruk bleeds."

Rekarafi stayed low and moved in a crouch to the right and left. He let Skorpe dominate the center of the arena as seemed to be the *gyanrigot*'s wont. He extended first his left hand, then his right, and watched the claws rise to fend them off. He cut to the left more quickly, as if to take advantage of the machine's blind eye. Skorpe spun fast, keeping the Viruk centered between its claws.

The Viruk brought his hands back in, resting them on his knees. He hunched his shoulders, then raised his rump, thrusting his face forward. He snapped his jaws open and shut, and the machine responded by clicking its claws. Like him, it leaned forward slightly. Then, in a blurred burst of speed, it charged.

Rekarafi leaped up and forward, his powerful legs propelling him well above the claws and beyond their grasp. As they closed noisily on emptiness, he soared above even the tail and its spike. As he began to descend, he extended his right foot and twisted in the air.

His left hand whipped around behind him as he turned and caught Skorpe's tail, right beneath the thickened bulb from which the stinger sprouted. With a flick of his wrist, the Viruk flipped the *gyanrigot* over onto its back. Planting his left foot, he completed his turn as his left hand stretched and locked on the tail. His right foot came down at the point where tail met body and snapped the appendage clean off.

Contemptuously he smashed the tail against the *gyanrigot*'s lifeless hulk. *"Nesrearck!"*

Utter silence greeted his victory, but the Viruk did not seem to care. He strode to the wall and pulled himself over it as easily as he'd vanquished Skorpe. He let spectators flee before him, laughing almost gleefully.

Ciras frowned. "How did . . . what did . . . I don't understand."

Moraven smiled. "He found the weakness. The *gyanrigot* looked like a scorpion, so Borosan struck at its head with a shot that would have killed a scorpion. It failed. Therefore, whatever drove Skorpe was not located in its body. The bulb on the tail, on the other hand, was far from damaged, and never used the way it should have been."

"I see that now, Master."

"Then you should also see something else, *Lirserrdin* Dejote." Moraven pointed at the *gyanrigot* and the men dragging it from the arena. "Disgust and dismissal prevent you from understanding your enemy. *Gyanrigot* may never be something you have to fight, but by understanding them and their limitations, you can be certain they will never defeat you."

Chapter Fifty

2nd day, Month of the Wolf, Year of the Rat
9th Year of Imperial Prince Cyron's Court
163rd Year of the Komyr Dynasty
737th year since the Cataclysm
Wentokikun, Moriande
Nalenyr

The sun had reached its zenith, but Prince Cyron still could not shake the dream that had awakened him nine hours earlier. He seldom had nightmares, and never believed in the prophetic powers of dreams, but this one disturbed him. As he recalled flashes of it, his mouth went dry and his head began to pound.

He had been the dragon and had lain in twisted coils on the ground—a rocky, desolate ground that had cracked beneath the sun or the impact of his fall, he could not be certain which. Every bone in his body felt equally cracked, and when he tried to move, the grating pain of fragments locking and shifting clawed through his brain. The frustration of his being crippled pained him even more than the agonies of movement.

His body lay rent and bleeding. Looking down his length he could see limbs impaled on stone spikes. Black blood welled up around them and flowed over him. He thought of the Black River and tried to remember Desei geography, to see if he, the dragon, lay with his spine shattered on the banks of the Black River, or if there was some other symbolism he was missing. It struck him as ironic that he was the master of the world's greatest power because of the

Anturasi charts, and yet his knowledge of geography had become so poor he could not identify where he lay in the dream.

While the significance of the land escaped him, none of the rest of it did. A massive hawk landed on his chest and dipped its sharply hooked beak into his entrails. It tore at him, supping on liver. Its left wing had two feathers clipped, but that had not hindered the bird. Down below it, a dog lapped at black blood. At his tail the Virine bear nibbled lazily.

Those symbols needed no translation, but two others did. Swarming around him and the bear, a living carpet of black ants moved steadily forward. Mindless and relentless, they devoured everything, and somehow he knew the desolation surrounding him was something they had caused. They attacked the bear and it yowled as white bones appeared, picked clean of meat and sinew. The dog barked and retreated, and the hawk took wing.

The black ants approached from his tail, but he could not study their progress too closely because of the vultures seated on his snout. He could snap his jaws at them, but never quickly enough to catch and crush one. They, in turn, struck at his eyes and ears. They tore bits from his tongue. The vultures blinded him. They made him deaf. They silenced him so he could not even scream as the ants ate him alive.

"Are you well, Highness?"

Cyron blinked and let the world swim back into focus. He sat on his throne, with Pelut Vniel kneeling off to his right. Both men wore white mourning hoods, though far enough back on their heads that conversation was not precluded. "Yes, Grand Minister, I am well."

"I know, Highness, that Grand Minister Lynesorat's death is a surprise, for we had all expected a great many more years from him. And the proper waiting period would have been observed before I was elected to serve you in the capacity he did, save that his widow's request and dire times superseded convention."

Cyron nodded. *Yes, best you think I am truly mourning than believe I am lost in ruminations about a dream.* "I have no fear, Grand Minister, that you will serve well in his stead. Serve greatly, even, for you know me better than he did. And you are more attuned to the needs of state."

The man bowed and pressed his forehead to the floor before

coming back up. "My only wish is to free you from the mundane so those decisions that only you can make become your primary concern."

And there are many of those, to be sure. Vniel undoubtedly referred to the Helosundian problem, which had become a tangled knot. Prince Eiran had taken Cyron's orders to heart and was actually winning the loyalty of his people. As he stepped into his responsibilities, the possibility of assassination increased. Pyrust would never do it, but Eiran's Helosundian rivals might, as well as Naleni malcontents.

But Cyron had a more pressing concern. Qiro Anturasi had continued to generate charts, but reports from the *Stormwolf* and the Ixyll expedition had become short and terse. To make matters worse, reports came from along the coast of raiding by ghost ships. His navy had been unable to find, much less engage, the ghosts. Merchants didn't want to send ships out without protection, and the resulting disruption in trade threatened to destabilize his government. Without money, he could not move forward. And, eventually, he would fall prey to Deseirion.

Vniel frowned. "You are preoccupied, Highness?"

The Prince hesitated for a moment, then nodded. "I have a concern, yes. Tell me what you know of prophetic dreams."

A little shiver ran through the minister, but otherwise he masked his reaction. "There are those who set great store in the symbolism. Prince Pyrust, as well you know, is one. I had not thought you believed in such, Highness."

"I do not, Minister. Have no fear for my sanity."

"I had none." The man smiled. "Was it a dream of yours, Highness, that concerned you?"

Cyron half closed his eyes and waved the suggestion away. "Hardly. I merely wondered if Prince Pyrust ever suffered nightmares?"

"I can inquire, Highness." Grand Minister Vniel let his smile broaden. "I do think, however, that Prince Pyrust will soon have news that disturbs his sleep. It is likewise my hope that this news will allow you to sleep that much more soundly."

"Thank you. I hope you are correct." Cyron gave the man a slight smile and hoped it covered the trickle of ice running up his spine.

You're one of the vultures, aren't you? I hear what you say, I see what you want me to see, and what I say goes through you. A sense of peace came over him as that bit of the mystery cleared up.

Now, who are the ants and from whence do they come? His eyes sharpened. *And when they come, can I stop them?*

Chapter Fifty-one

2nd day, Month of the Wolf, Year of the Rat
9th Year of Imperial Prince Cyron's Court
163rd Year of the Komyr Dynasty
737th year since the Cataclysm
Thyrenkun, Felarati
Deseirion

Sweet grey smoke drifted up over the soothsayer's face. The dim light allowed the incense's cherry glow to impart some color to his wrinkled features, but mostly it made his face a spiderweb of black. His eyes—half-closed, milky white, and all but sightless—glistened wetly in the smoke. Leathery skin hung somewhat loosely, as if he had once been corpulent but had wizened through years untold.

Pyrust sat there patiently, cloaked in the darkness of a hood. The soothsayer had only been told that he was one of the Prince's advisors. Pyrust had even donned a glove with two filled fingers to disguise his maiming. The incense's scent calmed him even as the smoke made his eyes tear. He kept his breathing shallow when the smoke drifted over him, then sucked in fresher air when the opportunity arose.

The soothsayer's voice sank deep, resonating with a strong timbre. "Beware, Hawk-Prince, the howls of the bitch in heat. She would rob you of all flight. Lairing in a den of earth, she would keep you from the nest and from soaring, as a Hawk must do. The Hawk thinks he understands her yapping, but his ears are made for better things."

The skeletal man reached beneath the small table between them and produced a brass bowl and an egg. The seer moved the egg through the smoke, letting the grey vapor wreath it. He held it up with his fingertips, then opened his hand and let it rest in his palm. With his other hand, he grasped the edge of the bowl. He cracked the egg with one hand and emptied its contents.

"There! See? See?" The old man cast aside the eggshell and held the bowl up with both hands so Pyrust could peer into it. The hanging candles above and behind him did cast enough light to show him a yellow yolk shot with blood. Pyrust recoiled and the old man lowered the bowl.

His voice returned to a whisper. "That egg was laid by a chicken in Thyrenkun. The chicken drank the urine of Princess Jasai. Her evil humors are thus revealed. It is a sign the Prince cannot be allowed to ignore. To heed her brings disaster."

"Does it?"

"Yes."

"I would disagree."

"You saw the egg. It is a sign from the gods."

"Hardly. The gods would never resort to base trickery." Pyrust shook his head. "You are old, slow. I saw the blood bladder in your left hand."

The old man blinked. "I need use no trickery to see the future."

"No? You do, however, when you are messenger to ministers." Pyrust lowered his hood. "You know who I am."

The man bowed his head. "Highness."

"I shall give you one more chance to read the future."

"Yes, sire?"

Remorselessly, Pyrust drew a very sharp, thick-bladed dagger. He thrust it into the man's belly, then ripped to the left before pulling it free. "Read your entrails."

The soothsayer sat there, his intestines a steaming tangle of white in his lap. "I see Death."

Pyrust laughed. "I almost regret killing you."

The man's head jerked up, as if caught in a spasm. His face contorted, then he began speaking in a growled voice, his words bitten off sharply. It was not the voice he had used before. It sounded like nothing that should have come from a human throat.

"The gates of my realm gape wide for your commerce, Prince Pyrust. You will offer me more and varied fare than any before you. Shrink not from this duty, and your desires will know fruition."

The soothsayer flopped back, gurgled, then lay still.

Pyrust sat there, the bloody dagger dripping onto the small table. *My realm?* The month of the Wolf: Grija, the god of Death. *Did the god of the Dead speak through this dying seer? My ministers made him a tool. Why should a god not do the same?*

The Prince shook his head. The world knew he set store by prophetic dreams precisely because he wished the world to believe it. As men came to accept that as true, they presented things to him in the form of dreams. It made spotting their attempts at manipulation that much easier. He often abided by what they told him, and he often manufactured a dream to explain some other decision or victory. Already people knew he'd dreamed of Princess Jasai before the battle at Meleswin.

"Are the gods as deceived about me as men, or did Grija speak to me?"

The dead man did not answer, but the Mother of Shadows appeared at his right hand and bowed. "The gods seldom speak. When they do, their requests are difficult to ignore. They are even more difficult to abide."

Two other forms in black emerged from behind her and dragged the soothsayer's body away. In no time, any evidence of the murder would be erased, and those who suspected anything would remain silent or pass through Grija's gates themselves.

"Did you hear?"

"No, my lord, nor do I wish to know."

Pyrust smiled and stood. "Do you fear the gods?"

"Only one." The cloaked form led the way from the building and into the night. "If commanded, I will enter the realm of the gods and slay Grija for you."

"He was not that insolent." Pyrust fell into step beside her. "You know which ministers filled that man's mind with their own prophecy?"

"Yes, Highness. Their death will come more swiftly than the whisper with which you order it."

"Hold off. I will let it be known that I had a horrid dream and went to a soothsayer, but he had vanished—just as in my dream. The ministers will wonder if there is a dissident faction in their midst that wished to deny me that message. They can kill each other and save me the trouble."

"As you wish, Highness."

Pyrust nodded. "I will ponder what else I heard. You may not wish to know it, Delasonsa, but part of the message was for you. As the god commands, you shall not lack for work."

Chapter Fifty-two

2nd day, Month of the Wolf, Year of the Rat
9th Year of Imperial Prince Cyron's Court
163rd Year of the Komyr Dynasty
737th year since the Cataclysm
Nemehyan, Caxyan

Before they traveled to the capital of Caxyan, Captain Gryst negotiated the release of the *Moondragon* crew. The negotiations proved surprisingly simple. Not only did the crew return to the ship and get started on repairs, but the artisan class of Tocayan accompanied them—to learn as much as they could and to help supplement supplies from local products.

Little substitution was required since the fleet carried ample supplies, but Anaeda accepted foodstuffs willingly. The artisans spent most of their time observing, and the Naleni learned that the Amentzutl had no maritime tradition to speak of. While they fished in rivers and from shore, they really looked upon the land as their source of bounty.

It was, therefore, not without a certain amount of trepidation that Tzihua and his entourage stepped aboard the *Stormwolf* for the trip north. Nemehyan had been constructed high on a bluff overlooking a natural harbor, and the reasons why the Amentzutl did not sail seemed clouded in the past—a past everyone seemed reluctant to discuss. But after reviewing maps and measuring distance, it was decided that what would have taken a week and a half on foot could be sailed in a third the time.

Jorim welcomed the warrior and his men onto the ship and conducted them belowdecks to their accommodations. He'd learned enough about their caste system to know that warriors occupied an elevated position. In preparation for the trip north, ships' carpenters had repositioned bulkheads such that the ten men Tzihua had brought with him would share living space with the *Stormwolf*'s own warriors. Tzihua himself would share Jorim's cabin, which seemed acceptable to all.

The giant had been forced to duck his head to enter the cabin, and stoop his shoulders to move about it, but this he took with good nature. It clearly intrigued him that, over the course of the trip, Shimik studied his mask, and the fur on the Fenn's face took on green-and-gold tones. More interestingly, furred tufts grew from his forehead in imitation of the feathers.

Jorim and Tzihua spent most of the time at sea closeted together in the cabin. The initial reason was because each wished to expand his knowledge of the other's language. Tzihua turned out to be a good linguist—perhaps not with Jorim's skills, but intelligent nonetheless—and very eager to learn. The various castes had their own dialects and Tzihua needed to practice the *maicana* dialect, as he had just been elevated to that caste.

This news surprised Jorim. "Perhaps I do not understand correctly how your society works. With us, moving between castes is all but impossible. A peasant could no more become a bureaucrat than an artisan or warrior." He hesitated. "Well, it is true that a peasant could become a warrior, but only after much training. And this is rare, so passage is rare."

Tzihua nodded. "The *maicana* are what I believe you call the *jaecai*. When one of us learns enough and is blessed with skill that allows us to draw upon magic, we become *maicana* with all the rights, privileges, and responsibilities."

"And the *maicana* rule the Amentzutl?"

"As it should be. They shield us from the wrath of the gods."

"Our gods are not that vengeful."

The big man let a smile light up his broad face. "You have nine gods, we have six. Ours have more to do, so become angrier."

"Ours do not often concern themselves with the affairs of men."

"As long as we sacrifice, they do not either. If we have pleased them, they bless us during the time of *centenco*."

"I don't know that word."

Tzihua tightened his dark eyes. "It is not for me to explain it, my friend. All you must know is that *centenco* is again upon us and the fate of the world will be decided once more."

The second reason Tzihua and Jorim had remained sequestered was because a storm roughened the seas on the second day of the journey. The Amentzutlian warrior's face drained of color, and Jorim was pretty certain he managed to vomit up half his weight. Shimik did his part by hauling off buckets and dumping them through the ship's heads, but quickly enough began to cringe when Tzihua began to retch.

Luckily the storm passed quickly and no word of his illness leaked out to his men. Though he said nothing, Jorim understood the loss of dignity that would ensue. He had a word with the ship's *bhotcai,* and the delivery of a particular tincture had the Amentzutlian warriors all vomiting the night before the ship arrived at Nemehyan. Tzihua was able to visit and tend them, which made him all the more godlike in their eyes.

If he ever suspected the deception, he said nothing to Jorim.

Though Jorim had seen Tocayan and most of the capitals of the Nine Principalities, nothing had adequately prepared him for Nemehyan. He'd carried in his head the image of a lone pyramid rising on top of a bluff, but no one had mentioned that the bluff had once had a mountain rising above it. That mountain had been leveled as if a sword had decapitated it, providing a plain roughly five miles square. Pyramids, as well as many of the roundhouses, rose from that plain. A causeway snaked up the inland portion of the mountain, crossing back and forth in an easily defensible pattern. The plains around the base of the mountain and to the north also had roundhouses and were cultivated. The nearest jungle had been slashed back north for several miles, and off to the east lay a vast marsh where workers harvested salt.

If Tocayan was home to a thousand... Jorim did a few mental calculations and wished he had Iesol to double-check them. This one city might have had as many as a hundred thousand people, which meant the fields would be insufficient to support it. *That means trade in food from faraway places like Tocayan.*

As the fleet came in, people gathered to greet it. They waved brightly colored cloth banners and sang songs. Jorim couldn't catch enough of the words to make sense of them entirely—the singers were not from the warrior or *maicana* castes, so his grasp of vocabulary hindered him. "As near as I can tell, Captain, it is a song welcoming the serpent, which makes sense."

Anaeda looked up at the purple sail emblazoned with the Naleni dragon. "I am glad they find this a good omen. I'm certain your robe will be seen as the same."

Jorim nodded. "Tzihua insisted I wear it. Otherwise, I'd be wearing my *Stormwolf* uniform."

"It matters not, Master Anturasi. We'll still claim you. The *Stormwolf* will lay at anchorage here. Some of our ships with more shallow drafts will conduct a survey, and we will see how close we can get. This harbor would be perfect were a quay waiting. We will have to make do with ship's boats. You are away first, with Tzihua."

"I will make certain they know you just seek safe anchorage, not that you fear treachery."

"In any other place it would not be the truth, but these are singularly peaceful people. I'm almost surprised they have a warrior caste, and one that is sufficiently trained to produce a *jaecaiserr*."

"It does bear investigating. And, as per our agreement, I have communicated none of this back to my grandfather."

Anaeda raised an eyebrow. "Does he suspect something?"

"He *always* suspects me of something, so I have things he can pluck from my mind after a little effort. He seems content with that now, and distracted." Jorim shrugged. "I imagine Keles is doing well on his survey, and that's occupying most of Grandfather's time."

"A blessing in disguise, then." She smiled. "If your brother were with us, I doubt we would have gotten along as well or as far with the Amentzutl. Go now; make certain we get along even better with them."

Jorim bowed to her, then turned to run to where the Tocayan contingent was descending into a boat. Shimik caught up with him in a bound. Not only did the Fennych have the furred tufts on his forehead, but he had grown out side locks the same as Jorim. The cartographer had braided beads into Shimik's fur and, with Tzihua's permission, had agreed to take Shimik along in the boat.

Lieutenant Linor ordered the boat away from *Stormwolf* and the sailors pulled hard. The bay remained placid and Tzihua weathered the crossing well. As they passed through the rest of the fleet, the crew and passengers raised cheers, and the Amentzutl acknowledged them with waves.

But the homage paid to the visitors by the fleet paled when compared with the greeting given them by the people of Nemehyan. The boat slid up on the beach and Jorim, riding in the bow as was his custom, leaped out and dragged it further up. Tzihua matched him, and quickly enough they had the boat high and dry. The other warriors poured out, split into two groups of five, and flanked the two men and the Fenn who, childlike, marched a few steps ahead and studied everything with wide-eyed wonder.

The people at the beach parted and, as the company passed, sank to their knees. They bowed deeply enough that many would rise with gravel still stuck to their foreheads. No one would look Jorim or Tzihua in the eye, but instead hid their faces. At the same time they all chanted *"Tetcomchoa,"* over and over again, in reverent and hushed tones.

As they came around to the base of the causeway, Jorim's jaw dropped open. There were people lining every inch of the two-mile causeway. Their attire and the shifting colors as the road wound higher matched the castes. Regardless of their standing, everyone knelt and bowed, breathing *"tetcomchoa."* Not only did Jorim have no idea what the word meant, but the level of greeting surprised him. Nothing of that sort had happened in Tocayan. *But the people of Tocayan knew Tzihua. Here he is arriving a new member of the* maicana. "Tetcomchoa" *must be an honorific of some sort, though why Tzihua would not have taught it to me, I don't know.*

They ascended to the city in a slow, stately pace. Once they arrived at the plateau, the line of people extended straight down a broad boulevard and up a staircase running up the front of a stepped pyramid easily a hundred and fifty feet high. They continued their march forward, accepting the homage of those lining the route. At the base of the stairs the honor guard stopped, but Tzihua continued to ascend. The people on the pyramid did not prostrate themselves, but they did bow deeply and add their voices to the chants from below.

Up and up Jorim climbed with Tzihua, and began to wish he had remained with the honor guard. *This is for him, and I sully it.* As they neared the top he reached out and took one of Shimik's hands. He drew the Fenn back to his side and smiled up at Tzihua as they reached the head of the stairs. From there, a red woven mat extended into a dark opening of the square building erected at the pyramid's summit.

"You go on, my friend, this is your honor. Thank you for letting us come this far."

Tzihua sank to his knees and gently tugged the Fenn into his arms. "The honor is mine, to have come this far. What waits within is for you." Tzihua bowed and his feathers brushed the stones.

Jorim's stomach began to roil. *Much as yours must have when the sea tossed.* Jorim almost looked back, but he could not bear to have confirmed what he knew lay there: tens of thousands of people with their faces in the dust. He had no idea why they had paid him that homage, and he was certain it was a mistake. Straightening it out wouldn't be easy, but he figured the place to start would be through that doorway.

That decision didn't make entering the pyramid any easier. He paused in the doorway's shadow to let his eyes adjust to the darkness, and relished the coolness of its interior. Large, blocky stone constructions became visible first, quickly followed by the more complex forms. The small chamber's rear wall was dominated by a huge disk, a foot thick at the very least, with thousands of symbols inscribed in it. He recognized them all as Amentzutl script, though he had no clue how to begin to make sense of them.

But any desire to do so faded as a woman detached herself from the shadows of a stone throne and approached. Tall and very slender, with long raven hair that fell to the tops of her breasts and half hid the gold pectoral she wore, she looked at him with large eyes harboring more sadness than reverence or curiosity. The loincloth she wore was entirely black, though woven with a raised pattern and decorated with gold buttons.

After several steps forward, she stopped and looked him up and down. Her gaze lingered on his green robe, where dragons were embroidered in gold over the breasts. Her dark eyes tightened for a moment, then an expression of resolution came over her face.

"It is as you foretold. It is *centenco*. You have returned." She bowed her head. "Tell me, Lord *Tetcomchoa,* how do we save the world this time?"

Chapter Fifty-three

2nd day, Month of the Wolf, Year of the Rat
9th Year of Imperial Prince Cyron's Court
163rd Year of the Komyr Dynasty
737th year since the Cataclysm
Opaslynoti, Dolosan

As he pulled on the protective clothing he'd been given, Keles Anturasi wondered if there was something truly wrong with him. Storm season had broken hard in Ixyll. The wild magic had begun to build to the west, raising huge walls of grey dust shot through with purple and black lightning. Even with the storms fifty miles off, the thunder cracks sent a shiver through his chest. Pressure built, and bits of rock and *thaumston* began to glow.

Opaslynoti became a hive of activity rivaling the Anturasi workshop when Qiro was in a rage. Half the people took to securing their homes and property against the oncoming storm. Canvas tarpaulins covered every door and window, fastened as tightly as possible. Each of them had the same mottled mushroom-grey-and-brown pattern that marked the clothing Keles had on—though only his outer layers were made of that same stiff fabric. Anything loose was taken inside or lashed down. While the young worked feverishly, older citizens with eyes that glowed to mirror the coming storm would chuckle and note that this "blow" would be the worst they'd ever seen.

The rest of the population—both workers from below and prospectors, traders, and free-miners—rushed around setting up traps.

These consisted of almost anything, from funnels and old lobster pots restrung with wire, to tall poles hung with metal cable across the presumed path of the storm. Each device was guaranteed to harvest as much of the magic as possible and charge up a supply of *thaumston*. Eventually the storm would sweep past them and refill the Well, but those who didn't want to pay for having their *thaumston* dipped took this chance at getting their samples in place.

The only difficulty with traps was that they needed to be tended. If one left samples out too early and didn't watch them, someone else might appropriate them. Getting out after the storm had passed and claiming one's samples quickly was a good idea as well. But both were fraught with danger, as the storms could come on too quickly or double back and catch the unwary in the open. While the protective clothing did help—or so he had been assured—it would be as effective as a wet nightshirt in a blizzard if caught in a storm.

Up until the storms had started, fierce headaches had prostrated Keles. His body had been wracked with pain, and while plenty of folks offered opinions as to why that was—the most imaginative being that a southern wind from Irusviruk had blown the stink of the Viruk over him—nothing anyone tried had managed to alleviate his condition. Almost with the first ripple of distant thunder, however, the shooting pains in his head ceased, and he felt better than he had since Rekarafi had carved his back up.

But the advent of storms seemed to have nearly the opposite effect on everyone else. For the citizens of Opaslynoti, he assumed it was because they were suddenly so busy. Those who erected traps were also preparing to venture into Ixyll as soon as the storm passed, so the anticipation of the race also heightened tension.

Some people who had been warped by the wild magic reported pains—and more sinister complaints. One man whose body was covered in tiger fur sprouted claws and had to be caged. A pregnant woman gave birth to a crystal egg—although her child seemed to be doing fine inside it. An old dray horse shed its skin like a snake, which made for quite a mess, but old-timers put all the unusual stuff down to the natural cycles of the storms. The last time storms had raged this strongly, Qiro Anturasi had been born—and thaumstoneers reported that the cycle had been building for a while.

Moraven and Ciras seemed the most affected among Keles'

group. Both of them grew a bit more distracted and cross, as if the storms were affecting their ability to concentrate. Borosan likewise became snappish, because the fluctuations in background energy made all of his little devices function oddly. He was disassembling them all rather quickly—at least the ones that could move on their own—and feeling frustrated because the new ideas he came up with could not be tested until well after the storms had passed.

Tyressa and Rekarafi were weathering things the best, but that still did not make them good company. The Viruk kept mostly to himself, refusing repeated efforts by the arena owners to fight another *gyanrigot*. They offered fortunes in gold and *thaumston,* and he rejected them all. While none of the men trying to employ him could understand, Keles had an inkling of how Rekarafi felt. After all, they were the offspring of slaves who wished to visit upon him the final indignity: fighting against toys for the amusement of people he would have whipped for such insolence millennia ago.

Tyressa, however, baffled him. While the others had gone to the arena to watch Borosan's *thanaton* fight, she had stayed with Keles and cared for him. She had applied cool cloths to his fevered brow and sung soothing songs. It made her hardly seem Keru at all. He'd found himself feeling utterly lost when she went away for even as long as it took to refill the water basin, and her voice admonishing him to sleep was the only thing that eased his pain.

Once he'd recovered, though, she'd vanished. He expected she was sleeping, but when he looked around to thank her for his care—and to offer anything he could to repay her—he could not find her. Only that morning he'd learned that she'd wandered Opaslynoti and—though she would say nothing of it to him—had located the bandits.

When the others came to visit him, they tried to be cheerful, but all seemed somewhat anxious that he be able to continue with their mission. Though Moraven Tolo had not been as adamant about his mission in the Wastes as Ciras had, Keles had noticed the swordmaster had not forgotten it. Throughout the journey, Moraven had paid attention to sites that were rumored to be old battlegrounds and possible burial sites. Deathbreathers were an anathema to everyone. Any cache of weapons that had been used in battles long ago would be a threat to the Nine.

In Ixyll they would find what Moraven sought, and quite likely have to battle Desei agents to secure the weapons. Keles still intended to do survey work in Ixyll, but realized that Moraven's quest had become more important. *I will do what I can to help him.*

Still, the advent of the storms revitalized Keles and emptied his head of the throbbing pains that had plagued him throughout the journey. He couldn't hazard a guess as to why that was, though he did suppose that the wild magic might have somehow reignited the Viruk magic and completed his healing. He moved more easily, and was able to think more clearly.

He wasn't certain why being in proximity to the wild magic should make him feel better. It clearly had the opposite effect on Moraven—though Keles figured that was because he was a Mystic. The whole concept of someone reaching that level of skill was easy to understand when it came to something as obvious as sword fighting or archery, but what would it mean in other pursuits? What would someone who was that gifted at math be able to do? Could they do things more quickly, or perhaps do more complex things? Singers, writers, artists—even cooks and farmers and courtesans—were easy to figure out. What of mapmakers, however? Could they become that good, and what would it mean?

He and his brother had spent some time wondering what that would be like, but they had always focused on other aspects of their art. Keles had always wanted to be very exact, which was why the Gold River survey had been perfect for him. Jorim liked discovering things. For him, what the land contained defined it better than any measurements.

Perhaps it was not possible for a mapmaker to know *jaedunto,* but that prospect did not daunt him. In some ways it was a relief, since the obvious candidate for *jaedunto* would be Qiro. While he did not wish his grandfather dead, the idea that magic might extend the man's life so Keles' sons and grandsons and great-grandsons might also labor under him was a bit terrifying.

Of course, I need to survive this survey and return to Moriande before it will be possible for me to worry about my children and theirs.

The protective clothing he'd been given for venturing into Ixyll was interesting, and explained some of the changes he'd seen in prospectors and free miners. It came in two layers, inner and outer.

The inner layer often was of silk or cotton, while the outer was heavy canvas and sometimes quilted. All of the fabric had been boiled in *thaumston* mud until the grey dust impregnated the fabric. This made it stiff and chafing, so often folks wore a third layer of untreated material against the skin, and Keles gladly followed their lead.

The inner layer consisted of stockings, trousers, and a shirt with long sleeves that had flaps covering the backs of the hands. Some people took to wearing silken gloves over that. A silken coif went over the head, covering everything from collarbones up, save for a narrow strip around the eyes. Breathing through that fabric brought an earthy smell with a sour tinge, as if urine were used in the dyeing. Most people wore normal leather boots to complete the inner layer.

The outer layer started with stiff canvas boots laced tightly over whatever footgear had been donned. Heavy canvas trousers, which came up to the low ribs and were held up by suspenders, tucked into the overboots. Another canvas coif covered the silken one, again leaving the eyes clear. A heavy robe went over that and belted in tightly, then mittens were pulled on and tied down at midforearm. Keles' mittens had a bilateral split in them, allowing two fingers to a sleeve, so he could nock and draw an arrow. Moraven and Tyressa just wore full mittens since it would not hamper their sword work.

The eyes, of course, were difficult to protect, and that explained why so many folks first reflected changes in that region. To safeguard the eyes, everyone wore a gauzy material slightly more dense than insect netting. It allowed a fair amount of vision, but reportedly became very hot in the summers. Many went without it, and the residual magic worked on them over the years.

In some ways, wearing the outfits was deemed unnecessary by many who saw the survey party getting ready—and Rekarafi seemed to set great store by these opinions. He chose to wear nothing more than the inner layer, and probably would not have worn that save for a certain amount of protection against the winter's cold. The experts in Ixyll noted that for a quick survey they'd not need the protection, and that if they were caught in a magic storm, all the protection in the world would not help them. Those who agreed with that latter point were often lumpen creatures, which made Keles gear himself up all the more completely.

While others sought the safety of deep caves, levels, and rooms as the first storm came in, Keles ventured to the surface and watched it arrive. He did not do so alone, for plenty of free miners waited until the last minute to make sure their traps were left untouched. Rekarafi joined him as well, which he had not expected; but he took some comfort in the Viruk's presence.

The storm chose to break out of Ixyll and flow down into the canyon just before sunset. The sun's illumination backlit the towering clouds of dust it stirred up, adding purple-and-red tones to a tableau shot through with black lightning. Keles wanted to liken it to a normal thunderstorm, but the lighting shot horizontally as well as vertically. And while it sometimes resembled the standard jagged fork pattern, it also sometimes swirled through and around dust columns, wreathing them with fire. The discharges of energy built, thunder cracks echoing sharply as the storm approached the curtain, then the curtain evaporated and the storm poured into the valley.

"I suggest we leave now, Keles."

Keles nodded, and Rekarafi led him back to the stable dome where the others waited. Tyressa's wanderings had turned up several groups she assumed might be the bandits. With Ciras' aid, she narrowed it down to one, then set about learning all she could. They had stabled their livestock at another dome, but were preparing to head into Ixyll the moment the storm passed Opaslynoti.

As nearly as could be determined, they had no map to provide them direction, which gave Keles heart. He himself was setting out lacking anything more definite than his knowledge of old tales and a variety of rumors in which he set little store. Jorim would have been able to ferret out the truth from the locals, or at least could have mined their stories for a useful fact or two. Keles settled for having a variety of stories from which he could draw correspondences.

Even in the dome, their protective clothes took on an unearthly blue glow—quite faint and the color of flameheart. Their horses, with canvas boots and caparison, shied uneasily as wind howled and dust rasped against the dome's shell. Borosan held some device in his hand, the purpose of which Keles could not discern, but the *gyanridin* watched it intently, then looked up.

"It's building beyond any scale I have ever heard of."

Keles glanced at him. "Old-timers said the cycle was reaching a peak this year."

"Yes, but it scales up arithmetically. This is building geometrically. It's bad. It's really bad."

Suddenly the wind's shrieking tightened to a painful squeak, then became inaudible. Its high-pitched vibration shook Keles' teeth, but he felt no pain. He glanced up at the dome, expecting to see it vibrating, but instead it had become transparent. A sheet of dust washed over it, obscuring the heart of the storm for a moment, then cleared again.

Keles studied the storm, barely aware of Ciras clawing at his coifs as he doubled over and vomited. Above him, the heavens opened and revealed a silvery ball shot with black highlights, spitting out lightning and deep crimson tongues of flame. The surface roiled, becoming a network of eggshell fractures. A piece of the mirrored ball would break away, then sink beneath a viscous, bloody fluid that would then turn black. Lightning would leap away, and suddenly the surface appeared smooth again.

Then the boiling of the ball's surface stopped and a round hole opened in it. Keles had the impression of an eye dilating in surprise. It watched him closely, then the pupil focused. Bloodred fluid filled the hole, then burned brightly before a jet of flame shot out and splashed over the dome.

The flame hit hard enough to shake the ground and topple Keles. Thunder blasted through the valley, and pieces of the dome's interior began to fall. Keles looked up, found the dome opaque again, and quickly mapped the spiderweb of cracks in his mind. *Just the inner surface spalling off.* There was no threat of the dome's collapse—and no hope of survival if it did.

The dying echoes of that blast took with them the wind's howling. The dome's doors no longer rattled, the shuttered windows ceased clattering, and dust slowly floated to the ground. Tyressa calmed horses, Moraven knelt at his retching aide's side, and Borosan again studied his device. He smacked it once with his hand, then shook his head.

"The storm is over. It can't be, but it's over."

Keles strode purposefully to the nearest door and threw it open.

The storm had ended, no question of it, but the dome itself glowed brightly enough to put the dying sun to shame. *Thaumston* dust covered everything, drifting into corners and against the door like snow. Even more impressive, the Well had been filled—and a rainbow riot of color splashed at the edges of the lowest level, threatening to flood the residents out.

Over on the other side of Opaslynoti, two dozen horsemen led a string of packhorses out and began the trek north. Among them would be the bandits looking for more weapons, corpses, and *thaumston*. What they had already stolen they'd likely cached, so if Moraven and Ciras could not find them and stop them in Ixyll, they had one more chance to deal with them—provided they could track them back to their hiding place.

But we'll stop them.

Then Keles' head came up. *Did I think that?* That was the sort of thing Jorim would think. Keles' job was to find a route through Ixyll and, if possible, find burial sites others had been despoiling. Adventuring was not for him.

But why not? Ryn was his father as well as Jorim's; the same blood ran in their veins. *Perhaps I've allowed myself too narrow a focus. Maybe what I need and what the world needs is what Jorim does, and what our father did before him.*

With that insight burning anew in his mind, he turned back and smiled at the others. "Our competition is already heading into Ixyll. If there is something out there, we'll find it first, I guarantee you."

Moraven nodded. "We may need more haste than your survey requires."

"No matter, Master Tolo." Keles waved a gloved hand to the northwest. "As you have labored to get me this far, it will be a pleasure for me to get you to your goal. I do believe it takes precedence—and, though my grandfather would not like it, I am completely at your service."

Chapter Fifty-four

3rd day, Month of the Wolf, Year of the Rat
9th Year of Imperial Prince Cyron's Court
163rd Year of the Komyr Dynasty
737th year since the Cataclysm
Anturasikun, Moriande
Nalenyr

It had to stop. Nirati knew things could not continue to go as they had been with Junel. She looked down at her wrists, the purple bruising bleeding out into yellow. The marks had remained even though he'd been gone for half a week. She'd covered them, but she was certain the servants had noticed.

They noticed. They told my mother.

The result had been easy to see. Her mother had offered to listen to anything she had to say. The invitation had come openly and even casually. She and her mother had often spoken frankly of many things, even things sexual. Her mother was the one who prepared the draught that kept her from getting pregnant. Even so, Nirati could not discuss what she was doing with her mother.

I hardly needed to, however.

Siatsi never had been a stupid woman, and her skill as a *bhotadina* was not inconsiderable. She easily deduced that Junel had been providing Nirati with draughts to beguile her. Siatsi added things to her own potions to counteract the Desei's work.

That is part of it, but I also think that whatever he gives me has worn off. My body is so used to it, greater and greater amounts are needed to keep me under its influence.

Nirati knew that Junel's potions had been losing their power over her. But she had liked that. It was not whatever drug he gave her that created her desire to be with him; the drug had only given her the fiction that she could not control herself. She was thereby freed to submit to his desires.

And his desires became my desires.

Junel held a hypnotic charm that built as his darker side was revealed. He could be forbidding and even remote, disciplining her where others would just indulge her. He showed her the limits of her endurance. He took her to the edge and held her there, teetering on the brink of oblivion, then dragged her back. The next time he would take her further, carrying her to new heights that threatened even greater crashes were she to fall, and she began to hunger for the thrill of those journeys.

She fingered the bruise on her left wrist, increasing the pressure until she could feel true pain. It hurt, but not as much as she would have thought. Certainly that pain was nothing on the scale she now knew herself capable of enduring. Junel had praised her tolerance for pain, noting that her real skill in life had been undiscovered until she began to explore. He even suggested she might be *jaecaixar*—capable of entering the realm of magic through pain.

Myriad thoughts had raced through her mind when he'd said that. First, she felt a burst of joy rip through her. The healing had worked. She *had* found her talent, and she wanted to push further and discover more. If she was good at something, she wanted to discover how good at it she was.

Flowing quickly behind that joy, however, doubts assailed her. What if he was wrong? What if she had clutched at the first thing that appeared to be a talent and prematurely ended her search? She'd spent her whole life rejecting possible talents, and if pain was not her talent, she would once again be good for nothing.

She might please Junel, much as she proved a comfort to her grandfather. That did give her some purpose, but what good would it be if it meant she never truly found her talent?

The question begged an answer. Junel had a need to control her, to make her do what he wished, to be able to do with her *as* he wished. And it pleased her to let him do so. She gave him pleasure by surrendering herself to his control. He showed her things about herself she didn't know—and had not even guessed at. She certainly never would have discovered them without his guiding hand.

But is Junel guiding me to my destiny, or leading me astray?

She thought her life was simple. Junel showed her that was an illusion. She was as mortal as everyone else, but she had an inner strength. She could endure more than others, and might well reach magic through it. She might well have found her means to realize her full potential. She could be *jaecaixar*!

Yet her pride in that accomplishment also seemed absurd. Of what use was someone who was Mystic of pain? Would the Lady of Jet and Jade have a use for her in dealing with difficult patrons? What other possible use could her skill have? It would create nothing. Perhaps if there were a way she could take away another's pain it would be useful, but that would treat symptoms, not diseases. Her mother's skill with tinctures could blunt pain and even begin to affect a cure. But even at the height of her powers—*if* she ever attained such heights—she could do none of that.

Another darker thought raced in. Just as these last bruises had lingered longer, and Junel had given her less of his drugs to increase her ability to feel pain, so had his need to inflict pain cycled higher. He would still be tender in the aftermath and attend to her needs, salving her wounds and caring for her. His tenderness even came in inverse proportion to his savagery. At some point, he would do something he could not soothe. He might lose control—the control she ceded to him—and do her irreparable harm.

That's why it has to stop. For the one thing the drugs could not shield her from was fear. She had been able to handle him being stern and even cruel, but when his face became a bestial mask, his eyes narrowing and face flushing, he no longer seemed human. She wondered if he might not be *jaecaixar* in his own right, having mastered the art of inflicting pain. The very idea sent a shiver down her spine.

Plus, the insanity of what she had been enduring had brought another insanity with it. Often in the aftermath, and more commonly now during her sessions with Junel, part of her escaped to Kunjiqui. Her own whimpers grew faint as she rested in her paradise. Cool waters soothed her flesh, and when the gentle wind no longer brought the sound of her own pleas for surcease, her physical body would slumber and she would remain there in her dreams.

Sometimes Qiro joined her, but neither of them needed to speak. Kunjiqui had somehow become their sanctuary from the world. Both of them felt betrayed: she by Junel and the unfairness of life, he by his son, grandsons, his Prince and—on any given day—a host of others. Somehow, through his visits with her—where they both dangled their feet in cool streams and let rainbow-colored fish nip harmlessly at their toes—his incipient paranoia all but vanished.

Without suspicions and hatred driving him, he was just a tired old man. It wasn't his fault that the world had thrust upon him the responsibility it had. The two surveys currently ongoing were expanding and redefining the world, allowing him to fill in huge blanks in the map and his knowledge of it, but there was still so much unknown.

She came to understand that it was not out of fear or hatred for Jorim and Keles that Qiro acted so coldly toward them, but a fear that all the pressures he endured would crush them inalterably. To protect them, he had to toughen them. This love formed the core of his being, but he only shed the layers in Kunjiqui. Only she knew the truth.

I have to tell them. I have to live to tell them. Nirati resolved to confront Junel when he returned from talks with inland nobles. She could no longer endure his depredations. It didn't matter if she would never learn if pain was her talent.

"I *may* have a talent, but I do have my *responsibility*. Responsibility to my family." She raised her wrists and kissed the bruises. "They do everything for me, and I shall do no less for them."

Chapter Fifty-five

6th day, Month of the Wolf, Year of the Rat
9th Year of Imperial Prince Cyron's Court
163rd Year of the Komyr Dynasty
737th year since the Cataclysm
Nemehyan, Caxyan

They think I'm a god. Jorim shook his head slowly, which Shimik mimicked with all the bewilderment Jorim felt. "They think I'm a god."

It didn't sound any better out loud, and hadn't sounded better no matter how many times he said it. The Amentzutl had a god named Tetcomchoa. His symbol was a feathered serpent, and he had lived with them over fourteen hundred years previously. He'd led them through what they called the Ansatl War. As near as Jorim could determine, it was a war against some reptilian creatures. At the end of the time they referred to as *centenco,* after the war had been won, he had gotten into a ship and sailed west.

Jorim wished Keles were there, because he could have made sense of everything, could have found a way to explain to the *maicana* representative, Nauana, how mistaken she was. Jorim, housed in the chamber atop the pyramid to Tetcomchoa, walked over to the giant wheel and traced his fingers along one of the circles of figures raised on the surface. Shimik climbed up on the big stone throne and crouched on the back of the seat.

Nauana had taken great pains to explain everything to Jorim—though whether or not she was convinced he needed to be reeducated in this incarnation or he was just testing her own knowledge, he couldn't tell. The Amentzutl used a cyclical calendar based on lunar time and the interplay of the red and white moons. While the black moon, Gol'dun, was not figured into their timing, Nauana assured him that all time began from the birth of the black moon, which told him just how far apart the Amentzutl and Imperial reckonings of the world were. Things continued on for a period of seven hundred thirty-seven years with simple progressions that made very good sense. At the end of a cycle, however, as the days spiraled down into the center of the wheel, they entered *centenco*.

Centenco was the beginning and ending of everything. It betokened great crises and cataclysms and horrors. The previous *centenco* had brought years without summer, and hideous winters. A savage tidal wave had wiped out the Amentzutl fleet—ending a proud maritime tradition that had been the reason they'd been able to defeat the Ansatl in the *centenco* before. The *centenco* before that had seen a horrible plague that killed hundreds of thousands. And still before *that* was the birth of the black moon, whence all time for them began.

Jorim would have liked to dismiss all of this as nonsense, but when he roughly translated the dates into the Imperial system, glacial melt ran through his bowels. Their years of no summer matched up with the Cataclysm. The Ansatl war corresponded pretty closely to the rise of the Taichun Dynasty, which remained in place until Empress Cyrsa created the Nine and went off to fight the Turasyndi. The *centenco* prior matched the arrival of True Men to beat back the Viruk and establish the first Empire, and the Amentzutlian dating of the birth of the black moon corresponded to when Virukadeen destroyed itself and the Viruk Empire started its decline.

To make matters worse, the rise of the Taichun Dynasty was supposed to have been led by a man who fought under a dragon banner. Prior to that, none of the warlords or princes had dared use a crest of the gods, and many said that Taichun claimed to be a god, or the son of a god. He was supposed to have arrived from the east on a ship and surrounded himself with a cadre of copper-skinned warriors.

Of course, later historians had explained that away as hyperbole.

His arrival from the east was meant to show he was extraordinary, since the sun rose in the east and he was the light that would banish the barbarism nibbling at the Empire at the time. His bodyguard was supposed to have been Turasynd, and Taichun's chief skill seemed to have been to make alliances with warlords, then betray them to their enemies while keeping the loyalty of their people. And so he forged a new Empire, created the bureaucracy, and dictated a book of common wisdom that governed the lives of many down to the present.

It was the Book of Wisdom that caused the most trouble, for as Nauana would offer one of Tetcomchoa's sayings, Jorim could complete it as easily as Iesol could quote Urmyr. She took this as a sign that Jorim was recovering his divine nature, while he was having trouble dealing with the total revision of history as he knew it.

Jorim sighed and Shimik giggled—an annoying habit he'd learned from the hordes of Amentzutl children who delighted in his company. Jorim frowned as he looked at the Fenn. "You're not helping, you know. Half of this is your fault."

Shimik's eyes got big, and he smiled, showing all of his teeth, but did not look wholly contrite. "Mourna mourna sad."

The cartographer growled at him. Jorim had tried to explain to Nauana that he was not a god and not divine, but she merely pointed to Shimik as obvious proof of his godliness. The Amentzutl did not know of the Fennych, so its very appearance meant Jorim was somehow special. Shimik had also picked up on the fact that the dragon was important, so when his fur developed a serpentine pattern, all who saw him were convinced that he was divine.

In some ways, he could have enjoyed the experience of being thought a god. There were places in Ummummorar where he was highly revered, especially after slaying Viruk. He'd been feted and saluted and offered wives by the score to breed more strong warriors like himself. He'd declined, but only because he had a taste for discovery, not power.

The problem with the Amentzutl was that they actually expected him to *do something,* because the world was dying. Only he could see them through the *centenco* cycle. The threat to the world was now the same as when he had been there before: strangers were invading, and the Amentzutl were not certain how to stop them without his help.

"My Lord Tetcomchoa, please forgive me."

Nauana's voice remained quiet, but filled the stone chamber, softening all edges and bringing light to even his darkest mood. She remained purposeful—and supremely confident in him—despite his best attempts to dispel her notions. She had filled his head with dire predictions about the rise of the seventh god—which could have also been a tenth god since three of their gods had tripartite aspects. He barely understood what Keles would have figured out in a heartbeat, and that thought provided him a place to gather himself.

He turned and reached out to scratch Shimik behind an ear. "Rise, Nauana. I will not have you on even one knee before me."

"As you desire, my Lord." The raven-haired woman rose slowly, her breath still coming a bit quickly given the exertion of the climb. "I have come to tell you that the Mozoyan Horde has come."

"From the northeast? As we expected?"

"As you *predicted,* yes, my Lord."

"And the defenses have been prepared?"

"As per your instruction, my Lord."

Jorim nodded and gathered Shimik into his arms. "Very good. Call the people."

Nauana nodded, then looked up. He caught fear in her dark eyes and for a moment dreaded it was fear of him. "My Lord, you will wish to see. They are as fog."

He nodded, then walked past her to the pyramid's flat top. He gazed north. To the northeast, slowly emerging from the jungle and filling the fields, hundreds upon thousands of small creatures became visible. He could see no banners nor crests—nothing that marked an organization, nor any leaders on horseback to provide direction. It heartened him that no giants or other monstrosities lumbered among them, but this horde of child-sized creatures was frightening enough.

The Mozoyan were not, as he had first supposed, barbarians like the Turasynd. "Mozoyan" did not mean from outside land, it actually meant from no land. The Amentzutl had no idea whence they had come, though refugees from Iyayan, a northern city akin to Tocayan, had said they had emerged from the sea almost like turtles coming up on the sands to spawn.

At Jorim's request, Tzihua had gone out on one of the smaller ships in the fleet, slipped into the area through which the Mozoyan were traveling, and brought back dead bodies. He'd not had to kill anything, just harvested cadavers from what had been the Mozoyan line of march. He'd gotten them back two days previously, then Jorim and some of the scholars from the fleet had conducted dissections.

From the very first, Jorim realized these were not the sea devils they'd seen, but he could not dismiss some relation between them. They had rudimentary gill slits, and while their flesh was not scaled, it did resemble shark leather. Their heads were not as narrow as sea devil heads, but they did have mouths full of shark's teeth, with several layers ready to pop up in place when one was lost. They still had webbed fingers and toes, though their feet were better suited to movement on land than were the sea devils'.

It looked to him as if these were distant cousins of the sea devils: as if the sea devils had mated with sharks and with frogs, then those offspring had been bred together. Eyewitnesses had reported that the creatures could leap prodigiously, and even their emergence from the forest showed signs of that. Their fingers ended in claws, but scratch tests on small animals showed no sign of venom, whereas the teeth could clearly deliver a nasty bite. They did use weapons, after a fashion, but only sticks and stones. They went without armor. Their numbers were their strength.

What disturbed Jorim most was that they reminded him of creatures that used to haunt his nightmares as a child. He had been two years old when his father had been lost at sea. When adults were discussing his father's death in his hearing, they said little, but a clever boy can hear things he might only partially understand.

And such things thrive in nightmares.

He'd had them off and on for years. His mother would comfort him when he was young, listening to his nonsensical babbling as if it were revealed wisdom, then lie down with him, holding him until he fell asleep. In later years he would awaken alone, drenched in sweat, and would huddle in his bed praying for dawn.

He finally confided in Keles when, at the age of ten, he'd fallen asleep in the Anturasikun garden and been awakened when a frog had snapped a fly from his face with its tongue. Once Keles had stopped laughing at his utter terror and Jorim had explained, Keles had been everything an older brother should be.

"Jorim, you are strong and fast, and they are amphibians. They are suited to water and swimming. On land you will outrun them. And their endurance? They will have none." Keles had tousled his hair. "Do what you do best, and you will beat them, Jorim. You'll beat them in your dreams and they won't bother you anymore."

"You're wrong there, Keles, because they are bothering me a lot right now," he muttered aloud.

"I beg your pardon, my Lord?"

Jorim smiled and turned back. "It is nothing. I was talking to my brother."

"I see." Her voice had all the conviction of someone agreeing for the sake of politeness. She understood he had a flesh-and-blood brother, and she accepted that, but also knew he had no divine brother. Everyone knew *that*. Since his brother was mortal, he could not hear such a spoken comment, so speaking aloud was just another idiosyncrasy she would have to endure.

"Nauana, you must understand something." Jorim pointed to the lines of the trenches that cut from the northwest edge of the jungle down to the southeast and the base of the escarpment. "My advisors and I have shaped the best defenses we can think of. Your warriors are going to fight hard, and I know the *maicana* will do all they can to contain the *oquihui*. There are no guarantees of victory, however."

She smiled in a way that made him want to take her face in his hands and kiss her senseless. Her faith in him could not be broken, and when she looked at him like that, he didn't want it to be.

"Your will shall be done, my Lord."

Down below, horns sounded and those few people who remained in the lowlands—save the soldiers—retreated to the causeway and began the long ascent to the heights. The last to leave had lit fires in the buildings—all of which had been emptied of supplies well before the retreat. The breeze coming in from the ocean blew the smoke back onto the Mozoyan, and Jorim hoped that neither their gills nor their lungs would function well under that assault.

The horde came on, angling down to reach the breastworks close to the middle of the line. The trenches themselves had been excavated with magic—the *maicana* working at night both so enemy scouts could not see them, and so their people would not be terrified by the power they wielded. Their magics would have been enough to cast the Mozoyan back into the sea—and might have been enough to send the entire horde to the Mountains of Ice—but they would not employ it that way. Warfare was the province of the Warrior Caste, and for the *maicana* to usurp their place would mean the utter destruction of the Amentzutl culture.

The warriors had plenty of time to prepare for the attack. The bottoms of the trenches and the faces of the breastworks were festooned with sharpened stakes. More importantly, the warriors had studied the battleground and knew the landmarks that would indicate the Mozoyan had entered spear-casting range. Using weighted sticks to effectively extend the length of their arms, the Amentzutl warriors launched spears and barbed darts in concentrated volleys as the grey masses drew closer.

The spears, tipped with obsidian points, sliced through Mozoyan flesh with ease. Creatures clutched at shafts and flopped on the ground, soon to be crushed beneath the feet of their advancing fellows. Showers of darts cut whole swaths through the horde. Bright crimson splashed over grey flesh as the Mozoyan went down.

But the holes in their lines closed and on they came. The Amentzutl warriors impressed Jorim with their discipline. If the trench line broke, the horde would pour through it relentlessly. Those northwest of the break might be able to flee into the jungle, but that sanctuary would only last so long. While the horde had emerged entirely from the jungle to fill the lowlands, they would certainly dispatch a part of their force to hunt down fresh meat. The warriors between the breach and the causeway might be able to fight their way up toward the heights, but it would be as part of a rear guard that would eventually be worn down.

The line had to hold, and would. Already, companies of Amentzutl warriors were moving southeast to bolster those soldiers running out of spears and darts. While new missiles arced above them, brave warriors mounted the breastworks as the first of the Mozoyan leaped forward. Many fell short, and with wet thuds impaled themselves on two or three spikes. Others, hit by a dart in midair, fell into the pit to die. Those that made the leap successfully faced no less dire a fate, for the stone-edged war clubs slashed more keenly than steel. Tzihua knocked one Mozoyan back into the pit. Other devil frogs sailed past him to be dismembered by the warriors where they landed.

Despite the heroic Amentzutlian effort, the horde pressed on. Dying Mozoyan filled the trenches with bloody grey flesh. A carpet of bodies would soon cover the breastworks and their spikes. Mozoyan would be able to walk over the bodies and crest the breastworks. While the Amentzutl would be able to beat them back once, perhaps even twice, the war of attrition would end up in the Mozoyan's favor.

Jorim looked over at the Naleni signalman stationed below him on the stairs. "Blow the first signal, please."

The sailor raised a horn to his mouth and blasted out a low, rumbling tone that echoed from the buildings and mountains. Below, on the edge of the escarpment, Naleni soldiers stepped to the edge, nocked arrows, and let fly on command. Hundreds of shafts filled the air, then fell among the Mozoyan. As had the spears and the darts before, the arrows cut down throngs of devil frogs. The archers concentrated on the Mozoyan closest to the escarpment and as the horde flowed to fill the gap, their entire line shifted laterally. They mindlessly shortened the line along which the Amentzutl needed to defend, buying them time and allowing them to concentrate their forces.

Jorim nodded. "Well, that is a help. The question is, is it enough?"

Nauana smiled again. "My Lord, you ask a question to which you already know the answer."

Jorim nodded. "I wish you were right." He crouched and set Shimik down, then pointed at the signalman. "Go tell him."

The Fenn's eyes brightened. "Twoooo?"

"Two."

Shimik scrambled off, taking stairs three at a bound. He howled "Twooo, twooo, twooo!" with an enthusiasm that sparked a smile on the signalman's face. He raised the horn again and let loose with another blast, this one broken and repeated as if matching Shimik's chant.

Jorim glanced at her. "Even that might not be enough, but it's the best we've got."

Chapter Fifty-six

6th day, Month of the Wolf, Year of the Rat
9th Year of Imperial Prince Cyron's Court
163rd Year of the Komyr Dynasty
737th year since the Cataclysm
Ixyll

Fear possessed Moraven Tolo, and this surprised him. He could not remember the last time he had truly been this afraid. But the faint copper taste in his mouth was something he'd experienced before. He recognized the voracious thirst. He felt very cold, and even the thought of food made him nauseous.

What compounded the fear was his being unable to remember the last time he'd felt this sort of terror. He found it too familiar, and he wanted to remember when he'd been this afraid, but it wouldn't come. It lurked beyond the veil of his amnesia, tantalizingly close, but insubstantial. *And if it has no form, no substance, I cannot fight it.*

The fear had begun as they set out from Opaslynoti, but the first giddy excitement of racing up the valley and into Ixyll before the *tavam eyzar* closed again helped him keep it at bay. Still, it chafed his psyche the way the clothes rubbed his flesh raw, and the tingle of magic grew into a torment.

They were not alone in making the trip, and studying the others did distract him somewhat. Rekarafi was not the most unusual creature in the Ixyll-bound rabble, though he was the only Viruk Moraven saw. The men they chased had ranged ahead of them, but

Keles had said he didn't think they had any more of an idea where they were heading than he did. Veteran thaumstoneers suggested that after such a fierce storm, anything that had been seen before could have been obliterated, so everyone was moving into virgin territory.

Dangers abounded, and disaster struck some of the stoneseekers the moment they set foot in Ixyll. Here and there, small cyclones of dust sprang up and danced playfully, much as dust devils would in the Nine. One lit a man on fire. Another turned a scrounger into a mass of beetles that actually managed to function as a man-shaped community for several hours. It might have survived longer, save for a hearty, congratulatory pat on the back. Moraven did not doubt that the beetles would eventually reconstitute themselves.

If they are not scattered again by a storm.

Quickly enough, the horde fragmented, as the beetle-man had. Keles pointed his companions toward the northwest. His choice made sense, as northwest was the direction of the old Spice Route, but no discernible track lay out that way. Keles' course took them into a rumpled blanket of hills with yet higher slopes beyond. Its only virtue was that the hills had a number of caves large enough to house their entire group, horses included. Scavengers had recommended seeking shelter underground, because while storms had been known to shift whole mountains from one place to another, rarely did the wild magic penetrate the earth.

The land itself bore countless signs of just how powerful the storm could be. Giant boulders had been rolled down or even *up* hillsides, then polished smoother than an infant's cheek. Trees had leaves that bled—not sap, but blood—and branches that curled around birds to devour them. Other plants grew up, blossomed, sowed seeds, and died on an hourly basis, sending circular ripples of flowers out—flowers of odd shapes and colors, with stripes and spots that shifted like oil on water, and would have been beautiful if they did not stink of swamp gas and decayed meat.

Ixyll's wild magic clearly did not kill everything it touched. Those things that had grown seemed to thrive. Places where storms had denuded a swath of land were quickly colonized by plants, or else insects raised great mounds that pulsed with life. Rekarafi pointed to one particular mound that rose like a volcano and had streams of yellow ants running like lava up and down the sides. He said those ants had not been seen in the world for hundreds of years. They used to be considered a delicacy in Virukadeen, but no one wanted to stop and sample them.

Those sorts of things did not increase Moraven's fear because they gave him points of reality to which he could cling. It didn't surprise him that insects that had been extinct had suddenly appeared in the storm's wake. Not only did he have the overwhelming sense of being *elsewhere,* but also *elsewhen*. It felt as if they were riding through a land that shifted and took form as their minds imposed order on it. Moraven *had* seen the shape that Rekarafi had called the mound, but it only took on definition when he named it, and the insects appeared as the Viruk pointed them out.

Would they have seen what I saw, if I had been able to point it out first? He shivered. He wasn't certain what he had seen, but it felt hauntingly recognizable. Memories were returning, clawing their way into his mind from some abyss. The scrabbling of their talons resonated through his fear.

Where are we? His stomach clenched. *When are we*?

For three days they rode through Ixyll in a fruitless search for tombs or traces of the old Spice Route. While they found caves aplenty—and some with signs of habitation—they didn't find so much as a Viruk burial, much less a catacomb full of fallen Imperial warriors. Granted, Moraven wasn't really certain what such tombs would look like, but to find no signs of anything predating the Cataclysm frustrated him.

If I knew what we were looking for, I know we would find it.

Worse yet, they came across no sign of the bandits who had preceded them. Keles' logic in heading northwest had been impeccable, based on history as well as tales like those of Amenis Dukao. The route northwest was well known; the Empire had outposts along it, so drawing the Turasyndi out that way would give Cyrsa's troops a better chance. But the lack of bandits suggested they might have other information. That meant they could be heading for a tomb complex while Keles and the others blundered around blindly.

The trip and the nature of Ixyll wore on them all. Rekarafi became hypervigilant and seemed to go without sleep at all. Ciras became more irritable and slept poorly, as did Tyressa. Keles, who seemed to be fully recovered from whatever had been giving him headaches, still approached things very cautiously. Borosan became uncharacteristically taciturn and obsessed with modifying his mousers and his new *thanaton*—Number Five—to guard them. Even the machines acted oddly, with the smaller ones riding on the back of the larger as it trotted along beside the horses.

All of them seemed to be waiting for something—and, in part, Moraven was as well. But for him, something felt different. They all faced a sense of the unknown and even unknowable. For him there was something out there that he knew, but just could not name. That sense of familiarity brought with it foreboding, and the foreboding came because he knew that thing was waiting for *him*.

But what is it?

Darkness began to fall on the third day, though dusk would linger this far north. They descended the northwest face of some hills and started across a flat, dusty expanse that might have once been a lake bed. A mile further on, already shrouded in shadows, a striated bluff waited. Despite the sun setting beyond it, however, Moraven caught sight of a flash of light—of the sort made by a signaling mirror. He pointed, but Tyressa and the Viruk had already seen it.

Is it my *light they see, or had they already created it?*

Keles had not seen, nor had Borosan, but that was because they were both studying the device the *gyanridin* used to measure the levels of wild magic. While Moraven pointed northwest, Keles swung around in his saddle and pointed to the northeast.

"There it is, Borosan, you're right. It's a storm, and a big one."

Moraven turned, and could see it even through the gauze veil. Most of the storms they had seen while in Ixyll had been small and far off, but this one was neither. Already the purple-grey clouds had screwed down into a serpentine funnel that lashed at the landscape. Red-and-gold fire shot through it, and black lightning clawed out. Thunder crackled, and the storm's roar vibrated in his chest. Ciras groaned, and Moraven reached out to steady him in his saddle.

Keles caught that. "We need to find shelter."

Tyressa pointed northwest. "In the bluff there was light. There, again, see? Flashing."

The cartographer nodded. "It's not reflecting the lightning, that's for certain. Let's ride. I think we can make it before the storm catches us."

The riders set spur to horse, but beneath their canvas caparisons the animals felt nothing. The horses, however, needed no real urging to flee the storm. Luckily the dry lake bed was flat, so the horses were able to race across it easily.

Moraven pushed past his own fear as best he could to keep Ciras in the saddle, but the storm would not be ignored. The winds it kicked up began to howl. An oppressive heat built, making him want to strip off his clothes. All around him, the magic was making the *thaumston* fabric glow. As riders moved and horses galloped, as cloth gathered in wrinkles, the edges and peaks would flash with silver or blue, while iridescent violets filled the darker valleys.

The storm would kill them, there was no question of that. But despite his certainty, it wasn't death he feared. It was something else. It came from the deepest recesses of his mind, a black creature, hulking and reeking of corruption. It wore armor that clanked, and a mask. An armored battle mask with the scales of a dragon. Its mouth gaped open showing sharp teeth, and from its throat issued a low laugh that blended into the wind's lupine shrieking . . .

Hoofbeats competed with thunder. Illuminated by the light of the storm's fire, the line of a path became visible. Not too steep and fairly wide, it cut up and across the bluff's face, leading to a large dark opening through which they would be able to ride without dismounting. Borosan's horse took it first, and the others followed. Rekarafi cut to the right and just scaled the cliff face, lurking beneath the edge at the opening until the *thanaton* chased the last of the horses within.

Moraven ducked his head to enter the cave, then vaulted from his saddle. Ciras sagged away from him, but clung to the saddle. Before he could fall, Keles and Moraven were able to ease him to the ground. Tyressa herded the horses deeper in and around the corner to the left, and their hoofbeats clicked and echoed from what sounded like the walls of a massive chamber.

Moraven tore away his veil and pulled the paired coifs back to a thick roll around his neck. "We need to get Ciras deeper into the chamber. Help me."

Keles nodded and took the young man beneath the armpits, while Moraven grabbed his ankles. They made their way slowly along the passage, relying on sound since the light from the opening faded the deeper they went. The Viruk's shadow played along the walls, effectively blocking much of the light. Moraven could understand the fascination with the storm, and knew the Viruk would not be so foolish as to linger there when it hit.

As they reached the entryway to the next chamber, Borosan ignited the *gyanrigot* lantern he'd brought along. Its blue light stabbed deep into the chamber, illuminating the tall, arched opening into yet another chamber, but it penetrated no further. As the *gyanridin* swung it around to the right, splashing it over the chamber's wall, it became obvious that what might once have been a normal rock formation had been worked long and hard by the hand of Man.

Moraven dropped Ciras' ankles and straightened up mutely. He wanted to speak, but words would not come. He found what the light revealed both glorious and terrifying. He knew in an instant that he had found the source of his fear. He had found what they had been hunting, what *jaecaiserr* Jatan had sent him to find. His knees buckled.

Borosan's light played over a wall that had been worked smooth, then had square chambers the height, width, and depth of a man carved into the face. Each one of these holes had been plugged by a slab of stone that had been cemented into place. On these stone slabs had been carved the names and deeds of the people entombed behind them. The lettering had been leafed with gold, so the names and legends glowed in the light.

Keles gasped. "That one there. It's the grave of Amenis Dukao. He died with the Empress!"

Before anyone else could offer a comment, the Viruk screamed. Moraven turned, unable to make any sense of his words, but it didn't matter.

The storm has finally caught us.

The Viruk's silhouette filled the opening. Rekarafi grabbed both edges of the entryway and hung on as the storm hit. A cloud of dust blasted in first, lifting the Viruk from his feet. His legs trailed out behind him, then a red-gold tongue of flame jetted in, wreathing him.

The rock in his right hand crumbled. Rekarafi, still anchored by his left hand, flew back and smashed into the entryway's wall.

No longer blocked by the Viruk's presence, a shimmering silver ball of wild magic bounced into the chamber. It floated for a moment, then sent tendrils of black lightning out in four directions. Their forks cracked and popped, moving like arms and legs as the ball crawled forward. For a heartbeat Moraven thought it had modeled itself on *thanaton* Number Five. *Or we made it do that, with our minds.*

Then a dark hole opened at the ball's center and filled with molten magic. The red dot swung back and forth as the ball came on. It looked. It searched.

It focused on him.

Then it exploded.

An argent wind slammed into Moraven and blew him off his feet. Agony sank into him as he tumbled through the air. Every muscle spasmed and locked, then sagged. When he hit the ground he bounced limply, his momentum unabated. He slid across the chamber floor, stirring up dust, then smacked up against the burial wall.

He remained dimly aware of all that was happening to his body, but it was of little consequence. When the magic hit, something entered his mind. It thrust deep, ripping harshly, and filled that wound with contempt.

<<It's you. You have returned. Good.>> Moraven's sense of the world faded, until only its voice remained. *<<You won't get away again.>>*

Chapter Fifty-seven

6th day, Month of the Wolf, Year of the Rat
9th Year of Imperial Prince Cyron's Court
163rd Year of the Komyr Dynasty
737th year since the Cataclysm
Thyrenkun, Felarati
Deseirion

Prince Pyrust found Jasai of Helosunde waiting for him in his audience chamber. The hearth contained only banked coals and produced minimal heat. Despite that, she wore nothing on her feet and only a nightshirt to cover her. Woven of thick wool, the nightshirt was not so heavy that he could not see the sharp outline of her erect nipples. She had been given to wearing this type of garment for bed, but had always favored the gay colors common in Nalenyr. Now she wore the garment undyed, as did the common folk of Deseirion.

She knelt as he approached and lowered her head. Her long blonde hair slid down to veil her face, but he sensed no fear or contrition in her stance. She wanted nothing—least of all forgiveness—and had no air of remorse about her. This surprised him, but he covered his surprise by slowly reaching up to undo the clasp on his black woolen cloak trimmed with a mantle of wolf fur.

It puddled at his feet.

Ignoring her for a moment, Pyrust bent to toss several logs onto the coals. They landed with a satisfying crunch, spitting a spray of sparks that drifted up the chimney. A burst of heat washed out, then flames rose, adding light to the dark room. The fire splashed a hint of gold onto Jasai's hair.

He drew off his gloves and tossed them onto his cloak. Holding his hands to the fire, he watched flames dance from between splayed fingers. He rubbed his hands together, then spoke, keeping his voice low.

"It is warmer over here. I begrudge you no warmth."

This did produce the response he expected. Jasai may have agreed to marry him and accompany him to Felarati for the sake of her brother, but she had still rebelled in countless ways. The first was to complain of the cold and to keep a fire roaring in her chamber day and night. Pyrust had explained to her that his was a poor nation and that such profligate use of wood was not permitted.

This did not stop her.

He let her have four days of constant fires, then she was provided no wood at all. When she complained, he told her she'd used up her allotment. He, on the other hand, had used less than most, so had more to spare. He told her that she could join him in his night chamber and that she would be kept very warm, but she'd said she would prefer the cold.

Her resolve lasted one more day, and might have lasted longer had he replaced the furnishings she'd burned. She had come to him. And despite a new ration of wood being made available to her with the turn of the week, she had chosen to remain.

Pyrust was no fool. They'd been hastily married in Meleswin and he'd consummated their union that evening. She had accepted him that night for it was part of their bargain, but she had rejected him again until the night the lack of heat had driven her to his bed. Even then he knew she had been coerced. Yet it really mattered not at all *why* she shared his bed, but that she did. Hatred, apathy, unquenchable desire—all of these things he could deal with. Just not disobedience.

Jasai did not raise her head. "You have explained, my husband, that valuable resources are not to be squandered here in Deseirion."

"But you did squander my wood until you learned I would be governed by the same laws as my people."

"I was foolish."

"And now you are wise?"

"Wiser, my lord." She raised her face and firelight flashed from the traces of tears on her cheeks. "I have news for you, Prince Pyrust."

The tears made little sense. He turned to face her and moved forward so the firelight would silhouette him.

"What news?"

She hugged her arms around her slender middle. "Your heir grows in my belly."

Pyrust clasped his hands behind his back, left in right, suddenly aware of his maiming. *What will my child think of it?* That thought came to him as if it were another message from the gods, and sent a shiver through him. What he had seen as his life and his future now projected further, on through generations to come. He had always been an *end,* but now he was a link in a chain, and his responsibility was to make that chain strong.

He narrowed his eyes. "*My* heir, or Helosunde's heir?"

Jasai's eyes widened, then her gaze dropped to the floor. "It should not surprise me your asking that question. You promised my heir the throne of Helosunde and said I would be his regent. That is the bargain I accepted. That was the goal I had in mind as I lay with you. I knew I would make any child hate you as I hated you, and the vintage of your life would turn sour and bitter."

The vehemence in her voice lacked the sharpness of before. Something had softened it. "If that was our bargain, why, Jasai, is he now *my* heir?"

She slowly exhaled. "I have been your wife for a month and a half. You told me that I would learn I could trust you, and this I have learned. You are cruel and capable of many things, including merciless murder, but you are not a hypocrite. You are good to your word. You would know the same cold as your people, the same hunger, the same dangers.

"My life has been spent in Nalenyr listening to lords and ladies proclaiming much, but their actions never matched their words. They wish to lead, but their method for doing so is to watch people, see the direction in which they move, then dash to the fore and announce they are being followed. My brother had no place being Helosunde's prince and everyone knew it—himself included. He was told what was expected of him and complied with those expectations."

"But now he does better because Cyron has set new expectations for him. That should give you hope for your nation and its return to power."

"But it never will return, will it?" Unbidden, she rose to her feet and fetched his cloak, which she pulled around her shoulders. "You cannot allow Helosunde to rebel, or Deseirion will be weakened and Cyron will no longer feel threatened. And Cyron cannot let Helosunde rise for fear of losing control over it. Our child on the throne of Helosunde is his worst nightmare, since it could unify our nations and leave his border open."

Pyrust turned and moved behind her, resting his hands on her shoulders. "Your analysis is good. You forgot to add that your son, as Prince of Helosunde, would be a rival to your brother, and the settlement of that rivalry would doubtless be the assassination of one or the other."

"Likely both, my lord, since the Council of Ministers will control neither." She glanced back to the left, then dipped her head and kissed his half hand. "This is why our child must be the Prince of Deseirion. I see this and accept it. I accept other things as well."

"Such as?"

"I must become Desei. The Council of Ministers expected to marry me off to someone—anyone. I did not matter. Being married to you, I am removed from consideration and consequence as far as Helosunde is concerned. By becoming Desei, your people will have a chance of loving our child—our children. Toward this end I shall adopt Desei clothing and custom. Like you, I shall do with less so others can have more. With your leave, I shall do things that shame other princesses into doing more for their people. If you approve, that is."

"Approve, yes." Pyrust lowered his mouth to her left ear and let his voice sink into a harsh whisper. "But the swiftness of your decision belies thoughtful commitment to it. You can understand my skepticism."

She nodded slowly. "Oh, be under no misapprehension, my lord. I do respect you and even admire you, but I still hate you. I will bear our children without ever coming to love you. But I will love them, and they shall be the outlet for my love. The fact is, however, that I hate you less than I hate those who put me in this position. They discounted and discarded me. I shall live to see them regret their folly. In this, I do believe, we are united."

He allowed himself a chuckle. "And how does this play into the gift you gave me? The promise that you would allow me to be Emperor?"

"These things are one and the same." She shivered and pressed herself back against him. "Our children should be more than either of us, and deserve more than either of us have had. You will become Emperor, and they shall have an empire. It will be best for them and for the world."

Pyrust kissed the back of her head. "I am pleased my children have so intelligent a mother." He reached down and swatted her bottom playfully. "Go now, wife of mine, and warm our bed. I shall join you momentarily."

"Yes, my husband. Then we will make our bed hot indeed."

Jasai swept from the chamber leaving his gloves, one whole, one deformed, lying flaccid on the ground. Pyrust kicked them into the shadows, then stepped forward to warm his hands.

It did not surprise him when the Mother of Shadows emerged from the darkness, bearing his gloves in a clawed hand. "Something bothers you, my Prince?"

Pyrust stared into the flames, knowing he would barely see her even if his night vision was unaffected. "Less than a month and a half and she is already pregnant?"

"You saw she was a virgin when you took her on your wedding night."

"Blood appears in eggs and appears on sheets by all manner of means." He frowned heavily. "Was she pregnant already?"

"Interrogations have revealed no rumors of her having a lover." Delasonsa's shoulders rose and fell in a shrug. "On the trip here she bled and has not bled again. It is highly probable she is pregnant and that you alone have lain with her."

"So, if she is pregnant, the child is mine?"

"Yes."

"Could learning she is pregnant be what has triggered this change in her?"

The Mother of Shadows chuckled. "It was not so much a change as an acknowledgment of reality. She seeks to make things better for her children. She is young, yes, but not frivolous. Maternity seldom changes a woman in that way; it merely awakens her to her true nature."

Pyrust nodded. "It is an interesting future she paints."

"Yes, my lord, but one yet unrealized." Delasonsa's voice came softly from within her hood. "She might miscarry, or the child could fail to thrive. Though no assassin will reach her, there will be attempts, and the least upset could trigger a disaster."

"You are right, of course." He turned to face her, taking his gloves in his half hand. "Rumors of her pregnancy must be quashed—and the rumor-mongers slain. Cyron would not kill her, but the Helosundian Council of Ministers would. Remind my ministers that their welfare depends on that of my wife, of whom I am inordinately fond. That will have them falling all over themselves to make her happy."

"You see clearly, my lord."

Pyrust sighed, tucking his gloves through his belt. "My dead brother's bastard will become a liability once my child is born."

She nodded solemnly. "I shall deal with Thyral."

"Don't kill him."

"No?"

"Delasonsa, you may think me a fool, but I am not a heartless one. His father died because he dared listen to Naleni agents and plotted against me. He had to be slain, as did his elder siblings. The boy was but an infant and now is six years old. He does not know who he is, so now is the time to train him. Tell him that I have selected him for a very special duty. He shall be your apprentice, then my son's bodyguard. He shall come to be the guardian of the Emperor."

The Mother of Shadows bowed low, held it, and came back up slowly. "You honor me by entrusting me with your blood to train."

"I dare do it, Delasonsa, only because I know you shall stand between ambition and my blood." Pyrust smiled slowly. "This future will come to pass. We both will have much work to guarantee it, but it shall come to pass. The gods will it, and so do I."

Chapter Fifty-eight

6th day, Month of the Wolf, Year of the Rat
9th Year of Imperial Prince Cyron's Court
163rd Year of the Komyr Dynasty
737th year since the Cataclysm
Nemehyan, Caxyan

The trumpet blast rolled over the smoky lowlands, then from the jungle to the northwest came a return call. Though the haze and distance made them difficult to see, five hundred Naleni warriors wearing bright scarlet uniforms rode from the jungle on horseback. Large golden dragons coiled on their chests and red pennants snapped beneath the heads of their light lances. Each man bore a round shield, similarly emblazoned with a dragon, and a colored cloth strip hung from the spikes atop his helmet—a different color for each of the five companies.

Nauana gasped, and a murmur arose among the assembled Amentzutl. In no conversation with them had Jorim found any evidence that they knew what horses were. The pack animals they used—*cunya* and their larger cousins *ayana*—struck the Naleni scholars as being more camel-like. While the *ayana* could sometimes be ridden, the Amentzutl had no stirrups and no martial tradition of fighting while mounted.

As the companies came forward they parted, with two to the left and three to the right, forming a space for a dozen war chariots. Drawn by four horses each, the chariots had a driver in the center and two archers standing on small risers that allowed them to shoot past the driver and horses. A trio of wickedly curved blades four feet in length protruded from the axle hubs and flashed brightly in the sunlight as they turned.

Nauana looked at Jorim, her eyes wide with wonder. "My Lord Tetcomchoa, you have produced a miracle. Strange beasts and stranger things. You have given us victory."

Jorim shook his head. "Just a chance. How good a one, Nauana, we'll see."

She stared back at the battlefield as the murmuring grew among her people. Not only did they not know horses but they had no practical knowledge of the wheel. Given that they lived in a mountainous land, where packing goods on beast back was more practical than building roads for wagons, relegating the wheel to their calendar and children's toys made an odd sort of sense. *Horses and chariots are as world-altering to them as discovering this continent was to us.*

The cavalry moved into a trot, quickly coming across cultivated fields. The way the smoke had spread over the fields, the cavalry faded in and out of view. Jorim was pretty certain that neither the Amentzutlian warriors nor the Mozoyan could see the Naleni troops. They could hear them, however. Their hoofbeats echoed like thunder.

Arrows continued to rain down, killing hundreds of the grey legion, and the Amentzutl held their line against the fearsome press of the enemy. A portion of the Mozoyan formation furthest from the escarpment broke north and west. At first Jorim feared they were going to form up to face the cavalry, but instead they just plunged toward the Amentzutlian line. They headed for a spot where the defenders had thinned and grey bodies filled the trench. Whether by design or accident, they rushed at the line's most vulnerable point, and in sufficient numbers to overwhelm the warriors set to oppose them.

The grey tendril charged out, but it never reached its target. The Naleni lancers burst from the smoke and slammed into the Mozoyan flank. Swift and strong, the horses crashed into unarmored bodies, snapping limbs and knocking Mozoyan flying. Lancers stabbed steel broadheads through slender bodies, then cast aside weapons weighed down by a half dozen impaled devil frogs. Swords filled empty hands, sweeping around in great arcs that scattered limbs and harvested heads. Shields batted leaping Mozoyan from the air, and steel-shod hooves scattered them.

Mozoyan surged into the gaps between Lancer companies only to face a new horror. The war chariots raced down upon them. The archers shot as swiftly as they could, and every arrow found a mark. In some cases, arrows ripped through one body to skewer another. But the Mozoyan that fell to the arrows were more fortunate than the survivors, because the wheel blades proved even more terrible. They scythed legs and chopped up bodies that had already fallen. Wheels, hooves, and Mozoyan feet churned the ground into bloody mud that spattered everywhere, coating the flanks of wheeling chariots and charging horses.

Disoriented, with no leadership, the Mozoyan on the flank panicked and fled screaming back to the main body. The alarm spread to the whole of the force. It surged away from the cavalry, like a school of fish turning from a predator, then squirted back north. The rear ranks leaped away as swiftly as they could. They disappeared into the smoke, and horsemen plunged in after them.

The grey ranks closest to the trenches turned and tried to flee, but had no room to maneuver. Darts, spears, and arrows harvested more of them. The Amentzutl warriors came up and over the breastworks and attacked the Mozoyan. Tzihua led a small knot of warriors over the filled trench and into the milling mass of the enemy. Their war clubs rose and fell, blood spraying in red arcs, carving a solid wedge from the Mozoyan troops.

The center of the Mozoyan formation remained in chaos. Some drifted northeast and the cavalry swept through them, slaughtering them in the hundreds. The war chariots did what they could, but eventually had to be withdrawn. The bloody mud became so thick it threatened to trap the wheels, and Mozoyan bodies offered little traction. Still the archers picked out individual targets, and toward the end of things challenged each other to more and more difficult shots.

The Amentzutl began to chant. Jorim could make no sense of what they were saying, as the dialects all blended, but the warriors seemed to draw strength from the words. Other warriors as big as Tzihua led their companies into the fray. The battle turned to slaughter, and the Amentzutl engaged in it with zeal Jorim had never seen before and hoped he would never see again.

Faster than Jorim thought possible, but not nearly soon enough, the battle ended. The ground nearest the escarpment lay covered two or three feet deep with grey bodies. Some Naleni and Amentzutl warriors had fallen, and more were wounded, some very seriously. But their casualties were insignificant compared to the enemy's losses, which were beyond numbering.

He shook his head. "I wonder how many of them there were."

Nauana looked at him. "You must surely know, my Lord."

"I do not. I wish we could have a head count."

"As Lord Tetcomchoa desires."

Nauana moved to the edge of the pyramid, caressed her throat with her hand, then spoke in a voice that easily filled the valley. Jorim could not catch all of the words, for she spoke in the most common of the caste dialects. But those below understood and the chanting stopped. What seemed to be the whole of the populace began to move down the causeway to the battlefield.

As they descended, the Amentzutl warriors again withdrew behind the breastworks and formed up in their ranks. They lay their dead and wounded before them, then raised their faces and voices toward the rest of the people. They uttered a ritual chant in one voice, repeating over and over again, "Our time is finished, yours has just begun."

The people reached the battlefield and began to spread out in groups. The laborers and slaves began to collect bodies and shift them around, not shrinking from such a grisly duty. Many paused to paint their faces or slick their hair with the blood of the enemy. That struck Jorim as odd, not only because he found it barbaric, but because their work soon had them covered in gore regardless.

They moved the bodies to areas where members of the artisan and merchant classes began to butcher them. With incredible efficiency, they stripped the skin away and piled it in one place. Others cut flesh from bone. Bones were cracked open, but were devoid of marrow, so ended up being hauled to vast piles. The viscera likewise were sorted and piled, sloshing into trenches from which the bodies and stakes had been cleared.

Most curious of all, however, was the duty performed by the

politicians. At the base of the escarpment, in a huge area that slaves cleared as quickly as possible, they began to pile the heads. In no time a great pyramid of skulls appeared, and he had no doubt that a careful accounting was being made of the construction materials.

He would have his head count.

Weapons got sorted out as well. The Amentzutl recovered their own weapons, then retreated to clean and repair them. The rudimentary weapons the Mozoyan had borne were tossed into a pile, but the Amentzutl refused to touch the arrows and lances of Naleni origin. It took Jorim a moment to figure it out, but then he realized only warriors would be allowed to touch weapons. He relayed a message to Captain Gryst, and she gave orders for her people to gather up their arms and clean them as the Amentzutl were.

The cavalry and chariots had withdrawn to the northwest and stood ready to react if the Mozoyan returned, but there seemed little chance of that. By midafternoon the Amentzutlian warriors organized themselves into patrols and entered the jungle. The Naleni troops used that opportunity to return to the ships and care for their animals. By nightfall, the first of the patrols returned and reported that the Mozoyan had disappeared, which began a round of chanted prayers of thanks, all of which rose to the heights of the pyramid and the god who peered down.

Jorim spent a long time watching the Amentzutl deal with the battle's aftermath. Kettles and smoking racks appeared. Strips of Mozoyan meat were boiled or laid out to be dried. Mozoyan leather was boiled and stretched. The bones, once dried, would be ground up for fertilizer. Even Mozoyan intestines would be dried and used to string *peptli*—crooked sticks with a net on one end that were used for an odd kind of ball game.

Nothing, it appeared, would be wasted.

The Amentzutl laughed and sang as they worked, and treated the butchery as a holiday. Even Nauana descended to the fields of carnage and helped harvest, returning at dusk, bloody and bearing roasted Mozoyan flesh for him to eat.

Jorim shook his head. "It is not a custom among my people to eat the enemy."

She frowned. "We are not cannibals, my Lord. We would not eat manflesh, but to waste Mozoyan or Ansatl flesh would be foolish. You have seen how they laid waste to jungle and fields. They have taken from us that which we need to live. Now what was their strength will be ours."

He thought for a moment and found her logic unassailable. He'd not eaten the Viruk he slew, but he knew their meat would make him sick. And the Mozoyan certainly were not men. He'd eaten with countless wild tribes of men in his travels who believed that consuming the heart of a brave animal would transfer that quality to them. While he really wanted nothing he'd seen in the Mozoyan, eating part of one was really the ultimate victory.

Or perhaps it will prevent me from having nightmares about them tonight.

He accepted the small skewer from her and nibbled. It wasn't too bad. It reminded him of frog, snake, and turtle. Remembering that the Mozoyan likely had eaten people they slew did send a ripple through his stomach, but he quelled it. Certainly if he tossed the meat aside and declared it foul, those below would do the same, even if it meant they would go hungry in the future.

Jorim smiled. "Is this how it is after every battle?"

"We have few battles. When we fight men, the warriors tend to their own. Twice a year we have migrations of *tohcho* going north and south. The warriors drive a portion of their herds to the nearest city and slay them. The others come out and harvest them. But the Mozoyan did not require us to drive them here."

"You have not dealt with the Mozoyan before, have you?"

"We have not seen them before this year." She smiled and a bloody streak on her cheek cracked. "We have remained as you bid us, Lord Tetcomchoa, always vigilant. You gave us victory over the Ansatl, and now over the Mozoyan."

"And thus ends *centenco*."

Nauana's smile died. "No, my Lord, this is how it begins. Our first encounter with the Ansatl was also a great victory, but merely presaged a war. The Mozoyan are the heralds of the seventh god."

"What do you know of this seventh god?"

She squatted next to where he sat, his legs dangling over the edge of the pyramid. Shimik came around and squatted in imitation of her but that did not lighten her expression. "You must understand, Lord Tetcomchoa, that our powers of foretelling are greatly advanced from when you were here before, but the time of *centenco* brings many visions. There are many things we do not understand and cannot puzzle out."

Jorim nodded slowly. "I accept this, and that it is no failing of yours. *Centenco* complicates everything."

"It does. The seventh god has two names. The first is Mozoloa."

"Mozochoa I would understand, for it would mean 'foreign god' or 'god of no land.' Why —loa instead of —choa?"

She sighed. "—choa does mean god. Omchoa is the jaguar god and you are Tetcomchoa.—loa means the god is dead. Omchoa ate and killed Zochoa, his shadow-twin, so has two aspects. Zochoa is now Zoloa, but is not spoken of since he is contained in Omchoa."

"I see. So Mozoloa would be 'dead god of no land.' "

"Yes. He is a dead god, not a god of death like Omchoa." Nauana scratched at her cheek, flaking off dried blood. "His other name is Neletzatl. It means he makes things new. It is literally 'he who names.' As he names it, thus it becomes."

"A homeless god who is dead and a creator. I see the confusion." Jorim handed the skewer to Shimik to nibble. "What else do you know?"

"Mozoloa has great hatred, and it is through hatred that he gains his power. He has great anger, too. He is dead but hates being dead. He has bided his time to return, and it has not been until *centenco* that this is possible. His power is growing."

Jorim arched an eyebrow. "But he has not returned yet?"

"No."

"Can we stop him?"

"You tease me now, my Lord. When you departed, you went west, for this is where you said Mozoloa would come from." She swept her left arm out to point at the lowlands. "You returned to save us from the Mozoyan so we could serve you. If Mozoloa is to be defeated, you will lead us in whatever action that requires. That *is* why you returned, is it not?"

Jorim shivered. He found it all too easy to forget she thought him a god, and his questions merely his way of testing her. Her faith in him, and belief in the destiny of her people, especially in the time of *centenco,* demanded he not try to disabuse her of the notion.

"Let it be enough, Nauana, that I am here, now." Jorim drew his legs up and hugged them to his chest. "I know much about the west. If this is where Mozoloa is located, and this is where we have to go to defeat him, I know how to get us there."

Nauana bowed low to him. "It is enough, my Lord. The Amentzutl have waited long for your return so we may serve. Lead where you will and we shall follow. We will serve to the last drop of our blood, and will not fail you."

Chapter Fifty-nine

6th day, Month of the Wolf, Year of the Rat
9th Year of Imperial Prince Cyron's Court
163rd Year of the Komyr Dynasty
737th year since the Cataclysm
Moriande, Nalenyr

Nirati's resolve to tell Junel Aerynnor that the nature of their relationship had to change died in the heat of his excitement upon his return from the interior. He'd not come to her, but had instead sent a messenger bearing a note that asked her to be at an inn called Kitorun by sundown. She arrived wearing the red cloak he'd told her to wear and was served a goblet of wine—a red of upland vintage. It was not very good, but she also knew it was better than the Kitorun normally served.

The innkeeper took her cloak when she sat, and when she finished her first goblet, brought her a black cloak with a hood. She started to complain, but the cloak had a small pocket in the interior, and in it she found another note. It contained more instructions, which she followed to the letter, wending her way across the river and toward the east, into some of the older portions of the city. In her red cloak she would have been a target, but the black one let her fit in perfectly.

As she walked to the appointed rendezvous, Junel came up behind her. He kept his voice low. "Nirati, this is very important. Turn left and left again, circling the block. The third left will be an alley. Enter it and knock on the second door on the right. You will be admitted. Go up the stairs, first door on the left. Do not falter."

"Why can I not walk with you?"

"Hush. I will watch to make certain you are not followed. They would not hesitate to hurt you to get to me."

His hoarse whisper sent a thrill through her. She did as he requested, keeping her gait even. She cursed the hood, since it did not permit her much in the way of peripheral vision, and she resisted the temptation to turn around and see if she was being followed. She really had no idea what was going on, but had to assume the *they* he warned about were Desei agents. *Did* they *get to Majiata, too?*

The prospect of that knotted her stomach. She would have put nothing past the Desei, having heard all the stories of atrocities in Helosunde. Even so, what happened to Majiata was beyond anything she had heard of. *Is that my fate?*

Relying on Junel to keep her safe, she walked through the alley, dodging puddles and looking for any sign of his passage before her. She saw none, but in the growing night's gloom, she had no light to see clearly in any event. She found the door and knocked. It opened and a twisted dwarf of a man admitted her. He said nothing, but pointed her to stairs, which she mounted with trepidation. She felt certain they would collapse with each creaking tread, but she made it to the top and entered the room.

Nirati had not been expecting much given the surroundings, but the room had been transformed through the legion of candles—thick and thin, tall, short, and scented—that flickered from every flat surface. Two even burned in the sconces on either side of a full-length, standing mirror. The bed had seen far better days, but the linen and bedding were fresh. A pitcher of wine and two goblets, as well as some cheese and bread, waited on a sideboard.

Nowhere did she see Junel, so she nearly jumped out of her skin as she felt his hands on her elbows. His arms slid around her and hugged her back against him. By reflex she grabbed his arms and squeezed, forgetting for the moment that she needed to have a serious talk with him.

He turned her about and smiled at her. "Oh, Nirati, I have

thought so much of you since I have been gone. You are even more beautiful than I remember. Too beautiful for a place like this, and I apologize for it. But I had to see you, and this was the only way."

She frowned, a bit afraid, and more concerned. Junel still was handsome, but he looked almost haggard, with dark circles beneath his eyes. He'd lost some weight during his journey, and he could ill afford it. His eyes had become restless, and the omnipresent hint of a grin had faded.

"What is it, Junel, what is wrong?"

"Sit, my darling." He guided her back to the edge of the bed and fresh straw crunched as she sat. "I've been to see the inland lords and there is so much going on. More than I suspected—more than you did, I'm sure. Not because you are stupid—far from it—but because so much does not reach the capital."

He crossed to the sideboard and poured her a goblet of wine. He took one himself and brought both to her, offering her the choice. She took the one from his left hand and sniffed before sipping. This wine had come from the interior as well, but south of the Gold River, and was of the finest quality. Best of all, its delicate flavor would not have hidden any tinctures, so she knew he was not drugging her.

Junel dropped to his knees before her and sat back on his heels. "There is so much I want to share with you."

"Share with me first who is after you? Has Prince Pyrust set his agents on you?"

The Desei exile smiled. "Oh, he has had people watching me since I've been here. In Moriande they were hard to detect, but in the interior they were simple to pick out. They are the least of my worries, however. At least, I think they are."

"I don't understand."

"You have seen the lords of the interior courting me. You so delightfully insulated me from them, and I did enjoy that. However, my accepting their invitations to visit was the best thing I have done since leaving my homeland." His voice dropped into a whisper. "The nobles of the interior are very angry with Prince Cyron. They get no money from foreign trade and are still required to pay taxes. Cyron sends that money back west to fund projects, like the dredging of the river, but they take it and do not spend it on such things. The inland nobles see those projects as things that will continue to enrich Moriande, so they think the Prince should pay for it from trade."

Nirati shook her head. "But these projects will make it easier for them to ship goods to the markets our trade makes available to them."

"Yes, of course, but they don't see that, my dear. Greed is driving them blindly." His eyes blazed as he spoke. "They wanted me to see if I could arrange for them to invest in shipments—shipments that would escape official notice, maximizing their profits. They also dropped not-so-subtle hints that if I were actually a Desei agent, they might look favorably upon an alliance with Pyrust, pitting the interior of Nalenyr and Deseirion against Moriande and the Helosundian exiles."

"But that is *treason*."

"Very much so." Junel sipped his wine. "If they had more forces under arms, or more weapons from Ixyll that would guarantee the superiority of their fighters, they would openly revolt. But as it stands, they need money to procure weapons, and they need a leader. A few even suggested *I* might fill that role, but it was flattery—and transparent at that. Each of them wishes to be prince of a new dynasty."

"That would be horrible."

"I agree, my dear." The Desei noble set his cup down and twisted the gold and jet ring on his right hand. "Prince Cyron is in a very delicate position. Erumvirine is a sleeping giant, with half again the population of Nalenyr. Were their harvest to fail, a hungry horde would pour north, and even all the gold Cyron gains from trade could not supply them rice. While Nalenyr might help Erumvirine's economy through trade, it is not enough to prevent them from acting in the face of a disaster.

"Deseirion and Helosunde create another problem. Cyron funds the Helosundian exiles and uses mercenaries to secure his northern border, but if his trade collapses, he will be without enough gold to do that. If Helosunde and Deseirion were to settle their differences and ally, Nalenyr would face an insurmountable threat."

He looked up at her, a smile growing on his face. "In fact, it is only your family, Nirati, that keeps Cyron from disaster. Everyone is awaiting the outcome of your brothers' journeys. If they find new treasures, the attention of the world will be diverted *and* Nalenyr will have enough gold to buy peace. They could even buy the inland lords, or buy those who would supplant them. Everything is balanced with an almost absurd precision, and all that will upset it is if your brothers fail."

She smiled. "But you are forgetting something that will make the balance less delicate, Junel. You know who the inland lords are. If you go to Prince Cyron and give him their names, he can neutralize them. He need no longer fear an alliance between them and Deseirion. This is where they failed. They thought you were a Desei agent and in that error they exposed their folly."

"It's not *their* folly that is exposed." Junel patted her left calf with his right hand. She felt a slight sting where his hand landed and jerked back. "It's your folly, Nirati. You see, I *am* a Desei agent."

He slowly stood as numbness raced up her leg. "More correctly, I am an agent of shadow, a *vrilcai*."

"What?"

Junel laughed. "Really, Nirati, you should have been able to pierce my disguise. Think about it. Those who did not believe the Viruk murdered Majiata thought it was Desei agents who did so in an attempt to get to me. But would Prince Pyrust, who wiped out every other member of the Aerynnor clan, allow me to live? Of course not. Not unless I was already his creature, the one who had betrayed my family's treason to him. Continuing in his service, I fled south, the last survivor of a butchered family, and here I was accepted most openly.

"That openness gave me entrée to Moriande society and the Phoesel family. Majiata died not to get to me, but to get me to you." He smiled as the numbness spread to her belly and made her legs twitch. "You played your part beautifully. Your desire to rescue me from Majiata much as you'd rescued your brother brought you to me."

Nirati slumped back on the bed, no longer able to sit upright. Her goblet fell from nerveless fingers, staining the sheets. "You . . . you killed her?"

He nodded solemnly. "Practice for you, my dear." He leaned over and pressed a fingertip to her numb lips. "My ring injected venom of the hooded viper. Your body will become numb and will not respond, but your mind will remain aware. I know you have been taking a tincture of gallroot to counteract what I have given you before, but it merely accentuates the effects of this venom."

Her head fell back on the mattress. She wanted to ask why, but her tongue filled her mouth thickly and her jaw would not move. *He is going to kill me. All that went before was prelude to this. All I endured, all I craved, it means I can endure more as he works. And now that I am numb, I will know no pain, just the mental agony of horrors as he takes me apart.*

Junel brought the standing mirror around and adjusted it so she could watch herself. He returned to her and gently released her from her clothing, stripping it off, neatly folding it and piling it in a sideboard drawer. She saw herself in the mirror, naked and beautiful. She wanted to close her eyes so that would be her last memory of herself, but her body refused to obey.

He opened another drawer and began to draw out a series of knives and a leather apron. "You'll want to know what and why. What I will do to you will make what happened to Majiata nothing. I will begin by stripping your flesh off and hanging it from the wall peg as if it were a cloak. You will live through that. You will live through the removal of some of your organs. Not your heart, I am afraid. But, so you know, I will leave your head and face intact, and position you such that the mirror will reflect your expression to those who enter here. They will see you in the mirror first, then in all your glory. It will be exquisite."

Junel pulled the apron on. "As for why, it should be obvious. Your grandfather loves you beyond all others, and you are the last anchor he has to civility. With you slain right here in Cyron's capital, his loyalty to the Crown will be sorely tested—especially when your killer escapes. He never will be found, you see, for I will have tried to stop your killing and will be wounded all but mortally, but my description of the killer will be useless."

His eyes softened. "When they tell me of your demise, I will be crushed. I hope you will appreciate that.

"In his grief your grandfather will stop creating charts, which will precipitate an economic panic. Chaos will reign, from which my master will profit." Junel held up a sharp knife. Candle highlights glinted from the edge. "I will make you a work of art. Your death presages that of your nation."

* * *

Nirati survived far into the morning hours, much longer than she or Junel would have guessed possible. In his intensity, he did not notice her slipping away well before she died. Nirati left that squalid little room and walked along the shore of a cool, crystalline stream, safe away in Kunjiqui. It felt good that her limbs worked again, and after a short time she had even forgotten why they had not previously responded to her commands.

She came over a small, grassy rise and found a man, strongly built with black hair, emerging naked from a pool. Mud was draining from his flesh. He laughed aloud, a joyous sound. He swept his long hair out of his blue eyes, then smiled at her. He clearly was not embarrassed by his nakedness and neither was she.

"My lady Nirati, I bid you welcome and thank you."

Nirati shrugged her shoulders, letting the gold silken gown she wore slip from her. "Thank me, why?"

"This is your sanctuary. Your grandfather fashioned it for you, but he has allowed me to reside here." He held a hand out to her and she took it, stepping down into the pool. "I owe you a debt, and I shall make good on it."

Nirati slid her hands over his broad chest and around his neck. She looked up into his strong face. "How will you do that, my lord?"

"You have been hurt. I shall see to it that you are hurt no more. I shall see to it you are avenged." He lowered his mouth to hers and crushed her to him in an embrace. She clung to him, raising her right hand into his wet hair, but he broke the kiss and murmured against her lips. "I am Nelesquin. I am come back from a very long journey. Your enemies and mine will learn to fear my return."

Chapter Sixty

6th day, Month of the Wolf, Year of the Rat
9th Year of Imperial Prince Cyron's Court
163rd Year of the Komyr Dynasty
737th year since the Cataclysm
Ixyll

The explosion of wild magic knocked Keles from his feet. He dropped Ciras' body and just barely ducked Moraven's flying form. Horses screamed, and shoes struck sparks from the floor. Borosan had fallen and his light had rolled against the wall, showing Moraven's slumped body twitching, his hair smoking.

Keles looked back at the cave's entrance, but could not see outside. A crystalline lattice had capped the cave with a honeycomb pattern. Each cell in the lattice was made up of hundreds of smaller hexagons, each of a different color, all shimmering. The storm's howl continued outside, but muted. For the moment they were safe, but Keles knew better than to expect that to last long.

The Viruk had fallen to the passage floor, but slowly gathered his limbs beneath him. He moved awkwardly, his limbs jerking and twitching, but he drew them in by dint of will alone. He hissed, but made no other intelligible sound.

Keles thrust Ciras off his legs, then scrambled toward Rekarafi. "Let me help you."

"No!" His voice sounded hollow, tinged with the roar that a fire makes. He held a hand out toward Keles, fingers splayed, and a red

light began to glow from within him. The bony plates of his exoskeleton had become black, as if they were made of night itself, but all around them this vivid red—the red of burning coals—built in intensity. His eyes filled with it, then golden highlights moved through them as if his thoughts had become a flow of lava.

"Stay back. I am not certain how much of this wild magic I can contain. Get the others away."

Keles withdrew slowly and dragged Ciras after him. He brought him to the base of the wall where Tyressa was straightening Moraven's limbs. "Ciras is alive. How about Moraven?"

"Alive, but barely. Shallow breath, very slow heartbeat."

Borosan came over and knelt with them. He held his device for detecting wild magic out so Keles could look at it. Previously the square device had appeared to have red sand trapped between two thin layers of glass. The sand somehow took on other colors, running from orange to violet, as the magic intensified. Now it had nothing but swirls of blue and violet rotating very quickly around the same central point.

The *gyanridin* shook his head. "We are at the heart of the storm. It is centered on us and has probably moved us many miles away from where we were."

Keles frowned. "That's not possible, is it?"

"I've heard stories."

"Borosan, shine your light at the far archway." Keles rose and pointed deep into the chamber. The *gyanridin* got up and joined him, playing the light over the arch as the two of them approached it. "I could have sworn it was open when we entered."

Borosan shrugged. "It might have been. It's not now, though." He reached out and ran his hand over the rock sealing the passage. "It's different than the other rock here. We are probably buried inside some mountain."

Keles touched the cool rock. "Limestone. It's everywhere, and this is pretty smooth. Could be we've not moved at all."

The Viruk dragged himself to the edge of the chamber. "We have moved. Can you not feel it, Keles?"

The cartographer tried to see if he felt anything, but he didn't. "I don't, Rekarafi. But it doesn't really matter, does it? We don't even know where this place is, much less where we have been relocated."

Borosan played the light over the wall again. "It's a burial site. The script is old."

Tyressa stood. "It's the Imperial script. You mentioned Amenis Dukao. You said he died with the Empress."

"I've read the stories of Amenis Dukao since I was a little boy. I know he was real, but the stories weren't. I didn't expect to find his grave here."

The Keru folded her arms beneath her breasts. "The grave is what waits for all living men, no matter how their lives are retold after they die."

Keles nodded and sank into a crouch. "Your point is well-taken, Tyressa. Accepting that Amenis Dukao is here means that these graves date from the time of the Cataclysm. I think I know what we might have here. Do you see any of the names that have hereditary titles?"

Borosan and Tyressa both studied the names they could see in the light, but neither reported finding a noble among them. Tyressa frowned. "Is that significant?"

"Could be." Keles smoothed dust on the floor and drew a diagram of the small entryway and the burial chamber. He ended it with a flat line where the stone had closed the archway. "This is where we are. My grandfather once commented that he hoped the Prince would ennoble the family; that way we would not have to be buried 'outside.' In Imperial times, this kind of chamber was an antechamber to a nobles' mausoleum. Loyal retainers and brave vassals would be buried out here, while the nobles would be buried in the larger chamber. It's not a common practice now, save with princes and some other families, but was the rule then."

He glanced back into the shadows. "Now Rekarafi says we've been moved, and Borosan agrees, but I don't. I think there is a huge burial chamber beyond that limestone slab." He drew the chamber in the dust and erased enough of the line at the arch to make it very thin.

Moraven and Ciras twitched. Rekarafi barked out a harsh laugh. "We moved, Keles."

"You're wrong, Rekarafi." He pointed back toward the entryway. "Did you forget the flashing light that brought us here? I think whoever or whatever shined that light is beyond that slab. The storm probably loosened it. It was designed to keep grave robbers out. I'm sure of it. We get through that slab and we're in. It's probably no more than a yard thick, and limestone can be chopped through."

The Keru nodded. "It can be, but we have no quarrying tools."

Keles' heart sank. "Borosan, how about your *gyanrigot*?"

The inventor shook his head. "With the storm on top of us, I cannot predict what they will do. But I doubt I have enough *thaumston* to let them burrow through even if the storm does go away."

The Viruk clawed his way up the wall and regained his feet. "Do not touch me, anyone. Not if you want to live." He looked at Keles with burning eyes. "A yard you say?"

"Standard for that sort of thing in an Imperial mausoleum."

The Viruk nodded, then shambled across the burial chamber to the tall archway. The air warmed at his passing as if he were burning with invisible flames. His flesh's red glow illuminated the limestone slab as his fingers crawled up it. He pressed his palms flat against the stone about ten feet above the floor. His voice, still hollow, rose and fell rhythmically in words both sibilant and powerful.

The light from beneath his palms shifted from red to yellow, brightening to white, then returning to its bloody hue. Each hand's light pulsed in unison at first and played through little spiderwebs of cracks in the stone's surface. Those lines grew larger as the glowing fell out of synch. Red energy traced them, only to be chased out by gold. The white light flashed, then sank from view. Pulse after pulse pummeled the rock and sent a humming through the air, causing the horses to shift restlessly.

Bits and pieces of stone began to crumble. Pebbles bounced from the Viruk's head and shoulders. Limestone dust greyed his hair. Larger pieces clipped him in the shoulders and ricocheted off his arms. The cascade of clattering gravel muted the first loud crack, but deep fissures appeared in the rock. A large, dagger-shaped piece shifted down, then began to twist. It caught for a second, then more stone came to pieces and it began to tumble.

"Rekarafi, *move*!"

The large stone hunk, easily as tall as Keles himself, fell forward and smashed into the marble floor. It would have crushed the Viruk, but he'd pushed off and sent himself flying backward. He slid across the floor, trailing limestone dust. Two bigger pieces of limestone fell in the other direction, leaving a ragged hole nine feet in diameter at a man-height from the floor.

Keles ran to Rekarafi but refrained from touching him. The glow had died, but his breath still rasped. "How are you? What can I do?"

The Viruk eased himself back against the wall. "You can do nothing but let me rest for a moment."

Keles looked at the opening in the rock. "What did you do?"

"The reverse of what I did back there."

"The crystals? You did that? How? You're a warrior."

Rekarafi coughed. "A warrior is what I am, but not what I have always been."

"But what you did is magic, and only female Viruk use magic." Keles frowned. "Sorry, I actually know nothing about the Viruk—nothing more than you have told me. Will you explain?"

"More fully, another time." He slowly began to roll to his feet. "Suffice it to say, not being *permitted* to do something does not mean one lacks the *ability* to do it."

Borosan pulled another light from a saddlebag and handed it to Tyressa. He then looked at his magic detection device, smacked it once against his leg, and shrugged. "Whatever you did, Rekarafi, the sand is all black now. It's broken."

The Viruk dusted himself off. "You will make something better. Come, let us see what Keles has found for us."

Tyressa nodded toward the two swordsmen. "Will they be safe?"

"From all but the ghosts, Keru." Rekarafi bent his arms and slowly pressed his elbows back until something cracked in the area of his spine. "They have nothing to fear. Come."

The four of them approached the hole, and Keles found his stomach roiling. He had felt certain the chamber was there, and as he looked into it, he found it laid out much as he had sketched in the dust. It was as if the wild magic had given him the ability to see the chamber and record it faithfully without ever having visited it. His grandfather would be certain this was nonsense, but he saw the evidence in the glow of the blue lights.

Tyressa entered first, then Keles. Borosan and the *gyanrigot* followed him, then the Viruk hauled himself through last. He paused in the hole, much as he had crouched in the entryway, sniffing. "Long sealed, long inhabited."

"Inhabited?" Borosan raised his lantern and let the light shine throughout the room. "Nothing living in here that I can see."

"I did not *see,* either." He tapped his nose. "So frail, Men."

Keles frowned as he looked around. The chamber not only had burial spots excavated from the walls, but standing sepulchres had been arranged in rows. They all had been carved of limestone, and several had effigies of the warriors within raised on them. The warriors stood out starkly, full-bodied but white as bone.

Then one of them moved. Keles leaped back, smacking up against Rekarafi's feet. "A ghost!"

The Viruk shook his head.

Pale as ivory and the size of a child, the creature came up into a seated position and wrapped skeletally slender arms around bony knees. The head seemed too large for the body, with the eye sockets overlarge and the heavy cheekbones slanted sharply down. Its two normally placed eyes matched the size of the third set high in its forehead. Above and below the two usual eyes were smaller ones, these of a golden color with a pinpoint black pupil—a contrast to the larger eyes, which appeared black save where gold sparks exploded in them.

Keles shivered. *Seven eyes, the future spies. Spy Gloon eyes, one surely dies.* The rhyme was one every child knew and accompanied stories of heroes who ventured into dark places to encounter Soth Gloons. The Soth, who had been highly valued by the Viruk Empire, went through life stages, and Gloon was the last and least common—at least as far as men knew. Their extra eyes were said to permit them a vision of the future, and to meet one was the harbinger of disaster.

"A Viruk here? This was unseen."

Rekarafi eased himself down from the hole. "Your eyes are too small to behold a Viruk's future."

"The Viruk have no futures to behold." The Gloon shook its head and closed the central eye. "You are in good company with these Men. Their futures are empty as well. In fact, death touches one of them right *now*."

Keles opened his mouth to protest, but pain exploded in the center of his mind. *Nirati? Nirati, no!* He felt himself falling and tried to clutch at anything to stop his fall. But nothing did, and the world crashed closed around him.

Chapter Sixty-one

7th day, Month of the Wolf, Year of the Rat
9th Year of Imperial Prince Cyron's Court
163rd Year of the Komyr Dynasty
737th year since the Cataclysm
Nemehyan, Caxyan

Jorim looked down on the city below and felt queasy. It was not just the Mozoyan flesh he'd eaten, or all the other things that went with it. The Amentzutl had put on a fine feast with soups and stews alternating with roasted strips of meat. The fleet had provided rice and other basics which, to the Amentzutl, were as miraculous as the horses and chariots. Even at the top of his pyramid, Jorim could hear sounds of singing and merrymaking as the sun began to peek up over the eastern horizon.

Anaeda Gryst looked toward the dawn. "Red sky in morning, sailor take warning."

"It's not the sky or the weather I'm worried about. It's not even being thought a god that worries me."

"No?" Anaeda smiled easily. "I think it would concern me. I merely accept responsibility for a fleet, but you have it for all these people."

"I am *not* a god."

"How do you know?" Iesol knelt at the top of the pyramid about a dozen feet to Jorim's left. "There are those who suppose that if one can reach *jaedunto,* perhaps there is a goal above that—divinity."

"Your idea invalidates your question. I've not reached *jaedunto,* so divinity would be beyond me."

"I would beg to differ, Master Anturasi." The minister pressed his hands to his thighs and spoke softly. "As the Master says, 'There is no destination that cannot be found at the end of multiple paths.' My idea merely described one way people think divinity is accessible. They are likely wrong. What you have told us suggests that divinity *is* something you can realize."

Jorim frowned. "I do not follow."

"It is simple, Master. Tetcomchoa, the first time around, sailed west and, you suspect, might have been Taichun—he who was Urmyr's Master. If you accept that Tetcomchoa was a god here, and a man in the Empire, then the path from god to man is open."

"But that does not mean the reverse is true. Nor does it mean that, because we accepted him as a man, he somehow divested himself of his divinity."

Iesol smiled. "But this would suggest that just because we have accepted you as a man you are not precluded from having always been a god."

Jorim held a hand up. "I don't mind semantic games, but not now. I've had far too little sleep and things are running riot in my head."

Anaeda crouched at his right. "I don't believe Iesol was playing a game. You don't want to accept the possibility that you are a god, or that you could become one. I understand this and even applaud your humility. The fact is, however, that these people do believe you are a god. They are also of the opinion that this Mozoloa is rising in the west. As the legends are explained to me, it is Mozoloa who each night inhales the sun and exhales the stars. Each night you send a serpent that squeezes him so hard that eventually he releases the sun and it rises again."

"We know that is not true."

"It doesn't matter what we know, Jorim. The point is simply this. For these people, Tetcomchoa is the god who makes all life possible. Tetcomchoa is core to their reality the same way the Nine Gods are to ours. Your problem is that they see you as Tetcomchoa *and* they expect you to lead them to where they can defeat Mozoloa."

Jorim sighed. "That is out of the question. We can't lead them to the Nine Principalities. Not only do they not have the means to get there, but they would be an invading force. For all I know they'd identify Prince Cyron as Neletzatl and make war on my home."

"Curious."

The cartographer glanced at Iesol. "What?"

"It cannot have passed your notice that Neletzatl and Nelesquin have similar sounding names."

Anaeda glanced up. "The Prince lost with Empress Cyrsa?"

"The Prince who was her rival, yes. There are stories—seldom heard, and almost never in the Nine—that parallel those of the Sleeping Empress. Nelesquin is said to sleep as well, but uneasily in his grave. It has been said he will return, but not as a help."

"Return to the Nine?"

"To what he once knew as the Empire—what he once thought he would rule." Iesol nodded. "If he has come back, perhaps the time for Taichun's return is at hand as well."

Jorim frowned. "And who else will return? No, don't answer that, Iesol, I was being dramatic." The cartographer groaned. "I don't believe I am Tetcomchoa. Still, every previous *centenco* has produced difficulties, and they match points in our history. Could it be that they are right? Is some threat rising to the west? Face it, between here and Moriande there is a lot of west, and most of it wet."

Jorim stared down at the shadows surrounding the pyramid's base. "If we accept that *centenco* has validity, then we know a threat exists. The Amentzutl know there is a threat, but the people back home do not."

"Can you communicate it to your grandfather?"

"No. I've tried. Not to tell him about the Amentzutl; we agreed I would not do that. But I tried to reach him to convey some basic weather information. I got nothing."

"How do you mean 'nothing'?"

He looked over at her, completely at a loss for words. He had always been able to find his grandfather and convey information. He'd largely been unable to stop his grandfather from plundering whatever else he desired—though the reverse had never been true. Parts of his grandfather had always been untouchable, and Jorim had learned to armor his private memories in layers of mundane trivia that his grandfather hated.

With distance had come a weakening of the contact, but always there had been *something*. Yet since the battle there was nothing. His attempts to reach his grandfather had fallen into a void, and when he sought his brother, things were no better—though he still could feel Keles out there somewhere.

"It is as if my grandfather has fallen off the edge of the world."

Her eyes narrowed. "Is he dead?"

"No, I think I would know that." He snorted. "There are times I have wanted it so badly that I know parts of me would rejoice in his death. Now I just feel isolated. Keles is still out there but not looking for me, so we are not communicating."

Anaeda stood and began to pace, her boots rasping on the stone. "If we accept that there is a danger, we have an obligation to warn Nalenyr."

"We also have an obligation to help the Amentzutl."

The ship's captain smiled down at him. "Spoken like a god taking responsibility for his people."

"That's not funny." Jorim clambered to his feet as Shimik came bounding up the pyramid's steps.

The Fenn leaped into Anaeda's arms, then pointed back down the steps. "Nauana comma."

Nauana was indeed coming, and at the head of a procession a dozen people long. Each of them wore feather cloaks and gold headdresses with long feathers rising from their brows. Each of them looked older than Nauana by at least a dozen years, and they ascended in age. The wizened man bringing up the rear could easily have been over a hundred and might have even been around when Tetcomchoa last walked among the Amentzutl.

The procession reached the top of the pyramid and spread out in a line. Nauana stood in front of them and bowed in the Naleni fashion. "These, Lord Tetcomchoa, are the Elders of the *maicana*."

The Elders bowed together and straightened up after a respectful time.

Jorim bowed to them and held it equally as long. Iesol and Anaeda likewise bowed, but remained down longer. These gestures brought smiles to the *maicana* faces—probably because they were happy to have mastered this new custom.

Nauana came up last of all, but smiled carefully. "This morning is a time for many momentous decisions." She gestured toward the north and moons glowing from within constellations. "We have much to tell you."

Jorim nodded. "As do we to tell you."

Nauana bowed her head. "Please, my Lord Tetcomchoa, tell us your will."

"We come from the west, where Mozoloa will present his threat. We must warn our people of it, and summon help to defend the Amentzutl from him." He glanced at Captain Gryst and she nodded. "Toward this end, we will be taking our fleet back west."

The young *maicana* woman solemnly translated his words for her elders, but they did not have the effect Jorim would have anticipated. He expected they would be upset that he was leaving, but instead his words seemed to elicit smiles and positive murmurs. Even Nauana smiled as she looked back at him.

"This is, of course, how it should be, Lord Tetcomchoa."

He frowned. "You know I will be going with them?"

"As we expected."

"And we'll be leaving inside a week."

Nauana frowned. "We do not think that is possible."

"There is no choice in the matter, Nauana."

"My Lord's resolve makes that apparent. We will work very hard, then." She nodded solemnly. "We shall begin now, shall we, my Lord?"

Jorim watched her face for any sign of deception, but found none. "Perhaps, Nauana, you need tell me what you all came here to say."

She nodded. "When you were here last, my Lord, and you took your leave, you shared your power with us. You created the *maicana*. You told us to hold your power and your art sacred. We were to learn and refine, create new things and make what you gave us as strong as we could. You said this was because one day you would return and we would have to show you our work, returning to you the vestiges of your power."

Nauana opened her arms, her cloak slipped back behind her shoulders. "When you came, I was certain you were Lord Tetcomchoa and worthy of your teachings to be returned to you. Others were not. The miracles you wrought on the battlefield have left no doubt. The Elders have confirmed it and have agreed to return to you what is your right."

"My right?"

"Yes, Lord Tetcomchoa. Though you give us only a week, we shall train you in the ways of the *maicana*." Nauana's face took on the expression of confidence that made his heart pound faster. "You came to us a god with the powers of a man. You shall face Mozoloa with the powers of a god. When we have returned to you what you lent us, nothing in heaven or on earth will be able to stand against you."

Chapter Sixty-two

7th day, Month of the Wolf, Year of the Rat
9th Year of Imperial Prince Cyron's Court
163rd Year of the Komyr Dynasty
737th year since the Cataclysm
Ixyll

Keles woke with a tightness on his forehead and pain throbbing in his head. Though he could remember nothing of what he'd dreamed while unconscious, bits of terror floated in a sense of contentment. It all had something to do with his sister, but the fading fragments made no sense. Pain chased thought from his mind and oblivion beckoned again, but he fought it.

He opened his eyes and it took a moment for him to remember where he was. Borosan's two lanterns illuminated only a tiny bit of the vast chamber. In the glow of one he could see Moraven and Ciras resting quietly, with the *thanaton* standing sentinel nearby, and the Viruk sleeping up against the wall.

Tyressa smiled at him. "He said you would be waking up now."

"He?" Keles tried to sit up, but his head began to swim. As he lay back down he realized he was stretched out on one of the biers, and that sent a shiver through him.

Tyressa pointed to where the Soth Gloon squatted beside Borosan. "His name is Urardsa."

Keles nodded once, then stopped. "How long have I been out?"

"Most of the night. You slept peacefully, as did Borosan. The storm has passed, but Ciras is exhausted. Moraven is unresponsive and Rekarafi says he needs more rest."

"How about you? Have you slept?"

She shook her head. "But I'm doing perfectly well."

He touched the stitches on his forehead. "Your handiwork?"

Tyressa nodded. "You'll have a scar on your front to match the ones on your back."

"Thanks."

The Gloon rose, leaving Borosan to tinker with his *gyanrigot*. "Your wits should be about you now."

"They're returning." Keles forced himself up on his elbows. "I thank you for saving us."

"What makes you think I did?" The pale creature cocked his head to the right.

"The signal light in the storm. You led us to sanctuary."

Urardsa opened his arms and spun around, displaying himself and the dirty rag of a loincloth he wore. "What do you see on me that would cause that glinting?"

"Nothing." Keles started to rub at his forehead, but Tyressa caught his wrist. "You're denying you saved us?"

"Have you any proof I did?"

"No." The cartographer lowered his hand. "Are you going to answer all my questions with questions?"

"Are you going to ask any questions for which there are answers?"

Keles looked at Tyressa. "You endured this for how long before you decided to let me wake up?"

She smiled. "How long do you imagine?"

He groaned and she laughed. Keles looked from her to the Soth Gloon again. "How is it that you are here?"

"I was entombed here with the others." He hopped up on the bier and squatted at Keles' feet. He pointed high up on one of the chamber's walls. "You can barely make out where they placed me."

A dozen questions immediately came to Keles, but he thought before speaking. If the Soth had been entombed, he clearly had been believed dead. Since the graves outside dated from the time of Empress Cyrsa, it would be logical to assume he had gone out from the Empire with the expedition. *And if he has not left here since he was entombed, he's been here for over seven hundred years.*

"You were taken for dead. Who did that?"

Urardsa shrugged his narrow shoulders. "I was beyond thinking at that point. I am now Gloon, but before that I was the life stage known as Myrkal. I was larger then than I am now, though not as large as when I was Anbor. As Anbor I had come to know some of the Empire's great fighters, and though I had become Myrkal, they invited me to join them. I could yet fight, but this was not demanded of me."

"Yet you were believed dead and entombed with warriors. What transpired to cause all these deaths?"

The Gloon smiled and his four small gold eyes tightened. "I find this fascinating, Keles Anturasi. I am able to see the future, not the past, so I do not know the details of how I came to be here. I do know the circumstances that led to it, and I shall share them with you, but first . . ."

Urardsa reached a thick-fingered hand out and passed it in front of Keles' face, over his head, down along his shoulders, never quite touching him. It was almost as if the Gloon were trying to catch an elusive insect. The expression on his face as he did this did not change, but the four gold eyes flicked quickly, often darting in different directions.

The Gloon lowered his hand. "When first I saw you, your future had dimmed. When you fell and struck your head, you should have been dead, but you did not die." He looked up toward the top of the chamber. "Perhaps the wild magic had something to do with it. It matters not. Now, though, you have a number of life-lines ahead of you."

"You see my future directly?"

The Gloon closed all of his eyes and shook his head. "You are a pearl on a chain. Your past forms links that are easily seen. For most, there is one chain into the future, and the length of it corresponds to their life. There are an infinite number of possible futures, but finite is the number in which anyone can participate. Your being here opened more futures to you when there should have been none—some great, some trivial. Unlike the others here, you may live a long time."

Keles frowned as much as he could, given the stitches in his forehead. "You were wrong about me. You're wrong about them. But you were telling us how you came to be here."

The Gloon smiled easily and broadly, almost as a child might. "You don't wish to know your future?"

Keles returned the smile. "You've already admitted that your vision is flawed, so why should I?"

The Gloon reopened his eyes. "It has been a long time since I have sparred with someone. My companions and their ghosts are not very inventive. Yes, my circumstances; I recall. I do not know what you have been told of the war against the Turasynd. Skirmishes raged across Deseirion, Solaeth, and Dolosan. The Empress kept drawing the enemy west, hoping that if the grand confrontation unleashed a wave of magic, it would be triggered far enough away from the Empire that her people would survive. Your presence suggests she was successful."

Tyressa nodded. "The Time of Black Ice was not easy, but we survived. It has been over seven hundred years."

The Gloon considered that quietly, then nodded. "Ghosts only discuss the past and do not mark the passing of time. The Empress—who is not here, nor has her ghost visited—wanted to be certain the Turasynd would not return to the Empire. She divided her force, leaving a third of it in Dolosan, hidden away. The plan was that when the Turasynd followed her onto the Spice Route, this force would come behind and catch them unawares. The barbarians would be crushed between both forces."

Keles looked at Tyressa, who nodded. "I understand her reasoning."

"Good, Master Anturasi. You are not alone, for all of us did, and applauded it. She was advised to put Prince Nelesquin in command of that force. What she did not realize was this: as a Prince of Imperial blood, Nelesquin resented her presence on the throne. To him and his branch of the family, she was naught but a concubine who had murdered her husband and usurped his place. That her husband was incompetent and paralyzed with fear was never believed by those with Imperial blood."

Keles nodded. The history of that era had emphasized how decisive and brave the Empress was. While it was known that she had killed her husband and met his bodyguards with a bloody dagger in hand, this was not dwelt upon. Moreover, because she had formed each of the Nine Principalities and some were still led by the families she had picked to run them, the bureaucracy and governments had a vested interest in maintaining that her actions were justifiable and legitimate. But Nelesquin's difference of opinion was understandable—especially as he was a contemporary of hers.

The Gloon leaped from one bier to another and crouched on the broad chest of a warrior's effigy. "Nelesquin entered into negotiations with the Turasynd. They were led by a god-priest of considerable power. Nelesquin trailed them into Ixyll, hoping to let both sides weaken themselves so he could destroy them and return to take the Imperial throne. The Empress, worried about a lack of communication from him, sent those entombed around you to see if he needed help. Under the leadership of Virisken Soshir, we discovered him in negotiations with the enemy. We struck at him and the Turasynd leader.

"We were greatly outnumbered, but fought valiantly. I do not imagine our bodies were recovered by Nelesquin and buried thusly. So I assume the Empress proved victorious, and that both the Turasyndi and Nelesquin were destroyed." He opened his arms. "This tomb is of Imperial style, so she must have had survivors who did this for us. It is her progeny that yet rule the Empire, is it not?"

Keles shook his head. "The Nine Principalities still exist. We are from Nalenyr and were sent to survey the old Spice Route. At least, I was. You said there were skirmishes. The dead were buried with their weapons. Would you know where those burial places are?"

"They might be possible to find. Why?"

Keles shifted around and slid his feet to the floor. His knees did not buckle, but he leaned back against the bier as Tyressa came around to steady him. "Their weapons have value back in the Nine. And we think there might be those who would use their bodies for corpse dust."

"I can show you what I know, but this would be as nothing compared to the place where the dead from the final battle were buried. You would have to venture further west to find that site."

Keles levered himself away from the bier and stood. "Then we need to get out of here. You said you have never been outside, but you have survived. What do you do for water and food?"

The Soth Gloon pointed toward the darker recesses of the cavern. "In there you will find seeps that suffice for water. There is also a colony of bats. I do not eat much, and they are filling when I do."

"If there are bats, then there is a way out."

Urardsa nodded. "There is a crack in the ceiling of a chamber through which they exit each night. I do not like heights, so I have not ventured forth."

"I'm going to go take a look."

Tyressa's hand landed on his shoulder. "Not alone."

Keles nodded, then looked over at Borosan. "Tyressa and I are going to take a look at a way out of here. We will be back soon."

Borosan looked up from his tinkering and nodded, but said nothing.

Keles took one of his lanterns and they headed off. The finished part of the complex narrowed deeper in, but the passage remained large enough that they could move without much more than stooping. Keles had come unarmed, but Tyressa had looped her sword belt around her waist. The scabbard kept slapping at rocks and caught a couple of times, but did not slow them much.

After a steep climb that leveled out into a narrow passage, Keles sat. "Just need to rest for a moment."

Tyressa knelt beside him and brought the lantern up to examine his face. "It's bleeding a little, but not too badly."

"It's not getting in my eyes." He glanced up at her. "What did you think of Urardsa's story?"

She shrugged. "It sounds true, and I have no reason to doubt it."

"But there are implications that I wonder about. The tomb complex, for example, was not easily built. Assuming the Empress survived, she must have had a considerable number of men to work on it."

"I agree."

"So why didn't she come back with them?"

Tyressa's breath caught. "I don't know."

"Do you think she's waiting out there somewhere as the legends say?"

"Does it matter?"

"Not really. I guess, as we go further west, we'll find out." He stood again. "C'mon, let's see if we can get out."

"And hope we find another entrance, because neither the horses nor Rekarafi are going to fit this way."

They scraped their way along a tight passage that then opened out into a relatively steep climb about thirty yards up. At first Keles welcomed it, but then a stench hit him. Halfway up, bat guano covered rocks and deepened as they climbed. Where the passage widened, the dung dragged at their feet. Insect larvae and dying bats wallowed in it and when Tyressa raised the lantern, the cavern roof seemed to heave and ripple with bodies.

Both of them moved through as quickly as they could, but that was not nearly fast enough. They found a narrow ledge that angled up and finally caught sight of a red streak they took to be the evening sky. This heartened them, and they moved more quickly. Being smaller, Keles was able to crawl up the crack swiftly and emerged into a cold evening. But the fresh air was bracing.

The landscape stretched out, painted in bloody tones by the dying sun, and would have riveted his attention, save something more close demanded it. As he emerged, a trio of men stood up. Two held crossbows leveled at his middle. They'd been sheltered in a small hollow beyond a rock, and had a small fire burning there.

Keles raised his hands. "Easy, I'm no threat to you. I'm Keles Anturasi and this is Tyressa." He half turned back as her right hand reached out to grab a rock. "We got trapped out here by a storm."

The man without the crossbow nodded. "They've been pretty fierce. Anturasi, you say? Of Nalenyr?"

Keles nodded. "Do I know you?"

"No, not at all." He pointed at Tyressa, half-emerged from the crevasse. "Shoot her. We've got what we want."

A crossbow twanged and Tyressa grunted. Keles spun and saw her disappear back into the cavern.

The leader snarled. "Make sure."

The two crossbowmen advanced, but before they could reach the opening, a cloud of bats exploded into the sky. Leathery wings snapped and tiny voices shrieked. The cloud became a blurred brown sheet pouring out, circling, rising into the sky. The crossbowmen yelped and dove for cover.

Keles turned and started to run, but a fist caught him behind the left ear and he went down hard. He twisted onto his right shoulder, hoping to prevent his head from hitting the rocks. He succeeded, but only at the cost of his collarbone, which snapped easily. He rolled onto his back and cried out, his left hand clutching at the break.

The trio's leader placed a booted foot on his chest. "Be quiet. You'll be taken care of." The man smiled. "Prince Pyrust would be upset if we let anything happen to you, Master Anturasi. You're safe now, under his protection. And before you know it, you'll be able to thank him yourself."

Chapter Sixty-three

9th day, Month of the Wolf, Year of the Rat
9th Year of Imperial Prince Cyron's Court
163rd Year of the Komyr Dynasty
737th year since the Cataclysm
Anturasikun, Moriande
Nalenyr

Prince Cyron felt the weight of the heavy white mourning cloak; it caught at his legs as he marched through Anturasikun. Similar cloaks shrouded the forms of the Keru before and behind him. White cloth covered painting and murals on the walls, hid furnishings, and otherwise obscured almost anything of color or interest.

Not only did mourning colors predominate, but grief pervaded the tower. Siatsi remained indisposed, and had not yet responded to the note of condolence the Prince had sent immediately upon learning of Nirati's murder. She had, however, had the messenger return her thanks.

Qiro Anturasi had not even done that much.

Cyron himself had been told of the murder and had gone to the scene of the crime. Even if he had been as battle-hardened as Prince Pyrust, he was certain he would still have vomited. To just look into the room and see the beautiful young woman's head perched on a mound of meat was an incongruity that offended even before one realized that the mound was the rest of her. She had been taken to pieces with incredible skill. Cyron's Lord of Shadows had estimated it would have taken five hours to accomplish that task, though how anyone could have remained sane that long was beyond any of them.

To compound matters, Count Junel Aerynnor had been found in a nearby alley with a dagger thrust into his back. An inch or two to the left and it would have severed an artery. He would have bled to death had rescuers not come across him. He had regained consciousness on the eighth, and told a tale of being kidnapped and brought to the murder site. He had been forced to look at what they had done to the Anturasi woman. He'd broken away from his captors—Desei agents according to him—and had been hit with a thrown dagger. Why they had not killed him he did not know, but—as far as he was concerned—in killing Nirati they had ended his life.

Cyron had immediately communicated his regrets to the Anturasi clan, offering to do all he could for them. He promised his people would find Nirati's killer, but with the murder of Majiata Phoesel yet unsolved, that promise sounded hollow even to him. Cyron had even gone so far as to promise Qiro he could leave Anturasikun to attend Nirati's funeral, and had opened his own family's crypt to allow her to be interred in the outer chamber.

The Prince had expected some response from Qiro, but got nothing. No doubt the man was grief-stricken. He likely was also trying to communicate with his grandsons to let them know of their sister's death. He had hoped the offer of freedom would bring some response—likewise the honor of having Nirati buried in the Komyr crypt—but still there was no word. Even sending stonemasons to ask after what sort of stone they would like for Nirati did not break Qiro's silence.

Cyron had been understanding, and was willing to allow the man his time to mourn, but almost immediately complaints had come from merchants who were waiting for Anturasi charts. They were slow in coming, or never arrived at all. On top of that, the captains complained that they contained no new information. If they were not getting the latest in navigational aids, they wanted to lower the percentage paid to the Anturasi family; but even their demands for renegotiation were going unanswered.

The Keru parted before the gated entrance to the tower's interior. Beyond it, the huddled form of Ulan Anturasi waited, his shoulders slumped and his hood fully obscuring his face. He dropped to one knee behind the bars, but remained far enough back that Cyron could not have reached through and grabbed him.

"Good day, Highness."

"Open this gate this instant, Ulan Anturasi! I must see Qiro at once."

"Opening the gate will do no good, Highness."

Cyron slipped the clasp on his cloak and let the snowy garment hit the floor. Beneath he wore a purple overshirt with a gold dragon coiled on it. "Look at me, Ulan Anturasi. You know who I am and what I represent. Do not play games with me. Do as I say. Open this gate."

The old man on the other side slowly rose from his knees. Palsied hands appeared from within the cloak and fumbled with keys. "It will do no good, Highness. Qiro is not here. I did not open the gate for him. He did not take my keys. He is gone. I don't know where, but gone."

The panic in Ulan's voice shocked Cyron much more than the news that Qiro Anturasi was missing. The information about Qiro's disappearance had been delivered almost matter-of-factly, as if this was not the first time Ulan had lost track of him.

Cyron played a hunch. "How long has he been gone this time?"

The man's head came up and red-rimmed eyes studied the Prince's face. "You know?"

"Nalenyr is my domain. There is nothing I do not know. How long this time, Ulan?"

"Since the other night. Since the night she—"

"Since the night Nirati was murdered." Cyron slapped the old man's hands away from the keys, fitted the right one into the lock, and turned it. The lock clicked open. Cyron stepped through the door, relocked it, then tossed the keys to one of his Keru. "No one goes in here. Get a company of Keru and surround the grounds. Another will search it for any sign of Qiro's passage."

"Yes, Highness."

Cyron started up the circular ramp. "No one heard anything, saw anything?"

Ulan wheezed as he struggled to keep up. "No, Highness, nothing. Last we knew he was working. Sometimes he would sleep in his workshop. We called to him, but got no response."

The Prince frowned. "What did you find when you searched it?"

"Searched it? Highness?" Ulan looked agog at him. "N-no one . . . We don't go in there unless he summons us."

"What if he died in there, Ulan?"

The man's lower jaw hung open and quivered. "He's not dead, Highness. I would know if Qiro was dead. He's not. He's just gone."

"Why didn't you tell me sooner? Why didn't you send for me?"

The man's voice became a tight squeak. "You are Prince Cyron, but he is Qiro. He has been gone before, but he has always come back. I didn't want to make him angry. You don't know what he is like when he is angry."

Cyron emerged at the heart of the workshop. The Anturasi paused in their work, looking at him. All seemed terrified, but Cyron thought it was less because of his possible ire than Qiro's wrath if a visitor were found among them in his absence.

That's it, mostly, but there is more. Some among them also feared Qiro's absence, for it left them without leadership. They might have hated him or feared him, but at least he gave them direction.

Cyron nodded slowly, knowing what he had to do. "I am Prince Cyron. You all know this. Until Qiro comes to overrule me in this matter, you will take orders from Ulan Anturasi. Understand something very important. Qiro would not have left if he did not trust that you could and would carry on the Anturasi mission. Do not let him down."

The Prince grabbed Ulan by the shoulder and pulled him toward Qiro's sanctum. They passed through the blue layer of curtains, then Ulan brought his hands up and beat Cyron's hand aside. The older man sank to his knees and bowed so low he seemed nothing but a discarded cloak wadded on the floor.

"Forgive me, Highness, striking you. Kill me if you must, but I cannot go in there."

Cyron resisted the urge to kick him. His hands tightened into fists, then loosened again. He squatted and kept his voice even. "Ulan Anturasi, you heard me tell the others you are in charge here now. So it is. I will not kill you. I *need* you. *Nalenyr* needs you."

The man stirred a little, but shivers still ran though him. "You mean that, Highness?"

"Yes, of course." The waver in Ulan's voice made Cyron doubt he would be up to the challenge. "Qiro could communicate directly with Keles and Jorim. Can you?"

"I have, in the past, but it has been so long. Qiro forbade it."

"Can you communicate with Qiro?"

Ulan's head came up and the Prince tugged the hood back so he could see the man's face. Worry made it an ashen mask. "I have not for a long time, Highness. I know he still lives, but he is faint and far."

"How far? Deseirion?"

The old man blinked, then looked down. "I don't know direction, Highness, but I would say further. Much further."

"Work at it. Work at reaching any of them. Now." Cyron stood and nodded toward the interior curtain. "I am going to see if there are any clues to his disappearance in there."

"Yes, Highness."

Cyron steeled himself for he knew not what and slipped past the last curtain. The room remained much as it had been when last he visited, save in one very important respect. The map on the wall had been modified extensively. A chain of islands curved down to the south to the Mountains of Ice. In the northwest an incredible amount of detail had been filled in along the Spice Route. As nearly as he could see, the old road remained useful well into Dolosan, and new routes had formed through the changed landscape. Both Keles and Jorim had been successful in their quests.

"And I had no idea how much they had learned. You *are* a bastard, Qiro."

These changes in the world should have warmed his heart, for these discoveries would guarantee the economic preeminence of Nalenyr through his lifetime and that of his children, grandchildren, and great-grandchildren—unto nine generations. He would be able to reunite the Empire and build it into a greater power than it had ever been before. He would make Pyrust his warlord and his domain would expand to include all of the known world and beyond.

One other detail on the map, however, sent icy dread coursing through his veins. There, in the empty quarter of the Eastern Sea, to the north of the Mountains of Ice, sat an island continent. Teardrop in shape, as if it had been wept from the mouth of the Gold River, it floated there to the southeast. Its landmass could have easily encompassed the Five Princes and Erumvirine as well.

Cyron stared at it, and the image took on definition as if some invisible cartographer were adding details. Mountains grew up and rivers flowed. Cities appeared, flourished, collapsed, and started the cycle again. Odd creatures decorated geographical features, and the name *Anturasixan* scrawled itself over the face of the continent in Qiro's strong hand.

And all of it was drawn in blood—blood that dripped slowly down the wall. Cyron thought it might just run in red streaks to the floor, but the fluid shifted and flowed differently, as if it had a life of its own.

It does, just like the place it has drawn. Cyron watched as letters formed into words. His mouth went dry.

Below the new continent a simple legend appeared, as it did on so many Anturasi maps. A warning, scrawled clearly and boldly, in Qiro Anturasi's hand. A warning to be ignored at the peril of the world.

"Here there be monsters."

About the Author

Michael A. Stackpole is an award-winning author and game designer whose first novel was published in 1988. He grew up in Vermont, and graduated from the University of Vermont in 1979 with a degree in history. He now lives in Arizona (though he is writing this on a day when it's 109 degrees in the shade, so he wonders why he's living in Arizona).

You can find his website at *www.stormwolf.com,* where, among other things, you can find a glossary of terms and a pronunciation guide for all the made-up words that no human mouth was ever meant to fit around anyway.